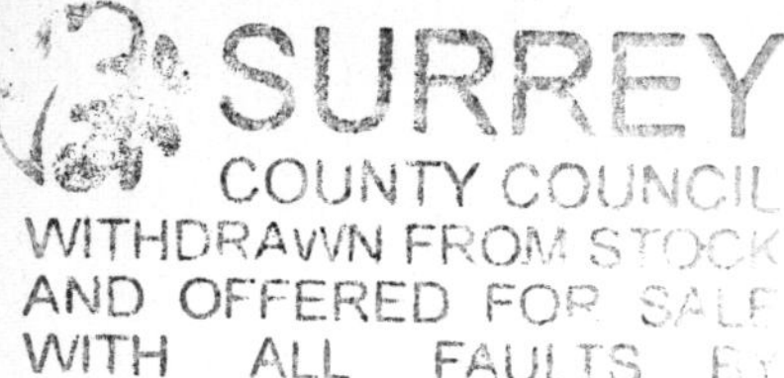

The Fox in the Forest

A motiveless murder, every policeman's nightmare. It is committed in a stretch of forest between two peaceful villages. Superintendent Lambert and his CID team can find few connections between the people who were around at the time of this death and a victim who seems to have had no enemies.

Before long, it seems that they have a serial killer on their hands, selecting victims at random and dispatching them in a manner which affords few clues to his identity. The press dub the killer The Fox and picture a rural community gripped by fear.

Lambert and Sergeant Hook are on ground they have not trodden before. The village closes in upon itself, preserving its secrets from outsiders. The solution when it comes is complex but satisfying.

by the same author

DEAD ON COURSE
BRING FORTH YOUR DEAD
FOR SALE—WITH CORPSE
MURDER AT THE NINETEENTH

J. M. GREGSON

The Fox in the Forest

THE CRIME CLUB
An Imprint of HarperCollins *Publishers*

First published in Great Britain in 1992
by The Crime Club, an imprint of
HarperCollins Publishers, 77–85 Fulham Palace Road,
Hammersmith, London W6 8JB

9 8 7 6 5 4 3 2 1

A catalogue record for this book is
available from the British Library

ISBN 0 00 232408 3

Photoset in Linotron Baskerville by
Rowland Phototypesetting Ltd
Bury St Edmunds, Suffolk
Printed and bound in Great Britain by
HarperCollins Book Manufacturing, Glasgow

CHAPTER 1

These woods are an ancient place. A motorway runs now along their edge, but within half a mile of the roaring traffic there are streams and pools that were here when King William the Norman sent out his men to compile the first inventory of his new kingdom.

The trees are 'managed' now, but not too fiercely or noticeably, and they impose their own leisurely time-scale. The last great impact was the felling of great tracts of oak to replenish the fleets of Nelson and repulse the ambitions of Bonaparte. Many of the oaks planted then still stand here, though other and greater wars have made claims upon them in this century of conflict. But the area escaped the worst of the evergreen mania of the 'twenties and 'thirties. Conifers supplement rather than overwhelm the deciduous trees.

The foresters who have worked here have been men with a feel for the place as well as skill in their work. The old bridleways have been expanded into wider routes, using the stone that is never far beneath the surface here. But entry is still forbidden to all vehicles save those of the Forestry Commission. So the forest remains a quiet, private place, where those seeking solitude will find it more easily than almost anywhere else in this crowded kingdom.

In summer, the woods throb with life. Irregular, conflicting bursts of full-throated birdsong from the deciduous areas blend into miraculous harmony. Streamlets dribble somnolently among rushes. Wild bees murmur on clover at the sides of tracks, where the gaps in the timber permit the sunlight to beam from above. The myriad, mysterious sounds of unseen small mammals amid the undergrowth surround the walker along the quiet paths, and deer will often cross the tracks ahead of him. And always above there is the sound of summer leaves, sighing softly in the lightest of breezes, whistling more briskly when the warm wind becomes boisterous.

In winter, the forest is a very different place. There are no leaf sounds overhead now, and only occasional scratchings in the dead, dry leaves beneath the naked trees. The few animals and birds that are still here make few movements over the cold, dark earth beneath the trees. Even the red kite, circling above the leafless twigs of the highest oaks, can detect little prey in the winter world beneath him.

On the shortest day of the year, little light penetrates to the floor of the woods from a sky sullen with cloud. Only at the few points where wide tracks meet is much of that sunless grey canopy visible. Elsewhere in the forest, this seems hardly a day at all, but rather a mere interval between long nights. Despite the cloud, there is a light north-east wind, driving down the temperature, ensuring that yesterday's drizzle has become a thin film of ice over the stony tracks.

The still, tall firs, which in summer are scarcely noticeable, seem now to dominate this part of the forest, dark and unchanging. It is a place for trolls, or those darker spirits of northern myth. This part of the wood might now be in Finland, an inspiration for the astringent strains of Sibelius rather than the Elgar who once trod here on summer days.

Yet there is a human presence here, still. When other men leave, he emerges from his hiding-place like one of the wild creatures of the forest. Then he stretches his limbs and studies the light that remains in the patch of winter sky which he can see between the trees.

The man heard the rabbit screaming long before he saw it. It lay upon its side, a broken paw preventing the wire from tightening to crush its neck.

He killed it with a single blow from the side of his hand. It died in mid-scream, its eyes still wide with surprise as he lifted it from the trap. He was annoyed with himself: the sound could have given him away to curious ears. Not that anyone was likely to have been near enough to hear; if they had, they would probably have assumed that a stoat rather than human interference was the cause of the rabbit's agony.

In any case, it could scarcely have mattered much. Any human listener here would be neutral, rather than hostile. But, knowing that he had made an error, he was angry, with the pedantry of the perfectionist.

He compensated by skinning the animal with self-conscious skill. As he disembowelled and dismembered the small body, his hands were as swift and accurate as a surgeon's. Only a very little of the warm blood coloured the fingers of his left hand. He shut his eyes for a moment, acknowledging the excitement he felt in the touch of flesh and blood that had been a living thing only moments earlier.

He made his fire now, before full darkness could make it a beacon to mark his presence in the wood. The temperature was dropping: this would be another night spent well below freezing point. He was glad to squat close to the small fire in the little combe among the trees, sheltered from that light but bitter wind and any eyes foolish enough to be abroad here at this hour.

The rabbit almost filled the square cooking tin. It took a long time in these conditions to bring the stew to boiling point beneath the close-fitting lid; at least there was no shortage here of tinder-dry sticks. He let his meal simmer for much longer, forcing himself to savour the food in anticipation, making the wait another discipline imposed upon himself.

While he waited, he set up the tiny nylon tent a little way from the fire, sheltered from the wind but towards the top of the slope, where he was least likely to be surprised. That had become a habit now. He was still dry and warm within his waterproof clothing. This would be his third night in the forest, but as he unwrapped the lightweight sleeping-bag, his hands were as dry as when he had come here.

The rabbit was worth the wait. The flesh fell from the bones without conscious physical action on his part, as if it were reacting to the impulses of his brain. It tasted better at this moment than the finest French cuisine. Tipping the tin steeply, he used his last crust of bread to mop up the gravy. Hunger was still the finest sauce: it had been many hours since his previous meal.

The ground was beginning to freeze, though in the damper parts the leafmould yielded still to the pressure of his heel through the outer crust. A few days of this and the whole surface would be iron hard. He moved to the top of the slope to look at his tent; even without the darkness, its faded green would have been almost invisible. He was well used to it now: he crawled into its shelter like a wild creature returning to its lair.

With the flap zipped firmly shut, the temperature built quickly within his tiny refuge. He read for a while; even the heat of the torch seemed abnormally high in that confined space. He was warm, even to the tips of his feet. He had kept dry throughout his time in the woods, knowing that dampness was his greatest enemy. Once it got within even the best clothing or boots, there was no easy way of getting rid of it in winter. Damp meant cold, and cold meant trouble; water was the greatest danger to his success.

Presently he put out the torch. He imagined the grey-green luminescence it must give to his tent, and was uneasy at the thought of detection, however unlikely it might be. This was the best time. He lay half in and half out of the sleeping-bag, indulging the lethargy he did not allow himself by day. In the streets of the town, the windows of the shops would be trimmed with Christmas tinsel, garishly bright amid the crowds. He was pleased to be out of all that; he took his time in relishing that thought. There were plenty of hours left for sleep in the long night to come.

At around midnight, a thin dusting of snow fell upon the trees. Then the sky cleared and winter clenched its fist even more tightly about the forest. The man slept dreamlessly beneath the white canopy, finding his progress thus far satisfactory.

CHAPTER 2

There are no houses now in the forest. The last charcoal-burner's cottage was abandoned early in the century, and has long since been obliterated by the saplings which pushed its humble walls aside.

The tiny village of Woodford lies almost within the shadow of the woods; indeed, in the last sun of a summer evening, the longest shadow from the great beech trees at the edge of the forest touches the roof of its first house. The crossing of the shallow stream which gave the place its name was replaced sixty years ago by a metalled road, but the place is otherwise little changed in its externals. The old stone church, too large like most now for the number of worshippers it attracts, still stands at its centre. The Crown inn opposite its lych-gate is nowadays in rather better repair than the church, as if emphasizing the ascendancy for the moment of Mammon in the perpetual conflict between this world and the next.

There are not many new houses here. Apart from a terrace of four council houses erected in the 'fifties, the only postwar building is a small detached house a hundred yards from the church; a discreet tablet by the side of its gate announces that this is now the vicarage.

If the Reverend Peter Barton ever looks with longing at the ivy-clad Victorian mansion that was once the residence of his predecessors, he keeps his thoughts to himself. Probably he does not do so, for envy has little part in his make-up. He is thirty-one, one of the new breed of clergy for whom progress towards things like the ordination of women is too slow and for whom action against social ills takes precedence over the liturgy and the order of service. The six bedrooms and the three-quarters of an acre of the Victorian vicarage, which now has a secular occupant, would be an embarrassment to him. And even his wife has to concede that they could not afford the heating.

Clare Barton concedes little else. She is a year younger than Peter, but already the doll-like prettiness which was emphasized by her blonde hair and light blue eyes is draining away. Her small, pert nose is becoming a little more button-like, the corners of her mouth turn habitually downwards, her figure is in danger of crossing that fine line from slimness into wiriness. She has the animation which first attracted her husband when they were students, but she seems nowadays to be more usually aroused by discontent than pleasure.

'It's not going to be a very lively Christmas, then,' she said.

Her husband had sensed from the start that the series of questions had been leading to this conclusion. He said carefully, 'It's a working time, you know, for a clergyman. He has to be at the disposal of his flock, to some extent. But that's no reason why it can't be a happy time.' He wished he hadn't added the last, obvious thought; it sounded like part of a sermon, hanging in the air, waiting to be developed.

He made a move as if to touch her, and she moved quickly away. 'It means we're stuck here. Tied to this house.'

'We can go out, if you wish, after I've finished my rounds on Christmas morning.' Like most country vicars, he was now a priest to more than one church and group of parishioners. The midnight service would be in Woodford, but he would conduct Christmas morning worship in three different churches. 'Or we could invite some people round here. Perhaps Boxing Day might be better. Most people will want to be at home on Christmas Day.' He tried not to imply a rebuke to her in the words.

'And what should we offer them to eat and drink? We can hardly feed ourselves, on what they mete out to you!'

'Oh, come on, Clare, don't exaggerate. We can have a

few friends in. Anyway, most of them would probably bring a bottle, and—'

'And patronize us as usual. No, thanks, I've had enough of that scenario, thank you.'

She was more annoyed by his calm than she would have been by the irritation he might have offered instead. Dimly, she realized that she had been looking for the full-scale row she was not going to get. Her frustration increased as he sought to console her, until eventually she stormed out of the room and up to the low-ceilinged bedroom, where he found it equally difficult to please her these days. It had all seemed to offer a different prospect when Peter had been a personable young theology student at university, in his final year when she was only in her first. Money had seemed an irrelevance then, perhaps because with her background she had never had to consider it. To Peter it was still an irrelevance, and she could not admit that that was one of their problems.

She knew that he would have preferred a city parish, where he could confront the most urgent challenges to his faith face to face and day by day. She had been secretly relieved when he had been sent to this rural backwater, though they both suspected it was a move to enervate his radical views on church reform. Now she hated the place. She found that she was not good at conversation with people of different generations and backgrounds from her own. Few of her contemporaries came to church, and those who did seemed to her generally rather wet. Perhaps she simply did not want to make the effort that was required to be a supportive vicar's wife.

Yet she knew she had a good man for her husband. She told herself that, repeatedly and ineffectively. And she put on her parish face with increasing desperation when she went out into the village, feeling like the woman in the song who kept her smile in a jamjar by the door. And the people of the village saw through her: she was sure they did.

She lay looking at the ceiling for what seemed to her a long time, though it was in fact no more than ten minutes.

Then she succumbed to the temptation that had been with her all day. She wondered as she changed her clothes in front of the full-length mirror whether she had decided to do so at the beginning of the day, whether her protests downstairs had been no more than an elaborate ritual of preparation for a course of action that was already determined.

She put her old clothes away carefully in the bedroom suite she had brought with her from that bigger room which had been hers at home. Then she took a last, cool look at herself in the heavy Edwardian mirror, adjusting the shoulder of her jacket a fraction, making the most of last year's smartness. These were clothes she rarely wore on her excursions into the parish; now she encased herself in her least dated, most formal outfit to get out of the place.

Peter was still there when she went down. He was like a man waiting to play out his part in a stage scene, she thought. Both of them would now go through the lines they had rehearsed too often before. She already felt the drama going stale as she launched this minor scene. 'I'm going out. I don't know when I shall be back.'

'Like Captain Oates.' His laughter was brittle as he tried to catch her eye. She understood the reference, but stonily refused to acknowledge it. He said more quietly, 'Do you have to go out?'

'You know quite well I don't have to. I choose to, which is quite different.'

He turned and came towards her; move stage right, she thought. She remained motionless just inside the door, as though she were preparing to upstage him in the dialogue to come. He took both her hands in his for a moment, in a gesture she remembered from the first days of their marriage. He was willing her to look at him, but she kept her eyes resolutely on the handbag he had made her put down. 'Clare, what's gone wrong with us?'

'With me, you mean. Nothing you can put right, I'm sure.' She willed him to accuse her directly of the damage she was doing, so that both of them might be forced to confront it. She flashed a look from her moist blue eyes full into his face, then dropped them again.

He was frightened by what he saw in her eyes. Frightened because he had no idea how to cope with it. There had been desperation in her face, and he had nothing to offer which would be strong enough to turn it away. He said, 'Let's sit down and talk it through,' and made a feeble attempt to draw her towards the sofa.

She shook him roughly away, angered more by his lack of conviction than by what he was trying to do. 'We've been over it often enough before. There's no point.'

Peter Barton shook his head. How could he be so competent, so helpful to others in distress, yet so unable to assuage this hurt that was close to him? 'I know things aren't right. But surely they can be put right. If only we had children—'

'It isn't that.' She was tight-lipped, not trusting herself to more than a simple rejection of the idea.

'I wish you'd consider adoption, you know. It isn't easy to get babies now, but we're the ideal couple as far as the adoption commission is concerned. If we put our names down, I'm sure—'

'No. I can't face that.'

'But everyone feels at first that it will be too much of a responsibility to take on. That's only—'

'Leave it, can't you?' She heard the hysteria in her voice. 'I'm going out.' She snatched up her handbag, fumbling for the keys of the car.

He walked behind her to the door. For a moment, he thought of asking her not to take the car, of telling her he needed it for his day's work. Then he shrugged his shoulders in a gesture of hopelessness which she could not see. 'When will you be back?'

She did not turn to look at him again. 'I told you, I don't know yet.' She paused with her hand on the handle of the door, watching her fingers whiten as she tried to fight down her tension. 'I—I know it's hard, Peter, but I can't help it.' She wrenched the door open and was gone, without looking at him again.

She forced herself to drive carefully through the village, presenting her jamjar smile to old Mrs Marsden as she crossed the road in front of her with her basket. She told herself as she drove to count her blessings. She would never starve, like the people on the other side of the world for whom she organized collections. She had no children to support. She had a good man for her husband.

She was lucky. Lucky to have Peter to rely on through this. Clare Barton told herself that yet again, as she drove away from him.

CHAPTER 3

The sign over the door of the village shop read 'G. G. Farr', but everyone called him Tommy.

A few people knew that the first initial stood for George, but not even his intimates were allowed the knowledge that the second one had inflicted Godfrey upon him. He had been born in Wales at the end of the war, when the memory of gallant Tommy Farr's contest with the great Joe Louis was still a fresh legend in the valleys. He had never minded that 'Tommy'; it had given him a kind of distinction among his schoolfellows.

It had meant he had had to fight sometimes, especially when one of his peers sneaked a glance at the register on the teacher's desk and caught sight of the Godfrey in her round copperplate hand. But he had never minded a scrap: his broken nose and misshapen right ear bore witness to the fact. During his National Service, in the very last batch of young men to be drawn in by that system, he had even boxed a little, fighting with gloves on for the only time in his life. But those days were long gone. He had been here now for almost thirty years, initially with a wife, but for the last ten years on his own.

He managed well enough, even when things were busy, as they were this morning with Christmas so close. He was never ill, and his broad-shouldered strength made light of the lifting of cartons of various sizes around the big, untidy storeroom which no one ever saw. In the shop itself, he had made himself over the years into an adequate conversationalist, recognizing the need to offer small talk as part of his alternative service to that of the supermarkets burgeoning in the towns outside the forest.

He greeted all the women, and all of the children sent on errands, by name. As the morning progressed, he gathered and then retailed various bits of harmless gossip—young Wayne's cut knee had needed stitches, old Mrs Hardman was having to go into hospital again, that young Sally with three kids already was pregnant again. If he saw himself playing a part, and occasionally derided what he saw, his hearers were not aware of that. They wanted only the odd snippet of news to sugar the extraction of their money, and he provided it satisfactorily. If he remained a secretive sort of man, few of them even registered it, let alone resented it.

He was putting a jar of cranberry sauce in his single display window at the end of a busy morning when he saw Clare Barton drive past. He studied her without any attempt at disguise, for she was too preoccupied to notice his attention. As she turned the old Escort round the corner by his store, she was hunched and intense over the wheel, with a strand of fair hair falling askew across her forehead. She missed her gear change before the car lurched away a little unevenly out of the village.

She was off out again, then. His deep-set eyes with their slight squint watched the thin blue smoke from the exhaust until it disappeared at the bend by Stonecroft Farm. Perhaps there was something in the rumours he had heard that all was not as it should be at the vicarage. He smiled a little at the thought. His teeth were his best feature, as the wife who had left had told him many years ago. So he was never afraid to smile.

Perhaps that clean-cut young Reverend Barton on whom

some of his customers doted was not giving her enough. She was a spoiled young bitch, from what little he had seen, but attractive. Perhaps what she needed was a bit of rough, and Tommy Farr could be as rough as most in bed when given his chance. He smiled again. As a man who lived alone, he was allowed his fantasies: in the secret small hours of darkness, he even indulged them. It was harmless enough, whatever his teachers and the chapel clergy had once told him. He liked to see his hot visions of Clare Barton as his revenge on the Chapel.

On the stroke of one o'clock, he bolted the door of his shop. He always gave himself an hour and a quarter for lunch, though he would open again just as promptly. He went through the storeroom to the old-fashioned living kitchen at the back of the building, where he switched on the kettle and cut himself a thick slice of bread to go with the cheddar cheese he had brought from the shop. The dark head which waited attentively by his knee vanished the rind with scarcely a sound.

He poured the boiling water over the teabag in the mug and subsided with a sigh into the big armchair. The head was on his knee now, and he fondled it as he ate; there was no one here to scold him about hygiene. It took him only a moment to rinse his cup and plate at the sink. The dog was waiting at the back door as he knew it would be, beneath the hook where his lead hung.

He walked briskly, relishing the release from the dark cave of his business, savouring the bitter air most of his customers had complained about as a reflex action as they came into the shop. There had been a little sun, which had melted the thin covering of snow in patches, but that had gone now. The cloud was high, but it would not clear again today.

He was in the forest in less than five minutes. The Doberman raced ahead of him, then swerved off the path into the woods, tail wagging furiously with the excitement of scents undiscernible to his master. It was colder than ever on the narrow track they followed, for the frost hung between the pines and no sun had penetrated here.

Farr did not mind that. He beat his arms a couple of times across his chest and ran for a moment, until he was thoroughly warm. He watched his breath wreathing in great tubes of steam into the branches above him. 'Come on, Kelly!' he shouted, and raced anew down the path as it sloped helpfully away in front of him. With the dog bounding at his heels, he was for a moment a boy again, racing along the hillside above the pit, conscious only of the exhilaration of the moment.

Kelly loped indulgently at his heels; he did not need to do more to keep up with the best speed his master or any other human could muster. He was a powerful dog, but gentle and well controlled. Not many people chose to test those qualities, for the reputation of his breed did not encourage the taking of chances. When his master slowed, he veered away again into the trees in search of something swifter to pursue.

The pair went a good mile into the forest before Tommy Farr looked at his watch and decided it was almost time for them to return. He whistled the dog, but was only accorded a distant bark in response. Usually Kelly returned to heel immediately. Tom hesitated a moment, then turned down an overgrown path that not many would have even recognized as a route. No one knew this section of the forest better than Farr.

He called again as he heard the sound of Kelly barking. 'Leave it, boy. Come on!' Probably the dog had found a rabbit or a fox. Tom had gone a hundred yards along the disused way, stooping under low branches and cursing to himself, when he saw the man. He had his back to Tom and his eye on the dog, watching it cautiously, prepared to defend himself if it sprang.

'Kelly, heel!' called Farr sharply. The dog, hearing the assertion of serious authority now, came reluctantly back to him. He fondled the soft ears without taking his eyes off the man ahead of him. He was no more than thirty yards away, motionless now that he realized he had been discovered. Tom Farr went a little nearer, then called gruffly, 'You're quite safe. He won't touch you with me here.'

The man looked without speaking from his face to the dog at his heels, weighed the situation, and seemed to accept his words. He nodded his agreement, but did not speak, as though waiting for Farr to make the next move. He had half a week's stubble on his chin and cheeks, a dark circle of hair which made his face look smaller. His hair was uncombed, protruding in a wild fringe beneath the edges of a cap which seemed too small to cover its exuberant disarray.

Farr said, 'He must have given you a shock, coming upon you like that. But he's harmless enough. We walk here nearly every day.'

The man knew it well enough. He had avoided them successfully until today. But he did not reveal that. He said only, 'Ay. I can see that now.'

His voice was not as rough as Farr had expected. Tommy had assumed he was a tramp, but he realized now that he had not seen a tramp in twenty years or more. They came from all sorts of backgrounds now, and they called themselves dropouts. Or other people called them that; he was not sure which. He cast a glance up at the square yard or so of sky he could see. 'Going to be cold again tonight. Not a night to be without shelter.' For a moment he panicked, fearing the man would suppose he was offering sanctuary. All the tramps he had met years ago had been expert cadgers.

'I'll be all right. I can look after myself.' There was a stubborn pride in the man's words. Perhaps, taken off guard by this unexpected meeting, he had spoken without thinking. It was his first human intercourse for four days. He glanced automatically into the undergrowth on his left, and the alert Farr caught a glimpse of the corner of what he thought was a small tent.

'I'm sure you can.' Tommy was anxious to be away now, obscurely afraid of involvement with the man, though he should have sensed the feeling was mutual. The tramp, if that was the right word for him, was younger than he had thought beneath the embryo beard. He looked fit and vigilant; the old army greatcoat he wore covered him well, but Farr fancied there was a hard, fit body beneath it.

Well, that was no business of his. He felt suddenly aware that this was a remote and lonely place, and was glad of the dog waiting obediently at his heels. 'Well, I must be off. I've a shop to open, you see.'

The man nodded. The quick half-smile he volunteered was the nearest thing he offered to acknowledgement or farewell. He did not turn away, but watched the retreating figures of man and dog until they disappeared beneath the dim evergreen canopy of the firs. Then he turned and set about dismantling the small grey-green tent. There were plenty of other places to camp.

Tommy Farr cast a look back at the woods as he reached the edge of Woodford. Even at just after two o'clock, twilight seemed to be descending. For once, he was glad to go back with Kelly into the shop which had sometimes seemed a prison.

CHAPTER 4

Peter Barton did not need to don his public face at the door as his wife did. He went out among his flock with pleasure. Even when he did not always like what he found, he remained an optimist about the possibilities of the human race.

Those in Woodford who had greeted him with suspicion —he had the twin disadvantages of being young and an incomer—had warmed, sometimes reluctantly, to his enthusiasm and his capacity to treat all souls alike. Those who attended his churches generally found him stimulating, once they had got used to his disturbing tendency to direct their attention to issues like starvation on the other side of the world. Most of them found themselves uneasy when asked to contemplate events outside the forest and its small towns, let alone beyond Gloucestershire.

Those who did not go to church were in the majority now in the village. There was a hard core of resolute atheists, but the majority had drifted into an ill-defined agnosticism when they found religion no longer provided answers they could accept. They used the church still for marriage, death and occasional christenings. They had expected the young vicar to chastise them for their sloth, and avoided him when he arrived, but had then been relieved to discover that he was not the aggressive crusader they had feared.

The Reverend Barton was ready to talk religion when they introduced the subject, but he never seemed to compel it upon them. He played cricket with the young bloods in the summer, coached the youngsters at football, played the occasional game of golf as a guest but had resolutely refused to join a club. After a distinguished performance in skittles, he had been welcomed into the pub circle. He could not afford to attend very often, but after one inspired evening at the dartboard, he was offered that ultimate male accolade in the village, an invitation to play in the Crown's darts team. He had modestly consented to becoming part of the 'squad', so that he might be called upon when the real giants of the arrows were not available.

He knew everyone in Woodford now, and faces young and old lightened at the sight of him on this bitter morning as he walked briskly among its houses. By the time he reached the church, he had four children trotting beside him. He gave them the key to the little room at the rear of the stone building, with instructions to carry the statues with extreme care along the path which ran beneath the old gothic windows alongside the church.

He stood for a moment looking at the front of the church before he went in, admiring the steeple which climbed towards the grey clouds, wondering what would happen to the place when the next major repairs were necessary. The moment took him back to Clare, for he remembered their honeymoon, and the way they had stood arm in arm, gazing like this at the soaring fronts of Rheims and Rouen, of Notre Dame and the Sainte-Chapelle. The parish church in Woodford had not the swirling detail of those great fronts, but its plainer elevations were balanced and agreeable enough to their latest incumbent.

And today at least, the doors were not locked. It was one of his abiding regrets that vandalism and theft in some of the richer churches had resulted in a diocesan directive that all churches should be locked when unattended. He would rather have locked away the church's modest treasures—mainly a pair of ornate Georgian candlesticks and a silver chalice—and left the house of the Lord open for quiet meditation. But there were more important issues for him to debate with the bishop than this.

He knew when he found the door unlatched that the ladies would be busy within. Mrs Jenkins was vigorously polishing the brasses. Mrs Coleman, who employed her on other mornings to clean her home, was unconsciously supervising her here as she did when she paid for the privilege. She stood with an amber chrysanthemum bloom in her hand, inspecting and admiring the sheen on the brass lectern. She did not see Peter Barton until he came forward.

'Good morning, ladies,' he called from the end of the central aisle, anxious to announce his presence early lest they should think him an eavesdropper. 'What a splendid gleam, Mrs Jenkins. I can see it from the back of the church.' The old Welshwoman's red cheeks shone with pleasure; her distorted reflection danced in the plate she polished like that of a benevolent sprite.

Deirdre Coleman said, 'I was thinking of doing the Christmas displays this afternoon, Vicar. You don't think it's too early?'

'In this weather, I'm sure the flowers will look as good as new on Christmas Day. As you know, we can't really afford to put the heat on until about six o'clock on Christmas Eve, ready for the midnight service. We shall all need our thermal undies on, even at that.'

Mrs Jenkins twinkled. It was a mildly improper suggestion, coming from a vicar, but that just showed how the young man wasn't stuck up. There were times when he said things her own husband might have said, even though Mervyn had left school at fourteen.

The children came in, carrying the crudely fashioned figures with elaborate reverence to the side altar where the crib was to be set up. Young Meg had made sure she got Baby Jesus for herself. With her dental brace, her jeans and her patched anorak, she made an unlikely Madonna, apart from the sentimental affection she conveyed upon the plaster figure as she cradled it carefully in her arms.

Peter Barton was soon on his knees, spreading straw carefully around the floor of the improvised stable, putting just enough of it into the small wooden manger to set off the figure Meg waited patiently to deposit there. It was better not to let straw get into the hands of over-enthusiastic children, lest it spread into the aisles the ladies had just swept. After eight years as curate and vicar in different settings, he was an expert on the temperaments of voluntary church helpers.

'Any chance of a little greenery round the crib when we've finished setting it up, Mrs Coleman?' he called to the now invisible presence behind him. He knew the children would regard their work as downgraded if it did not receive the accolade of decoration by the floral artists.

Deirdre Coleman appeared behind them, surveying their work without comment. 'We might not be able to run to chrysanths,' she said. These children must be kept firmly in their places.

'Oh, that wouldn't be appropriate anyway,' said Peter Barton. 'I thought a little holly and ivy to garnish the edges —the kind of thing you did so effectively last year.'

Mrs Coleman glowed. 'That's easy enough. There's plenty of holly, and it's berried up nicely this year.'

'That's good. Traditionally English rather than historically accurate, of course, but that's entirely right.'

She watched them critically for a few minutes as they set

the figures in place. 'Pity you've only got two wise men. Young Florence Brown dropped Balthasar a couple of years ago, you know.'

'It doesn't really matter,' said Peter. 'There's no real evidence for the three kings being at the stable anyway. And it leaves us room for this rather appealing donkey.' He moved the beast a little nearer to the manger, so that it looked quizzically at the Christ-child. Not surprisingly, thought Peter: this Jesus, with his lengthy brown locks, looked at least eighteen months old. He hoped that Joseph did not look quite so villainous from a few yards away as he did at close range; he moved him back a little further into the shadows.

He watched the children's rapt concentration on their task and felt again the lack of a family of his own. Would it have made much difference to him and Clare? He wondered bleakly just where she was at this moment, then turned resolutely back to the task in hand.

In one of the village's four council houses, two people who never set foot in Peter Barton's church were preparing for their own kind of Christmas.

Charlie Webb was fiddling with the lights on the Christmas tree, taking out the tiny bulbs one by one and replacing them. 'It can't be more than a connection, Gran,' he said over his shoulder. 'They were working all right yesterday when I got them out.'

'Damn Japanese rubbish!' said old Mrs Webb. She spoke without rancour; indeed, with satisfaction, for the thought that all things unreliable should be made abroad was one dear to her heart.

'They weren't made in Japan, Gran. If they had been, they'd be a lot more reliable.' He looked at the side of the carton on the sideboard. 'Made in Taiwan,' he read, by way of enlargement.

'There you are, then! I told you. Damn Japanese rubbish!' She dabbed extra-large allocations of mincemeat into the last two pastry cases, as if in triumphant celebration of her vindication.

Charlie opened his mouth to correct her misapprehension, then closed it firmly. She wouldn't accept his geography; it would provoke only a diatribe about cheap labour and her father buying Japanese fire-crackers at sixty-four for a penny in the early years of the century. The lights lit up suddenly as he screwed in the last bulb. He looked at them gratefully, knowing that his small reserve of patience had been precariously preserved. Then he said, 'I'll go and put the washing out,' and took the basket down the narrow garden.

The thin veil of snow in the shadow of the house struck chillingly at his feet through his thin plastic trainers. The clothes wouldn't dry much today, for it was much too late to put them out really, but Gran would fret if they weren't put out, and he didn't want her trying to do it herself after he'd gone to work. He pegged her long pink bloomers among his shirts, checking anxiously over his shoulder that he was not observed by the neighbour's children.

Gran was the nearest thing he had known to a mother, his own having left when he was scarcely two. They never spoke of her. Gran had buried her husband twenty years ago and her son, Charlie's dad, when Charlie was ten. He was the only thing she had left; as she shrank into old age, the fear that this last male presence would be balefully removed from her like the others was one of the few things which animated her.

Once his last pair of socks was on the line, Charlie went swiftly between the rows of drunken Brussels sprouts to the shed at the bottom of the long garden. Within the privacy of its thin wooden walls, he held his most prized possession up to the light of the small window and revelled in its softly gleaming perfection.

The barrels of the shotgun shone darkly in the pale winter light. He broke it open over his arm, studying the empty cartridge chambers, enjoying the scent of the oil he had applied yesterday, savouring the spotless perfection of the engineering. The box of number 6 cartridges was dry and unopened on the shelf. Tomorrow perhaps, he would take some of them with him and go into the forest . . .

He went back into the house and ate the meal the old lady had ready for him. She watched him affectionately, not eating herself. 'You don't want too many of them chips,' she said, ignoring the fact that it was she who had piled his plate with them. 'Bad for your spots, they are.'

Charlie ran his hand automatically over the small outcrops on his forehead and neck; tact was not a quality to be associated with the aged. He made a note to use the ointment tonight, so that it could have its opportunity to work before he went to the dance on Christmas Eve. He was twenty now, and in a year the spots would be gone, as a confirmation of the manhood he pretended to have attained some time ago. But he did not know that: the pink and purple excrescences still filled him with a hot adolescent embarrassment.

He put down the black leather bomber jacket and his gauntlets. 'It was time to be moving'; Gran had left the plastic container with his sandwiches by the door. 'I may get a couple of hours' overtime, so don't wait up. And don't worry if I'm late.'

'I have to worry when you're on that motorbike,' she grumbled. 'Noisy, dangerous things. Ought not to be allowed.'

He didn't bother to argue, nor did she expect him to. Her protests had become a ritual for both of them. She had been through the same business thirty years earlier with his father. Both of them knew really that there was no way he could get to his employment at the electricity works without the bike. Public transport to the village had ceased ten years ago, and there was no way be could afford to run a car.

Charlie took the polythene cover off the Honda and pushed it round the side of the house. He looked at the watch Gran had given him on his birthday before he pulled on his goggles. He was on the last minute again. He would have to use the road through the forest, as usual.

It was well after dark when Peter Barton returned to the vicarage. He called upstairs, 'Clare, I'm home!' but he knew because the front of the house was in darkness that his wife had not come back.

He went to check that the garage was empty, hoping against hope that she had come home and gone out again into the village. Its absolute stillness and carless concrete floor seemed sinister on this icy evening, as if emphasizing the presence that had been removed.

He felt a sudden, futile indignation that she could have taken the car and not returned it. She had left him to make his calls on foot, without checking on his schedule to see if that was possible. It was not the absence of the car itself which irritated him, but the petty selfishness involved in its removal like this. He was not a man used to feeling sorry for himself, and the emotion only disturbed him.

The house tonight seemed to echo cheerlessly around him, as if reflecting his misery. He was tired out, emotionally as well as physically. He had spent almost an hour with a man who was dying of lung cancer, wrestling with the problem that while the central figure now accepted his fate, his family was still fighting it. He wanted to ring Clare's mother, to see if she was there. Instead, he forced himself to make the phone call to the hospice, knowing it would press upon his mind through the night if he left it for the morrow.

He made himself beans on toast. He was a man for whom food was not important, who became embarrassed indeed if it was dressed up for his consumption with too much care and ceremony. Yet tonight, he would have liked to have a fuller meal than this; above all, he would have liked it to have been prepared and served to him by his wife.

Watching the television without seeing it, he wondered again where Clare was at that moment.

CHAPTER 5

The Old Vicarage in Woodford was an architectural embodiment of changing times; sociologists, of which there was a merciful scarcity in Woodford, could have dwelt upon the fact at tedious length.

Even after the sacrifice of some rooms to the demands of en suite bathrooms and more spacious servants' quarters, it had six bedrooms and four reception rooms. Its ivy-clad elevations bespoke a permanence, a faith in solid money and sensible investments. The grounds were large enough and mature enough to have full-grown copper beeches at their boundary. In spring, the magnolias held their purple-flushed cups confidently aloft and huge Pink Pearl rhododendrons made fifty-foot-high pyramids of opulent bloom on the closely mown front lawn. In summer, the spacious lawns at the rear called out for cucumber sandwiches and afternoon tea.

In these dead days of winter, there was little colour evident in the long borders, but the huge Victorian conservatory, in decline for many years, had recently been restored to its pristine glory. Hyacinths filled the place with heavy, exotic perfume, and the bowls of paperwhite narcissi would be out for Christmas Day. The temperature was kept at sixty degrees, comfortably above the level at which the last vicar who had lived here had been able to keep the house itself.

The Old Vicarage had long since ceased to be owned by the Church of England.

Peter Barton did not hesitate between the high wrought-iron gates because of envy. He had no regret for times past, no desire to live here with the comfortable social position of his predecessor a hundred years earlier. When he confronted the sparse audience for his Sunday sermons, he had an occasional nostalgia for the teeming pews of Victorian

England, but he knew how he would have been appalled by the poverty and exploitation of that era. His grandfather had been an early Labour Party man, and he was proud of that, though there were some environments where he bit his lip and concealed it.

The Old Vicarage, ironically enough, was one of them. But the people here meant well enough, he told himself resolutely as he marched up the long drive. He was seen before he arrived at the broad mahogany door. The maid, Mary Cox, was one of his parishioners. She smiled a shy welcome and ushered him into the drawing-room. Colonel Harry Davidson, JP, was holding forth at length on the penalties appropriate to young offenders, but he broke off to greet his vicar affably enough. 'Come and sit down, Peter. We're just rustling up some t-tea.' He had a slight speech impediment which caught him out when a t came at the beginning of a word; it went oddly with his general air of control.

Davidson was a Gloucestershire man, but he had been away from the county for over twenty years in the service of his country. Woodford had been glad he had chosen the Old Vicarage when he retired a few years ago, and not only because money and employment were always welcome in a village where both were in short supply. Harry Davidson had managed to distinguish himself in the Falklands, leading a landing party in the crucial action at San Carlos in 1982. He said modestly that he would have retired as a major had he not been in that place at that time, but Woodford was glad of a whiff of military glory.

His army pension would never have stretched to the Old Vicarage, but Colonel Harry had made a good, late marriage when he came back from the Falklands. Rachel was from a relatively minor Swiss banking family, but she brought with her considerable riches. She was striking rather than pretty, but she had the equable personality and intelligence which her husband was shrewd enough to recognize as more valuable to him in the setting he now dominated.

Two-thirty was a strange time for tea, but she had long since reconciled herself to the English habit of offering it at any hour as an assurance of welcome. So she now pushed a plate of scones towards the young vicar, who she thought looked drawn and strained. 'Sit down and get warm, Peter, for goodness' sake! You look as though you need it.' Her Swiss accent was scarcely detectable now.

He was more glad of the hot tea and the newly baked scones than he knew. Perhaps it was the feeling of being cosseted that his human weakness really appreciated. 'I was hoping the four of us might form part of a fund-raising group.' He looked round hopefully at the Davidsons and Mrs Graham, the widow who had been listening to the Colonel when he arrived.

'I don't see why not,' said the Colonel comfortably. 'Which church fabric is in need of repair now?' He waved aside the offer of more tea from his wife.

'I wasn't thinking of our buildings. Sooner or later we're going to have to abandon one of them—probably St Thomas's at Ashbridge—but we can debate that in a larger assembly in due course. It's the famine in Ethiopia that should perhaps be our immediate concern.'

Davidson frowned. 'None of us likes looking at pictures of starving children, I agree. But Ethiopia seems in danger of becoming a perennial problem. Are we sure that all this aid gets through to where it's needed? Some of these African governments simply can't be t-trusted.'

'I think organizations like Oxfam and Christian Aid know the score on that,' said Peter firmly. 'They've a lot of experience of ensuring that money and food get through to where they can do most good. It's just the scale of the problem that threatens to overwhelm them. It needs vast sums to make much impact; I'm glad to see the Princess Royal is throwing her weight behind the Appeal.' He aimed this last shaft at Mrs Graham, a determined royalist, though he took care not to look at her. He was delighted to see her responding out of the corner of his eye.

Rachel Davidson said, 'The young people would be interested. If someone could organize a disco in the village hall, I'd provide them with refreshments.' She took up her silver cake-server and slid two more pieces of scone deftly on to Peter's plate.

Her husband had enough sense to realize when he was outnumbered. He prided himself on his capacity for swift decisions, not recognizing that it could sometimes be a weakness as well as a strength. 'Well, if you're all happy to give the project your energies, we might as well get on with it,' he said, cheerfully enough.

Cut your losses early and people don't even realize you've been defeated. It was the most valuable lesson he had picked up from the course on managerial skills the Army had offered him to prepare him for civilian life at forty-five. He used the tactic often on the Rural District Council; not that as Chairman he had to concede defeat very often there.

Peter was relieved to find his objective so easily achieved: he had expected quite a struggle to carry the day. It was agreed that he should mention the crisis and the fund which was to be their local response at his sermons at Midnight Mass and on Christmas morning. The two women came up with ideas of their own, and the Colonel promised to pass the hat round at the conclusion of the Boxing Day hunt. Peter watched the logs burning cheerfully in the wide inglenook fireplace, sipped his second cup of tea, felt pleasantly drowsy and supported.

He had not realized quite how drained he was until Mrs Graham said to him conventionally, 'And how is Mrs Barton? Looking forward to Christmas?'

'Er, yes, I think so. I've been too busy to see much of her these last few days.' He managed a weak laugh. He could not tell them that she had not come home last night and he did not even know where she was. 'Well, I must be going. I want to get over to Ashbridge to set up a similar collection for Ethiopia.'

'But you didn't bring your car,' said Rachel Davidson.

So he had been observed as he thought as he walked up the drive. 'No. Clare's out in it, actually. But I'll walk over to Ashbridge: it won't take me very long.' He moved towards the door.

Davidson sprang up. 'You'll do no such thing, Vicar. Arthur will run you over there in my car.' Ignoring Peter's protests, he seized the internal phone and explained what was required to his chauffeur-handyman, who lived in the flat over what had originally been the stables. 'He'll have you over there in t-ten minutes.'

'But I may be a couple of hours. Really, it's not necessary, I'm quite used to—'

'Nonsense.' Harry Davidson was in the masterful mood he regarded as his military vein. He enjoyed taking control, especially when he knew the two women thoroughly approved of his magnanimity. 'Arthur will wait and bring you back when you're ready. He's nothing better to do, I'm sure. Or better still, he can walk back through the forest, and you can bring the car back at your leisure. You can d-drive the Rover OK? It's an automatic.'

'Yes, but I couldn't possibly ask Arthur—'

'Of course you could. And if you couldn't, I could. Do him good to get a bit of exercise. He gets too little in the winter. He'll be running to fat.' He sniggered to the ladies at his jest: Comstock was as lean and hungry in appearance as any Cassius. 'Besides, he can get back here in daylight, whereas you'd be in the dark by the t-time you've finished over there.'

It was true that Peter did sometimes wonder how Arthur Comstock managed to fill in his days. With odd jobs around the house and grounds, he supposed, though he knew the Davidsons had a full-time gardener. The chauffeur looked cheerful enough when he collected him at the front door three minutes later, though Peter wondered how far this was a front for his employer.

Ashbridge was five miles away by road, on the other side of the wide tongue of forest which separated the villages. On foot, it wasn't much over two miles, if you took the road through the forest which was barred to cars. That was the way Peter had planned to use, the way on which Arthur had been directed to return by his imperious employer.

Peter chatted to Arthur Comstock as they drove through the landscape with its thin covering of snow. He found him polite but uncommunicative. Knowing that Arthur had been a regular soldier like his employer, he tried that track. 'Cold enough today for it to be the Falklands!' he said rather desperately.

Arthur, negotiating a tight bend carefully in the big Rover, took a few seconds to reply. Then he said, 'You're right there, Padre.' He clung to the Army address, treasuring the memory of his service like many long-time regulars. 'But the sickness was worse than the cold—I'd never been at sea for any length of time. I was only an RASC Sergeant in the UK at the time when the war blew up.'

'You weren't with Mr Davidson in the Army? I somehow got the impression you'd been with him in the Services.'

'Faithful batman sort of thing? I'm afraid that went out a long time ago, Padre. I just saw the job advertised here and went for it.'

'Yes, of course. Stupid of me.' At thirty-one, Peter could be no more than fourteen years younger than the man beside him; he suddenly felt immeasurably less experienced than this worldly-wise veteran. As they ran into Ashbridge, he caught the chauffeur stealing a look at his watch. 'Did you have something else planned for this afternoon? I'm sorry you were hauled out like this. It wasn't my doing, it was Mr Davidson who insisted.' Peter resolutely refused to use the title of 'Colonel' which was almost universally accorded to the man whom he was determined was now a civilian.

He felt weak explaining himself like this, but Comstock seemed to appreciate the thought. For the first time in a quarter of an hour, he was prepared to reveal a little of himself. 'It's only that my sister's coming down from Yorkshire for Christmas. I was hoping to meet her bus in Cheltenham.'

'What time is she due in?'

'Four o'clock. But she'll just have to wait a while.'

'No, she won't! Why didn't you mention it earlier, you silly devil—pardon the unclerical expression. Look, there's no problem. You take the car back as soon as you've dropped me off at St Thomas's, and I'll walk through the woods when I've finished in Ashbridge. That way, I needn't rush, and it's what I intended to do before Harry thrust transport upon me, anyway.'

'But it could be dark when you finish. I can't— '

'You can and will.' It was a relief for a man who spent so much of his time being diplomatic to assert himself so decisively. 'I know the tracks through the forest well enough, and I have a torch here if I need it.' He patted the pocket of his anorak. 'You can pay me back by helping me to get a collecting box for the famine appeal into the Crown. Drunken heathens are often the most generous givers. I'll explain to Mr Davidson that I insisted you left me, if that's what's worrying you.'

'Oh, it's not that.' The thought that he might be considered in fear of his employer seemed to decide Harry. 'All right, if you're sure. I'll go straight through to Cheltenham when I've dropped you. If you change your mind and want a lift just ring my flat—I've got my own number.' They came to a halt outside the old church and he put on the handbrake while he scribbled the number on the back of a petrol receipt.

Peter Barton watched the rear lights of the Rover as they wound away from him over the undulating lane. They seemed unnaturally bright on that dim afternoon. When he turned the other way, the drunken tombstones seemed almost threatening in the cheerless shadow of the church.

He walked briskly to the first house beyond it, trying unsuccessfully to thrust away conjecture about the whereabouts of his wife.

CHAPTER 6

Clare Barton did not return to the Vicarage until the next day.

She had been away for forty-eight hours. Absence had seemed at first to confuse her emotions rather than clarify them. By the second day, there had come to her a dim realization that her problems were within herself, and that therefore she would have to confront herself before they could be solved.

Perhaps she had hoped despite her conduct that her absence from Peter would really make her heart grow fonder, as it had been used to do in the early years of their marriage. That had not quite happened: life as she got older did not seem to be as simple as it had once been. But she returned full of a bleak determination to try harder. She would throw herself wholeheartedly into the work of supporting Peter. It was not the first time she had so resolved, but this time she felt very determined.

Her arrival back in the village was noticed. The vicar's old red Ford was known to everyone, and in the quiet middle of the day several pairs of eyes remarked the strained white face of his wife behind the steering-wheel. She drove very slowly when she reached the village, turning the tight bend by Tommy Farr's village shop with elaborate care, working out what she would say to Peter when she re-entered their sterile little house.

As soon as she turned her key in the front door, she sensed that the house was empty. She called her husband's name up the stairs and into the kitchen, but already she knew that there would be no reply. She walked round the ground-floor rooms, looking for the note she could scarcely expect to find. It was she, after all, who had left Peter wondering where she was for two days.

She went into the kitchen, half-hoping that she would

find the units in a mess, so that she could emphasize her contrition by cleaning the place up before he returned. The place was as orderly as a hospital operating theatre. Not even a piece of cutlery relieved the surface of the stainless steel sink; there was no sign of even a cereal packet on the grey formica surface of the table. She felt the electric kettle: it was stone cold. Tipping the lid of the rubbish bin, she saw only an empty baked bean tin as evidence of her husband's use of the kitchen while she was away. She smiled, for the first time in two hours. Peter hadn't much idea of how to look after himself. The thought of his vulnerability was a comfort, a support to her new resolution.

She went over to the single small bag she had carried in with her. She put the cricket book she had bought for Peter in the corner of the lounge; with its gaudy Christmas wrapping it became immediately a point of interest. Later, on her way through the village, she would call in at Tommy Farr's and order a Christmas tree, that pagan symbol so beloved of her Christian husband with his schoolboy enthusiasms. She had told him the artificial one they had upstairs would be quite adequate for their needs, if he must have some such childish symbol. Now this would be the first of her concessions.

The second one would be more important. She picked up the phone and tapped out the number of the secretary of the diocesan adoption society. Her fingers flicked impatiently over the panel: her resolution must not fail before the thing was accomplished. Within two minutes, she had set in motion the first stages of the adoption procedure which for five years she had adamantly refused to contemplate.

It was much easier than she had expected. While still buoyed up by her relief, she sat down at the kitchen table and wrote her message on the jokey Christmas card she had brought for Peter, indicating that she was willing now to adopt. She said nothing about the phone call she had just made; she would tell him that, as the confirmation that she was serious in her intention. This would be her real Christmas present.

When she had sealed the envelope and put the card on top of the book in the corner of the lounge, she washed her face, put on some light make-up, and prepared to go out into the village. Looking at her pale features in the mirror, she saw herself don the smile she was accustomed to wearing on her village rounds. Well, that was all right: it was too early yet to expect anything else. If things worked out, the smile would become more genuine over the months.

She walked briskly through the village, calling as she had determined to do at the stores to order her tree. Tommy Farr promised that there would be a four-footer ready for her on the morrow. She kept her eyes alert as she went on for any sign of Peter. If she could find him, she would plunge enthusiastically into support of whatever he was doing, as a public demonstration of her new attitude.

The church's heavy wooden door was open. She was disappointed to find that her husband was not within the place. Frosty Mrs Coleman had not seen him today; she was putting the final touches to her Christmas floral display. The older woman stood looking thoughtfully after the vicar's young wife from the church porch, wondering what could be the source of her new animation. Strange woman; the vicar deserved better, she thought protectively.

Clare decided that her husband must have gone over to one of the other churches. She felt a pang of guilt that he had not had the car. It was still drizzling a little: perhaps she should take the car and try to collect him. But she did not know for certain where he was, and she would hate not to be in the house when he came home.

She took home the vegetables she had bought at Tommy Farr's and began to prepare a meal which would be an elaborate one by her recent standards. Activity was an effective therapy. For the first time in years, she was actually enjoying a domestic task. The drizzle on the window made her feel warm and protected in the warmth of the small brick house.

It looked as though there would not be a white Christmas, after all.

In the forest, the rise in temperature brought a smell of damp vegetation which overwhelmed all other scents. The drizzle was scarcely more than a dampness in the still air, but it had been present for most of the day, so that the trees dripped steadily on to earth which was soft with the residue of the melting frost.

Despite their initial reluctance to come, the children were glad to be here, releasing their abundant holiday energy. It had needed all the persuasive powers of an overworked mother to get them out into the open air and away from her festive preparations. Now they were glad of the change from waiting for Christmas and what it might bring. In less than thirty-six hours now, it would be Christmas Day; to young minds, the interval seemed interminable. But racing along the tracks in the woods, throwing the stick for an enthusiastic dog, even they could forget Christmas for a while.

There were three of them, two brothers of eleven and nine and the elder boy's classmate. The dog was a black labrador, not yet two years old, more delighted to be here even than they were. He dived in and out of the trees, retrieving the stick when it suited him, ignoring it when more interesting scents or sounds diverted him. Sometimes he made longer expeditions into the undergrowth, rejoining his young companions further down the wide stone road when they had almost despaired of his return.

The boys had brought a mountain bike with them. They took turns to ride it, bouncing crazily over the stones which protruded from the earth, coming to grief occasionally in the ruts left in soft areas by the heavy forestry vehicles. The young one, as usual, had to fight hard to get his turns on the machine. His shrill tones, sometimes near to tears in his frustration, soared piercingly over the tops of pine and beech as the boys moved towards one of the clearings where wide tracks crossed, then curved away again until they disappeared beneath the trees.

The boys were so preoccupied that they forgot the dog for a while. The eldest one eventually realized that the animal had been missing for several minutes. They called his name in high, wailing tones. It became a contest of decibels between them as the labrador failed to appear. Gathered around the bike, they took turns to bellow, each one straining his alert young ears for the response which would show that his cry had been the successful one.

Eventually, they caught the faint sound of a bark through the heavy air. All of them called together then, and the bark came again, made eerie by the distance. But still the dog did not return. The sound was from their left, down the track which had just met them at the crossing place. They set off towards the tenuous notes of the dog, calling as they went to make sure they were correct.

The labrador was a good quarter of a mile away; they were quite breathless when they reached him. Only his excited snuffling told them where he was, for his sleek black fur was almost invisible beneath the ferns which covered the ground below the leafless oaks. The boys called his name again, but still he did not come to them, acknowledging their presence only with an excited half-bark.

The eldest boy called, 'Come on then, lad! What is it that's bothering thee?' in what he thought was a fair imitation of his father's unflappable tones. Then he scrambled down the bank and crossed the shallow ditch between him and the dog.

When he saw what the dog was tugging at, he felt again the child he was rather than the man he had pretended to be. It should not be children who discovered things like this.

The man was sprawled upon his back, his eyes gazing unseeingly at the ferns which brushed his face. One arm was twisted beneath him, the other stretched wide and stiff on his other side, as if it was ready to embrace the boy who had come so unexpectedly upon him. The boy backed fearfully away, feeling his legs which wanted to run turn suddenly to lifeless sticks.

In the nightmares which beset him in the weeks to come, it was the huge raw wound in the chest and the great red hole where flesh should have been which woke him screaming in the dark hours of the night.

Clare Barton was impatient to see her husband. The meal was almost ready; she had set the table in the little dining-room which they had so rarely used. Now she put the two cut-glass goblets beside the place settings and positioned the reading lamp on the sideboard beside the table. The claret glowed richly against the winking crystal in the subdued light: it was almost like a scene from one of the magazines her mother studied so avidly.

She was glad she had lit a fire in the lounge: it transformed the square room with its welcome. Standing on a chair, she pushed the drawing-pin through the last of the Christmas paper chains at the corner of the low ceiling and looked at her handiwork with satisfaction. It was a good start.

She was taking the apple pie which was his favourite out of the oven when the doorbell rang. She knew the sergeant, but not the rather nervous-looking policewoman at his side.

It was the sergeant who said, 'May we come inside for a few minutes, Mrs Barton?' And then, as she stared without comprehension at them, 'I'm afraid we have some bad news for you.'

CHAPTER 7

On the morning of Christmas Eve, the forest throbbed with unaccustomed activity. Or at least, that part of it did where the body of the Reverend Peter Barton had met his death.

The barriers at the edge of the wood which were designed to prevent access by four-wheeled vehicles had their padlocks removed for a time. The white police vehicles drove swiftly down the unpaved road, but parked a respectful distance from the thing the boys had found in the bushes beside the wide, unpaved track. There might be other wheel tracks here, even footprints, which must not be obscured.

Only the ambulance inched cautiously nearer to the body. It stopped about ten yards short of it, waiting like a large, patient animal until the men around the corpse had finished their business and given the signal that it could be moved. Presently, what remained of Peter Barton was slid into its black plastic sack and zipped scrupulously from sight. Four men lifted the bag carefully but unemotionally into the ambulance and shut the doors against the prying eyes they might meet once they left the shelter of the woods.

The pilot of the police helicopter which circled above the forest watched the process going on below him, seeing human detritus swallowed into a dustbin bag and stowed for disposal like so much kitchen rubbish. Then he swung the craft away on the light breeze and resumed his survey of the forest. He was more than a mile from the scene of the crime when he found something to interest him in a tiny gap between the lines of tall firs.

Behind him, the uniformed officers directed by the Scene of Crime sergeant began to move methodically outwards from where the body had lain, their progress almost indistinguishable from above, searching the ground minutely for any tiny sign the killer might have left of his presence. Fibres from brambles, a rusting paperclip from the ground, the plastic top of a ballpoint pen, all found their way into plastic bags to be tagged, documented, filed. The painstaking groundwork of the investigation had begun.

It was another twenty minutes before John Lambert parked the big Vauxhall at the edge of the forest, nodded to the rather nervous young constable who prevented entry by the public, and walked into the woods with Hook at his side. Among superintendents, he was a survival from an earlier age; sometimes his juniors made him feel like a dinosaur. He was unable to keep away from an investigation, unable to sit in his CID office and marshal his forces towards the defeat of homicide like a general behind the lines.

His Chief Constable indulged him, so far. Perhaps it was because he produced results: the CC was a statistician, as the current perception of his office encouraged him to be. Lambert solved a high proportion of the serious crimes which came his way, using his own idiosyncratic methods as well as the modern police machine. It worked, and as long as it continued to do so, Douglas Gibson, with one eye on his Committee and the other on his pension, was content to indulge his Superintendent's eccentricities.

On this bleak, damp day, when most men of his rank would have welcomed a centrally heated office, Lambert marched with the sturdy Detective-Sergeant Hook at his side, looking thoughtfully at the pewter sky above the firs at the edge of the forest. If he pulled his coat more closely about him against the cold, he sniffed the air of a new inquiry with the slightly guilty enthusiasm it always prompted in him.

He liked to approach on foot, getting the feel of a crime as he moved towards the scene. It was an illusion of course, but he felt that he sometimes picked up small nuances that way that more precipitate arrivers missed. Now Superintendent and Sergeant rounded the gentle bend in the wide track and saw the machinery of the investigation set out before them.

The police ambulance had passed them as they approached the forest, moving with extreme care over the narrow lanes so as not to disturb its gruesome burden in the plain fibreglass coffin it had been accorded, proceeding at a pace appropriate to the hearse it had become. So the pathologist had already been and gone: Lambert frowned at the thought of the scent of murder growing stale before he had even reached the place. If it was murder.

Sergeant Dickenson, who was in charge of the scene of crime team, gave them the white paper zipper overall and overshoes he doled out to all who came through the limits of the roped-off area around the innocent-looking ditch. Lambert and Hook stood for a long, silent moment beside the spot where the body of Peter Barton had lain. The imprint of the corpse, with its arm thrown crazily sideways, was still visible in the rushes which covered the soft ground on the side of the ditch.

The men who were conducting the search for clues affected not to notice the chief's presence as they worked methodically away from the spot. They grunted sometimes with the effort necessitated by the cold and uneven ground beneath the trees, but even their curses were subdued once they realized that the Super was around. Their eyes fastened to the ground in conscientious diligence, they examined its unrevealing surface; their breath rose in white clouds through the few brown leaves which clung still to oak and beech, a badge of their conscientious exertion.

'We couldn't do much last night,' said Dickenson, as though apologizing for the fact. 'We lit the place overnight and put a guard on, of course, and the fingerprint officer got busy. But DI Rushton thought we'd be better doing most of the scene of crime work this morning.'

Lambert nodded. The dead were never in a hurry. To avenge them, one had sometimes to be patient. 'How long had be been dead when he was found?'

'Dr Burgess didn't commit himself on the spot; he's making us wait for the autopsy. But the police surgeon said last night that the body had been there for some time—probably overnight, he thought.'

Lambert nodded glumly. The longer the interval between a death and its discovery, the greater the chance of a culprit escaping detection. 'Could he have been dumped here?'

'Dr Burgess thought not. There's quite a lot of blood here.' Dickenson pointed to an innocent-looking russet patch on the sparse grass beneath the low branches. The police photographer, a civilian in huge wellington boots, was taking his last shots of the area, a pair of tyre prints twenty yards down the track which were probably unconnected but just might be crucial. He had a film in his pocket which would be developed within two hours, showing the body and its spillage of gore from every conceivable angle.

'We took a video early, but I doubt if it will show much—it's very dark under the trees.' Dickenson was of an age to resent the new technology, or at least hope that traditional methods proved more effective. 'Don't rush it,' he called to the backs of the men combing the ground, 'I don't want to have to bring you back tomorrow!'

There were muffled groans from the undergrowth, and one more daring anonymous voice muttered that only bloody policemen would spend Christmas Day like that. 'A better way to spend it than the Reverend Barton,' said Dickenson quickly. 'Or his wife.'

He turned almost apologetically to Lambert, as though he was in some way tarnished by his contact with the crime. 'Bad business, this,' he said conventionally. It was an odd sentiment to come from a policeman, inured as he was to worse things than this. Yet Lambert knew how he felt. To find a gangland victim with half his torso blown away was but one more manifestation of an underworld of violent evil. To find a woman treated thus still shocked them. To find a man of God shot so brutally in this quiet place jolted them still more. A bad business, indeed.

'Do we know how many people come regularly into the forest?' said Lambert. For once he was adopting his administrator's hat, wondering about the size of the operation he would need to mount. They all knew that this might be the work of a person who never came here, save for this specific criminal purpose. But those who did would need to be eliminated from the inquiry, to be questioned about anything unusual they might have seen around the hour of the death. Lambert frowned: that hour might be difficult to establish with precision, which always meant that the net had to be trawled more widely.

Dickenson said, 'DI Rushton has set up the door to door stuff in the three nearest villages. I think he'd appreciate some more men, for that and a couple of road blocks, if you can squeeze him a few from somewhere.'

Lambert pulled a face: manpower was never easy. He said, 'Barton was based in Woodford, wasn't he?' He had only had time to glance through the preliminary reports of this killing before he went off to a divisional CID conference called at the other end of the county.

'Yes, sir. But he apparently served what used to be three parishes, until well after the war. The house-to-house squads are trying to establish his movements on the day of his death. Apparently his wife was away at the time, which will probably make it more difficult.'

'We'll go and have a look round the village,' said Lambert, wanting to feel himself involved in the business of detection as it gathered pace. The first step in any murder investigation must be to get to know the victim and his habits. That surely shouldn't be too difficult with a country vicar. It was the first optimistic thought he had been able to afford himself.

They walked slowly back towards the edge of the woods and their car. Lambert at fifty was beginning to develop the slightly stooping shoulders of the tall man; his hair was plentiful still, but flecked a little more with grey with each year that passed. His height and Hook's solidity made the Sergeant look shorter than he actually was. Bert Hook walked with the unhurried tread he had used for twenty years to trudge the twenty yards back to his bowling mark, impressing nervous village batsmen over four counties with its quiet menace.

The carrion crow which had seen all and could tell nothing watched them from the leafless twigs of the topmost tree. Back at base, the helicopter pilot typed his report, and the first suspect of the case was established.

CHAPTER 8

The big old car cruised quietly into the silent village. Lambert parked it beside the tiny children's playground, where swings hung motionless in the dank air.

There was not a soul to be seen on Christmas Eve. Lambert was reminded of the mining disaster which had been one of his most difficult assignments as a young, uniformed policeman. The community then had shut itself off in its grief, as though outsiders, however sympathetic, were intruding upon emotions they could never understand. Only one man had died this time, but it was a small village, and he had been its vicar.

Even in these harsh and hedonistic days, the cloth should afford a man some protection. And Peter Barton had been a man who had loved his flock and been loved himself. Perhaps his parishioners realized this only with his brutal removal from their midst. The thirst for revenge, that most primitive and insistent of human reactions, would gather force as the day drew to its close. But the village now was still shocked enough to resent intruders. Lambert and Hook were observed from curtained windows, but no one came willingly to offer them help or opinions.

Half unconsciously, they moved towards the church, as much because it was traditionally and physically the centre of village life as because it was the working place of their victim. It was a stone church with a surprisingly elegant steeple, which seemed taller than it really was because of its slenderness. Even on this day of grudging half-light, the local stone had the soft orange glow which gave the place a serenity appropriate to its purpose.

Lambert stood for a moment at its gate before he walked along the flagged path between the mounds and the lichened tombstones; fifteenth-century, he guessed, though no doubt there had been a church on the site for much longer than that. Restored and modified a little by the Victorians, who had replaced two narrow windows with the soaring neo-Gothic they so favoured, but without the virulent stained glass that disfigured some of their more opulent additions. It was a small church; no doubt it was still too large for its modern congregation, but scarcely unique in that.

The big wooden door opened readily when he turned the heavy iron ring of its handle. The two big men stood a little awkwardly in the aisle, as though they felt they should explain their presence here if they were not going to kneel and pray. The empty church was ready for Christmas, looking incongruously joyful, as if it had not yet heard of the fate of its incumbent. Brasses gleamed brightly on the altar; the patina of the mahogany communion rail was deep enough to reflect the colours of the opulent chrysanthemums which stood in tall vases beyond it. The front of the pulpit which Peter Barton would never occupy again was flecked with a multitude of deep red holly berries.

Lambert walked over to the side altar where the crib had been set up. An appealing collage from the village primary school covered the wall behind the crib. Three small wise men followed a huge star which had been exuberantly smothered with tinsel. An anorexic angel, with his trumpet clasped at an unlikely angle, flew uncertainly across a navy sky, like a Lowry drunk on his way home from a Christmas binge. Its innocence was a world away from the scene they had left in the woods.

As if to echo that sentiment, a voice behind them said tremulously, 'The church seems so empty now. And all of this seems useless. Worse than useless; it's an insult to his memory. I feel like taking it all down.'

'Oh, I shouldn't do that, Mrs—?'

'Coleman. Deirdre Coleman.'

'John Lambert. Superintendent Lambert, I'm afraid, CID. And this is Detective-Sergeant Hook.'

'Oh, I see. Yes, of course.' The woman looked as if she did not see at all, or only very dimly. She was probably in her fifties, but at the moment she looked older. She had been crying; the flesh around her eyes was puffy and her make-up was in ruins. She made an effort to pull herself together which was curiously touching because it was so transparent. 'I was here when I heard, you see. I sent Mrs Jenkins home. Then I just sat in the vestry. It's true, then, about Peter? I couldn't believe it, at first; then I sat in there and prayed to God it wasn't true.'

'I'm afraid it is, Mrs Coleman.' He wondered how much she knew of the detail of the killing. Probably everything: the body had been discovered by village children, and rural imaginations, bred on the abattoir disposal of stock, would pass on and enlarge the gruesome particulars. Melodrama like this was unique in the lives of most of them.

She looked past them, staring unseeingly at the altar she had dressed so lovingly over the last few days. 'He was such a lovely man,' she said dully. 'Who would want to kill him?'

For once the banal sentiment which was so familiar to policemen rang true. Hook said gruffly, 'That's what we're here to find out, Mrs Coleman.' She reminded him in her distress of the aunt who had died when he was a boy, the only relative he could remember before he went into the home. He resisted a temptation to put his arm round the hunched shoulders as a sob shook them: the woman was quite obviously middle class, and he was on duty. 'The Reverend Barton was well liked in the village, then?'

She looked at him resentfully, as though it was vicious in him even to ask for confirmation of it. 'You won't find anyone with a bad word for him,' she said. Her chin jutted resolutely as she took courage from her assertion of his reputation; it was all she could do for him now.

'How long had he been here, Mrs Coleman?' As usual, Hook was the better of the two at getting information from people in distress.

'Four years.' The reply came so promptly that they suspected a no doubt highly respectable passion on her part for the young vicar. 'He seemed very modern at first, but he was so gentle and polite with everyone. And when we got to know him—' Her voice caught and tears gushed in new channels through the powder on her cheeks.

Hook said, 'I'm sorry to upset you, but all this is most helpful information to us, Mrs Coleman. We can hardly bother his widow just now, though we shall have to see her quite soon.'

For a moment she looked as though she was about to offer them a view on Mrs Barton. Then the tragedy fell again across her mind, and she looked down at the pew in front of her. 'Clare's been taken to identify the body, I believe.' The village grapevine was flourishing healthily, as they had thought it would.

As Deirdre Coleman dabbed at her face with a tiny handkerchief which was wholly inadequate for her grief, Hook said gently, 'Please think carefully for a moment, then we'll leave you in peace. Is there anyone at all, inside or outside the village, who might have a reason to wish him dead?' He held up a hand as she rushed to refute the idea. 'Think about it for a moment, please. It's the last service you can offer to Peter Barton.'

The use for the first time of the dead man's full name, which she took as an acknowledgement of her closeness to him, stilled the denial in her throat. She accepted Hook's guidance as meekly as any child, and thought dutifully for a moment before she spoke. Perhaps she desperately wanted to find a culprit for them, to render an intimate service in death such as the personable young vicar had never permitted to her in life. After a moment, she shook her head miserably. 'He hadn't a single enemy round here. Or anywhere else, I'm sure.'

Hook looked at his chief, collected the briefest nod of acquiescence, and said, 'Thank you for your help, Mrs Coleman. We'll get the person who killed him, in due course.'

They left her behind them with her grief. When they looked back from the church door, she had fallen on her knees before the altar, with all thought for the appearance she had checked so carefully before leaving home now gone.

Her elbows sprawled across the pew in front of her, providing support for shoulders almost collapsed by her grief. One of her shoes was almost off, its heel worn flat on one side. Her head was so bowed that all they could see was a few wisps of grey hair.

Yet her grief in the deserted church gave her a dignity that struck home to both of them as they closed the door upon it. Peter Barton could have had much worse representatives to his memory.

In the deserted Crown, they drank two halves of bitter and tried to collect a different impression of Peter Barton from Keith Harrison, licensed to retail spirits and ales.

'He was one of us,' he said with conviction. It was not clear who were 'us', and still less who were the unspeakable 'them' that his use of the phrase implied. But it was plain that his approval of the dead clergyman was as unstinting as Mrs Coleman's, and from a totally different section of the community—basically male and non-churchgoing.

They heard about skittles and darts, and how Peter Barton respected beliefs which ran contrary to his own. Harrison polished horse brasses vigorously, and the noise rang round the empty hostelry almost as resonantly as if they were still in the church across the lane. Eventually, Lambert said desperately, 'But he must have had enemies. Everyone has.'

The landlord swept his hand over his balding head, then scratched it thoughtfully, as if he had removed a non-existent cap to permit himself the indulgence. He prided himself on being a worldly-wise, realistic man, and he collected his share of confidences and freely offered views on the world and its denizens, particularly the local ones. He wanted to offer suggestions to the police, feeling obscurely that his self-image as a village sage might be at stake here.

Yet in this single respect, Peter Barton failed him: he was unable to scratch up enemies of any kind, let alone any bitter enough to have killed him. Eventually he said gnomically, 'No man is an island. Perhaps he had enemies we don't know about here. I don't know much about his private life.' For a moment, they thought again that they were about to be offered some speculative thought about Mrs Barton. Then the landlord seemed to reject the idea. He said almost reluctantly, 'But you won't find any to say a word against him around here.'

As policemen, it was not what they wanted to hear.

They came to the village store almost in desperation, and met there the kind of cautious hostility with which as policemen they were more familiar. It was almost a relief.

After enduring a few moments of surly non-cooperation, Hook produced his notebook and affected a more formal approach. 'It's Mr G. Farr, isn't it?' he said, flicking to a new page and preparing apparently to record the words of the shopkeeper in detail.

'Everyone calls me Tommy,' said Farr. It was a small gesture of conciliation, and they took it as such.

'You see a lot of what goes on around here,' said Lambert.

'People come in and out. They don't talk a lot.' Lambert reflected that they were probably not encouraged to do so. As if he read the thought, Farr said, 'I run this place on my own, so I don't have a lot of time for gossip.' In fact, he made it his business to be pleasant, but he saw no reason why he should volunteer so much to the police.

'Perhaps not. But you don't strike me as a fool, Mr Farr, so I need scarcely remind you that it is your duty to offer whatever help you can to the police when they are investigating serious crime. I'm asking you what you thought of the Reverend Barton, and what other people thought of him.'

Farr looked at them coolly. 'He weren't my type. His wife might have been.' He bit his lip, banishing the surly smile of male complicity, regretting immediately the streak of himself which had been betrayed.

Lambert let the moment stretch, allowing what might

have been no more than a rough masculine boast to gather a heavier significance, pushing his man a little more on to the defensive. Then he said, 'You didn't like Peter Barton?'

'I didn't like or dislike him. I said he wasn't my type. That doesn't mean I took a shotgun to him.'

They both looked him full in the face then, watching the broken nose, the surprisingly regular white teeth, the blue eyes beneath the tightly curled grey hair which now had only traces of red in it. Lambert said, 'So you know how he died, Mr Farr?'

If Farr thought he had made a mistake, he did not acknowledge it. The steely eyes held theirs, almost insolently. 'The kids described the body. Their mothers have been in here.' It was as though he spoke in shorthand.

Hook said, 'But you said they don't talk a lot.'

'You try keeping them quiet over something like that.' It was a fair defence, but he spoke of his customers with contempt.

'And they told you the vicar had been killed with a shotgun?'

Farr had the sense to pause before he replied. 'They talked about the injuries. It didn't take much knowledge to guess they had come from a shotgun.'

'I see. Do you have a shotgun yourself?' If the man wanted to be insolent, Lambert could return the attitude with interest. Ultimately, he held all the important cards in this game.

Perhaps Farr realized that. He said sullenly, 'Yes. You can see it, if you want.' Without waiting for a reply, he turned and walked through the door behind him.

Both of them knew the shotgun would be of no interest, or he would not have volunteered it so readily, but they were not going to turn down the chance to see how this aggressive curmudgeon lived. They followed him without even needing to look at each other.

The storeroom behind the shop was surprisingly untidy after the neat displays of merchandise they had left. Probably Farr knew his way around its clutter well enough.

They were almost through the next door and into his living quarters when the menacing growl and bared teeth stopped them in their apprehensive tracks. 'All right, Kelly, they're friends. Back in your box!' said Farr. The Doberman loped away, obedient but seemingly disappointed; Farr's smile of secret amusement convinced them that he had deliberately not warned them about the dog, which now stared at them from its bed with baleful brown eyes.

Farr went into a small pantry near the back door and emerged with a double-barrelled shotgun which he almost tossed into Hook's hands. They gave it a token inspection, but Lambert was more interested in its owner. 'You said the Reverend Barton wasn't your type,' he said. With the shotgun now back in Farr's hands, it seemed an appropriate moment to return to the shop-owner's assertion.

Farr acknowledged the thought with a mirthless smile. 'I've no time for organized religion. Perhaps he was just the representative of that. I'd nothing against Barton personally.' He said it as though it was an admission of weakness rather than anything to his credit.

'But you like Mrs Barton.'

Tommy Farr shrugged his wide boxer's shoulders, pulled briefly at the distorted lobe of his flattened right ear, and put the gun unhurriedly back into its place in the pantry. 'I'm not sure I said that. I think I said I fancied her. That's different. I could do her a bit of good, if she'd let me.' He smiled in lubricious speculation, but his amusement was for himself, not his audience.

Lambert, watching him closely and refusing to react, said, 'You live here alone, Mr Farr?'

He looked at them suddenly then, for the first time since he had brought them into his own quarters. 'Yes, unless you count Kelly.' He went over and fondled the dog's soft ears; it wagged its tail and lifted its slim, powerful head towards his hand after he had stopped caressing it. 'And to save you asking, my wife walked out. Fifteen years ago. I haven't seen her since.'

He said it aggressively, as though he expected them to

pursue the matter with further questioning, but Lambert merely nodded, almost absently. Farr, with his air of barely suppressed energy, did not seem a man who would find it easy to sublimate his sexual instincts. If he regretted his unguarded reference to the vicar's wife, he had carried it off forcefully enough, in line with the terms in which it had been couched.

Lambert looked through the small window beside the rear door towards what now seemed the brooding presence of the forest. The nearest trees were scarcely two hundred yards away. He said, 'I suppose you see most of the people who go into the forest from your shop.'

'There are other ways than the lane in front of my shop —footpaths across the fields. And anyway, I have a business to run; I'm too busy to watch all the comings and goings.'

'Nevertheless, you would no doubt be aware of most of the people who regularly go into the woods.'

Farr weighed the thought of denying the suggestion, then decided that was not possible. 'There's plenty. Most of the children go in there sometimes, especially now they're on holiday. Like those kids who found Barton.' He seemed to find this a convincing demonstration of his argument, but they said nothing to encourage the notion. Farr said, 'I go in there myself, nearly every day, with Kelly. Do a mile or two, I suppose.'

'And who else do you know who goes in there regularly?'

Farr paused, whether in a genuine attempt to give them the best information or in a consideration of how best to conceal something, it was impossible to say. Perhaps he was conscious of this ambivalence, and pleased by it. He smiled as he said, 'There's young Charlie Webb, of course. He takes a short cut through there on his way to work at the Electricity Works.'

Hook raised his eyebrows. 'Long way for him to walk, even with a short cut.'

'He doesn't walk.' Farr was delighted to expose their naïvety. 'He takes his motorbike. Pushes it under the barrier. Easy done, that is.' His South Welsh accent came out more strongly in his contempt for their ignorance.

Lambert said, 'You say you go into the woods yourself on most days. Did you go there yesterday, and the day before?'

'Yes. I told you, I walk Kelly in the forest most days.' He had not even hesitated. Probably he had anticipated the question from the moment when he first heard the news of the shooting.

'And did you see or hear anything which now seems significant in the light of the Peter Barton's death?'

'No.' Farr paused, preparing to make the maximum impact with the piece of information he had known from the start that he would have to reveal to them when the time came. 'I saw a tramp in the forest though, the day before that.'

Lambert had to control both irritation and excitement. 'Where was he sleeping?'

'In the forest, I think. He had a little tent with him. Ain't no haystacks for tramps, nowadays, I suppose.'

Lambert said heavily, 'You'd better show us just where. Bert, there's a 1:25,000 map in the car. Would you—'

'I can do better than that. I can show you the place, if you've got half an hour. It's ten minutes into my dinner-hour already. The shop should be shut.' Tommy Farr had decided to help the police. He didn't want to shop anyone, but murder was murder. And he'd made one mistake in mentioning Clare Barton like that, and another one in letting on about the murder being done with a shotgun. He was in need of a bit of credit with the police.

The entrance to the forest was under police guard, though Lambert reflected wryly that it must be impossible to cordon off the whole of the perimeter and deny the possibilities of entry and exit where no tracks ran. The young uniformed constable did not know Lambert, but fell back when he heard the exalted rank like a footman before a duke.

Kelly moved ahead of them, seemingly a dog who knew exactly where he was going. They matched Farr's brisk marching pace for a mile, then ducked after him under low branches, down a side-track which was so overgrown that they would not have known it was there.

They moved a hundred yards at least before Farr hesitated. 'It was around here, I'm sure. It was Kelly that found him.' Because his mind was on other things, his pride in the dog leaped out at them like that of a small boy, catching him as well as them unprepared for it.

The dog had moved a little to their left, and Hook, following it, called a little breathlessly, 'There's been a fire here, and a tent, I think.' They pushed through behind him into the tiny clearing. There was a small rectangle of flattened ground, a trace of ashes where earth had been roughly spread over the remnants of a fire.

Lambert had turned already towards the way out of the forest and the investigative team he should be heading. Over his shoulder to Farr, he said, 'We'll need a full description.'

CHAPTER 9

A murder investigation exposes many secrets, most of them unconnected with the death.

Clare Barton would find this in due course. For the present, she was in shock. Even the sight of her husband's pale features had not seemed real; the voice which calmly confirmed the identification to the pathologist had seemed to come from someone else; the explanation that this was necessary for something mysteriously called 'continuous evidence' seemed to be meant for other ears than hers.

Now she trod the carpets of her house on limbs that seemed hardly hers. Once she looked for the imprint of her foot in the plain deep-pile carpet of the lounge, as if in search of some tangible evidence that a real creature trod here and was experiencing all this.

Her elder sister watched her anxiously, wondering how

much of this was shock and how much evidence of the sedation the doctor had given her. It was a bad time for this to happen, she thought, rebuking herself for her selfishness. She must get Clare out of this house and back home with her: that much was obvious, despite her sister's protests. But she could not be other than a damper on Christmas for the children. She was not a very natural aunt at the best of times, and with this behind her . . .

At least she was not hysterical. Indeed, she was as docile as a small child on her best behaviour; Barbara, who was eight years her senior, could recall many happier occasions in the past when she could have wished her sister as easy to control. She busied herself in the small kitchen, salvaging what she could from the food Clare had prepared so diligently on the previous day and never eaten.

Clare came obediently to the dining table when she was asked to do so. She was waiting there, sitting bolt upright, when Barbara carried the two bowls of soup in from the kitchen. She did not touch the food as it steamed in front of her. Barbara felt guilty that she should be so hungry herself. She waited until she was half way through her own helping before she said, 'Clare, love, you've got to eat. That's good chicken soup; it'll pick you up a bit.' The banalities reminded her of her dead father, who could never bear to see anyone fast.

Clare did not look at her, but she began to take her soup. She spooned it into her mouth slowly, but with a regularity which became dreadful. It brought back to Barbara a long-buried image of a glass-cased mechanical model in an amusement arcade, lifting a spoon to its plaster mouth in mechanical response to children's pence.

The impression was fostered by Clare's doll-like appearance. Her yellow hair had not moved since she had combed it to go to the mortuary several hours ago. The warmth of the house and the sedative from the doctor had restored her colour, so that her cheeks were almost unnaturally red, with a patch of high colour at the top of each cheekbone. Her light blue eyes might have been made of glass, so unblinkingly did they stare past her sister towards the abandoned Christmas tree in the corner of the room. Barbara felt that if she bent the stiff upper body backwards, those eyes would close automatically at some point, like those of her favourite childhood doll.

Yet the food seemed to have some effect. Clare refused anything else after the soup, but she drank most of the coffee which Barbara brought to her, sinking gradually towards a more relaxed position in the armchair which seemed far too large for her slender frame. Barbara was relieved when she looked in from the kitchen. She began to think about Christmas Day again. She would ring her husband in a little while, after she had persuaded Clare to talk.

The phone was quite near to Clare's armchair, but for a moment she did not know where the sound came from. She had picked it up by the time Barbara reached the door, and she waved an airy acknowledgement that she would deal with this. It was a reassuring, even an amusing gesture to her sister, who took it as evidence of a return to something like normality. She shut the door carefully behind her when she saw that Clare was coping; eavesdropping had never been one of her faults.

Clare listened for some time without speaking, not taking in all of what the voice on the other end of the line said. 'So you see,' it concluded desperately, 'it's vital for both of us that you don't say you were with me at that time. I've got too much to lose, you see.'

'I see. Yes.'

'And so have you, really, haven't you?'

'Yes, I suppose so.' She spoke like an automaton.

'I'll go now, then. Look after yourself. It will be better if we're not in contact for a while. So make sure you don't ring me. Leave it to me to get in touch in due course.'

The line went dead. She stared at the mouthpiece dully for a moment before she put it carefully back in its holder. She felt cheated: she had wanted to tell him that he was never to ring again.

*

A hundred yards away in the block of council houses, Charlie Webb was thinking also about a telephone call. In his case, it was a call he needed to make.

They had no phone in the house, but it was not far to the public box near the Crown. He wanted an excuse to escape his gran's watchful eye, and his store of invention was almost exhausted. It was his day off. It had seemed a good idea at the time to tack it on to Christmas Day, but now he would much rather have been at work. He ran his hand rather desperately through his thick dark hair.

It was cut quite short at the front, in the current spiky fashion of the young. Old Mrs Webb, who was pretending to read her tabloid newspaper, said, 'Mind you don't scratch yourself on that hedgehog!' and cackled with satisfaction. She had made the joke many times before, but was delighted to catch her grandson in the gesture when he thought himself unobserved.

'So who killed the vicar, then?' she said for the third time. She was fascinated by the violence of the killing, so that her unpredictable old mind kept coming back to it. She was almost housebound now; a dramatic event so close at hand brought a touch of sickly glamour into her home.

Yet death in the village always worried her, reminding her as it did of the death of her son and the fragility of all life. It meant that even young Charlie had but a tenuous hold upon it, and he was the only one she had still to lose. She watched him now as he moved restlessly about the house, stooping to look for the twentieth time through the window of the living-room towards the centre of the village.

Just when she thought he had ignored her question, he said with rough affection, 'How the hell should I know who killed Reverend Barton? We never had anything to do with him, did we?'

'No time for it,' she said promptly. The impersonal pronoun embraced all religions and their representatives. Her spiritual world had been demolished piece by piece with the death of her loved ones; since the death of her son ten years ago, she had reviled all clergymen as the representatives of an institution that had cheated and deceived her. Unable to venture out, forbidding entry to her house to Peter Barton, she had remained proof against the charm the young vicar seemed to have exercised over the rest of the village She dismissed reports of his achievements as so much more evidence that the world was populated by credulous nincompoops.

'The police will find who did it,' said Charlie. He had seen two large men going from church to pub earlier in the day; they had looked like plain clothes men to him. He was not sure, but he thought he had seen them leaving the village when he was in the back garden, walking with Tommy Farr and that damned dog of his. If he was right, it was probably safe to go to the phone-box now. He had no wish to be observed, least of all by them.

'His wife will be at the bottom of it, somewhere, you mark my word,' said Gran. She spoke it into her paper, as though it were a reflection not meant for him, but she was delighted when he reacted. Sometimes the generations fell away and they were like husband and wife, with him making the necessary punctuations in her monologues.

He grinned. 'Why on earth should you think that, Gran? You don't even know the woman.'

'Too pretty for her own good, that one!' said Mrs Webb, nodding as though she had produced the most convincing possible argument. 'Blonde hussy!' All blondes were hussies to her; the notion had an obscure origin in her youth, when the cinema had brought impossible excitement to country towns and Jean Harlow had been followed by Veronica Lake.

Charlie knew the script and delivered his next line with impeccable timing. 'But what about Grace Kelly?' he said.

'Princess Grace, you mean,' she corrected him loftily. 'She was all right, so they killed her.' She made haste to relate this irrefutable logic to the particular local event. 'I'm not saying that Mrs Barton killed him herself, mind, though she might have. But she'll be involved in it somewhere.' She ceased her pretence of perusing the paper, folded it upon her lap, and rocked slowly back and fourth on her chair, gazing contentedly into the fire. Hollywood scenarios with poor Clare Barton as a *femme fatale* began to seep into her delighted imagination.

Charlie was never sure how seriously she entertained the wild speculations she retailed to him. Perhaps they were all part of an elaborate comic world she created to compensate for her lack of mobility. He scratched his long nose and threw back his narrow shoulders: if he was to feature in one of her fantasies, it had better be as the handsome hero. 'It's still fine,' he said. 'I think I'll go for a little spin on the bike. I've put a new plug in this morning.'

'Damned Japanese rubbish! Always breaking down: I tried to warn you,' she said with immense satisfaction.

He was quite relieved. There wasn't a lot wrong with the old girl's brain if she could switch her ideas as promptly as that. 'But the Japanese make the best bikes now, Gran.'

'Triumph was good enough for your Dad. Norton's still the best in the world. Got to be.'

For a moment he saw her as Supergran on the telly, astride her machine like a dark avenger. He went and started up the Honda and rode it slowly through the village. He had thought he might ride over to Ashbridge and use the phone-box there, but there was a police road block where the lane from Woodford joined the road to the next village. He turned the bike in the space where a five-barred gate led into a field of winter barley and rode slowly back to the village, feeling as though a net was being drawn tighter about him.

Tommy Farr was back in his shop; the lights glowed gold in the gloom of the afternoon. As he stopped his bike and took off his helmet, he toyed with the idea of going in and trying to find what Tommy had been doing when he saw him with the police. But he knew he would be unable to do it casually. Tommy had that way of looking straight through you and seeing what you were really thinking. He treated Charlie with the amusement of an adult dealing with an inexperienced child, and Charlie felt himself grow more gauche even as he tried to shrug it off.

He went instead to make his phone call. For a moment, he thought there was going to be no answer. Then the connection was made and he said, 'Dave? It's Charlie. Listen, don't forget I didn't ever leave work that night . . . I know . . . I know our arrangement . . . I know you wouldn't. It's just that it might be more vital than usual this time. So remember, if the police come asking questions . . . the police, yes. Just tell them I was there the whole time, all right? I'll explain when I see you.'

He took the bike home and wheeled it into the shed at the bottom of the garden. Out of the view of his gran, he began to clean every particle of mud from the treads of its tyres.

CHAPTER 10

Back in the CID section at Oldford police station, the Murder Room was filling with material at the usual surprising pace.

The dead man's clothes and shoes had been bagged and labelled. A bewildering number of small bags of fibres and other objects discovered in the area around the body by the Scene of Crime team had been tagged and stored for later comparisons. The photographs had almost all been developed and numbered; already enlargements of the more interesting ones, which might in due course become evidence, were being attached to a pinboard by the civilian police photographer. The three word-processors in the room had been kept busy, so that the first of the reports which Lambert thought kept superintendents for too long at their desks had already been typed and filed by those concerned.

Lambert was closeted in his office with Detective-Inspector Rushton, to receive the latter's account of his attendance at the post-mortem on the Reverend Peter Barton. A senior police officer had to be present throughout the autopsy, and Lambert's squeamishness in the face of Burgess's abattoir skills was as well known as the pathologist's robust parading of them.

Cyril Burgess had found the autopsy less fun with Rushton than when he had Lambert's delicate sensibilities to play on. It was in any case one of his less interesting examinations, as far as he was concerned. As an enthusiast for the detective fiction of the 'thirties and 'forties, he looked for complexity in the corpses he dissected. But he was usually disappointed, and this shattered cadaver seemed unlikely to disturb the pattern.

Rushton said, 'We shan't have Dr Burgess's report until the twenty-seventh, because of the holiday, but he warned me that it will almost certainly add nothing to what he was able to tell me this afternoon.' Rushton found it regrettable that even murder had to defer to the demands of Christmas and Boxing Day. Lambert had stood down all but a skeleton staff of the murder team over the Bank Holiday. Rushton disapproved, because he suspected that the Chief would use it as an excuse to become even more involved than usual in the direct business of the investigation.

'No doubt the irrepressible Cyril brandished various organs before your very eyes,' said Lambert, suppressing a shudder of distaste at the thought.

'Not quite, sir, but he didn't spare me much of the detail.'

'Well, spare it for me, Chris. Let's concentrate on the important things for the investigation. Was Barton killed where he was found?'

'Yes, sir. Almost certainly. Burgess says there is no evidence that the body has been moved. The hypostasis indicated the body had fallen where it was found, and had been there for some time.'

Lambert was confirming what he already suspected. It would have been a bonus for the team if the body had been moved, for the killer or his accomplice might well have left a trace of himself or his clothing on the flesh or clothes of the deceased. The simplest deaths were usually those most difficult of investigation.

Rushton looked at his notes. 'Details of the injury. A shotgun, as we surmised, sir. A twelve-bore, I'm afraid.' This was bad news on both counts. If the weapon had been a rifle, the bullet would have left evidence which was often as individual as a fingerprint. A rifle could be identified from its ammunition easily enough, and there were many fewer rifles than shotguns around. They were much easier for the police to trace, even though shotguns had now to be licensed. Shotguns were nothing like so distinctive, and much more widely held. And the twelve-bore was the most common of all.

'What about time of death?'

'The body had been there for some time before it was found. Burgess hazards between eighteen and twenty-four hours, but he warned me that he wouldn't be pinned to that in court. He went on at some length about the digestive organs and the stomach contents, though, sir.'

Lambert wished he could prevent the younger man calling him 'sir' so persistently, especially with no one else around. It was more his own fault than Rushton's. Why did the moment never seem right to tell him to drop the formality? He watched the Inspector studying his neat, flowing handwriting again. Rushton was only thirty-two, a representative of that younger generation which would eventually ease—or thrust—men like Lambert and Hook into retirement. The Superintendent was well aware that a little at least of his resentment had its origin in that.

Rushton was one of the few officers who did not look like a policeman in plain clothes. When he wore a suit, as he did now, he could have been a confident young industrialist. His dark brown hair had no hint of grey; on the third finger of his left hand, he wore the broad band of wedding gold which Lambert had never affected. He said, 'I think if we put what Burgess will report about the stomach contents together with our own inquiries about the Reverend

Barton's last movements, we should be able to establish the time of death fairly accurately, sir.'

'What do we know so far about his final movements?'

Rushton looked again at his notes, though Lambert was sure that he did not need them for this. 'He was dropped off in Ashbridge to visit a Mrs Wheeler. We've seen her. She confirms that he attended a shortish meeting at her house to organize a fund for famine relief in Ethiopia. Apparently he was going to mention it in all three of the churches he serviced at Christmas and he wanted the organization set up before then.'

'You say he was dropped off in Ashbridge. Didn't he have his own car?'

'No. He owned a car, but he didn't have the use of it that day, apparently. We should know why that was by tonight.' Always when a victim's normal routine had been disturbed before a murder there was a possibility that it was connected with the crime. In this case the removal of his car had left a man walking through the forest at night.

'What time did his meeting finish?'

'About five, Mrs Wheeler thinks. There were other people there, who should confirm that. The door-to-door team have a note to check it.'

'And Barton chose to walk home through the forest, in darkness?' It was not a journey that Lambert would willingly have made. But then, he had been brought up in London; his earliest memory was of his grandmother's dead arm across his face when their house had come down in the Blitz. Even when he had become familiar with it as a young policeman, he had never learned to relish the dark. He tried unsuccessfully to remember whether there had been a moon on the night when Barton died.

Rushton shrugged. 'Apparently there was nothing unusual in the vicar walking around alone. He would have been home in about forty minutes that way: it's three times as far by road. The track through the forest was a route he used quite often, though no doubt usually in daylight. But he had a torch with him: the Scene of Crime boys found it near the body.'

'How near, Chris?'

For once, Rushton did not riffle though his papers for the answer. 'Five metres. It was switched on, though the battery had run out, of course. So presumably he was using it at the time he was shot. The print boys got a good set of dabs from it, but they're Barton's of course.'

They were silent for a moment, picturing the scene on that bitter night, with the torch bobbing through the shadows of the trees, making the man who carried it an easy target for the killer who lay in wait for him in the blackness beyond its faltering beam.

Then Rushton, as though determined to bring them back abruptly to police practicalities, said, 'Burgess said the stomach contents indicate some food taken roughly three hours before death. According to Mrs Wheeler, the vicar only had a cup of tea in Ashbridge. Said he'd had tea and fresh scones immediately before he arrived, in Woodford. The stomach analysis confirms that.'

'So that would give us a time of about five-thirty for the shooting. On his way home from Ashbridge.'

Rushton knew where his chief's thinking was leading, and was anxious to show that he did. 'Yes. That indicates that the body lay where it fell for approximately twenty-one hours before the children found it. Burgess says his thermometer readings would support that. Rigor hadn't set in, but the body temperature had declined to that of the environment.' The DI was back in his notes again.

'So why did no one report the vicar's absence in those hours?'

'We should know that by the end of the day. It seems Barton's wife was away at the time of his death. We got that much from the WPC who went round to break the news of the death.'

'Has the wife been interviewed yet?'

'No, sir. She had to identify the body. And she was so distressed that—'

'I'll see her myself. Tonight, probably.'

'Yes, sir.' For once, Rushton was glad to see the older man becoming so directly involved. His wife would not relish his absence from their neighbours' party on Christmas Eve. He wondered if Lambert even realized for the moment what day it was, so immersed did he become at this stage of an investigation. Well, let the old devil see the bereaved wife: that was always the most difficult of the interviews, where the police presence seemed most intrusive. Like all CID men, Rushton knew how high a percentage of killings had a domestic origin. But surely not this time, with a clergyman's wife?

A thought was nagging at Lambert's mind, but for the moment he dismissed it. Facts first, he always told his juniors; speculation only when facts have been exhausted. Who had the opportunity came always before who had a motive, because opportunity was clear fact. Lambert could be a Gradgrind about facts until all the available ones had been established. He began to tick off the remaining ones. 'Any money in Barton's pockets?'

'Two pounds and forty pence. What seems to have been quite an expensive presentation pen in his inside pocket. Blown apart by the impact of the cartridge, actually.' Both of them looked automatically towards the cabinet where these grisly trivia were filed.

'Fingerprints?'

'Almost certainly nothing of interest, sir. I've mentioned the torch. There are a few other prints around the area, including one quite good set from a plastic bottle, but it had almost certainly been there well before the murder. We're checking it, of course, and we'll keep it as evidence against an arrest. My guess is that it will turn out to be totally unconnected with this.'

'What else, Chris?' Lambert fed in the Christian name rather self-consciously, hoping to breach the formalities which lay between them, but he still could not give the simple command to drop the 'sir'.

'Not much, sir. The photographer came up with a couple

of interesting footprints as well as eliminating those which belonged to the children.' He gestured towards the pin-board away to their left. 'I've got my doubts, though. Quite a few other people use that road through the woods.'

'You must have a pretty good idea by now where the murderer stood. I thought I could have made a fairly accurate guess even when I was there, without a body.

'Yes, sir. The police surgeon gave us a fair idea, and Dr Burgess confirmed it after a detailed examination of the death wound.' He turned to the relevant page of his notes. 'Twelve-bore shotgun. The spread of the pellets indicates it was fired from three to four metres. Fired from the front right of the victim. I had a good look myself at the scene of the crime, before the SOCO took over completely, and it seemed pretty obvious where the assailant had stood.'

'But you found nothing of interest?'

'No. Certainly no sign of a footprint, though the top half-inch of the ground was quite soft. It's possible he's worn polythene bags or something similar over his feet.'

'Or her feet. No sign of a weapon, needless to say?'

'Not so far, sir. Nothing in the immediate scene of crime area, certainly. We're checking around the villages for shotguns, but I'm afraid there'll be plenty of twelve-bore shotguns in an area like this.'

'Any cartridge cases?'

'No, sir. Certainly not in the area round the corpse.'

'So he—or she—probably covered his feet, and almost certainly picked up the empty cartridge cases before he left.' A carefully planned crime, with no panic afterwards by the perpetrator. Not an encouraging scenario, for those charged with detection.

Lambert returned reluctantly to the less specific consideration which had remained patiently at the back of his mind. 'I know it's early days, but have you turned up anyone yet with a motive for getting rid of Peter Barton?'

Rushton paused a moment before he shook his head. He would dearly have liked to suggest a line of inquiry which others had missed, but there was no possibility of that this time. 'No, sir. So far, he seems to be that creature we're often told about but rarely discover, the man without enemies.' He allowed himself a small, sardonic smile at his own expense: only policemen could find a man without enemies a depressing prospect. 'But there are obviously a lot of people who know a vicar, people we haven't even begun to eliminate from the inquiry yet. We may get some pointers in the next day or two.' He was asserting his right to be around, even if it was Christmas.

The DC who came hurriedly into the room after his token knock was as full of his news as a schoolboy. They knew from his very bearing that he brought good news. He tried unsuccessfully to keep the excitement out of his voice as he spoke. 'The man in the woods reported by the helicopter, sir. White and Burrows have found him. They're bringing him in now.'

Rushton looked at his watch. It was twenty-six hours after the hour they had tentatively established as the time of the killing. All his training and experience bade him to keep an open mind. Yet something deep beneath those things told him insistently that they were about to talk to a murderer.

CHAPTER 11

Although all of Woodford was stunned by the death of its vicar, the Davidsons were perhaps more shaken than anyone.

Possibly it was something to do with their residence within the ivy-clad elevations of the Old Vicarage. A little guilt that new riches should have removed the building from its ecclesiastical owners still lurked in the recesses of Colonel Davidson's psyche, though he would have been loath to admit as much, even to himself. He was a Gloucestershire man, with a deep consciousness of his Anglican heritage, even when he chose to ignore it.

Probably the disturbance the Davidsons felt was more connected with the abrupt and brutal removal from their midst of a young man whom they liked and respected. The shock of the news was emphasized by the fact that only hours before his death Peter Barton had been with them in their house, enlisting their support for his efforts towards famine relief. Colonel Davidson let it be understood that he had seen death on a greater scale during his military career. Nevertheless, it was obvious that he was considerably shaken by the death of the cheerful young clergyman, who had seemed so at ease with them on the last occasion he had sat with them in this room.

Harry Davidson had sent for Arthur Comstock, his chauffeur-handyman. While he waited for him, he stood by the big Victorian bay window of the drawing-room, his lips no more than a dark line against the grey-white flesh of his face as he turned to the light. The house was floodlit, partly for reasons of security. His brown, watchful eyes stared down the long expanse of lawn, its dull winter green now brighter in the artificial white light, to the stone wall beside the high wrought-iron gates. Behind them, the tops of the forest trees in the distance were invisible in the early winter darkness.

Rachel Davidson studied him from her chair by the hearth. The room was high, but warm: the central heating system which her money had installed was more than adequate for the purpose. Yet she had twice caught herself shivering. Shock, she supposed; it was still no more than half an hour since the maid had come back in tears from the village with the news. She was more upset than she would have expected by this violent removal from their midst. Barton was a young man to whom she had accorded increasing respect as she had learned more of his work.

Perhaps, she thought, as she pulled her woollen stole more closely about her shoulders, it had something to do with her race. Though she had been born and bred in Switzerland, her Jewish banking family had been an extensive one, and the Austrian branch had been almost wiped out in the holocaust. She had grown used as an adolescent to finding her mother in wet-eyed mourning on two or three days in the year. Perhaps this jolting distress she felt at the violent, unexplained removal of a young man in the prime of a blameless life was part of her heritage.

She watched Arthur Comstock as he came into the room and walked over to stand facing her husband. To her surprise, he seemed to evince an unspoken aggression, as if he was determined no one was going to blame him for the extinction of this young life. Shock took people in different ways; perhaps its waves affected this normally quiet man in this way. She did not see a lot of him, but she had found him taciturn but accommodating in his dealings with her.

Perhaps he had picked up something from her husband's attitude, for Harry began as if he held Comstock personally responsible for the tragedy. 'This is a bad business, Arthur. You should have seen him safely home to his house in the village. That's what I asked you to do.'

'That's what I intended to do. It's not my fault that it didn't happen.' Comstock was taller than his employer by a good four inches, and he held himself erect as a Guardsman. His small black moustache seemed to make his features more severe rather than relieving them.

Davidson continued as if he had never spoken. 'You weren't asked to make your own arrangements. You were asked to t-take the Reverend Barton to Ashbridge, wait for him there until he had finished his business, and t-take him home. If you had done that, he wouldn't have been killed in the forest.'

Comstock breathed hard in the pause that followed, as if he were controlling himself for his reply. He said, 'We don't know yet that he was killed that evening. It was well into the next day when he was found.'

'Come off it, Comstock. You and I have both heard where those boys found him. It's on the route he would have t-taken home from Ashbridge.'

Rachel had never heard her husband call this man or any other servant by his surname before: it was as though he was back in the Army. She deliberated whether it was yet another undiscovered byway in the labyrinth of the British class system she had striven so hard to negotiate. Watching the men breathing unevenly and staring into each other's faces, she decided it was not.

She said, 'Surely we want to hear what Arthur has to say, Harry. Getting excited won't bring Peter back.' She spoke diffidently, for her Swiss and Jewish background did not encourage her to interrupt the men of the household when they were about their business. Her friends found her reluctance to assert herself either amusing or irritating, according to the intensity of their feminism.

The two men looked round at her as if they had almost forgotten her presence. For a moment, she thought Harry was going to make the situation worse by checking her for her interference. Then he said with a forced smile, 'You're right of course, dear. By all means t-tell us what happened, Arthur.' His stammer as always was more noticeable under the stress of emotion, and his use of the forename now seemed to necessitate a deliberate effort of will.

Perhaps Comstock picked that up, for when he said, 'Very well, sir,' Rachel thought she caught the faintest ring of irony in the use of the title. But he went into the explanation he had plainly been anxious to give since he came into the room. 'I was planning to do exactly as you instructed. But on the way to Ashbridge, the Reverend Barton got me talking about my plans for the rest of the day. I let out that I had been intending to pick my sister up in Cheltenham. You may recall that I had mentioned the arrangement to you earlier in the week: she's staying with me for Christmas.' He looked to Rachel for confirmation, and she nodded an acknowledgement.

'I wasn't going to tell Reverend Barton at all, but somehow he managed to get me talking and it came out.' He looked at both of them in turn, as if in apology for the banality, but they nodded a confirmation that it was a quality the dead man had had. 'I said my sister would just have to wait for a while at the bus station, but he wouldn't hear of it. Told me I must meet her as planned, that he'd intended to walk both ways, so that the lift to Ashbridge was a bonus anyway. He said he'd explain to my employer that it was his idea to walk back, not mine, but I told him that that would not be necessary.'

Rachel detected a curious truculence in the last phrase, as though Comstock were determined to assert his independence. Perhaps it was another nuance of class: the British seemed absurdly sensitive about service. As her husband said nothing, she said, 'And of course it wasn't. None of the blame for what has happened can attach to you, Arthur.'

Harry Davidson accepted that view grudgingly. He said, as though offering it as a punishment, 'The police will want to see you. They've already been here.'

Comstock nodded coolly, a small smile touching the edges of his wide mouth for the first time since he had come into the room. 'They've already been to the cottage, too. They took a preliminary statement about times, and said a more senior officer would probably want to interview me in due course. I expect they'll want to talk to you, too. Apart from the three church people he met in Ashbridge, we're the last people he saw.'

He had somehow reversed the positions, for it was his employer who now looked discomforted by the thought. Harry Davidson dropped his eyes to the carpet and said, 'It's a bad business, Arthur. Barton was a fine young man.' Death conferred unreserved approbation upon a man; the fact that Davidson had found many of the young vicar's liberal ideas misplaced could be forgotten now. He looked up at his listeners, but neither of the faces revealed any sign that they suspected him of hypocrisy.

Comstock said, 'I'm sure everyone would agree with that. I'm not a churchgoer, as you know, but everyone seems to have liked and respected the Reverend Barton.' He seemed now to be making a conscious effort to relax.

Rachel Davidson said gently, with her faint accent edging the just too perfect English, 'Have you heard any views in the village as to who might have done this thing, Arthur?'

Comstock shook his head. 'Not so far. But I've hardly spoken to anyone. I thought I might pop down to the Crown for a pint later on tonight.'

Davidson said stiffly, 'Pub talk won't be reliable. That sort of conjecture is best left to the police.'

'I agree, sir.' Again Rachel thought she detected the tinge of irony in the form of address. 'But Peter Barton suggested I organize a collecting-box in the pub for his famine relief fund. It seems the least I can do, now.' He made his intention sound like a rebuke of his employer's insensitivity.

Davidson went back into the bay of the window when Comstock had gone. She watched him brush away an imaginary lock of hair from over his left eye, a gesture he always made when under stress. Perhaps long ago, before she had known him, a real tress had been prone to stray there. She suddenly found the empty, comic gesture very moving.

Eventually he shook his head sharply and said, 'I'm going out for a walk. Need a bit of fresh air.' For a moment, she thought he was going to kiss her forehead, as he did when leaving for a whole day or longer. Then he recollected himself and moved briskly past her, as though anxious to be gone before his resolution could weaken.

He took with him the springer spaniel which he usually left others to walk. He looked back at the house through the darkness as he went. Its orange lights seemed warm and beckoning as he turned into the raw night, but he turned resolutely towards the journey he had determined to make.

He had gone no more than half a mile when he heard the car coming towards him from the edge of the woods. He moved to the narrow band of grass between road and hedge and stood back to allow the vehicle the full use of the narrow lane. Then a small motorbike came noisily from the other direction, the beam from its headlamp wobbling a little when its rider saw the car and slowed.

The car stopped beside Davidson to allow the bike to pass, and he realized that the white saloon with its red banding along the wings was a police vehicle. Beside the policeman on the back seat of the car, he saw in the reflected light a dishevelled figure with a half-formed beard. It stared straight ahead without expression.

Presumably this mysterious figure from the forest was being taken in for questioning. Harry Davidson was within a yard of a suspected murderer in the darkness. The prisoner in his cocoon of warmth could perhaps not see beyond the window to the man outside. Certainly he gave no sign of having noticed him as the car eased forward and drove on.

Davidson stood for a long time in the darkness, pondering the implications of what he had seen.

CHAPTER 12

Because he was planning to use him on Christmas Day, Lambert had sent Bert Hook home to a grateful wife and the boys upon whom he doted. When the patrol car brought in the tramp from the forest, he took Rushton with him into the interview room.

It was a new room in a modern extension, but it had already acquired the characteristics of all police interview rooms. With its single small window, its harsh fluorescent ceiling light, its small floorspace and its gloss-painted walls, it had a claustrophobic atmosphere. But that was not the fault of the architect: these rooms, rightly or wrongly, were conceived as claustrophobic. It was one of the weapons considered legitimate to a police force who found that society charged them with upholding the law and then conspired to stack the odds against them in the execution of that duty.

The two detectives stood for a moment and surveyed the figure who might provide them with instant success in a case that was bound to get lurid publicity. There was no hurry; the pressures were all upon the man who already sat on the hard, upright chair at the other side of the small table.

At the moment, he did not seem unduly affected by them. The public has a romantic idea of what a tramp should look like. It is anything up to forty years out of date, and even in that historical context it owes as much to fiction as to hard fact. The 'knight of the road' was an urban conception; he was mainly rural, highly independent, nomadic and harmless. He was half-envied by townsfolk for his contact with nature and his independent spirit. Countrymen were always more suspicious of a figure they regarded as parasitic and unreliable.

Whatever the realities of the various pictures, the rural tramp is a figure almost but not quite extinct. The overwhelming majority of those whom the police meet who have 'no fixed abode' are urban derelicts. They are often squatters, often guilty of various forms of petty and not so petty crime, often in physical or mental ill health. This is frequently self-induced, in that an ever-increasing number are brought low by drugs or drink. And as the end of the century approaches, they are often homeless as a result of their omissions and addictions, rather than by any independent decision on their part to cast off the burdens of regular home and employment.

This was the context in which Lambert and his detective-inspector now estimated the man they had come here to question. It was quickly apparent to them that he was not one of the derelicts who came broken and confused into rooms like this. He watched them with wary brown eyes, refusing to be cowed by the room or the situation. He did not look undernourished; he was squat and powerful. Five feet nine and over twelve stones, Rushton estimated, but not fat. The arms he now placed with deliberation on the table in front of him were thick and muscular. Without being asked, he had slipped his waterproof anorak off his broad shoulders and on to the back of the tubular steel chair he occupied.

He had a week's beard on his face, and a half-grown

beard gives to the most innocent man an air of villainous licence. He had a small scar above his left cheekbone, which was partly hidden by the sideburns he had allowed to grow down in front of his ears. He had a broad nose and rounded, rather coarse features; altogether, Lambert decided, a face which would not be improved by a beard, even a fully-developed one.

They looked at his feet beneath the table. They wore boots; not the Chaplinesque apologies for boots, with perforated soles and gaping toes, which popular imagination accorded to tramps, but serviceable leather boots with padded tops and commando soles. His thick woollen trousers looked as though they would keep out rain and cold for a long time; a single tear below the knee had been expertly repaired.

There was one other unusual thing, which at first Lambert could not define for himself. He had been in the room for almost a minute before he realized what it was. There was no noticeable smell from this man. It might seem insulting to the homeless men and women the police had occasion to bring in, but it was a fact of life that many of them brought with them a pungent, unwashed odour. There was no such scent from this man or his clothes. If he had been living in the forest for some time, that was something of a feat.

Rushton spoke into the recorder mike to indicate the time that the interview was beginning with Superintendent Lambert and DI Rushton. If the man was impressed by the top brass that was being brought to bear upon him, he gave no sign of it. Rushton asked him his name and he said, 'Dougie Robertson. My friends call me Robbie.' It was not clear whether this constituted an invitation to policemen to do the same. He had an Edinburgh accent which was fainter than his name might have warranted.

'Have you any documents which would give us proof of your identity?'

He looked at them for a moment before replying, 'No. Nothing.'

Rushton said a little desperately, 'Letters? Driving licence?'

He gave them a sour smile, all the negative he thought the question needed.

Lambert said, 'How long had you been in the woods before our men brought you in?'

He looked puzzled, ran a hand through his unkempt hair. 'I'm not sure. About a week, I think. One day merges into another when time doesn't matter.'

It was true enough, Lambert supposed. Yet he suspected Robertson knew quite well how long he had been there; his gestures were those of a man playing a tramp rather than those of genuine confusion. Lambert said, 'Mr Robertson, you must know why we have brought you in here. A serious crime has been committed in the forest.'

He nodded, serious but apparently unconcerned. 'A man was shot. Your uniformed men told me on the way in.'

An interesting tramp, who distinguished between CID and other policemen like this. A man, perhaps, who had been in trouble with the police before. 'A local vicar was shot, on his way home through the woods. Very close to the spot where you were found.'

The brown eyes looked at them evenly from beneath the bushy brows, giving nothing away. Rushton said, 'You could be in trouble, Robbie. Big trouble.'

Robertson looked down at his thick fingers, seeming to approve the absence of grime as he turned them over. 'For something I didn't do?'

Lambert spoke as though this man and not his questioners had been responsible for the leisurely, watchful pace of their interchanges thus far as he snapped, 'Progress at last. You're saying that you didn't kill the Reverend Peter Barton. Can you offer us any opinions then on who did?'

Now the stubby hands turned palm upwards. 'Sorry. I heard nothing. I saw nothing.'

'When?' The word came like a rifle shot.

'Sorry?'

'When did you hear nothing? We haven't told you when this killing took place.'

For the first time, Robertson looked confused. After a moment he said, 'I assume it was last night. Anyway, whenever it was, I heard nothing.'

Lambert caught and held his eye, looking for knowledge which should not have been there. 'It was at about five o'clock in the evening, Mr Robertson. The day before yesterday. You should have heard the sound of shooting.'

'Well, I didn't. I might have been in my tent at the time. Or further away: I have traps for rabbits. Most of them live above ground during the winter now, you know.'

It was possible he might not have heard the shotgun. His tent had been located about a mile from the scene of the crime; Lambert had exaggerated its proximity to put pressure on the man. He said, 'Do you have a shotgun, Robbie?' He tried out the familiarity of the nickname, but it did not fall easily off his tongue; there was no genuine intimacy. It was rather a participation in a charade which the man on the other side of the table had initiated.

'No . . . He was killed with a shotgun, then? That might explain why I didn't hear anything. There's plenty of those in the country. A lot of them are used around the edge of the woods. I hear them quite often; I might not even have registered the sound of a shotgun.' He looked from one to the other, challenging them to deny him. Whatever else he might be, this was certainly not a man broken down by drugs or meths.

Rushton said, 'How long have you been on the road, Mr Robertson?'

He looked cautious, even evasive. Perhaps he realized that this was not a situation in which he could refuse to answer. It was a moment before he said. 'A few years now, off and on. I was made redundant from the steel works in Corby in Northamptonshire. One of the last to go when it closed.'

Lambert could see him working in a foundry; and a lot of Scots had come down to Corby and found themselves redundant. But that was many years back now. He said slowly, 'A long time ago, Robbie. A long time to be on the road. A long time to keep yourself together as well as you seem to have.' He looked him up and down, taking in his warm, functional clothing, his serviceable boots, his obvious good health.

'Oh, I've worked a bit, here and there. Never more than a few weeks, mind.'

'No insurance stamp, and no records for us to trace, you mean?'

He shrugged. 'The Lump isna' my fault. If the employers won't offer you anything else, you have to take it.'

It was true enough: the fringes of the building industry were a jungle which provided trouble for the police as well as the hospitals and social services. Lambert said, 'Are you married, Mr Robertson?'

'No. I'm not dodging the maintenance. And I've no family.' For a moment, the sturdy figure was like an insolent small boy, delighted to be unhelpful to them. Then he said, in a more conciliatory tone, 'I don't draw the dole. I don't get in anyone's way. I don't mug old ladies.'

It was probably all true. It would have been more winning if it had not emerged as a prepared speech. Lambert had again the impression of a man playing a part he had devised for himself. He said rather desperately, 'Have you camped in the same place in the woods for the week you've been there?'

Robertson paused before replying, as if he was estimating the possibilities of incriminating himself. 'No. I've moved around a bit.'

'Why here?'

'I worked for a while on a building site in Gloucester. They laid us off at the end of November, when the winter set in.' There was no note of complaint: he seemed to accept such things as facts of life. A hard man, this.

'If you've been in the forest for about a week, you must have seen other people in the forest. Tell us about them.'

'I'm not going to fit you up with a suspect. You can do your own—'

'Look, we're talking about murder, not shoplifting, Robertson. At the moment, you're in the frame yourself. You're the only person so far who's admitted he was in the area at the time of a brutal killing. I should remember that. And forget all that stuff about innocent until proved guilty. That's for the courts. We're conducting a police investigation.'

Robertson looked at them sullenly, but without fear. He seemed almost relieved by the aggression suddenly turned upon him. After a moment, he nodded his willingness to cooperate.

Rushton said, 'You must have seen other people in the forest during the days before the murder. Tell us about them, please.' He had a clean sheet of paper in front of him, its blank whiteness a challenge to the goodwill of the man on the other side of the table.

'I haven't seen many. A couple of forest workers: they were cutting up trees which had fallen in the gales. I kept away from them. Kids, of course, I've seen since the schools broke up for Christmas.'

Lambert said, 'For a man who claims not to know quite how long he's been in the forest, you are very precise about such things.'

Robertson grinned. This time, he felt, he had caught out this tall man who watched him so hard. 'It doesn't need great powers of deduction. You hear kids in the woods during the day. They're either wagging it, or they're on holiday.'

Lambert smiled briefly in acknowledgement. Policemen, too, were always aware for a variety of reasons when the school holidays began. More empty buildings to protect, and, as the number of working mothers grew inexorably, more young, unsupervised minds which idleness might lead into mischief. He said, 'Who else did you see? Who else would know the woods well enough to be there at night, waiting for a man on his way home?'

Robertson said, 'The tracks are quite wide: you wouldn't need detailed knowledge of the forest to have done this. And your killer might not have waited there, you know. It might have been a chance meeting.' He was almost teaching them their job now, and perhaps he caught Rushton's resentment, for he went on hastily, 'One or two people came through there fairly regularly. It's a short cut, you know—probably the clergyman who was shot was treating it as that.' He paused, as if overcome for a moment by the immensity of the part played by chance in life and in death. 'There's a lad who comes through regularly on a little motorbike.'

'Which way?'

'Both ways. I think he probably starts from Woodford.'

'Times?' Rushton's pen was poised to add the information to what he had already written on his white sheet.

'Don't know. Don't know if there was any regular pattern to them or not. I only remember him because of the noise of the bike. He must push it under the barrier; cars can't get into the woods, except for the forestry vehicles; their drivers have keys.'

Lambert wondered whether he was conscious that he was feeding them information they had already, wrapping his nuggets of valuable reportage in useless packaging. 'Did you speak to anyone?'

'Only one man, all week. I keep myself to myself, you see, except when the Old Bill interfere with me.' He had sensed their interest; the aside was a deliberate postponement of the gem of information he had saved until the last. 'But this chap's dog came and found me. Ugly brute, like a police dog. Doberman, it was. But he had it under control, I'll say that for him.'

'When was this?'

'Two days ago.' For once, the information came promptly. He gave them a description which was a surprisingly accurate depiction of Tommy Farr, from Woodford village stores. The time tallied with what Farr had told

Lambert of the meeting: they concealed their disappointment behind a professional inscrutability.

They took him through an account of his movements at the time of the murder, but there was little for him to tell them. He had been in the forest, possibly cooking himself a meal: he had a tiny stove for emergencies, but he preferred a fire of dry sticks whenever it was possible. He had neither seen nor heard anything suspicious, he repeated.

For the moment, at least, they were going to get no further with their number one suspect. Rushton said eventually, 'Well, we'll be keeping you here over Christmas. You can see whether a police cell helps to jog your memory.'

'It can't dig up what isn't there.' Robertson stroked his embryo beard and afforded the Inspector a bland smile.

'You're in trouble, Robbie, make no mistake about that. Do you want a lawyer?'

'What for? I haven't done anything. You won't be holding me here for long.' Again he gave the impression that he knew far more than a vagrant should about his rights. Rushton had already made a note to check criminal records, and not just under the name he had given them. Some young DC could have fun with hundreds of mug shots.

As if he read the thought, Robertson said, 'I might even pass the time by shaving off these whiskers. I'm sure you could find me a razor.' His fingers played speculatively for a moment over the small scar beside his eye.

They took him down to the cells; he would with luck be the only occupant over the Bank Holiday, if the good sense counselled in the latest drink-driving campaign prevailed. Rushton ushered him within the painted brick walls with a little vindictive satisfaction: the man's calmness irritated him more than he liked to admit. 'Christmas Day in a cell. Not my idea of fun,' the DI said, as the uniformed constable prepared to slam the heavy door.

The man in front of him looked round the stark little room, with its barred window and narrow bunk. 'Dry and warm after the forest. There are worse places to spend

Christmas Day. Christ himself might have been glad of this.'

Rushton's last image as the door shut was of Robertson smiling benignly at him, conscious that the captive had made the final small thrust in this bout with his captor.

CHAPTER 13

When there are small children in the house, Christmas morning begins very early. If Lambert had forgotten that, it was brought to his attention by the cries of infant delight which woke him soon after six.

He lay for a while adjusting to this special day and the fact that another year of the allotted span had ticked away. He was still trying to adjust to being a grandfather. He qualified all right when the babies were there. He treated them as a father might, dandling them self-consciously upon his knee as though they were late and wholly delightful additions to his own family.

But he could not think of himself as a grandfather, even in those congenial moments when the grandchildren departed and he and Christine went back into a house grown magically quiet. The daughters whom he still thought of as vulnerable children were mothers themselves now, wiser and more responsible in the mysteries of parenthood than he would ever be himself.

He knew that Christine was awake beside him, alert with that primeval female instinct to the nocturnal whimperings of a small child. He lay motionless for several minutes, listening to the gurglings of infancy from beyond the walls and wondering if his wife was thinking as he was of the child they had lost a generation ago. Eighteen months old Sue had been, when she died: he would not have that 'taken from them' phrase which well-meaning fools still occasionally tried to use. She would have been twenty-five now, but for them she would be eternally a beaming infant with an infectious chuckle.

Like the child whose innocent awakening they listened to now. Perhaps that death had sealed a pact of reconciliation between the young Inspector and the wife who had hated and fought the Force. It was around that time that they had almost broken up. But he refused to accept the bond brought by that death as being in any way part of a grander design. That would have put an awful burden upon them; and neither of them had been able to accept a God malignant enough to proceed by such means.

He went to the kitchen and made some tea, creeping back past the door of the room where Jacqui was talking gently to her daughter in the cot. Christine lay and watched him without moving as he poured the tea. She noted with the ruthless precision of her affection how he stooped a little now as he entered the room, as tall men will as the years advance, how he set down the tray and poured the tea with a little more care than he would once have used, guarding now against the accidents which morning stiffness might induce.

Whatever he was like at work, however much he chose to ignore the advance of the years there, he was a grandfather now to her, who saw him resolutely in the context of the family. For a moment, she thought she could see how he would be as a septuagenarian. Physically, that did not need any great projection; mentally, she remained unsure how well he would cope with growing old. To strangers, he deprecated his job and the demands of modern police work, and looked forward to retirement. To his intimates, of whom there were few, he was occasionally more revealing.

'I have to work today. That killing in the forest, over at Woodford.' He was still reluctant to bring the word murder into the house, as though the very thought of that oldest and darkest of crimes could contaminate the place.

At one time she would have been resentful, not of him so much as of the job, which took him away without forewarning whenever it chose to assert its demands. Now she accepted it as a part of him: perhaps the most vital part. She sipped her tea, listened to the gathering sounds of the crowded house awakening, and said with a smile, 'You'll be glad to get out. Away from all these women!' She often wondered how much he missed having a son; he had always professed himself perfectly contented with their daughters.

He grinned down at her as he sat on the side of the bed. 'Away from the noise, perhaps,' he admitted. 'But I'll be back for the meal. About three o'clock, we said, didn't we?' It was always a minor triumph when he remembered domestic arrangements of this kind. Once, when she had been tied at home with small children and the running of the house was her only challenge, she had resented his forgetfulness about such things. Now, many years into a highly successful resumed career as a teacher, she saw them in almost the same light as he did: necessary maybe, but essentially trivial, compared with the greater concerns they were both fortunate enough to deal with in their work.

By the time he had shaved and dressed, the whole household was busy. Caroline, his elder daughter, had already fed her four-month-old girl and eaten her own small breakfast. She had made Lambert the bacon and eggs which Christine nowadays forbade him except on special occasions. Father and daughter sat like conspirators at the round pine table as he ate them. He was reminded of the days when she used to bring her baking home from school and sit with wide and anxious eyes as he sampled it and gave his verdict.

Jacqui and her daughter came in as he moved on to toast and marmalade. The child he had heard mouthing experimentally an hour ago was twenty months old, able to walk rapidly around the kitchen and explore regions which had been inaccessible to her on her previous visits. His sons-in-law, waiting patiently for their allotted spans in the bathroom in this female household, would no doubt appear in due course.

By the time he was ready to go out at eight-thirty, they had returned in tracksuits from their morning jog, and the house was full of noisy self-congratulations and banter. The children, anxious to maintain their centrality in the attentions of this gathering, asserted themselves excitedly, and female voices rose in shrill approval of their efforts. Lambert, easing himself into the driver's seat of the big old Vauxhall and directing the car towards Bert Hook's home, was quite glad that he had an occasion to depart.

Clare Barton's Christmas morning was very different.

The two pills the doctor had left for her had cast her quickly into a deep sleep. But she woke unrefreshed. Lying alone in the bed which seemed now much too large, she had to remind herself again of what had happened on the previous day. Of what had happened to the man who had shared this bed with her on every previous night when she had slept in it. She lay waiting for the light to creep into the square room with the chintzy furnishings she had once thought so important, bitter in heart and mind that this should be Christmas Day.

She listened to Barbara ringing home, trying to help a harassed husband to cope with the children by the advice she offered from a distance. 'I can't leave here yet,' she ended in a low, urgent voice: Clare could see her casting anxious glances up the stairs towards this sister who must be handled like wafer-thin glass. 'I may have to bring her with me when I do come . . . Oh, come on, Dennis, it's not her fault this has happened.'

So she was a package that had to be carried around, until it could be abandoned without embarrassment. Was what had happened indeed not her fault? What she had done must be in some way connected with Peter's death. This was divine retribution for her own behaviour, surely. For a moment, her mind moved out of her body and she stood at the foot of the bed, studying her own small form lying motionless as a mummy beneath the spotless white counterpane.

Perhaps wives should be burned on a pyre when their husbands died, as she heard they still were in parts of the

East. If their functions stopped as abruptly as this with the death of a husband, the counterpane might as well be a shroud. She lay absolutely still in the centre of the bed, trying to feel her heartbeats slowing as she had done when she was a child, seeking the trance which might dispel the desolation she felt.

When Barbara crept tentatively into the room and studied her, she was scarcely conscious of her. Then her sister said, 'You're awake, then,' in such a tentative tone that she was stirred by the very banality of it.

Clare sat up, took the cup of tea, and fought hard not to let her face register the distaste at its sweetness. It was her first small step outside herself and back towards the normal world of consideration for others. 'I'll get up now,' she said.

Barbara did not try to dissuade her. 'Those detectives are coming here this morning,' she said. 'They said it's standard practice in cases of sudden death. I—I suppose they're like doctors, in a way. They have to get used to horrible things like this, I mean.'

'I'll see them. I want to do everything I can to help them find who did that to Peter.'

To her elder sister, she looked childlike in the middle of the big double bed, like a painting of a Victorian waif victimized by a malignant fate. 'I'll stay with you when they come, if you want me to.' Her sheltered life had allowed her no experience of policemen. She half-expected the worst strain of TV aggression in their questioning.

When she opened the door an hour and a half later, she saw two men in dark grey suits, with apologetic faces. The taller one said, 'I'm Superintendent Lambert, and this is Detective-Sergeant Hook. He spoke to you last night, I think, to arrange this. I'm terribly sorry that we have to intrude at such a time, and on such a day, but I'm afraid we do need to see Mrs Barton.'

Clare Barton was sitting very upright in her armchair when they were ushered into the lounge. She acknowledged the arrival of the two large men as if she were a monarch granting an audience. The high-backed chair seemed too large for her; even the crown of her fair hair did not reach the top of it. With her youth, her fair skin and her gravity, she reminded Bert Hook of the picture of Alice in Wonderland he had just left behind him.

'Do come and sit down,' she said. Her voice had the evenness of a child delivering a rehearsed line. 'We shall be all right now,' she said to her sister, who was lingering protectively by the door.

Barbara hovered for a moment, then said, 'I'll make some tea. If you want me, Clare, I shall only be in the kitchen.' She had no idea what her rights were in this matter, and plainly neither of the policemen was going to tell her.

Clare estimated the CID men with a calmness deriving from the mixture of shock and sedatives. It is a volatile cocktail, and she might at any moment switch moods if the balance of the two altered. For the present, she felt she saw everything with more clarity than she could ever remember. It was not a sensation she retained for very long.

She listened carefully as the tall man introduced himself and his sergeant. He had plentiful, frizzy hair, which must once have been very black but which was now liberally flecked with grey. His eyes too were grey, but dark enough indoors to seem almost black. They watched her steadily and without apology, as if they hoped to pick up information more important than what might come from her tongue. There was kindness in the eyes, she thought, as though he understood her situation and would alleviate it if he could: but perhaps that was a part of his technique.

The other man, rather shorter and broader, was trying to encourage her with his slow, awkward smile. He sat on the edge of the chair, as if he had no right to be there at all. He was a big, genial man, she decided; with a few white whiskers and the all-enveloping red robe, he would have made a wonderful Father Christmas. Perhaps she would tell him so, when the time came for him to go.

She watched Superintendent Lambert's broad, humorous mouth as he began to speak, as if it were divorced from the words it pronounced, as if she were studying the movements of a lizard in a terrarium. Although she saw his lips with this abnormal, dispassionate clarity, his words seemed at first to come to her from the other side of a glass screen, so that her reaction to them was delayed. But by the time he had introduced the two of them and said a little about police procedures, she was beginning to follow him almost normally. She was pleased with herself for that. He was telling her that Peter had died instantly, that he hadn't suffered, or even known much about it. He seemed to be offering her that as consolation, so she agreed that it was good.

Then Lambert was saying, 'It was quite some time—at least twenty hours, we think—before your husband's body was discovered. No one reported to us that he was missing, you see.' He waited for a reaction from her, so she nodded sagely to show that she understood. He said gently, 'You weren't here yourself at the time, Mrs Barton?'

She thought he would have known that. Perhaps there had been a breakdown in communications somewhere: no doubt that wasn't his fault. She said, 'No, I was away.' He seemed to be waiting for her to go on. Perhaps he wanted her to tell him where she had been. But she couldn't do that, could she? Michael had asked her not to.

Lambert smiled at her, explaining himself like a patient uncle feeling his way with a niece he seldom saw. 'We need to know where you were in those eighteen hours, you see. And in the day before that.'

She smiled at him like a cheerful, slightly mischievous child, who does not see the need to cooperate. It was a relief to him when her sister came in with a tray of tea. He said, 'Please sit down and stay with us, Mrs McLean. There is certainly no objection to your presence here from us.' He would be glad of it, indeed: people in shock sometimes reported things quite eccentrically to their relations when the police had gone.

Barbara poured the tea and went to sit at the other end of the hearth from her sister. It was Clare who then said calmly, 'I would rather do this on my own, Sis, if you don't mind.' It was years since she has used the diminutive; Barbara could not remember hearing it since Clare had got married. She looked at her, then picked up her cup of tea and went back to the kitchen. There was something compelling in her sister's calm obstinacy.

Bert Hook, who had so far written nothing in the notebook he had opened expectantly, said to the younger woman who sat primly in the big chair, 'We need to know where you were, love. It's standard practice when there is a death like this, you see.'

Lambert did not think that quoting the requirements of bureaucracy would have any effect, but he was wrong. Perhaps Hook's reassuring Gloucestershire tones were more important than the words he used. She looked at him, studied the ballpoint poised over the pad as if she had never seen such an implement before, and said, 'I see. What exactly would you like to know, then?'

Hook took over the questioning without a glance at his chief. 'When exactly did you leave home?'

'On Monday. I didn't come back until yesterday.'

So she had been away for two days and two nights. She did not seem to realize, and he must not tell her, that the movements of a spouse were always of great interest in cases of violent death. He said, 'Did you go by car?'

'Yes. I took the Escort. I should have left it for Peter: he wouldn't have been walking through the woods then.' There were no tears after this calm assertion. They would come later, no doubt.

Hook said, 'You couldn't know that at the time, though. You mustn't blame yourself—you didn't kill him.'

'No. But I feel as though I did. Have you any idea who did it, yet?'

There was a childlike simplicity about her, even now as they approached the key facts. He felt as though he were taking advantage of her, like an unscrupulous hypnotist abusing the trance he induces. But whatever her confusions, she seemed anxious to help them. She had even pointed out in her naïvety how the removal of the car had left her husband vulnerable to a murderer who knew of his habits. Hook said, 'Where were you in those days, love. We need to know.'

She shook her head. 'I can't tell you that.'

'I'm sorry, you're going to to have to. You see, when there is a serious crime like this, we check the movements of everyone involved, and we get the people they were with to confirm those facts. In that way, we can eliminate them from our inquiries.' He was glad to be able to feed in the jargon phrase; it made him feel a little less as though he were taking advantage of a child.

She looked at him, serious and unblinking. The brilliant blue eyes were very round in the unlined face. Framed in the corn-coloured hair, her features looked more than ever like those of an expensive Christmas doll. She said, 'You mean, I have to have an alibi?'

He smiled at her, smoothing away the harshness of the thought. 'If you like, yes. We never use the term. But it does help us if we can eliminate people from all suspicion. It saves us a lot of time, and we can then devote our energies to the people we have left.' He was talking desperately now, trying to preserve them for a little longer from the curtain they felt she must surely ring down between them.

She nodded, digesting this. 'Yes, I see . . . It's awkward for me, you see. He didn't want me to tell you.'

They tried not to show the spurt of excitement her simple words shot through each of them. Lambert, sensing his colleague's desperation, said, 'But I'm sure that when he said that he didn't realize how important it would be to us. We're going to find who killed Peter, you know. We're already making progress. But we need the help of those who were closest to him. Can you give us the name of anyone who can confirm your movements in the time you were away, Mrs Barton?'

For the first time, she dropped her eyes; it came as a

considerable relief to them. Then she said, perfectly clearly but in a lowered voice, 'I was with a man.'

Lambert put all his energies into maintaining the same even, unhurried tone. 'Was this for the whole of the time you were away?'

'Almost all, yes. We spent the nights together.'

Hook said, 'We need his name, I'm afraid, as we said.'

'He's married. He doesn't want our affair made public. I was only a bit of fun for him, anyway.' It was the first time she had been prepared to admit it to herself. The scales that might have clouded her eyes for months had dropped away in minutes with Peter's death.

Lambert said firmly, 'We'll have to have his name, please. This is a murder inquiry.' The formality of the reminder was a relief after the perilous empathy into which she had drawn them.

She nodded, a responsible rather than a frivolous child again now. 'His name's Michael. Michael Crawley.'

She gave them his address, assured them that she knew of no one who would have wanted to kill her husband—apparently she did not even consider Crawley as a candidate—and offered them her sister's address as the place where they could contact her if she was not here. As they rose and took an awkward leave of her, she looked round the stark room and said, 'Barbara seems to have taken down my Christmas decorations. Perhaps she thought they might upset me now.' She looked towards the corner of the room. 'She's moved the book I bought for Peter, too. There was no need, really.'

They were in the hall, thanking the sister for her efforts and the tea, when they heard the first sobs from behind the closed door. The three of them were arrested for a moment by that ancient, intimate sound. It came as a relief to all four people in the house.

CHAPTER 14

The English village still has a romantic image. Town dwellers muse fondly on the scents of summer hedgerows, thrushes in joyous song, and the sound of willow on leather on the village green.

It is not entirely a false image, even today, though it ignores the ubiquitous internal combustion engine and the malicious translation of rural cottages into city-dwellers' weekend residences. But it is essentially a summer image. Winter is different: only those who live in the country know how different. And even countrymen have mercifully little experience of the changes wrought when violent death clamps itself upon a village community.

Woodford had its village green. In summer, they even played cricket upon it. But on Boxing Day morning the grass here looked grey rather than green; after the brief and sunless mildness of Christmas, the frost was on its way back. The green was deserted, unkempt, unloved.

Lambert and Hook looked across the green for a moment without speaking, towards the churchyard where the bishop with whom Peter Barton had argued so fiercely would presently murmur conventional obsequies over the vicar's mortal remains. Then they turned the other way and went round the back of the Crown to seek out the house they wanted.

Council houses do not generally age well. The four properties here had been erected in optimistic postwar days by a council determined to do right by the virtuous underprivileged. They were showing their age now. They had been neglected for twenty years; their stuccoed walls were grey with dirt and veined with scores of tiny cracks, the blue of their paintwork was peeling where the summer sun had blistered its surface. These residences had none of the raddled dignity of Victorian houses in decay, none of those echoes of architectural exuberance which sounded still in the buildings of earlier eras. They waited like crippled beasts for some stronger outside will to revive them or despatch them.

The only concessions the designer of these houses had made to anything beyond utility were the small red-tiled porches which hooded the front entrances of each of them. Some of the tiles were cracked now, but the little pitched roofs over each door remained the one tiny flamboyance in these exteriors, as though ageing harlots had dashed on a hasty lipstick in an attempt to perpetuate attractions now long gone.

The porch was so small that the two large men in dark suits almost filled it. To Charlie Webb as he opened the door the sky seemed to have darkened with their presence. Lambert looked him up and down for a second before he said, 'Mr Webb? We need to ask you a few questions.'

They had to wait for a moment of stupefaction to pass from Charlie before he said, 'You'd better come inside.' He peered past them at the other houses and the back of the Crown, trying to see who might have observed their arrival here.

The old woman in the rocking-chair looked them up and down, then split her narrow face into a delighted grin, full of the mischief of the girl everyone but her had long forgotten. 'It's the fuzz, Samuel!' she told the black and white cat. It stretched itself on the window-sill in deference to this new presence, putting the tinselled artificial Christmas tree in grave danger as it did so. Granny Webb held her wrists out together and said, 'I'll come quietly, governor. Put the bracelets on.' Then she cackled heartily at the excellence of her wit, while Lambert sighed inwardly about the side-effects of television crime series.

Charlie said wearily, 'Behave yourself, Gran,' like a parent struggling with a hyperactive child. He was unable to keep the affection out of his tone, and for an instant only, the anxiety left his face. He tickled the cat beneath its chin and it rubbed the side of its head luxuriously against his thin arm.

'What you been doin' then, young Charlie?' said the old woman. Virtually housebound nowadays, she was delighted to have a little drama brought into her house with the advent of these men. It must be harmless excitement, because Charlie was a good lad. So she might as well have a bit of fun out of it. Pity old Margery next door but one had gone last year: she'd have no one to tell now about this. 'Don't you go framin' 'im. I've heard all about bent coppers, you know.' She grinned with satisfaction at this demonstration of her grasp of the underworld patois.

Then she clasped her arms across the place where her waist had once been and laughed again, to show it was a joke. Coppers who framed the innocent were part of that fictional world she now found more attractive than the real one. She could not believe that any real policeman would behave other than honourably; her sole experience of the species was in the form of the village bobby of an age that was gone. 'Ask the fuzz to sit down, then,' she called to her grandson, waving loftily towards the single armchair on the other side of the hearth.

Bert Hook grinned back at her, almost conspiratorially. Then, looking at her grandson for the first time since they had come into the crowded living-room, he said, 'Like to show us your bedroom, son?'

The boy led the way gratefully upstairs, while the old lady remained in her chair and cursed her arthritis and the ineffectiveness of modern medicine. The bedroom was surprisingly spacious. These had been designed as family houses, and this had been the main bedroom, designed to afford parents the privacy and status which was still thought appropriate in the families of the late 'forties. There were two windows, and Charlie's four-foot bed and single bedroom suite left plenty of floor space. He had been able to install a table, an upright chair and two bulbous old leather armchairs without overcrowding the floor.

If the dimensions of the room were surprising, its tidiness

was even more so, in view of its occupant. There were no clothes on the floor, no washing awaiting removal from the furniture. A pop group poster with a lean, earnest blonde girl in the forefront was attached with Blu-Tack to the back of the door. A coloured photograph of a rider cornering in a motorcycle race, knee almost touching the tarmac, helmet and goggles making him anonymous as a spaceman, filled the space between the dressing-table mirror and the corner of the room.

This was not just a bedroom, then. It was a den to which the boy could retire when the generations stretched too dangerously between him and that suffocating compound of love and bewilderment downstairs. An insulation against the battered pensioner syndrome which was the kind of 'domestic' the police were called to ever more frequently in the 'nineties. A place where he might occasionally bring a friend to listen to the records stacked neatly by the player on top of the chest of drawers. They were finding out a little more with each minute about this young man and his way of life.

Lambert said, 'We know some things already. You're Charles Webb. Aged twenty. You live here with just your gran. And you work shifts at the Electricity Works.'

The implication was that they knew much more than that, but were not going to waste time airing the full extent of their knowledge. Charlie, who had things he wished to conceal, gulped and nodded. He wondered if he looked quite as pale as he felt at that moment.

The two men sat in the armchairs and motioned him to sit on the upright chair by the table. He found that he was facing the morning light as it fell upon him from the window, and wondered if this positioning was deliberate or accidental. His face felt as exposed as if it had been beneath a spotlight. Lambert said, 'You know why we've come here, I'm sure. We're investigating the murder of the Reverend Peter Barton on Tuesday last.'

'I guessed it must be that. But I don't think I can—'

'We're questioning everyone in the village, as you might

expect. But your movements interest us more than most.'

They watched Charlie as he licked his lips. Investigations were always urgent, and yet within that urgency there were moments when one had to behave as though there was no earthly reason to hurry. Moments when time was on the side of the investigators, and silence could be allowed to stretch until it became unbearable.

The small purple eruptions of Charlie Webb's spots became more noticeable as the sallow skin around them seemed to whiten and stretch. He said, 'I can't think of any reason why my—'

'You go into the forest regularly. Past the spot where a man was shot. You can think of reasons why: you're not stupid, lad. Neither are we.'

'Just because I use that track sometimes doesn't mean—'

'You were there on Tuesday?'

'Yes. I went to work that way.' He didn't make any pretence of having to think about it, as he had planned to do. His nerve hadn't held for very long. He hadn't thought it would be like this. Lambert's grey eyes seemed to be looking right into his brain, and discovering a grim amusement in what they saw there.

'On your motorbike,' said this omniscient tormentor. Webb nodded and the Superintendent said, 'We found the tracks, near the body. Someone will need to match your tyres with them presently. In case they're needed in evidence.'

He was too well used to working with Hook to need to give him any sign, so that he was able to keep his gaze steadily upon the unlined, adolescent face as Hook said, 'Time?'

For a moment Webb looked uncomprehendingly at the point to which the attack had been switched. He saw the Sergeant with ballpoint poised impassively above the page of his notebook and understood. 'It would be about twenty to four. I was on at four o'clock.' Watching the pen moving rhythmically over the paper in Hook's round, precise hand, he was drawn into further words by a compulsion to fill the silence with which these men seemed so much at ease. 'The shift is six to two, you see, but I was doing two hours of overtime. So I was at work well before the vicar was shot.'

He knew he had made a mistake as soon as the words were out, but they seemed in no hurry to exploit it. Lambert allowed two rooks outside the window to conclude a raucous duet before he said, 'And how would you know what time that was, Mr Webb?'

Charlie looked at the heels of the 'trainers' he could see peeping from beneath the bedspread where it just failed to reach the carpet. He felt he would never again look into the faces of his tormentors. 'I—I thought everyone knew when he was killed.'

'It took us a post-mortem examination and a lot of interviews to establish the time of death with reasonable certainty. Yet you seem very confident about it.'

'I heard he was shot on the way home from Ashbridge—I can't remember where.' Charlie Webb's voice sounded very surly as the confidence seeped from him.

Lambert said, 'Are you telling us that you weren't around at the time this killing took place?'

'I was at work. I've already told you.'

'Indeed you have . . . What kind of work do you do, Mr Webb?'

Charlie glanced at him suspiciously, forgetting his resolve to keep his eyes on the carpet. 'General maintenance, they call it. Sweeping round machines. Checking from the dials that they're working as they should be.' He preferred to be vague, even here when it was in his interests to be precise. He was reluctant to admit to anyone that the job wasn't much more than cleaning. It had been supposed to be a route to better, more skilled things when he took it on, but he had never got round to taking the exams. Had never worked for them properly, in fact. He made a resolve to begin studying systematically in the new year. When all this was over.

'The kind of work that allows you to nip out for an hour when things are quiet, is it, Mr Webb?'

Charlie thought he was going to faint. He gripped the table beside him hard to stop the room from moving. They couldn't know, surely? If they were trying to trap him, there was still a chance, if he kept calm. When he spoke, the voice seemed for a moment to come from another person, behind a screen to his left. 'I was there all the time on that night. I don't know what you're on about. Ask—ask anyone at work.'

An outsider would not even have noticed the tiny nod with which Lambert indicated that his sergeant should take over the questioning. Hook said quietly, 'We did ask, Charlie. That's how we know you were missing from work for over an hour. At about the time when you've just told us that Peter Barton was murdered.'

Webb's voice was so low that they could scarcely hear him as he said, 'Dave Jackson told you. He said he wouldn't.' His face set like that of a small boy whose parent has broken a promise.

'Dave Jackson did no more than his duty, Charlie. He'd have been in big trouble if he hadn't. He wasn't sneaking on you to a teacher. He was assisting the police in a murder inquiry.'

Webb said dully, 'I'll lose my job.'

'You'll lose more than that, Charlie, if you're not careful. A man has been brutally killed, and we haven't arrested anyone for it yet.'

Hook was reasoning with him as if he were no more than a difficult child. Lambert would have been much harsher in these circumstances, but he knew Bert had a way of getting results with lads like this. Hook's own background as a Barnardo's boy made him effective with lads like Webb who had lost their parents. Sometimes he could be too sympathetic, but that could be adjusted in due course, if necessary. He spoke almost like a father as he said, 'Where were you, Charlie? We need to know: you can see that, now.'

Webb nodded miserably. He said, 'I went out to meet a girl. It's difficult here, you see, with Gran. I only meant to be about twenty minutes, but we had an argument.' He seemed to be rehearsing his explanation to the Works Manager, still unaware of the seriousness of his position.

Hook said, 'All right. We'll need her name, Charlie.'

Webb looked up suddenly. 'No. I can't do that. Her parents don't know, you see. I can't drag her into this, not even to save me.'

Hook said, 'You can and will, Charlie.' He was very quiet, very persuasive. Lambert would have snarled at the lad: the last thing he needed at this stage was a pimply youth going quixotic upon him.

But Hook's way won. Webb gave them the name and address quietly enough a moment later. They were on their way out, ducking under the chains of coloured paper which were strung diagonally across the room downstairs, before Lambert spoke again. They had taken their leave of Granny Webb when he turned back to Charlie and asked, 'By the way, do you happen to have a shotgun, Mr Webb?'

The old woman, who had been disappointed to see them departing, was highly amused. ''Course he has. Spends all morning, sometimes, just cleaning it. Keeps it in the shed down the garden, don't you, love? With his motorbike, it is.'

Her cackle came to Charlie like a cracked bell tolling his doom.

CHAPTER 15

Douglas 'Robbie' Robertson, if that was his real name, should have been cowed by captivity. Instead, he was in truculent mood.

Perhaps living rough inverts men's normal standards. Certainly he was not impressed when he was confronted again by the top brass in a murder investigation, Superintendent John Lambert and Detective-inspector Christopher Rushton. He called them that himself when he came into the interview room; they were struck again by his familiarity with police ranks and his refusal to be unnerved by the cramped harshness of the cheerless room with its bare, windowless walls.

His acquaintance with their methods suggested an old lag, though he had not that air of prison darkness about him which most CID men think they can detect in such men, and the newly computerized fingerprint records had produced nothing. They had persuaded him to shave, and then set two young detective-constables to work on the books of mug shots, to see if they could turn him up as a criminal. The exercise had produced nothing. The files of British Steel had thrown up two Douglas Robertsons who had worked at the Corby plant before its shutdown over a decade earlier, but there were no details extant, and, of course, no photographs.

They were going to have to release him, unless they could unearth something quickly. Or bluff him. Rushton, who was more and more convinced of his guilt, was determined to try that. In answer to Robertson's softly voiced opinion that it was time for him to be moving on, he snapped, 'Don't think you're going anywhere until we're ready to release you!'

'Oh, I think I am, you know.' The man seemed positively to relish the moment. 'I enjoyed my Christmas dinner, and your cells feel quite well heated after the forest in winter. Because of that, I've been content to let you hold me for considerably more than twenty-four hours without charging me. But it's time to be off now, I think. Unless you think you can arrange a magistrate's order on Boxing Day to hold me.' He smiled at them blandly, challengingly.

Lambert thought him so confident of his ground that he might go on talking, perhaps giving away unwittingly what he had so carefully guarded during formal interrogation, but the man was too shrewd for that. His brown eyes became wary as the older man tried to lead him towards revelations. He looked younger than they had thought him at first, for he had allowed his long, unkempt hair to be trimmed short at the same time as he shaved off his beard. His appearance now reinforced the feeling Lambert had had all along that this was a man playing the part of a tramp, rather than the genuine article.

Rushton acknowledged for the first time that they were going to have to observe the due procedures and let Rushton go. 'We'll need to know your whereabouts,' he said, 'and you'll need to inform us if you leave the area.'

Robertson's brown eyes twinkled. 'I am "of no fixed abode", I'm afraid, Mr Rushton. Makes it difficult for me to give you an address. And we knights of the road are men of sudden decisions, not possible for ordinary citizens like you. We're creatures of impulse, moving about the country as the fancy takes us.' He looked steadily at Rushton and folded his arms, contriving to make it seem a gesture of insolence.

Lambert looked at the squat frame, the powerful forearms clasped before him as though presented for inspection. Whatever his background, this man had kept himself in prime physical condition, well nourished but not overweight, hard, confident, observant. When Lambert had hoped a few moments ago that the man might overplay his hand, Robertson had been instantly aware of the danger. He wore up to date clothing and boots, well chosen for his way of life; there was not an article about him that was a cast-off from a more affluent society. He did not seem a man to spend a week in the forest without some definite objective.

Yet they could not hold him. He knew that, had indeed just told them how thoroughly he knew it. And they had turned up no hard evidence to take to a magistrate, even if a court had been available to them. Lambert told him as much, grudgingly.

Robertson afforded him another of his humourless smiles. 'That's because there's nothing to find, Superintendent.' He managed to invest his pronunciation of that rank with something like contempt.

It was probably that which made Lambert think of a new

tack when the man had gone back to his cell. 'That fellow must know something, whether or not he was involved himself. And he certainly knows all about us and the way we operate, Chris.'

'But we haven't turned up a record for him. I doubt whether he's been inside for any length of time.' Rushton searched feverishly for an idea which would demonstrate his mettle to Lambert. Even as a DI, he still felt the need to prove himself to the older man: it was a strain in him which irritated both of them. 'Do you suppose he's ever been a JP? Or a lawyer of some kind?'

It was a desperate suggestion. Neither of them entertained it seriously, but Lambert could not dismiss it as summarily as he would have done had it come from someone like Bert Hook. There was a stiff politeness between these two which got in the way of his normal style. 'Not a JP. He's hardly old enough, for one thing. I suppose it's possible he had a dose of legal training somewhere along the way. Quite a few jobs give a smattering of that. I think you might be right that we've been chasing the wrong hare in assuming a criminal record. What if he was on the right side of the law in this mysterious previous existence?'

Rushton nodded slowly. 'It's a possibility, I suppose. We tend to assume that potential murderers have always been bad lads. But if he wasn't a wrong 'un, where do we look? Especially at this time of the year, when all the records offices are either closed or operating on skeleton staffs.'

'Closer to home. Let's have a look at ex-coppers.'

Rushton grimaced. 'There's a hell of a lot of coppers leave the force, sir, as we know only too well. If we're going back ten years and more—'

'But the number who are actually officially discharged rather than being persuaded to resign is much smaller. And recorded carefully, in case such men are ever tempted to try to rejoin the force. Let's start with them. It's a long shot, but worth trying. If it turns up nothing, we might try Army records: the Services dispense with a number of psychopaths each year; injured policemen in various parts of the country can testify to that.'

'I'll set the wheels in motion.' For once, as he watched Rushton making a note on his pad, Lambert was glad to have this man behind him; there was no more efficient or diligent officer in following through this kind of task.

For the moment, he could dismiss Douglas 'Robbie' Robertson from his mind, just as he would shortly have to lose him physically from his sight: the machine was doing all they could think of to check on him and his past. Lambert said a little wearily, 'What else have we turned up, Chris?'

'Not a lot that seems significant at the moment, sir. The Scene of Crime team have found nothing very helpful. A couple of twelve-bore cartridge cases, almost certainly the ones discharged at Barton. Fibres on the corpse's clothing which tally with a sweater worn by Arthur Comstock on the day of the murder. Sounds exciting, until you remember that Barton travelled in Comstock's car only a couple of hours before he was killed.'

'Have we checked out Comstock's account on his whereabouts at the time of the death?'

'I saw his sister myself, sir.' Rushton was faintly pained that his Superintendent could even entertain the idea that such an obvious procedure might not yet have been implemented. 'She confirms that he picked her up in Cheltenham —had to wait for her there, because her coach was half an hour late—and took her back to his cottage. I've checked that with the bus company, and it's correct. Unless we presume conspiracy between the two of them, there doesn't seem any easy way he could have been back in the forest at the time of the shooting. But he did take the car down to the village shop as soon as they got into the cottage. He could have gone into the woods instead, or afterwards, I suppose. I'll check with the shopkeeper myself to see just what time he was there.'

'Man called Farr. Doesn't like the police and keeps a Doberman.' Lambert grinned at Rushton's wry face.

'There was a slip of paper with Comstock's telephone number on it in Barton's pocket. He said he gave it to Barton in case he wanted to ring for a lift home from Ashbridge.'

Lambert said thoughtfully, 'He's the only person we've located so far who knew for certain that Barton would be coming along that track.'

'And at that particular time.'

Lambert said, 'I suppose there was no joy with young Charlie Webb's shotgun?' Rifle-shootings often left evidence as strong as a fingerprint; shotguns were much less distinctive, as well as much more widespread.

'Nothing very useful. It could have been the weapon, and it's probably been fired recently. That's as far as the ballistics boys will go. It's a twelve-bore, like the murder weapon, but there are plenty of those around as well as Charlie's. Mind you, we haven't found any other young men who were absent from work at exactly the time of the killing.'

'But only people on shift work, like Charlie, would have been noticed. Most other people could simply have left work a few minutes early. There aren't too many large works with clocking off systems round here. What about Webb's girlfriend?'

'We found her easily enough. These liaisons aren't as secret as young people like to think. She's a typist in an estate agent's office; he met her when she'd finished work. She bears out his story, more or less. She's vague about the time they met and how long they were together. No doubt it would have been possible for Webb to ride his motorbike into the forest and shoot the vicar, then see her to establish an alibi of sorts.'

It didn't seem likely to either of them. Compared with the man who had sat defiantly opposite them in the interview room a few moments earlier, Charlie Webb seemed a slight candidate for homicide. But panic or desperation can lead to violence in the most unlikely people, as the annals of murder document in awful detail. It is such individual, 'one-off' crimes which can be the most difficult to solve.

'Have you turned up anyone else who might have been in the forest at the time?'

'The house-to-house hasn't turned up much, so far. There are a couple of Forestry Commission people who were working in the woods all week, as you would expect. One of them lives in Ashbridge, one of them in a village five miles further on. They left the woods at about four on the day of the murder. They could have gone back, of course: they know their way about the forest at night much better than most. One of them says he was in his house on his own at the time: his wife was away for the day. But God knows why either of them would want to kill Barton.' Rushton shrugged his shoulders hopelessly. He knew the Chief did not like to discuss motive until opportunity had been established, but the absence of it worried him more than usual this time.

'Anyone else from Woodford or Ashbridge known to have been in the forest at the time?' Lambert was aware that he was beginning to sound desperate: any other possibilities they were able to discuss sounded very thin when contrasted with the massive, sinister presence of the man the station sergeant was at this moment releasing.

Rushton said, 'No one is known to have been there. Almost anyone could have been, of course, particularly from Woodford. The place is less than twenty minutes' walk from the village, and most of them know the tracks through the woods well. Tommy Farr had shut the village shop by the time of the killing, and he goes into the woods every day. Webb and the foresters we've already talked about.' Rushton counted them off on his fingers as he spoke. 'We've seen Michael Crawley, Clare Barton's lover. He certainly wasn't anywhere near here at the time of the killing: there are witnesses to that. He could have hired someone to remove the husband, of course.'

'And do we think that's likely?' Lambert took a small, malicious pleasure in putting Rushton on the spot. He was unlikely to have interviewed a man who lived sixty miles away himself.

'I haven't seen him myself, sir, as you'll appreciate. The officer who saw him thought not. He seems to be a married man who saw his chance of a bit on the side and took it. He's appalled to find himself drawn into a murder case and devastated by the thought that he might have to give evidence in court. It might all be a front, of course. I told Bath CID that if further evidence emerged you might want to see Crawley yourself in due course.'

Lambert noted that the tables had been turned neatly on him in that last sentence. Rushton had not made detective-inspector at thirty without learning much about the intricacies of working relationships. The Superintendent said, 'There is, of course, Mrs Barton. With a lover in the background, she has more of a motive to kill her husband than we've unearthed so far for anyone else.'

The thought of that pathetic, doll-like figure waiting in the darkness of the forest to release the barrels of a shotgun upon her innocent spouse was chilling, even for a man habituated now to the depths of human evil. But there was no need for such melodrama. Like Crawley, she could have hired someone to fire the shotgun and made sure she was miles away herself at the time. Or she could have colluded with her lover. Sex was the most frequent element of violent murders, and Clare Barton had almost volunteered its presence to them in this case.

Lambert said heavily, 'Has anything emerged from the people who were with the vicar on his last afternoon?'

'No. At least, we have only negative findings. Barton did not seem at all nervous or upset. There is no evidence at all that he entertained the idea that anyone might be trying to kill him. On the contrary, if we believe what Arthur Comstock says, Peter Barton insisted on walking home alone through the forest in the dark when he need not have done so; it's difficult to believe that any man who had had even a hint that his life was in danger would have done that.'

'And you didn't find any motive among those who were with him that afternoon? They were as far as we can tell the only people who knew he was going to go home through the forest at that time.'

'No. The meeting at Ashbridge was with three pillars of the church there. They didn't know he would be walking home through the woods until he told them at the meeting. I suppose it's conceivable that one of them could have cut through the woods at a faster pace than the vicar and waited to ambush him, but all of them are over sixty and two of them are ladies.'

They allowed themselves a brief smile at the picture of these worthy elders bent on such unlikely violence. Then Lambert said, 'What about the Davidsons, back in Woodford? They must have known his plans.'

Rushton shook his head. 'Not entirely. The only person at that earlier meeting who knew Barton would be in the woods is Comstock, and as we said, that wasn't until almost the moment when he dropped Barton off in Ashbridge. Colonel Davidson arranged that Barton would drive back in the Rover at his leisure. It was Barton himself who changed the arrangements.'

'And none of them saw anything in the vicar's behaviour which now seems significant?'

'No. He was organizing a village fund for the famine in Ethiopia, and was delighted to get their cooperation. Rachel Davidson said he looked tired and strained, but she put that down to his wife's behaviour.'

'From what I heard when I interviewed Clare Barton, she was probably right.' Lambert came back to the issue which worried them both. 'Are we any nearer to establishing why anyone should want to kill Peter Barton?'

'No. On the contrary, it's been difficult to find anyone to say a word against him. Even among the people who never go to church—a majority nowadays, even in the country—everyone is full of praise for what he was trying to do and the way he behaved. He seems to have been a man without enemies.' Rushton smiled apologetically, not for the cliché but for the detectives' nightmare it presented. Almost always a murder victim had men or women who hated him. If there was one in particular, the investigation was easy and short. Where, as often, there were many, it took longer, but the lines of inquiry were marked out for them to follow.

The sudden dispatch of a man whom everyone seemed to like, whose death seemed to have benefited no one, was a CID nightmare. Rushton voiced the thought which neither of them wished to contemplate. 'We may have to face the fact that it might have been a nutter, sir.'

Lambert nodded reluctantly. In a lower rank, he would have dismissed the idea without ceremony as defeatist; in a conscientious and experienced officer like Rushton, it might be no more than realism. It was what every investigating officer feared. Motiveless murders by unbalanced men—such crimes by women are virtually unknown—are difficult to pin down, since the murderer is often unacquainted with his victim. They both excite and terrify the public, so that they bring accusations of police incompetence and demands for success which are often unreasonable.

Worst of all, such killings rarely come singly.

CHAPTER 16

Arthur Comstock had enjoyed his Christmas. It had been nice to have a woman about the house, taking over his kitchen, spoiling him with richer and more elaborate fare than he bothered to prepare for himself. He and his sister had always got along easily enough, though there had been long periods when they scarcely saw each other.

Now that his army service was over and Molly was growing accustomed to her widowhood, they felt themselves closer than at any time since the days when she had watched over his boyhood from her lofty adolescence: she was the elder by eight years. Certainly the manner of her husband's sudden, violent death had brought them closer together, the more so as Arthur had also been in the Falklands at the time. Sailors did die in wars, but no one had expected this one.

They had already arranged their next meeting, which would be at her cosy Yorkshire home when the winter was over. He would be quite sorry to see her go on the morrow and would look forward to Easter. Yet he knew also that he would be relieved to have his cottage back to himself.

Service habits die hard, and he had got used to his own domestic routine, his own small forms of tidiness. The wife who had left him years ago had seen his neatness as an obsession rather than a virtue, and he saw now that it could be irritating for a woman to live with. But he had come from a home which was always untidy, and the barrack-room rectitude instilled in him as a boy soldier had been a delight to him when it was a burden to others.

Now, after years of travelling about the world at the Army's dictate, he appreciated his own home and the opportunity to settle into it. The cottage might belong to Harry Davidson, but it was a permanent home as far as Arthur was concerned. He did not intend to vacate it until it suited him; he had no doubt that that would be many years hence.

As his sister busied herself in the kitchen, he had to control his urge to follow her about and replace things exactly where he thought they should be. When she caught him re-positioning the teapot, her grimace was a mixture of irritation and affection, but he read it as a warning sign. 'I think I'll just go for a stroll into the village. I've been inside all day and I'm not used to it,' he said. 'The Colonel usually keeps me pretty busy on normal days.' He used his employer's rank self-consciously, testing out the idea of his new job on Molly. He had fallen on his feet here all right.

He went out past the main house now. The Old Vicarage looked picturesque on that Boxing Day afternoon, with its holly wreath on the door and its brightly lit Christmas tree reaching almost to the ceiling of the high old drawing-room.

Harry and Rachel Davidson had guests—his brothers and their families, Arthur believed—and there was animated conversation and laughter behind the bay windows of the drawing-room. No sounds emerged through the new double glazing, and the silence gave the scene a macabre touch, like the haunted house scenes Arthur had set moving with his pennies in the amusement arcades of the 'fifties. There were no curtains drawn as yet, for none but he could observe the movements in the house.

It was bitter cold as the evening dropped upon the valley; there would be hard frost as usual around the turn of the year. From the gates of the Old Vicarage, Arthur took a last look back at the glittering cameo in the drawing-room. From a hundred yards away, the small figures looked even more unreal, as though their lives might be switched off at the turn of a switch. He smiled in the dusk, then set off briskly towards the village.

He was nearing the junction of the lanes by the village shop when he saw the figure coming towards him from the forest. It looked both taller and more sinister with the last of the light behind it, a silhouette which seemed to grow in size and menace as its outlines became more definite and it took on the shape of a man.

It was within ten yards if him before he recognized it. 'It's you, Tommy!' he called. 'Didn't recognize you in this light.'

'Nor I you, Arthur boy.' It pleased Tommy Farr to play up his Welshness when the whim took him. He watched the Doberman come loping up from behind at the sound of Comstock's greeting, knowing the dog would not harm Arthur, enjoying the moment of apprehension he noticed in the man as the dark shape materialized from the hedge and moved to his side.

It was characteristic of Farr to defy the small conventions of village life. Since the murder of their vicar three days earlier, no one in the village had cared to be seen abroad with a shotgun. Tommy carried his negligently now across his shoulder, though in fact he had not used it during his brisk walk along the edges of the forest. Kelly was not a gun-dog, and he rarely discharged the weapon when the dog was around.

Nevertheless, in view of what had happened, it would not do for people to get the idea that he owned a shotgun he did not use for legitimate purposes. Although he would never have acknowledged it, least of all to himself, Tommy Farr had the beginnings of that troublesome paranoia which sometimes besets men who live along and fancy themselves to be at the centre of community gossip.

Arthur, confident now that he would not be savaged, fondled the dog's soft head and spoke gently to it in the darkness. Tommy, watching the two of them indulgently, recognized with a shaft of insight that was both ridiculous and disturbing that he and Comstock should have been fathers. There was a lot of talk about women deprived of children, but no one ever gave much attention to men and the brutalizing effect that deprivation might have upon them.

The two fell into step and moved past Farr's shop. Comstock called at the village shop for small purchases, no more than once a week. The two men did not meet regularly, or for very long. Yet the bond of their bachelor status, in a village dominated by the family and its periodic births and bereavements, was stronger than either of them cared to acknowledge. Both of them had had wives, and each of them had unburdened himself to the other about the circumstances of the departures of those wives, revelations they had denied to anyone else in this small, tight community.

That knowledge united them in a half-humorous alliance against the intrusions of the villagers into the lives they had worked out for themselves. There was an unspoken assumption that women in particular needed to be kept at bay, that the less they were told about life in general and emotions in particular the better. It was a vague, often jocular stance, which they had never troubled to define, because their understanding meant they never had to do so. Perhaps it enabled them to give an element of drama to attentions which were no more than friendly and sympathetic.

They walked to the Crown, without needing any agreement that they were going for a pint. The pub had only just opened. They moved to the table they had used before in the alcove between the inglenook and the small window. They sipped Welsh bitter appreciatively, interspersed terse dialogue with untroubled silences, and impressed the landlord with their air of deep, unhurried collusion.

Peter Barton's death overhung all other village discussion still, even on Boxing Day, when many families had visitors from outside. The collecting-box for the famine relief which he had organized as his last act was beside the publican on the bar: he remembered almost guiltily that it was Arthur Comstock who had come in to organize it, only hours before the vicar's shattered body had been discovered. Kelly had draped himself invisibly behind his master's heels; the shotgun, gleaming darkly in the low orange illumination of the shaded wall lights behind the two men, seemed more than usually ominous in this context.

It would not have surprised the landlord to know that the two men were discussing the death which preoccupied his regulars. Tommy Farr said, 'The police took in the chap I saw in the forest on the day before the murder. I'm not surprised at that. But I heard from Bill Evans that they're going to have to let him go. He's probably out again now.'

There was a considerable silence, which neither of them felt any need to fill. Bill Evans was the uniformed constable who lived in the village, so the information would be reliable. Then Arthur Comstock said, 'He didn't do it, then.' He had a faith in the efficiency of the police, because he regarded them as the civil counterpart to the Army which had been his life for so long.

Tommy Farr did not share his respect. 'That don't follow, boy. They have to let him go if they can't pin it on him, see? If you ask me, they don't know who done it.' The thought seemed to give him a perverse satisfaction.

Comstock looked guiltily round the bar, but there was no one watching them. Then landlord had taken advantage of slack trade to watch the Boxing Day television programmes with his wife: they could hear the sounds of studio laughter through the open door behind the bar.

Neither of them was a heavy drinker nowadays. Within twenty minutes, they were talking in quiet tones in the deserted car park. Arthur Comstock left Farr at the rear entry to the village stores. As Kelly nosed his way through the gate and up the familiar flagged path, the two men looked automatically towards the dark outline of the woods, scarcely three hundred yards away and clear beneath the first stars of a frosty night.

They needed no words. Each know the other was conjecturing upon the presence within that dark mass of the man the police had questioned and released.

The man who called himself Robertson was there all right. But no one else went into the forest until the next morning.

The temperature was still below freezing at ten o'clock when Charlie Webb walked there. He was on holiday, having taken the three days to bridge Christmas and New Year, as most of his fellow workers tried to do. Now he was wondering why. He came on foot, wishing as he had when a boy that he had a dog to run with. He did not know why he was drawn here, for he shivered as the bare twigs closed out the sky above his head, knowing that the cause was not just the bitter cold.

He had wanted to bring the shotgun with him, but he had left it behind in the shed; he was still disturbed by the way the police had questioned him so closely about it. He had a vague notion of going to look at the spot where Peter Barton had fallen, but now he hesitated, then turned away at the junction of the tracks, so that his route took him away from the scene of the death and along a smaller path, running roughly parallel to the edge of the forest and emerging on the other side of the village.

His movements were observed with curiosity and wry

amusement by Robertson. He watched the slight figure in his bomber jacket and motorcycle gauntlets walking without rhythm down the undulating path. The youth moved as though when deprived of his motorcycle he had no confidence in his movements. Robertson observed him until he was out of sight. Then he went back to his tiny camp in the undergrowth, like a tortoise withdrawing its head after deciding it has seen enough of the world for the moment.

He did not realize that Charlie Webb had seen him, had registered not only his presence here but its exact location. It was easy to underestimate that slender, uncoordinated figure. But Charlie was a country boy, born and bred round here. He had registered the smell of stale smoke which spoke of an extinguished fire before he turned the bend to follow the track past the place where Robertson had slept and breakfasted. When his youthful peripheral vision picked up the movement which was not quite behind him, he was astute enough not to register it. So the police had let this man go. He was disappointed about that.

Behind him, the man who used the name of Robertson was also disappointed. Although he knew it was early, he had hoped this might be the walker he awaited. He had made the call under the cover of Boxing Day darkness, and he was confident no one had intercepted it. Secrecy had become a habit with him: he carried it like the other tools of his trade. He hid the radio telephone carefully beneath the brambles, where it had lain safely while he was in the police cell.

The person he waited for would come: there was no question about that. It was time for a reckoning.

CHAPTER 17

If Arthur Comstock was secretly glad to have his home back to himself, Rachel Davidson in the Old Vicarage itself was not.

She saw off her guests from the wide stone steps of the old house. Harry's brothers had come in their own cars; they drove away now with their wives and children crowding the cars, uttering noisy thanks and valedictory injunctions to visit them in due course. Harry was delivering his two aunts to the station in Gloucester himself, rather than entrusting them to the less personal care of his chauffeur Comstock. He installed them solicitously into the back seat of the car, then watched them take a muted but affectionate farewell of their hostess.

Rachel watched the Rover until it disappeared between the two high wrought-iron gates, answering the genteel flutterings of the gloved hands with a more vigorous wave of her own. Then she went sadly back through the wide oak door to the silences of the big house.

Rachel had been brought up in a mansion in Switzerland that was continually full of people. They entertained her father's business associates on long winter evenings when cut glass glinted in profusion on their big mahogany table. They entertained friends and their numerous relatives on the terrace in the summer, when the scarlet fire of the sunsets over the silver Alps seemed perpetual in her memories of childhood. The winter Cotswold landscape seemed by comparison drab and featureless, the silent expanse of the six-bedroomed Victorian house felt like an airless prison with the windows shut against the end of year cold.

She stood in the bay window and looked sadly at the leafless borders and grey-green lawns which stretched away in front of the house. The depression which had beset her since the death of Peter Barton surged softly back into the room with the departure of her guests. She had thought herself insulated against death after the awful years of her childhood and early youth, when half her race and the whole of the Austrian side of her family had perished in the holocaust. The postwar years had seemed to bring each week the details of the deaths of relatives who had disappeared years earlier into the concentration camps of the Third Reich.

Yet the sudden, violent death of the young vicar she had been so concerned to help seemed to bring the disturbing grief of those harrowing years vividly back to her when she thought she had exorcized it. Why had it happened? She asked herself the question anew. She wondered if evil that had no apparent motive was more disturbing to a Jewish woman than to others. Perhaps she should ring young Clare Barton; but she had no confidence yet that she could contain her own emotions, as she must when they met.

Hearing a movement in the house behind her, she was suddenly conscious of how little she wanted to be alone. She found her maid Mary, whom her husband called a 'general purpose domestic' and took her upstairs to begin stripping the beds the guests had occupied. The undemanding rhythms of the work, the folding of the linen and the re-making of the beds, helped to calm her physical restlessness. She asked Mary about her own Christmas in the village and found the girl anxious to talk. Her queries released a torrent of domestic trivia about the girl's family and their occupations, which ensured that her side of the conversation needed to be little more than a series of promptings.

It was not enough to still her spinning mind, and when Mary took the sheets off to the washing machine below, she wandered irresolutely from room to room, arriving eventually as she knew she must at the room in the north corner of the house which her husband had converted to a study.

She scarcely ever came here, not because of any prohibition from her husband—that might well have been counter-productive for one of her temperament—but because her upbringing had included the belief that men needed time and space for their own concerns. These might be trivial, occasionally even ludicrous or risible, but it was better for women not to interfere with them. Rachel would have hotly disputed the principle involved, yet she applied it without even assessing her actions.

Harry Davidson's study was indisputably a man's room. The desk was tidy enough: only two or three letters, held together with a bulldog clip and presumably awaiting replies, broke its smooth, leather-blocked surface. There were school photographs on the wall. The picture of Harry's passing-out group at Sandhurst looked scarcely more than another of these to the casual glance. There was a picture of a mess dinner night in 1981, when Harry was still a major, with the officers trying to look comfortable in their blues.

She looked at the pictures with affection, marvelling again at how Englishmen fulfilled the need to create clubs of some kind wherever they went. The Constable and Munnings prints seemed mere afterthoughts, gestures towards the convention of what a study should be. There was nothing from the last few years of Harry's service, when he had had his own command at last. And nothing at all from the Falklands. But she did not find that curious: her parents had been at pains to wipe all traces of that earlier and greater conflict from the great house in Switzerland. Harry spoke less of the battle in the South Atlantic nowadays, and she understood his need to be rid of it.

Her husband was still to some extent an exciting stranger to her. They had married late, when his military career was behind him. Unlike many women, she found tales of life in the regular Army fascinating, an insight into a strange male world which could never be hers, a contact with a warrior psyche which was as foreign to her as though it belonged to a different species. She was secretly disappointed that Harry spoke less and less of the dangers he had endured, even when they were alone. But she understood his need to make a new life here.

She was amused, and sometimes secretly a little dismayed, by the importance to him of his standing in the local community. Sometimes also—usually when she was depressed—she felt she still knew very little of the world of men. A split-cane fishing rod, mounted high on the wall above the photographs, was more a remembrance of things past than a modern implement: Harry's father had been a keen and skilful fly fisherman, but Harry had never really pursued the sport. Apart from the photographs, there were no obviously military memorabilia; the pair of antique pistols mounted on the wall over the fireplace scarcely qualified.

They were not the weapons that attracted Rachel's attention. She walked over beyond the desk and studied the two shotguns which stood in the corner of the room. She was a better shot than Harry; better even than Arthur Comstock, who had won Army competitions in his time. Nowadays she never fired at live things.

The beautifully polished butts of the weapons glowed like antique furniture from the darkness near the floor. They would not be loaded, of course, but she could not bring herself to touch them. She opened the top drawer of the narrow chest beside the shotgun, registering the half-full box of cartridges before she slid it shut. It meant nothing, she knew. Why then did she cudgel her brain energetically and unsuccessfully to remember the last time that Harry had taken the shotgun out with him?

She looked down over the leafless oaks and the stable block to the roof of the neat service cottage. Arthur Comstock was emptying his kitchen waste container carefully into the dustbin. He was in shirtsleeves, despite the cold. She saw the thinning of the hair about his pate which she had never noticed before; he was lean and upright still, though he must be almost as old as her husband. He stood and looked round for an instant, then glanced up at the sky, so suddenly that she shrank back hastily from the window, lest she might be detected and thought a spy.

She brushed her dark hair back from her face, angry with herself that she should behave so guiltily without reason. It was a moment which made her realize quite how much on edge she was. It also crystallized a resolution. She went to the mirror on the landing and combed her hair; she was surprised how white her face was, accentuating the prominent nose, so that it looked to her much too large. She was glad the mohair sweater came high up her slim neck, so that she could not examine it for wrinkles. Then she went down the wide staircase with its mahogany banister, moving briskly before her resolution could falter.

Arthur Comstock answered the door immediately; no part of the small cottage was very far from the front door. He was surprised to see her: Colonel Davidson came here quite often with the details of his requirements, but his wife, on the rare occasions when she needed his services, used the internal phone system.

'May I come in for a moment, please?' she said. She was surprised at the tautness of her voice. He noticed her accent, more pronounced than he had ever heard it before.

She followed him into the scrupulously tidy parlour; after the spaciousness of the Vicarage drawing-room, it seemed a tiny chamber. He did not know quite how to treat her. She had been invariably courteous and considerate towards him, but with an edge of reserve he had never attempted to challenge. It took him a moment too long to ask her to sit down.

She perched on the edge of an upright chair. With her bright black eyes and strong nose, he thought she looked in profile like a bird which might take off at any moment.

Then she told him what she had come to talk about and his face turned to stone.

CHAPTER 18

Lambert had never thought he would be sad to see his house emptied of infants. Now he was, and it was disturbing. His daughters had driven away with his grandchildren; the house was suddenly silent. And he felt old.

As usual, Christine divined his feelings without any word from him. For the second day in succession, he was presented with the bacon and egg breakfast he was nowadays not allowed. Then she stole softly away, lest he should see the smile she could not resist. She had always told him he would make a good grandfather, but it was nice to see it coming true.

A better grandfather than father, he reflected ruefully as he pretended to read the paper. On Christmas Day and Boxing Day, he had been able to come home from a murder investigation which was obstinately retaining its secrets and switch himself immediately into family life. He had joked with his daughters and played delightedly with their babies. A generation ago, he had never been able to switch off and play with the girls like that. He had missed most of their childhood, had almost lost the wife everyone now said was the perfect partner for him.

Today, he had even been prepared to delay his return to work until he had seen his daughters leave, on the grounds that he had been working on the case over Christmas. It was an indulgence he would once never have permitted to himself.

If he mused on these things as he ate his very late breakfast, he was as single-minded as he had ever been once he left the house. Motoring through the quiet lanes to pick up Bert Hook, he scarcely noticed even the beauty of the frost-edged trees. His brain had room for nothing but this disturbing case which so obstinately refused to give up its secrets.

Bert's house had not emptied. His two boisterous boys overflowed its small modern confines exuberantly, but they were indubitably still in residence. One of them was lovingly inspecting the tyres of a gleaming Christmas bicycle; his smaller brother fenced with plastic sword and shield against a myriad imaginary foes on the driveway between house and fence.

Bert's rubicund countenance appeared behind him at the kitchen door. 'The sword hasn't slept in that little blighter's hand since he unwrapped it!' he said as he eased his bulk into the old Vauxhall. 'Though I doubt very much whether he intends to build a new Jerusalem.' He took a last affectionate look at the children, who were more precious because they had come to him when he was approaching forty. Then he said, 'Sorry, I've been trying to catch up on my Blake assignment since early this morning.'

He was studying for an Open University degree, much to the secret delight of a superintendent who pretended to be threatened by the development. Lambert scratched up a Blake quotation to keep up his end:

> 'When the voices of children are heard on the green,
> And laughing is heard on the hill.'

He took a last look at the clamorous boys as they drove away, thinking of his own children and how they had disappeared into women, resolving to enjoy his toddler grandchildren as they moved through childhood.

'I thought we'd go and have another nose round Woodford,' he said. 'Visit that surly Tommy Farr and see if we can prize any more out of him. Allow you to have a go at young Charlie Webb. Probe Colonel and Mrs Davidson a little more. Even go over Arthur Comstock's story with him. And I want to see if the landlord of the Crown has noticed anything new over the last three days.'

It all sounded a little desperate, and both of them knew that it was. Sometimes the only option was to go over old ground again, while the team around them spread the net of suspicion further and further. Each of the pair was so preoccupied with his own thoughts that he was startled when the radio crackled and blared into raucous life.

Even through the distortion, they caught the excitement in Rushton's voice. 'Something's come up, sir. Are you coming in to the station?'

They were at a T-junction with the main road. Lambert flicked down his indicator and swung the car abruptly in the opposite direction from the one he had intended ten seconds previously. 'We are now, Chris. We'll be with you in five minutes.'

Rushton could not control his excitement when they arrived in the CID section. 'It looks as though you were right about chummy in the forest, sir! He was an ex-copper.' He might once have been resentful that Lambert and not he had thought of the possibility, but now his instinct to catch a villain rode fiercely over such unworthy considerations.

They went quickly through to the Murder Room and he passed over the teletext message. One Ian Sharpe had been discharged from the force in Leicester eight years previously, when holding the rank of sergeant. He had been guilty of brutal treatment of prisoners in custody and trying to extract confessions by unlawful means.

Lambert's face hardened as he read the phrases and translated the shorthand. A bully, or worse, who had brought his violence to work. The worst kind of bad apple in the force's barrel. The one in a hundred—Lambert still preferred the statistics of his youth—who brought contumely upon his colleagues and justified the hostility of the louts who obstructed their work at every turn. Lambert, although he had long trained himself in impassivity as part of his professional equipment, hated such men. He said in a level voice, 'What has he been doing since?'

Rushton picked up the scrap of paper with the notes he had made during a telephone conversation concluded only minutes earlier. 'The people in Leicester kept tabs as long as they were able to. As far as we can gather, he had a period as a mercenary soldier in Africa after he was kicked out of the police. No one seems to have heard of him in the last four years.'

The three of them were silent with conjecture for a moment. Hook said, reluctantly allowing the possibility, 'It might just be that he has genuinely taken to the road in the way he tried to sell to us.'

They considered the notion; none of them saw that hard, confident man as the dropout who made the typical modern vagrant, but they knew enough to be aware of the danger of generalizations. Rushton answered the key question before it was even voiced. 'We haven't found any connection with Peter Barton yet. Except that Barton seems to have worked in a hostel for derelicts in Leicester for a short period before he was actually ordained as an Anglican priest. Sharpe must have been in the police there at that time.'

Lambert said grimly, 'Let's go and get him.'

The forest seemed unnaturally quiet. There was not a breath of air, and the cold was clamped hard upon it. No bird sang, and those small mammals who were not in hibernation had more sense than to be active on days like this, when no food was available. And since the death of Peter Barton, most of the dog-walkers and horse-riders had chosen other places for their exercise.

The CID were not naïve. The law had forced them to release the man who called himself Robertson, but they had put a tail upon him when he left them without volunteering an address. They knew exactly where he had made camp in the woods, and Rushton had a note of it.

It did not take them long to reach the place. Lambert's quick march became almost a run in its last stages, so anxious was he to come to grips again with the man they now knew as Ian Sharpe. He was already planning the lines of the vigorous interrogation he intended. Rushton wondered if they should have come here armed; their quarry had a history of violence and he must surely realize now that the game was up.

They heard nothing and smelt nothing that prepared them for the scene they found. Sharpe had struck camp; his tent was tightly rolled and fastened to the framed rucksack containing his spare clothes and cooking tins. The man himself lay beyond the small paraphernalia of his mysterious life, with his arms and legs thrown wide and spattered with red.

His head was blown almost completely away.

CHAPTER 19

A serial killer was at work. The press, not the police, decided that.

From the point of view of the CID, this dead time of year between Christmas and New Year is the worst possible time for brutal murders to occur. International wranglings take their only break of the year at this season; Parliament is not in session; even the incessant din of political exchange is blessedly stilled.

So the tabloids fell upon the forest deaths like famished hounds upon a succulent quarry. They transformed kind Peter Barton into a modern Francis of Assisi, 'beloved by the birds and animals of the countryside he loved to walk'. The mysterious tramp who had been the second victim became 'Old Dougie', a harmless recluse, living at peace with the wild creatures of the forest, until his pastoral idyll was so brutally terminated by a twelve-bore cartridge.

The police, of course, were baffled, anxious, or looking desperately for any kind of lead, as tradition again demanded. As the inquiry's net spread wider and more and more men had leave cancelled to join the inquiry, the papers began to talk of police complacency in the face of the danger to innocent citizens.

The columns told of woods eerily deserted, of villages blanketed in fear, where every family locked its doors at dusk and the elderly were too fearful to venture forth at all. Pictures of parents collecting their children from Christmas parties were used as illustrations of the terror gripping the heart of every mother in the Forest of Fear.

Once the crime reporters had decided a maniac was in the woods, they had to give him a name. An animal was favourite, but most of the best ones—the panthers and the leopards—had already been used for previous psychopaths. There were badger setts in plenty around the places where the victims had fallen, but the badger has an appearance and a folk-tale history which is too unthreatening for the purpose. The beast of the woods became The Fox of the Forest: within three days of its first, tentative appearance, all the nationals had adopted the name.

It had not the fierce, flesh-tearing associations of more exotic foreign predators, but at least the ideas of random, wanton killing, of carnage spread ruthlessly merely for the pleasure it afforded the killer, could now be exploited.

And foxes, of course, were cunning; everyone knew that. As the days drifted by, the headlines became more scornful about PC Plod and the way The Fox was so much more subtle, ingenious and successful than those engaged in his pursuit. Soon, if he was not unmasked, the killer would acquire the charnel-house glamour of the mass murderer. And sick young men in different parts of the country would begin books of cuttings about his progress.

Lambert had been through it before. He was irritated, and sometimes more than that, but he had to pretend to the team he led that he was unruffled, that the kind of publicity their work was getting was no more than a routine accompaniment to murder. He spoke to journalists at a press conference on New Year's Eve—television had for the moment left the murders alone, except for a routine report and a few pictures of the area. Presumably camera crews like many others had used holiday allocations to bridge Christmas and New Year into a ten-day break.

He fed the reporters enough detail of the vigour with which the case was being investigated, of the murder of officers engaged and the number of people being questioned about their movements, to allay rumours of police complacency, but even as he spoke he could see that the hardened men in front of him were not interested in such detail. They had already published their routine pictures of men fanning out in a ground-search for evidence around the place where Robertson had fallen, and they were not here to act as public relations officers for the police.

Lambert said rather desperately that he was not yet convinced they were dealing with a maniac. It might be difficult to see reasons for the killing of the Reverend Peter Barton, but the CID thought the second killing was clearly motivated. But when he refused to be drawn on what the motive was, or to release any detail of the direction their inquiries were taking, he could feel the cynicism abroad in the room. He pointed out a little desperately that two killings scarcely constituted a series. Then he offered the thought that he had not yet ruled out the possibility of a woman as killer, either directly or as an agent.

But the gentlemen of the press—there were no ladies yet to leaven this male monopoly—refused to take the carrot. Sex was always an attractive angle, but the whiff of it which Lambert had offered them was too faint to divert them from the beast they had created. The Fox held sway still in their columns, moving quietly about the forest, patiently awaiting the chance to savage his next innocent victim in what they were now pleased to call the valley of fear.

When the pressmen had disappeared, Lambert journeyed thirty miles to a suburb of Bristol to interview Clare Barton's lover. He took DI Rushton with him; Bert Hook was on a four-day break in Cornwall between his Open University courses. Lambert, knowing the University year began in January and that Bert had not been away from home for two years, was reluctant to recall him. He was scarcely prepared to acknowledge to himself the memory of those years long ago when his own marriage had nearly foundered on the rocks of his commitment to his work before all else. Bert Hook was a different, in some ways a sounder, man. But there was no need to test how far his wife could take the strain.

Michael Crawley met them in his office at a deserted factory, at his own request. 'We've closed down until January 2nd,' he said. 'It's not worth running the machinery, you see, for what we could produce with a skeleton staff.' His nervousness, like that of many others before him, took refuge in irrelevant explanations, and for a moment or two they let it run its course without comment.

Crawley stood and looked down into the car park, with its sixty spaces marked off by stark white lines. Only his own Jaguar and Lambert's old Vauxhall were there today: the bleak expanses of tarmac made him feel very lonely. He said, 'I'm sure I could rustle up some coffee and biscuits, it you could give me a few minutes.' He looked uncertainly towards the deserted outer office; like many male executives, he was helpless in a working environment without his secretary.

'That won't be necessary,' said Lambert. His sternness made it sound as though Crawley had offered an improper suggestion. He looked round the office, and was pleased to find it so characterless: that suited his purpose. It had a swivel chair behind the broad teak-topped desk, two armchairs where the detectives now disposed themselves, an empty wastepaper basket, a small cupboard by the single window which probably contained drinks for those deemed to merit them. The only picture on the wall was a print of the ramshackle shed which had been the firm's original works.

This office was not so very different from the interview room where Rushton and he had spent many an hour of interrogation. It was bigger, admittedly, and sumptuously carpeted. And it had not the stark grey-green walls which induced useful feelings of claustrophobia, even panic, in those assisting police with their inquiries. But the room was almost as characterless as those small cubicles which were deliberately devised to be so.

They pulled the armchairs close to the desk, so that although Crawley in his swivel chair sat slightly above them, their faces were not far from his. From behind them, the wan sunlight of late December fell upon the anxious features of the man they had come here to question.

Crawley said, 'My wife thinks I've come in here today to attend to business matters. It won't be necessary for her to know anything about our meeting, will it?'

Rushton said, 'We can give you no guarantees, Mr Crawley.'

'But I understood—'

'Then you understood wrong. This is a murder inquiry.' His voice cut like a whip across Crawley's uncertainty. He had smelled fear on the man, and fear was weakness. And weakness was there to be exploited. Lambert, recognizing the situation, decided to give the younger man his head. Good CID men were always intelligent opportunists. He saw some of himself in Rushton now, even if he did not much like it.

Crawley opened his mouth, but found no more words. It was a weak mouth, curiously in contrast to the firm chin beneath it. He must have been about the same age as Rushton, but against the confident vigour of the Inspector, he suddenly seemed older. He was finding it difficult to keep still. He folded his arms but then immediately let them drop to his sides again. In another moment, the hands were kneading each other nervously below the cuffs of his cashmere sweater.

Rushton was in no hurry. He watched his man impassively, carefully concealing the contempt which was building within him. Eventually he said, 'You know why we're here?'

'I understood it was in connection with the death of poor Peter Barton. Though what I could tell you about that I can't—'

'I understand you are conducting an affair with the dead man's wife, Clare Barton.'

'Was, inspector, was.' Crawley tried to shrug the matter away, but his smile was that of a febrile child. 'I made it quite clear to Clare on the phone that our affair was over.' In the silence which followed this assertion, he ran his hand through his wavy hair, then pinched the greying strands beneath his right temple briefly between finger and thumb, in what was clearly a habitual, unconscious gesture.

Lambert said quietly, 'Mrs Barton also made it quite clear to me some days ago that it was her intention to end the affair.' He was anxious to prevent Rushton following false trails, but this came out as though he were trying to defend the woman he had interviewed on Christmas morning. He could see her now, her pretty, doll-like face smeared with her grief beneath her blonde hair, her resolution to end the infidelity which could no longer hurt her husband giving her a strange sort of dignity.

Rushton said, 'At any rate, you were lovers at the time of Barton's death. Indeed, it seems that Mrs Barton spent the night of her husband's death in bed with you. That she left you to go home on the day that his body was discovered.'

Crawley wished he had a glass of water. He gripped the edge of his desk hard as he said hoarsely, 'We didn't know that. If we'd known he was going to be killed, neither of us . . .' Words failed him and he lifted his palms hopelessly. He had hoped to find them men of the world, perhaps even prepared to enjoy a male snigger and a little envy of his bit on the side. But these men were not here to offer him help or understanding.

Rushton said, 'How long had Mrs Barton been your mistress?'

Crawley had scarcely thought of pretty, vulnerable Clare in so serious a context. He had spotted her as a blue-eyed blonde with that brittle gaiety which springs so often from an unhappy marriage. Her inexperience had been an invitation to a man like him; the excitement of the affair had come from the sexual education he had been able to initiate in her. He said, feeling as though the line was required of him in a bad play, 'I can't see how all this can be of any interest to—'

'I'll tell you how, if you wish, sir. Barton was a good man, according to people who knew him better than you. So good that we've found it difficult to find anyone to suggest a motive for blowing him apart. But you have one.' He had not bothered to keep the contempt out of his voice this time. Lambert realized for the first time that his deputy was probably an old-fashioned Puritan in sexual matters.

'You mean that I—that we . . .'

'I mean that sex is a factor in many violent killings. The commonest of all, along with money. So don't pretend to me that you've nothing to explain.'

'But you've said yourself that I was with Clare at the moment when Peter was murdered. Surely—'

'I haven't mentioned the time of Barton's death. It's interesting that you should be so certain of exactly when it happened.'

It was a cheap point, which a moment's thought would have answered. But it broke Crawley's frail resistance, because it convinced him of their hostility. He looked at the middle of his desk and said sullenly, 'I might be a bit of a womanizer, but I'm not a murderer.'

Rushton, dark eyes narrowed, studied the weakness of his man unashamedly for a moment before he said, 'Where were you between six and ten p.m. on December 22nd, Mr Crawley?'

Crawley did not even look up as he said quietly, 'I was here until about half past six. From seven onwards, I was in the Crossed Keys Hotel with Clare Barton.'

'Witnesses?'

He looked up, angry for a moment, with the desperation of the cornered animal. 'Clare herself. No one else. We were being discreet, you see.' His voice was bitter with the irony of it.

'Pity. Means that each of you only has the other to corroborate your story. So far.'

Michael Crawley said wearily, 'I suppose the hotel could confirm at least our arrival there. We put the "Do not disturb" sign on our door. I suppose you'll say we could have—'

'Could have, yes, sir. That's all. If you didn't leave the hotel, it will probably be fairly easy for us to establish that.'

'In that case—'

'There are of course other methods of killing an inconvenient husband than doing it yourself. Well-documented methods, often involving shootings.'

'You mean that we might have got someone else to—'

'I mean that contract killings are becoming much more common in Britain. Unfortunately for those of us who have to investigate them. Professional killers are more difficult to pin down, you see. But we get them, in the end. Usually by finding out the details of their hiring.'

'But you surely can't think—'

Crawley was looking for some kind of reassurance, however minor. He got none. The two tall men watched him impassively as he looked from face to face. He might have been a butterfly pinned upon a board.

It was Lambert who at length said to him, 'You may not yet be aware that a second body has been discovered in the forest, not far from where Peter Barton was killed. I'm now asking you formally, Mr Crawley, whether you were involved in the deaths of either of the men at Woodford, either directly or indirectly?'

'No. I swear I'd never have got involved with Clare if I'd thought for a moment that Peter—'

'And have you any idea who might have committed either of these murders?'

'No.'

They waited a moment to see if stress might induce any useful indiscretion. When none came, they rose unhurriedly at a nod from Lambert. Rushton said from the door, 'If you have any occasion to leave the area, Mr Crawley, please be good enough to let us know the details of your movements.' He managed to make even that sound like a threat, a final assurance that he neither believed nor trusted the man they were leaving alone in the deserted factory.

They drove a full mile before either man spoke. Then Rushton said, 'I wouldn't trust that bugger as far as I could throw him. On the make with women, deceiving his wife, prepared to drop Clare Barton like a hot potato as soon as the going gets tough.' He stared through the windscreen at the damp paving stones where mothers muffled against the cold pushed prams, aware that he was voicing his distaste rather than any constructive idea.

Lambert said mildly, 'An adulterer isn't necessarily a

murderer, Chris, thank God. Nor is a coward who drops a woman as soon as she becomes an embarrassment.'

'But he's the only one we've found so far with any convincing motive for getting rid of Barton.'

'Agreed. We'll need to check him out. But did he seem to you as though he felt strongly enough about Clare Barton to commit a crime of passion?'

Rushton sighed. 'No. He seemed like a crafty shit, who took what he could get and dropped it like a hot brick when it looked as though it might burn his fingers.'

'He might of course be a very good actor. But that would require Clare Barton to be one too. She was adamant she wasn't going to see Michael Crawley again, and she convinced me she meant what she said at that moment. Of course, if either one of them had arranged for Barton to be murdered, it would be policy to pretend the affair meant less to them than it did. And I agree it's the nearest thing we've got to a motive for killing Barton. That vicar's becoming more and more like a saint as we question everyone in the village. Irritating, for CID cynics like us.'

It was an olive branch: he had come dangerously close to accusing the younger man of a failure in objectivity, that ultimate sin in detectives. Both of them were too sensitive with each other, still. He would not even have had to think about these things with Bert Hook.

They were driving away from the city now, through the last of the suburbs. Lambert would normally have felt a sense of release as they moved back into the country he loved. For a little while, he did. But as they approached Woodford and the forest closed tightly around the roads, the shadow of brutal, motiveless murder fell back upon them.

At that moment, the teeming city they had left seemed a cheerful and innocent place, the silent village a centre of faceless evil.

CHAPTER 20

Tommy Farr was still one of the few villagers who ventured freely into the forest.

He went there indeed at four o'clock on New Year's Day, when the low sun had already dropped from sight and his fellow-villagers were shuttering their houses against the night and the north wind. And against The Fox: country-dwellers are as susceptible as their urban counterparts to the suggestions of the media.

Tommy swung briskly along the road, as though he had no thought of danger. He had two forms of insurance against any attack. Kelly bounded ahead of him, with head erect and energy rippling from every line of his carriage. The Doberman sniffed the bitter air as if it was the sweetest he had ever savoured: he had been waiting for this walk ever since the hour of his normal lunch-time exercise had come and gone without his master stirring towards the door. The dog bounded into the forest as into a Paradise regained, forcing his indulgent master almost into a run to keep pace with him.

The second form of protection which Farr took with him towards the scene of the late murders was more obvious, and perhaps more sinister. Slung almost negligently against his left shoulder was his shotgun. The dark polished metal of its twin barrels gleamed briefly in the diminishing light. There were cartridges today in both barrels of the twelve-bore. Tommy had seen to that before he left the privacy of the kitchen at the back of the village stores. He found the butt of the gun solid and reassuring now between his palm and fingers.

Two miles or so away, on the other side of the long tongue of forest that ran down to Woodford, a lane traced its erratic course towards Ashbridge. It was not even the main route between the two villages, though that was by no means a major thoroughfare. The road was metalled, but patches of grass poked their blades through the ridge at its centre. In the years between the two great wars which had taken men from this quiet region to a greater and more violent stage, the lane had linked small farms to each other, winding crazily along the boundaries. Now these small homesteads had long been deserted, their lands merged into larger holdings which still struggled to balance their books in the 'nineties.

At dusk on the first day of the new year, a car lurched cautiously along this quiet way, reluctant to put on even its sidelights as the gloom stretched inexorably across the valley behind it. It was not the most well-adapted car for such a place: a Land-Rover would have managed the route better than the long Rover saloon, with its soft springs and low ground clearance.

But the care and skill of the driver ensured that it reached the appointed place safely enough. Beneath a low-branching chestnut, it would have been easy to miss the narrow break in the straggling hedge which marked one of the less frequented ways into the woods. But this man was on the lookout for it. He did not park next to it, but ran the big car thirty yards further on, to where a patch of grass just off the road allowed him to leave it almost out of sight beneath an overarching conifer.

He shivered a little as he left the warmth of the car, then zipped his anorak tightly against the sudden cold. He hesitated a little before he moved beneath the winter canopy of twigs and branches, as though he was reluctant to shut out the sky and the remaining daylight.

But as he plunged a moment later down the path into the forest, it was behind him that he cast his eyes, down the lane on which he had arrived. He wanted to check for the last possible time that he had not been followed here. There was no sight of any following figure, no note of an engine engaged in pursuit of the Rover. It was as much comfort as he could offer himself in this lonely setting.

As he turned towards the area where two men had lately met such violent deaths, this man had not the safeguards which surly Tommy Farr had afforded himself. No large dog was at his side, and he carried no weapon. He dug his gloveless hands deep into the pockets of his anorak, and began to hurry towards his assignation. There was not much light left for him now.

CHAPTER 21

On January 2nd the world was back at work. Notes on Lambert's desk told him that Central Television and the BBC would both like to set up interviews. He pushed them resolutely to one side and brought Hook up to date with what had happened in his absence.

At 9.30 Dr Burgess, the pathologist, was ushered into his office, trailing policemen and policewomen behind him like a consultant upon his rounds. He had insisted upon bringing in his official post-mortem report on the second victim personally, though Lambert expected it would add little to the details he had already taken over the phone.

He had long since despaired of introducing reality into Burgess's lurid and literary impressions of modern CID practice. He humoured the silver-haired, patrician figure because in his autopsy work he was both efficient and alive to the urgency of police requirements. And because he liked the old boy, though he never admitted it. And perhaps just a little because it annoyed the ascetic Rushton to have a civilian present even on the periphery of police deliberations.

He had a good excuse for involving Burgess this morning. A scientist from the forensic laboratory would arrive at any moment to tell them what he could about the weapons and ammunition he and his colleagues had been examining in connection with the two killings in the forest. At least all the specialist scientific evidence could now be set alongside the meagre evidence the police had so far turned up.

'I come most carefully upon my hour, like the ghost of Hamlet's father,' said Burgess with a benign smile.

'Let's hope you are not the precursor of the kind of carnage introduced by that unfortunate presence,' said Lambert drily. 'Do find yourself somewhere to sit down.'

His office always seemed much smaller when Burgess came into it; the pathologist was scarcely six feet tall, four inches shorter than Lambert, but his urbane presence made the piles of documents and statements awaiting the Superintendent's attention seem more untidy than ever. The pathologist picked a shred of white thread from his immaculate navy suit, set three closely typed sheets on the edge of Lambert's desk, and said, 'So The Fox is still eluding his dedicated pursuers?' He settled himself in the room's single battered armchair with every appearance of satisfaction at the thought.

It was typical of him to seize upon the press's label for the killer, which Lambert had scrupulously avoided in his briefings to the team. The Superintendent said sourly, 'First animal I know that kills its prey with a shotgun.'

Burgess waved a hand airily. 'You mustn't expect too much from the gentlemen of the fourth estate, John. You should know by now that they never let facts get in the way of a good story. Still less a good metaphor. And at least The Fox has brought a little glamour into a life made dull by petty fraud and public house brawls.'

Lambert was fortunately prevented from any rejoinder by the arrival of the forensic scientist. He was a slight, intense man with a closely trimmed brown beard. His narrow features appeared sharper than ever because they were pinched with cold. Greatly to Burgess's delight, he introduced himself as Sam Johnson; Lambert winced mentally in anticipation.

'We shall be able to look to you to lighten the "inspissated gloom" with which this case seems to be beset!' said Burgess affably. The bewildered Johnson had obviously not investigated his illustrious namesake's wordier pronouncements. The scientist opened his briefcase and took refuge in a sheaf of notes.

Burgess watched the move with interest. After a few seconds, he offered innocently, 'Your celebrated namesake thought that "Notes are often necessary, but they necessary evils". I think I'm inclined to agree with him, aren't you, Mr Johnson?'

'I find it difficult to operate without notes,' said Johnson acerbically. He found the pages he was looking for and smoothed them upon his knees, setting the briefcase down beside his upright chair.

Lambert was relieved when the return of Hook with Rushton diverted Burgess and allowed the informal meeting to begin. He said briskly, 'Perhaps I could ask Dr Burgess to begin with a summary of his findings about the death of the man we now know to be Ian Sharpe.'

Burgess raised his elegant eyebrows a fraction. He had not heard the new name before; the corpse had come into his laboratory as the remains of Douglas Robertson. But he was aware that he was here on sufferance, so he was careful not to ruffle Lambert by asking for detail. 'I would guess your man died between ten and eleven on the morning of 27th December. I couldn't be definite about it under oath —you'll see that I've put between nine and twelve in my report.' He nodded towards the pages on Lambert's desk. 'But both body temperature and stomach contents indicate that he had not been dead very long when you found the body.

'I'm assuming he last ate at about eight a.m. It's hardly likely that he'd be eating before daylight, living as he was. He'd been eating rabbit, incidentally. Easy enough for him to trap, I should think, now that so many rabbits live above ground all winter.'

Rushton said, 'He'd been living as a tramp. Do you think he was one, Dr Burgess?'

The elegant shoulders shrugged beneath the dark worsted. 'Who knows what a tramp is nowadays, Inspector? If he was a dropout, though, he was a remarkably fit one. Not much fat on him, despite his powerful, stocky build, and his muscle tissue was in excellent condition. Well above average for a man of his age. What was he? Late thirties?'

Lambert said, 'About that, yes,' and all of them thought wryly of the press's picture of harmless 'Old Dougie' and the white-haired, helpless pensioner they had created as the second victim of The Fox. 'He was a steelworker, a long time ago. Then a copper, for a while. After that, we're not quite sure what. Probably a mercenary soldier, for a little while at least.'

'A bent copper?' Burgess was delighted to air his knowledge of the vernacular.

Lambert gave him a grim little smile. 'Not in the manner you probably mean, Cyril. He seems to have been prepared to take short cuts to get convictions. To have been too fond of violence for his own or other people's good. Contrary to popular opinion, that isn't something we encourage. There wasn't any evidence of his accepting bribes or other inducements. He was found unsuitable for further service as a police officer, but there was no prosecution.'

He realized with a spurt of irritation that he was speaking not for Burgess or the meeting at large but for Rushton, proving to his deputy his credentials as a defender of the force. Had the two of them been alone, he would not have felt the need to say these things to Burgess. A little too hurriedly, he said, 'Could you tell us about the forensic findings, Mr Johnson?'

When invited to speak from his own area of expertise, Johnson was suddenly confident. 'Shotguns,' he said with distaste, as though he were pronouncing a mild obscenity. 'They're the bane of our lives. Far too anonymous for anyone's good. Both your men were killed with twelve-bore cartridges, probably fired from about four yards in each instance.' He looked interrogatively at Burgess, who nodded confirmation from his PM findings. 'Unfortunately, as you probably know, we cannot pin down a particular weapon from the ammunition used when it's a shotgun. It's quite possible we've handled your murder weapon in the last day or two, but there's no way in which we could be sure which gun it was.'

Hook said, 'Is there any chance that you could be certain that it was the same weapon that was used in each case?'

Johnson shook his head mournfully. 'The most we could say is that our findings indicate it would be probable. And you know that "probable" is totally useless in court. The same sort of cartridge was used in both killings. But it's the commonest type of ammunition, so it doesn't mean a lot.'

Rushton said, 'Did your examination of the twelve-bores we brought in from the surrounding villages throw up anything that might be useful?' He turned to Burgess to explain, 'We collected all the known twelve-bores from the district to see if they would reveal anything, because the murder weapon was not found anywhere during an extensive search of the forest.' Lambert thought with amusement that it sounded like an official press release, but Burgess was delighted as always to be involved in the machinery of an investigation. He retained a schoolboy's enthusiasm for the processes of detection, despite all his contacts with corpses.

Johnson said, 'We haven't come up with anything that seems particularly significant. Except . . .' He searched feverishly through the notes he had said were vital to his operations. 'You gave us particulars of the owner's statements about when the shotguns had last been fired. There was one of your villagers whose account did not seem to tally with what we found when we looked at his twelve-bore in the lab.'

Lambert said carefully, 'Which village?' trying to eliminate optimism and excitement from his voice. This business had been so obstinately retentive of its secrets that he distrusted hope.

'Woodford.'

'And which shotgun?'

Johnson ran his index finger feverishly down the page until he located the name. 'The gun from number four, Gladstone Terrace. Owned by a Mr Charles Webb.'

'Charlie Webb,' breathed Hook softly. He was thinking not of that strange young man, but of his old grandmother, cheerfully mischievous and so obviously fond of her grandson, even as her mind wandered into decline.

Sam Johnson looked up a little petulantly, as if he did not like being interrupted when he had finally found his place. 'According to the statement you collected from Mr Webb, he had not used the shotgun since December 18th. That is several days before the first of the shootings in the forest, that of the Reverend Barton. But our examination indicated that it had been fired within the last day or two before we saw it. It had not been cleaned, you see, so we could test the powder traces. They were quite fresh. Is Webb the sort of chap who would normally be careless about cleaning his shotgun?'

Hook said quietly, 'I wouldn't know about that. He's scarcely more than a boy.'

Rushton said acidly, 'That scarcely indicates whether or not he would be careless about cleaning a murder weapon.' He too was searching through his sheets of notes now. He had a much thicker sheaf of them than Johnson, for he had the task of co-ordinating the written reports of the sixty officers now engaged upon the inquiry as they arrived in the murder room. He tried not to reveal his excitement: that would not suit the image of himself he was anxious to create.

Lambert said with a hint of irritation as he watched this search, 'Do you have something to add to what Mr Johnson has said about the gun, Chris?'

Rushton pulled out the relevant sheet with the relief of a conjuror who has not been quite precise enough with a trick. 'It's a report from the house-to-house team, sir. You remember that we were trying to get the names of anyone who was in the forest on the morning of the murder of Ian Sharpe. This came in last night: a Mrs Baker was in her garden on the edge of the village when she saw Charlie Webb going into the woods. Incidentally, he hadn't told us that himself, when we questioned him about his movements.'

'What time was he seen?' Lambert's voice sounded perfectly calm: he had practised these things for much longer than Rushton.

'About ten o'clock, the lady says.'

Lambert looked at Burgess. But now that it had come to it, the pathologist did not care to pin down a suspect with his findings. It was left to the Superintendent to say, 'So he was at or near the scene of the murder at exactly the time when you think Ian Sharpe was killed.'

CHAPTER 22

The council house blue paint on the door within the small porch was in much better condition than the paintwork on the windows. It had been washed down quite recently. That was a surprising thing for a boy of Charlie Webb's age to think of doing. They remembered the almost obsessive tidiness of his bedroom.

They had ample time to study the door, for they knocked upon it three times before there was any sound from within the house. Then Granny Webb's voice called with surprising strength to ask who it was who hammered so vigorously. Most of her visitors, aware of her immobility, were accustomed to walk straight in after knocking.

Now Hook tried the door, found it unlocked, and opened it a cautious two inches. He called through the gap, 'Please don't be alarmed, Mrs Webb. We're the police. It's Superintendent Lambert and Sergeant Hook, come back to see you again!'

There was an immediate delighted cackle. 'It's the fuzz, Samuel. Whatyer been up to out there? Under age kittens, wos it?' Peals of broken laughter at the excellence of her wit rang round the room as they entered. The black and white cat sitting on her lap conducted an unhurried appraisal of the newcomers. Apparently it was not impressed; it jumped softly down, stretched in elastic slow motion, and stalked with dignity towards the kitchen and away from their view.

'Charlie not about?' said Hook unnecessarily.

'Be 'ere any minute, if you want 'im. Just gone round to Tommy Farr's to get our shopping. Sit yourselves down, you're hurting my neck up there.'

They did so. There was a stale odour about the room, more that of old age than old cat. Lambert said, 'We knew Charlie wasn't at work. We rang there, you see, before we came round here.'

''ere, what you want 'im for? 'e ain't done nothing. 'e's a good boy, is Charlie. Good to 'is old Gran, too.'

'I'm sure he is, Mrs Webb. We just need to ask him a few questions, that's all.' Lambert wondered a little desperately how long it would be before the boy returned.

It was Hook who saw his absence as an opportunity. 'He has a shotgun, hasn't he, Mrs Webb? Does he use it much?'

She gave the question serious consideration. She liked being called Mrs Webb by these careful, polite strangers. Everyone around the village called her Gran, as though for them she only existed in Charlie's shadow. 'Mrs Webb' took her back to the days when she had got around more, when she had sometimes gone into the clothes shops in Gloucester just to hear the assistants call her 'Madam'.

She said, ''Orrible dangerous, smelly thing. I don't let him keep it in the house. He bangs away with it sometimes. Brings home the odd rabbit. Never a pheasant.' She leaned towards them confidentially. 'My uncle used to breed pheasants, you know, in the old days. For the shooting, up behind the hall. All gone now. Never the same, after the war.' Her voice was a dirge for her lost youth and innocence.

Hook drew her gently back. 'Fond of his gun, is he, Charlie?'

She was suddenly suspicious. 'What you want to know about that for? Took his gun away, the fuzz did. Got it back though!' She chortled again, then nudged a non-existent companion in celebration of her cleverness, as though her cunning had outwitted the entire police force to secure the return of the weapon. Then, with another of her bewilderingly swift changes of mood, she glared at them and said aggressively, 'What you picking on Charlie for? He's a good boy, I told you.'

Hook grinned back at her, not at all abashed. 'You told us when we saw you before that he enjoyed cleaning his shotgun.'

'Always at it, he is. Takes it to pieces on the kitchen table. Oils it and polishes it. I can't be doing with it.' She was grumbling now, slipping as he had hoped she might into a familiar routine.

'These youngsters just don't think about the mess. I expect he's the same with his motorbike.

'Damned Japanese rubbish!' She produced the phrase triumphantly, as though it were the winning conclusion to a word game. 'Norton's the best. Always was. Or Triumph: 'is Dad always 'ad Triumph.' She rocked backwards and forwards on her chair with folded arms and considerable content.

'But he needs his bike to get to work, doesn't he?'

'Not been speeding, 'as 'e? I told 'im the fuzz would get 'im if— '

'Oh' nothing like that. He's a good boy that way, as you say. All taxed and insured properly, not like some youngsters I could tell you about, Mrs Webb. We'd just like to know a bit more about the way he uses the bike, that's all.'

She said he went to work on it every day, used it indeed when he went anywhere outside the village, as might be expected. Hook teased so much out of her with a little more prompting. But they wanted to know whether he had gone out on the bike on the morning of Sharpe's death, and that was hopeless. Granny Webb had no idea of whether things had happened yesterday or a month ago; pinning her to what had happened on the morning of 27th December at ten o'clock or thereabouts was quite impossible.

When confusion was at its height in the warm, airless

room, Charlie returned. Lambert had left the Vauxhall in the car park at the Crown, so that he did not know as he came up to the gate that there were visitors in the house. But he heard the noise of voices as he came up the path, and hurried protectively into the house as he caught the old lady's agitation.

He stopped dead in the doorway of the living-room when he saw who the visitors were. He was certainly disconcerted, but it was too dark where he stood for them to see whether he was frightened.

Lambert said, 'We wanted to talk to you, Charlie, about a couple of things.' He felt guilty in his relief to be speaking to someone who was of sound and consistent mind. 'First, your shotgun. You told the officer who asked you about it that you hadn't used it since two days before the Reverend Barton was killed. Would you like to reconsider that information?'

Webb's gaze flicked from one to the other, then round to the steadily nodding head of his grandmother, as if he might find somewhere among them a clue as to how he should answer. Seeing none, he said, 'No. What I said when they took my shotgun away was correct. Why should it be important to you, anyway?'

Hook said quietly, 'Because we now know for certain that that gun has been fired more recently than that. Fired, you see, at about the time when a second man was killed in the forest.'

Webb gulped and snatched at the back of a chair, pulling it out so that he could sit down on it and face them. He was certainly pale now; he looked as if he might have fainted if he had not found himself a seat. His white, scared face was totally unlined, so that he looked for the moment much younger than his years. Like a frightened child, Lambert thought. The first murderer he had ever arrested had looked like that, nearly thirty years ago, standing in a wet city street with a pistol still in his hand and looking down aghast at the policeman he had killed.

Webb's voice cracked a little, then recovered, as he said, 'I can't explain that. I haven't fired the gun.'

They waited to see if he would volunteer any suggestion as to how this might have happened. Even the excuses chosen by men driven into a corner could be significant. On this occasion, Webb offered them nothing.

Hook waited for a nod from his chief before he said, 'Where were you on the morning of the 27th of December, Charlie?'

Webb looked at them as if they were closing upon him a trap which he had not seen or understood. His right hand shot suddenly upwards and across his spiky hair, as if it had a will of its own. He looked down upon it when it came to rest again across the top of his other hand in his lap, studying the long fingers and bitten nails for a moment as if this was someone else's hand. Then he said, 'I was on holiday. Not at work, I mean.'

'Yes. Where did you go, that morning?'

'I went for a walk.'

It was like prising information out of a guilty child, but Hook was patient. His tone of voice remained the same throughout the exchange. 'What time was this, Charlie?'

'I—I'm not sure, exactly. About ten, I think. I remember I was at a bit of a loose end.'

'And where did you go on your walk?'

The room seemed stifling now. A coal on the heaped fire tumbled softly and sent a little cloud of white ash into the throat of the chimney. Granny Webb gave it a wide, almost toothless smile; not one of the other three in the room was certain whether she was listening to them or was in some quite different world of her own.

Charlie Webb's long neck, poking from his polo-necked sweater towards the spots beneath his chin, made him seem vulnerable, even fragile, as if he might disintegrate with harsh treatment. It seemed a long time before he said, 'I went into the forest.'

Hook's voice held no note of triumph in the admission he had secured. He said, almost wearily, 'But you told the constable who saw you about it that you had been nowhere near the woods on that day.'

'Yes. I was scared. I knew the man in the woods had been killed. It was all round the village.'

Something in the phrasing interested Hook. Webb had stared dully at the carpet through most of his questions; he waited until the youth looked into his face at last. Then he said, 'Did you know there was a man there, Charlie? Before he was killed, I mean.'

'Yes. I saw him that very morning.' Webb looked as though confession had relieved his tension. His face was despairing, but relaxed.

'What time was this, Charlie?' Hook might have been a doctor, treating an accident victim whilst he was still in shock.

'About ten o'clock, I suppose. Perhaps a bit later.'

If Webb was telling the truth, the murderer must have been very close behind him. If he was not, he was putting himself in the dock. Hook kept the excitement scrupulously from his voice as he said, 'Did you speak to him, Charlie?'

Webb said, 'No. He didn't think I'd seen him, see. He came out behind me for a moment on the track, then went back to his camp. He didn't make much noise, but I knew he was there. I'd smelt his fire, see, although he'd put it out by then.' There was a little flash of pride in his country boy's skills, the first he had shown since he came into the room.

Lambert, knowing Hook had come to the end, said in a different, harsher voice, 'You went into the forest with your shotgun that morning, didn't you, Charlie? And you didn't just see the man, but shot him. We know he died at around the time you were there.'

'I didn't! I was there, just as I've told you. I lied before because I was scared, but I've told you the truth now.' Webb did not shout, as from experience they would have expected him to. His voice rose, but he retained control over it, as he had had difficulty in doing at the beginning of their interrogation.

As they went through the tiny porch, Granny Webb flung after them, 'Come again soon. Always glad to see the fuzz.' Lambert wondered if a mind wandering like hers was capable of irony. Perhaps it was a genuine invitation; she had so few visitors now to bring breaths of excitement into the confusion of her old age.

Hook was silent in the car, even after they had driven out of the village. He did not want the lad to be guilty, though the policeman in him longed for the quickest possible arrest. Webb was too like the youth he had once been, when he scrambled towards manhood in the years after he had left the home. Lambert knew his man well enough now to divine most of this. He glanced sideways at his sergeant's troubled profile and smiled.

Then he said gnomically, 'The crucial question about Webb is the one Sam Johnson from forensic asked.'

CHAPTER 23

The tabloids moved into a new year with their Parliamentary comedians still in recess. So they homed in on Woodford.

Margaret Parkin, who had helped out behind the bar of the Crown on New Year's Eve, became 'attractive fun-loving barmaid Meg Parkin'. For a small consideration, she informed a reporter that: 'Every woman in the village is frightened to open her door. We go in terror of The Fox. Our fear grows every day as we wait for him to strike again. The police may be trying their best, but they can't protect us: we've already seen that, haven't we?'

These observations from the voluble Ms Parkin were received in the area with a mixture of derision and outrage. In the Crown and the Women's Institute, those twin centres of village enlightenment, she was rumoured to have been in more beds than ground elder. Perhaps the deaths in the forest had indeed cut down her nocturnal activities. But even the most charitable were driven to compute that she must now be at least sixty-two.

The photographers had to go to the primary school in Ashbridge on the day when the schools re-opened, because Woodfood's tiny village school had been closed for twenty years. They got their pictures of anxious mothers meeting their children and hurrying them home, conveniently ignoring the fact that the Woodford children now without exception travelled on the school bus.

When invention flagged, there was always the ritual pillorying of the baffled police. THE FOX IS FOOLING WITH PC PLOD! the tabloids decided, while even the serious papers ran articles on previous serial killers and the omissions of the authorities. The press now got hold of the news that the second victim had been held by police for thirty-six hours, then released to be gunned down in the forest. HOW WRONG CAN YOU GET? roared the next day's headlines.

Lambert was glad that his Chief Constable was enjoying a well-earned rest on a Caribbean cruise.

On a bitter grey January afternoon, almost everyone in the village attended the funeral of Peter Barton.

Behind the coffin, three people wept steadily, losing not a shred of dignity as they did so. Barton's parents had come down from Newcastle to a country world which they did not understand. They felt the warmth of the sympathy around them, but on this bitter day no heat would have been enough to burn away their outrage at the senseless obliteration of the boy who had promised to achieve so much.

In front of them and immediately behind the coffin as it made its short, slow journey down the aisle of the packed church, Clare Barton walked as though in a trance. The crowded pews of the little church brought home what she had always known but not cared to acknowledge, the hold that Peter had taken upon the affections of his flock in four short years. Four years, she thought, when he had worked unremittingly, with only the most sporadic and ineffective support from the wife who should have been at his side.

The bishop spoke over the coffin of the man who had been such a thorn in his side. And because that is the way of these things, he spoke movingly and well. Whatever the frustrations of the Anglican Church in the final quarter of the century, it had offered him thirty years of practice in the art of oratory. He had honed his skills, until he was effective now in almost any situation. He said generous things about the young man's ministry. And, to be fair to the bishop, he meant them, even if they came a little too late. He was not insensitive to tragedy, and he felt it here, suffusing the very air of this village church above the multitude of bowed and weeping heads.

A television camera crew waited outside the church, but its operations were carefully, almost apologetically, low-key. Some of the mourners did not even know the cameramen were there until they saw the brief sequence of the coffin and the grieving widow and parents on the regional evening news bulletins.

Although there was only the lightest of breezes in the churchyard, it blew from the icy north-east. This congregation had supported Peter Barton only sporadically in his efforts during life. Yet only the most elderly and infirm among them failed to move to his graveside for the final rites of his death. Ashes returned to ashes, dust to dust, in the bishop's high, clear tones. The coffin was lowered into the grave from the frozen fingers of the bearers, and the crowd broke up into small groups for the final, conventional regrets. There were no floral tributes: such monies had gone, as Peter would have wished, to famine relief. In half an hour, a rectangular mound of yellow earth would be all there was left to see of a man who had worked so hard for the people who mourned him.

Lambert and Hook watched things from the edge of the crowd. They were more interested to see who was absent than to count those in attendance: the theory that the murderer likes to see his victim finally interred has long been dismissed by the CID as a romantic fiction. Charlie Webb was there, despite his grandmother's robust dismissal of all things religious. Arthur Comstock, ramrod straight and looking even taller as a result, stood quietly at the back of the church, looking over the heads of everyone to the austerely decorated stone altar, speaking to no one during the ceremony in the churchyard.

Tommy Farr was not present, though there could have been little custom in his village shop. More surprisingly, Harry Davidson, JP, that pillar of the local community, was neither in the church nor at the graveside. His wife, handsome and upright in the black which suited her, had an empty seat left beside her which made his absence conspicuous, for the villagers had obviously expected that he would have come. Rachel went over and said a few words to Clare Barton as they moved away from the grave, taking the small hand for a moment between both of hers.

Clare's face was very white, throwing the intense blue of her tear-washed eyes into vivid relief. A little of her golden hair had pushed itself obstinately out from beneath the tight black veil; she brushed it away from her small, perfect nose with her free hand. Rachel Davidson was a generation older than Clare, but an infinity of experience seemed in this moment to stretch between them. With her strong nose, her dark eyes and tightly bound black hair, Rachel stood erect and proudly Jewish in an ancient English churchyard. And she seemed to carry with her some of the suffering of her race, as though she were here to set this domestic English tragedy within the context of the millions in this century of savagery who had perished as Peter had, violently and without cause.

As the crowds drifted away from the church, Lambert said, 'Let's go to see Tommy Farr.'

They walked swiftly towards the village store; vigorous movement was a relief after the enforced stillness of the graveyard in temperatures below freezing.

Hook, whose only contact with the case during his four

days in Cornwall had been the newspapers, said suddenly, 'Do you believe in The Fox?'

Lambert did not bite his head off, as he had half-expected. After a few seconds, he said, 'No. If there were another killing of the same kind, I might be forced to. I'm almost afraid to voice that thought, in case it ushers in more blood. Not a proper quality in a detective, superstition.'

Hook said, 'What I can't find is any connection between the two murders. Both of them in their different ways seem quite senseless.'

'Hence the press's creation of The Fox,' said Lambert. 'Motiveless killings are always the work of a maniac. What our journalistic friends don't wish to realize is that very few murders are motiveless, but occasionally the motives are not immediately obvious.' He was rehearsing the things he would like to say to the press, which he would probably never see translated into print. Perhaps there was something after all to be said for those television news conferences which made him so uneasy: at least you couldn't be misquoted when you delivered your own answers to the camera.

Hook said, 'Very few of the men we've regarded as close to the killings have wives.'

'Sexual frustration turning a man into a maniac? You're beginning to think in tabloid terms, Bert, and I'm not sure I like it. In any case, someone as unbalanced as that kills women, not men, in my experience.'

'Unless, of course, the unbalanced psyche is that of a woman—she might kill men.' Bert Hook produced the idea triumphantly. Was it not Lambert who had told the press that he hadn't ruled out the idea of a woman killer?

'I'm going to put in an official complaint to that Open University, if it encourages detective-sergeants towards lateral thinking. I'm not sure that official police policy allows sergeants to think at all. All right, let's have your thoughts about our deprived men.'

'Well, there's Tommy Farr to start with. His wife left him years ago. Arthur Comstock's wife apparently left him earlier still—long before he came out of the Army. Both of them are divorced now. Charlie Webb has no wife yet. Even Ian Sharpe didn't have a woman in tow, as far as we've been able to tell.'

'And Peter Barton's wife was perhaps on the way to leaving him. Well, Holmes, what do you deduce from all this celibacy, enforced or otherwise?'

Hook was ready for the question. 'Nothing, really. I was just throwing up the idea. In case a superintendent could make more of it than a sergeant!' Bert stared straight ahead with the slightest of smiles. It was the smile he had once allowed himself on the area's village greens when he clean bowled a public schoolboy.

Lambert grinned. Rushton would neither have understood nor approved this exchange. Well, he might be tomorrow's man, but he could wait a while yet. 'Our only husband and wife who have endured are Colonel and Mrs Harry Davidson.'

'Not exactly endured. They only married five years ago, when Davidson was finished with the Army.'

'True enough. But they appear to be pillars of the local community.' Both of them were silent for a moment then, thinking of the Rachel Davidson they had just seen, that cosmic tragic profile as she consoled the vulnerable, venal Clare Barton. Because they were detectives, the impressive cameo suggested to them among other things that Mrs Davidson was a woman with the nerve and intelligence for this sort of murder, if she thought it justified.

'Why wasn't Colonel Davidson at the funeral?' said Hook.

'I've no idea. I'm surprised he wasn't there, though. In his role as leader of the local community and Chairman of the Parish Council, it was almost obligatory. Particularly as I rather think he enjoys that role. No doubt there was some good reason. We might ask him what it was, later. Tactfully, of course.'

They were at the door of the village stores now. Lambert

paused only momentarily before they went in. 'Let's give Farr a hard time first, though.'

The man didn't look as though he would be easily intimidated. He lounged behind the old-fashioned counter inside his shop with his bottom supported by a high stool. Perhaps it was his broken nose that twisted his small smile of welcome into something nearer to a sneer, but Hook did not think so. Farr said, 'Found your Fox yet then, PC Plodders?'

Lambert looked him coolly up and down with a mirthless smile. 'Do *you* think our man is a maniac, Mr Farr?'

'Asking Tommy Farr for his opinion now, is it? God, you must be as baffled as they all say you are!' His voice was deep, even musical, taking the edge off the insult he intended, suggesting the male voice choir in which he had long ago held his corner against the Welsh tenors.

'You didn't answer me, though, did you, Tommy?'

Farr glared at them aggressively for a moment, as though they had accused him of something. 'I don't have to, do I? But no, I don't think you've got a maniac to catch, if you really want to know.'

'I don't suppose you'd be so eager to go into the forest if you did, would you, Tommy?' said Hook.

Farr whirled to confront him. He had been concentrating his contempt upon Lambert, not expecting any rejoinders from the stolid presence which had been examining the bank of cereals away to his right. For a moment, his features were twisted with the suspicion and hostility he did not trouble to conceal. Bert thought his pugilistic nickname was appropriate, even if it was obvious: Farr would not have been the man to take on in a pub brawl.

The shopkeeper forced himself to relax: they could see the physical processes of it. 'Keep your spies out, do you, Lambert? Bloody police state we're living in now.' It was delivered sullenly, without passion, being no more than a ritual hostile response.

'A double murder inquiry is in progress, Tommy. You must expect us to keep our eye on Woodford, and other villages in the area as well.' Hook was probing for a significant reaction, but he did not get one.

'Fat lot of good it's done you, so far.' Farr gave his sneer free rein, but his words sounded a rather hollow note of defiance. He was wary of committing himself to more, wondering furiously how much they knew of his comings and goings. It was hardly news that he went daily into the woods still with Kelly: he would have expected so much to be observed by the more nosy among his customers, as well as by any more official presence. But did they know of his meetings in the wood?

Lambert was smiling at him, baiting him a little even as on the face of it Farr was taunting him. He let the silence stretch now, surveying the broad wooden counter, the old-fashioned cash register, the neatly priced packets of flour and dried fruits. 'It's your duty to help us, not obstruct us, you know, Mr Farr,' he said without rancour. 'You go just as freely into the woods as you did before these things happened. Some people would think that in itself suspicious. After two brutal murders, you seem to have no fear that you might become a third victim of The Fox, you see.'

He had taken the name Farr had used in his opening jibe and thrown it back at the man. Tommy felt himself on the defensive; he was not quite sure how it had happened. He said, 'I'm not going to let any bloody Fox spoil my way of life, see? And anyway, I have Kelly with me when I go in there.'

'Proof against shotgun blasts, is he, Tommy? Remarkable dog, that.' Hook had moved round towards where the door led through to the storeroom behind the shop. There was a low whine from the Doberman in the kitchen as he creaked a board; perhaps the dog had caught his master's use of the name.

Farr said now, 'Kelly would go for anyone who attacked me.' But he knew he had not answered Hook's point.

'And you take a shotgun with you, as an additional precaution, on occasions,' said Lambert quietly. 'One of our problems, of course, is that we haven't been able to pin down the shotgun used in these killings. Yet.'

'You took mine in and examined it. Eliminated it,' said Farr roughly.

'Not eliminated, Tommy. We can't do that with shotguns.' Lambert was wondering just how much Farr did know about shotguns and their forensic implications. 'We haven't found a murder weapon for either of these killings. Probably it's still in this area.'

It sounded like a threat, and at least it succeeded in making Farr cooperative. He sounded almost conciliatory as he said in a low voice, 'I saw Charlie Webb going into the forest.'

'When was this?'

'On the morning of the second killing, whenever that was.'

Hook said, '27th December. We knew about Webb, Tommy. We also knew that you had probably seen him. It's taken you until now to tell us. Not helpful, that.'

Farr was silent, staring sullenly at the counter in front of him. A hundred yards away down the lane, a car pipped its horn. The village was coming to life again after the funeral. Soon there would be other people in the shop. Lambert said quietly, 'And was young Webb carrying his shotgun at the time?'

Farr looked up at them then, searching each face in turn in an attempt to follow their thinking. They were professionally inscrutable. He said hesitantly, 'I—I don't think so. He was well past the shop when I saw him; perhaps a hundred yards away. I didn't see that he had his shotgun with him. But it didn't seem important at the time, see. I suppose he might have been concealing it. Or it might have been already in the woods.'

It was their turn to watch closely, trying to divine whether this man suddenly so anxious to be helpful was speaking the truth, whether his hesitancy about Webb was assumed, whether his new attitude had anything of his own guilt in it.

Lambert said suddenly, 'Do you know why Colonel Davidson was not at the funeral?'

He was rewarded with a tiny start of surprise from his man. Whether this was because of the question or because of his sudden switch away from Charlie Webb it was impossible to say. Farr said, with an attempt to recapture his early surliness, 'No. Why should I? He doesn't tell the likes of me about his plans, you know.'

Lambert studied him coolly for a moment. Then, without taking his eyes off him, he said, 'I think we'd better go to see Colonel Davidson right away, Sergeant Hook.'

There was a flash of something in Tommy Farr's eyes in the instant before he cast them down. Lambert could not for the life of him be sure whether it was alarm or elation.

CHAPTER 24

There was not much of the short day's light left by the time Lambert turned the big Vauxhall between the high wrought-iron gates of the Old Vicarage and drove carefully up the gravelled drive. The lights were on in the high Victorian conservatory, lighting the old glass more brilliantly than ever in its heyday. Inside it, they could see Colonel Harry Davidson, watching the approaching car.

Mary showed them straight into the conservatory to see him when she answered the door. Normally she would have asked visitors to wait until she consulted her employer, but she had had no formal instructions in these matters, and in her book the police overrode these social conventions. But if she hoped for a little vicarious excitement from the visit of detectives, she was to be disappointed.

Davidson looked a little put out when they were ushered in, though he must have known they had seen him through the slight distortions of the old glass. He said stiffly to the maid, 'You can go home now, Mary, before the dark. We won't need you again today.' The girl thanked him and withdrew. There was nothing Victorian about the relationship of master and servant; far from bobbing her acceptance, she thanked him almost as though they were equals. Yet Davidson did not seem quite at ease with her. Lambert fancied he had been used in the Army to giving orders only to men. Perhaps it was Mrs Davidson who normally gave Mary her instructions; that would account both for the girl's lack of servility and Davidson's awkwardness with her.

Harry Davidson turned to them after the door had closed behind the maid. 'What can I do for you, Superintendent?' he said. The genial squirearchal pose which had become habitual to him was no more than skin deep; the caution about his eyes belied the smile he carried beneath them.

'You can answer a few questions for us if you will, that's all,' said Lambert. He looked round the conservatory, with its heavy scent of hyacinths and bowls of paperwhite narcissi. 'Very pleasant in here, especially when it's so bitter outside.' He was in no hurry to remove Davidson's unease.

'Do sit down,' said Davidson, waving his hand towards the comfortable cane armchairs and taking one himself. He sat incongruously on the very edge of a chair designed for lounging, as if he expected that at any moment he would have to spring into action. Bert Hook wondered if this was a military mannerism or whether he was really as much on edge as he looked. He was not a tall man, and his eyes were scarcely level with those of his visitors, even though he sat so determinedly upright.

In this place of ferns, greenery and heavy scent, with its bright white light and its extravagant heat in the depths of winter, it felt strange to be talking of the dark, frozen forest and the darker deeds that had taken place within it. Lambert said, 'You are no doubt aware that I am investigating the deaths of Peter Barton and Ian Sharpe.' He caught a little twitch of surprise on the second name, but it might have been no more than a reaction to a name not so far revealed to the public. 'I know you have been asked before about your movements at around the time of those deaths, but we now have a more precise time for the second of them, and I should like to review our information. I am doing this with other people as well as you, as you would expect.'

It was a leisured assurance, which he had delivered more times than he cared to recall, but the slow pace of it seemed to put Davidson on edge rather than reassure him. He said, 'I am only t-too anxious to help, of course.' His slight speech impediment, which made him struggle for just an instant with his t's when they came at the beginnings of words ambushed him now, making his bland statement sound less assured.

Lambert said, ostensibly waiting for Hook to turn to a pristine page in his notebook, 'We've just come from Peter Barton's funeral.'

Davidson said, 'I see. How did it go?'

'As well as these things can. Not a happy occasion. Your wife was doing her best to comfort Mrs Barton after the service and interment.'

'I'm glad about that. Rachel was very fond of young Barton. I'm only sorry I wasn't able to get there myself. I've had a heavy cold, though that's much better now. But I had to drive over to T-Tewkesbury, on business. Couldn't get out of it, I'm afraid.'

It had the ring of an apology, though they all knew he had no cause to apologize to them about this. Lambert let the man's embarrassment hang between them in the humid warmth, but Davidson enlarged no further upon his excuses. Eventually Lambert said, 'Well, there were plenty of people there: the church was packed. Probably you weren't missed by most people.'

It was a conventional white lie, but it hardly comforted Davidson, who looked as though he had been offered an insult. The moment confirmed to Lambert how important his position as a cornerstone of the local community was to the Chairman of the Parish Council. Davidson, apparently feeling a need to offer something, said, 'Rachel was going on to the reception at the Bartons' house afterwards. She will have given my apologies.'

Lambert said, 'And I'm sure the family will be glad to have her there. Now, could you tell us exactly where you were at the time of the vicar's death, Colonel Davidson?'

If he had hoped to throw his man off balance by the sudden switch, he failed. Indeed, Davidson seemed relieved rather than otherwise to be asked to account for himself in this way. He smiled with the confidence of a man who has nothing to hide. 'I was here, Superintendent. In the house, I mean. As I told your man a few days ago—Inspector Rushton, I think? If necessary, both my wife and Mrs Graham, who was here that afternoon, could testify to that.'

'Oh, we are not speaking of testimony; not at the moment, certainly. The statements of both your wife and Mrs Graham confirm that you did not leave the house that afternoon. So does that of your maid, Mary Cox.' Harry Davidson looked slightly disconcerted that his innocence should have been investigated so thoroughly by the police. 'I have to ask you, though, whether you have any thoughts on who might have killed your unfortunate vicar. You are, after all, probably more familiar with the residents of this neighbourhood than almost anyone else in the area.'

It was a shameless piece of flattery, and Colonel Davidson rose to it. 'Oh, I'm not sure that's t-true, you know. We've only been here five years. I'm a local man, in a way, but I was away in the Army for t-twenty years and more. But I suppose it's fair enough to say that I have a good working knowledge of the people round here, what with the Parish Council and my work as a JP.' At last he relaxed his posture a little, settling back into the wickerwork of the chair. For an instant, he steepled his fingers and looked at them. Then he discarded the gesture, as if he thought it demonstrated his urbanity a little too obviously.

Perhaps he was too concerned with his image of relaxed control, for he apparently forgot the question which had stimulated it, and Lambert had to say, 'Quite. That is why I thought you might have some idea who had perpetrated such a shocking crime. There seems to have been nothing quite like it in this district before.'

'No. Well, I'm afraid I can't help you there. There's no one I can think of among our local villains who might come up with a killing like that.' His reply came a fraction too quickly, when set against his previous easy assumption of a comprehensive knowledge of the neighbourhood. A man who implied as he did that little escaped him might surely have shown a willingness to offer some suggestions before the matter was abandoned. But perhaps he had thought about the question over the last few days and been forced to acknowledge that he was as helpless as everyone else.

Hook said, 'And Mrs Davidson is as baffled as you are?'

Fury passed like a storm cloud across Davidson's face. For a moment, Hook thought he was going to come out like the military man in a bad play with 'You leave my wife out of this, Sergeant!' They still met that attitude often enough around the small-town world where they operated. But the anger passed as swiftly as an April cloud. Davidson merely said rather woodenly, 'She has no idea who killed our vicar. We've discussed it, of course. But you must understand that she is not as familiar with this world as you and I are, Sergeant.'

'Murder is abnormal wherever it happens, Colonel. It turns ordinary worlds upside down.' Lambert's own passion against this darkest of crimes flamed for an instant through his detachment. He had spoken quietly, but his words had come like a reprimand. He recovered his calmness as he said, 'Are you suggesting that someone from outside this area perpetrated Peter Barton's murder?'

Davidson looked suddenly full into his questioner's face, but found no clue there to his intentions. The grey eyes stared steadily back at him, watchful but neutral. The brow beneath the crinkled iron-grey hair was lined, but not furrowed with puzzlement or hostility. The Superintendent's wide mouth neither smiled nor grimaced. Yet Davidson felt he knew for the first time what those infantry squaddies must have felt when they stood before him, capless and at attention, on a charge. He said, 'I couldn't really say, Superintendent. You have more idea about these things than I have.' It cost him an effort of control to deliver even so much.

Lambert studied him for a moment, while Hook made an elaborate play of writing down the details of this negative reply. Then he said, 'Where were you when the second man was killed, Colonel Davidson?'

Normally, Harry Davidson was glad to hear his title used. It was a reminder of his standing in the community, of the eminence he had achieved in the service career which was a prelude to this, of past military glories which he played down but loved to hear recalled to him. From Lambert, the title came differently. It kept him at a distance when he wanted to be friendly, to be assured that suspicion of him was no more than a formality of police investigation. He wanted the assurance Lambert would not give him that they were on the same side in this. He said hesitantly, 'Where was I when this man—Ian Sharpe I think you said just now—was killed?'

Lambert nodded with a fleeting smile. 'You have an excellent memory for names, Colonel.' He made it sound as if he was suggesting more than that. He was thinking back over thirty years to his days of National Service, when he had been a gangling youth in an ill-fitting uniform and colonels had held their noses in the air as though he carried a bad smell when they inspected parades. But he knew this was not the moment to indulge himself with retribution. He waited patiently for an answer: he was not going to repeat the question they were both perfectly aware had been asked.

'When Sharpe was killed, I was out in the car.' Davidson smiled at them with what he hoped was disarming frankness.

'Driven by Arthur Comstock?'

'No. I'm afraid I can't alibi him for you.'

'Nor he you,' said Lambert drily.

'I suppose not!' Davidson laughed uneasily, as though

they were playing a game. The silence into which the sound fell only made it more obvious that they were not.

'Was Mrs Davidson with you?'

'No. I was on my own. I like to drive the Rover myself sometimes. Comstock isn't just a chauffeur, you see. He does all kind of jobs about the place.'

In a curious way, he seemed to be trying to justify his employment of the man. But perhaps he was merely seeking to divert attention from himself to the man who lived in the service cottage. Lambert said, 'And where did you go in the car on the morning of 27th December?'

'I took my old aunts to the railway station in Gloucester.' He produced it with a little flourish. Perhaps he had been playing with them, keeping a cast-iron alibi up his sleeve while he enjoyed his fun.

'What was the time of their train?'

'Eight fifty-eight.'

That put him back in the frame. The murder had been mid-morning. 'So you returned here at about ten o'clock?'

Davidson took a deep breath, like a man composing himself to steadiness. 'No.' Now he stood up suddenly, as though the moment had been forced upon him by some pressure outside his control. He stood for a moment in front of Hook, as though he was studying the Sergeant's neatly rounded record of his answers. But then he moved across to the shelf by the north window, where a row of cyclamen reared impressive heads of bloom. He began to test the soil surface with his fingers. 'I didn't get back here until late morning. About eleven-thirty, I suppose.'

Lambert watched those fingers as they played around the top of the plant pots, wondering if the brain which activated them could still them if it wished to do so. He asked the question they all knew had to come as though he were delivering a cue in a play. 'And where were you during those two hours, Colonel Davidson?'

The fingers never stopped. Lambert could see the reflection of the oval face in the double glazing of the window as Davidson said, 'I walked around Gloucester for a while, looking at the shops. Then I had a cup of coffee. The place was crowded, though. It was the first day the shops had been open after the Christmas break. Some of them were already beginning their sales.' It was delivered quite evenly and unemotionally. Too evenly, perhaps; it had the ring of a prepared statement. But perhaps there was nothing sinister in that: an intelligent man would expect to be called on for an account of his movements on that morning.

He gave them the name of the café, a crowded place near the centre of the town. Lambert said, 'Did you purchase anything else in Gloucester?'

Davidson was turning to him almost before he had completed the question, holding out the scrap of paper those nervous fingers had twitched from his pocket. 'I bought a small electric propagator. I told your colleague about that. I found the receipt today.'

Lambert looked at it, then handed it without a word to Hook. It had the trade name of the propagator and the date of the purchase; no time, of course. He said, 'Where did you park in Gloucester, Colonel Davidson?'

'Well, I delivered my aunts straight to the station, of course. But then I parked in the multi-storey short stay park near Southgate.'

'Do you have the ticket?'

'No.' Davidson turned back to face them now, with a thin smile. They all knew that ticket would have recorded the precise time he had spent in the car park. 'I probably left it behind with my payment. I usually get rid of litter as soon as I can. It's an old Army habit, I suppose.'

Lambert smiled in turn, recalling the vast drill squares from which he and other basic trainees in that Army had long ago removed every shred of paper on winter mornings. 'And of course you had no idea at the time that it might be useful.'

'No. I kept the receipt in case the propagator was defective, of course. There was a reason for that.'

'Did you go anywhere else after you left Gloucester?'

'No. I drove back here through the lanes in a very

leisurely fashion, enjoying the day. It was a glorious winter morning, you may recall, bright and frosty.'

'I do indeed. Sergeant Hook and I were out in it ourselves, rather belatedly. Unfortunately, Douglas Robertson, alias Ian Sharpe, was killed some time around the middle of that splendid morning. The shotguns from this house which our forensic team examined were perfectly clean. Has either of them been fired in the last few days, Colonel Davidson?'

Davidson sat down again. Plainly he felt the crisis, if that was what it was, had passed. 'As far as I am aware, neither twelve-bore has been fired in the last month, Superintendent.'

'And have you any idea at all who might have perpetrated this second violent killing?'

'None at all, I'm afraid. I've thought about it, like everyone else, no doubt. But I've neither seen nor heard anything since the crime took place which seems to me significant. Perhaps after all it is this maniac the yellow press is talking about as The Fox.' He smiled wryly, seeming perfectly at ease with himself now. It was a long time since he had stumbled over a word; Lambert wondered if his brain filtered out the T-words when he framed his speech, as he had known happen with stammerers much worse than this man.

'We shall have to see Mrs Davidson in due course.'

Davidson frowned, then thrust away his irritation with a deliberate effort. 'If you must, then you must. But I'm afraid she will be able to offer you no more assistance than I have been able to do.'

'Probably not. But sometimes when one puts several accounts together, they suggest something we might have missed. Thank you for your help. No doubt if you come across anything you think might be of interest, you'll get in touch with us immediately.'

They left him in the conservatory. As they reversed carefully over the crunching gravel to point the car down the long drive, Bert Hook saw him staring steadily at the bank of bright Indian azaleas on the other side of the structure. Hook said, 'He has a cast-iron story for the vicar's murder. He could have been anywhere when Sharpe was killed. I doubt whether anyone in the place where he says he had coffee at Gloucester will remember him. His appearance is too average. The uniform men have already checked the purchase of that propagator. The shop has no recall of the time it was sold.'

'No.' Lambert drove a full mile before he said, 'But I always distrust a man who begins with a lie.'

CHAPTER 25

Mary Cox was a sensible girl. She had lived all her young life in Woodford, so she was not afraid of the dark. Those who have not been accustomed to street lamps have less fear of shadows than city-bred folk.

Still less did she fear the forest. It was the scene of some of her most happy memories of childhood and adolescence, a place of innocent laughter, dappled sunlight, and the warm, resinous scents of woodland in summer. Even the short memories of twenty-year-olds have a habit of filtering out the duller and harsher moments from the past.

As she walked home from the Old Vicarage, she looked at the outline of the evergreens against the sky on her left. The wood sprawled against the blue-grey sky like some huge recumbent animal. This dusk was too cloudy to allow her a glimpse of the early stars. As she marched briskly along, she thought of the man the papers called The Fox: she would have been less than human had she not done so. But you couldn't believe everything you read in the papers; every one said that. Mrs Davidson, who was so easy to talk to that sometimes you forgot she was an employer, did not believe in The Fox: she had told Mary that only this morning.

In any case, the place where the murders had taken place

was well away from her route, over on the other side of the village: she reminded herself of that now. All the same, she was glad that Colonel Davidson had told her to go home early. The dark would drop in swiftly today, for the sun had never shown itself. That stiff man who hardly ever spoke to her had given her the last streaks of grey light to help her home. She wrapped her thick woollen coat around her and walked briskly, wondering what it was that the CID men were talking about with the Colonel.

The wood crept closer to the lane here, until it was only the width of a narrow field from her. As she approached a gate in the high, straggling hedge, she became aware of a snuffling presence and checked her step for a moment. But it was only a curious, wide-eyed highland cow, its breath condensing in long snorts between its wide-set horns, its outline in the semi-darkness like the pictures of medieval oxen she remembered from her school books.

Two days ago she had walked this very lane with her boyfriend. It had been a brilliant frosty day then, with a robin following them in little swoops along the hedge at noon and the sun picking out the details of the winter scene with an almost unnatural clarity. Now her boyfriend had gone back to his work in Leicester, and the sun seemed to have departed with him.

But she was not far from home now; half a mile, at most. She could see the first lights of the village over the low hawthorn hedge to her right. In a couple of minutes, she would reach the little rise where she would be able to see the illuminated sign of the Crown. She looked forward more than usually to that comforting picture today; it was bitter cold indeed.

She was still two hundred yards short of the point where she would see the sign when she heard the rustling behind the hedge on her left. She thought at first that it was some small wild creature. Then she realized that the sound was following her progress along the road. It stopped when she stopped, moved forward when she chose to walk on. Mary fought to control an urge to run, struggled with a dread of the unknown that plunged a sensible girl straight back into the nightmare of childhood. But this time she would not wake up to the warm darkness of the small cottage bedroom and the steady breathing of the smaller sister who slept beside her.

She snatched a quick glance behind her. The lane wound away blank and empty towards the Old Vicarage. There was no relief from that quarter; her racing brain told her that those two tall detectives in the big car would not be coming this way yet, even if they turned towards the village when they left the house. She listened for a moment with ears strained towards the invisible village ahead of her, hoping to hear the sound of Arthur Comstock and Mrs Davidson returning in the Rover.

There was only that deep silence of the country on the edge of dark, which sometimes seems more significant than any sound. It seemed so now, for it gave Mary the message that she was here utterly alone. Or very nearly alone: the rustling on the other side of the bushes began again as she moved forward urgently.

Something illogical but utterly convincing told her that if she could reach the abrupt rise of the road which would show her that bright red neon outline of the Crown and the fairy lights which surrounded it, she would be safe. She could see the grey ribbon of tarmac for all that distance now. It had almost a sheen upon it against the dark, high hedge and the hidden presence it screened.

It was not far to the ridge, but the metalled road seemed to stretch beneath her feet like elastic as she thrust her steps along it. She wanted to shout, but the noise caught in her throat and was trapped there. And suddenly she knew that if her scream was ever released, she would lose all control of her limbs and fall a helpless prey to whatever it was that was moving so closely beside her.

It was at that moment that she heard the first chuckle. It seemed to her outraged senses so near that it was nearly in her ear. She told herself she was imagining the sound, that she was being stupid and childish. Then, as she tried to picture her mother's comforting face, ridiculing her fantasies and banishing her fears with comforting contempt, the chuckle came again. It was low, unmistakable, instinct with an obscene, dangerous mirth.

Now Mary Cox abandoned all pretence and tried to run. Her legs, which had earlier been so anxious to charge forward, now refused to obey. Her limbs flailed disjointedly, so that her arms whirled wildly in an attempt to activate the rest of her body into the racing movement which was now her only thought. And the chuckle roared into a laugh.

It was at a small gap between two straggling willows that the thing confronted her. It was too dark now for her to see more than a dancing outline against the dark sky. She saw ragged legs, a cloak which reared itself above her on the outstretched arms like an immense bird of prey. And she heard laughter; crazy, insane laughter, which terrified her more than any threat in the world.

But it was what she saw at the top of this awful vision that finally doused her raging senses. The last image that imprinted itself on her mind as she fell into unconsciousness was that of the head which topped her attacker. It had russet cheeks, pointed snout and bared fangs. It had rough red hair flaring about its edges.

The face of The Fox.

CHAPTER 26

'He won't be pleased,' said DS Hook.

'Lambert? He'll be bloody furious,' said DI Rushton.

'That's what I said,' said Bert Hook.

Both of them looked at the uniformed man who sat at the next desk, united for once in their understanding of where the blame for this catastrophe could be laid. Policemen in such circumstances are not without sympathy, but they tend to be clear-sighted. A training with so much emphasis on the retention of a clean nose has its effects.

Sergeant Williams gave up his pretence of being engrossed by the report form in front of him. He was newly made up to sergeant, unsure of his status yet with CID men in a serious crime inquiry. This was his first murder, except for a single obvious domestic crime. 'It's my fault,' he said. The two heads alongside him nodded as though activated by a single string. 'I'll have to carry the can.' If he was looking for comfort, he had chosen the wrong quarter: the two faces inclined together again with glum satisfaction.

Rushton looked at the columns of print beneath the picture of Mary Cox's drawn face. FRISKY FOX FOOLS THE FORCE proclaimed the headline. And beneath it:

> The fox is getting bolder. Last night he came out from the forest, came almost into the hamlet which the folk in the region are now calling the village of terror. A young woman was assaulted by him, saved from death only by whatever it was that surprised the monster at his play.
>
> The girl was still too shaken last night to speak to me. But her mother told a horrifying tale of The Fox laughing crazily as he prepared to despatch another victim, of his sadistic mockery of a girl who had done him no harm and was merely going about her innocent business.

There was more in the same vein, then a portrait of quiet Mary Cox through her mother's eyes as a girl who was universally popular around the village, given to helping old and young with equal willingness and cheerfulness. The folk-tale of Beauty and the Beast was skilfully if conventionally evoked. The copy ended with the ritual denunciation of police inefficiency. It was the omissions of the force which had so emboldened The Fox as to bring him right into the terrified village, defying the police who were supposed to be protecting its frightened occupants.

Lambert took in the scene at a glance. 'Get that rag out of here!' he said to Rushton, who had folded the paper too late to conceal it. 'Into my office,' he said to Williams. The others heard 'How in hell's name—' before Williams got the door closed. Lambert, unlike most senior officers, was not a big swearer, even when things went wrong. It made his anger more fearsome, less of a ritual, than that of those for whom obscenities and blasphemy had become the normal safety valves.

Williams said as soon as he could get a word in, 'The man's in the cells now, sir.'

'Shut the bloody stable door then, have you?'

'We'd questioned him before, sir, during the house-to-house. He was obviously an oddball, but—'

'Why wasn't I told about him?'

Williams took a deep breath, knowing they had reached the nub of the matter. 'He is mentioned, sir, among the other reports.' He gestured his head towards the pile of sheets on the left of the Superintendent's desk.

'You mean you think you've covered yourself. Well, it takes more than a scrap of bloody paper to do that. You didn't see fit to mention the local nutter when we had our conference and you reported the findings from the house-to-house team.'

'No, sir. At that time, we had cleared him, to our own satisfaction. I'd still stake my pension that he wasn't involved in either of the killings.' Williams spat the phrases out quickly, afraid that he would be interrupted if he did not do so. He was standing rigidly at attention still, his thick fingers stretched towards the floor as though he was afraid to move them, his eyes kept rigidly to his front.

His appearance spread Lambert's irritation from the Sergeant to himself. 'Oh, for God's sake! Sit down, Dave. Tell me why you thought he was no danger. And you'd better make it good.'

Williams perched himself on the edge of the chair, as though he was afraid it might bite his substantial bottom. 'Johnny Pickering, his name is,' he said. 'He's admitted it was him. He hadn't much option: we found the Fox mask straight away in the drawer of his sink unit. He was so delighted with himself that he hadn't even been able to bring himself to throw it away. He's not twelve pence to the shilling, you see, sir.'

'So I understand,' said Lambert sourly. He wondered how long it would be before the vernacular went decimal. 'So why have we left him roaming the lanes and frightening harmless girls half to death?' He felt vaguely guilty himself, having watched the girl begin her journey only a few minutes before the incident.

'We—we had no reason to hold him, sir. In any opinion, he's not fit to be living on his own, but the law doesn't allow us to bring him in because of my opinion.'

Lambert sighed resignedly. 'Fill me in on the background, Dave.' With this second use of the forename, both of them were aware that Williams was half way to safety.

Sergeant Williams needed no notes. The details of the man they had questioned and dismissed from their deliberations were etched upon his mind now. He had thought what had happened last night had lost him the rank he had worked for years to secure; now it seemed he might after all get away with it. He did not look Lambert in the face yet, lest his reactions might impede the smooth delivery of his defence.

'Johnny is forty-three now. He hasn't had much out of life. He was born retarded. Classed as educationally subnormal at the age of eight and sent to a special school. While his parents were alive, he lived at home and didn't get into any trouble. Did various labouring jobs, but never anything permanent. Always someone better to employ, I should think.'

'Was this in Woodford?'

'No. Away on the far side of Ashbridge. He had an aunt here, that's all. He was born when his mother was forty-three. His father died when he was twenty-four, his mother about ten years ago. Johnny moved into a house in Tewkesbury, with a warden. There was about half a dozen of them there, and he managed well enough, as long as there was someone to keep an eye on him. I spoke to the man who used to be the warden myself. He said Johnny was quite harmless, as long as there was someone around to give him a bit of guidance. The tests said he had a mental age of twelve. The warden reckoned it was more like nine or ten, especially under stress.'

'How did he come to leave?'

Williams almost smiled. These CID men were insulated from the day to day troubles of men on the beat. A uniformed man would have guessed what had happened to Johnny: they came across plenty of his kind. 'The law changed a few years ago, sir, as you know. Our masters decided that people like Johnny were able to fend for themselves in society. The group lost the warden. Johnny was bound over for shoplifting not long afterwards. He came to live near his aunt, in an old farm labourer's cottage which had been empty for several years. The aunt died two years ago.'

'But Johnny's still in the cottage?'

'Yes. It's not much more than a hovel, with a hole in the roof. About a hundred yards from where he sprang out on Mary Cox. We'd interviewed him about the murders, but more in the hope that he'd have seen something than been our villain. It's—it's like going back a century when you go into that place, sir. I don't know how he survives there.'

'Doesn't he have any help at all?'

'The social worker goes in from time to time. I spoke to her this morning. Apparently she had some accommodation lined up for Johnny in a home a few months ago, but he refused to go. I think she's rather given him up since then, but she can't admit that, of course. One or two of the villagers used to go in to see him, but they're busy most of the time with their own concerns. And I don't think he always made them very welcome.'

Lambert thought for a moment about the complications introduced by this pathetic flotsam of the welfare state. 'You've researched your man very thoroughly, Dave. It would have been useful if you'd let me know about his existence, that's all.'

'Yes, sir. Thank you, sir.' Williams could scarcely believe

it. He was going to get away with it, after all. He still didn't see how anyone could have prevented what had happened to Mary Cox, but he knew that if you were unlucky enough to be in the wrong place at times like this, the system made you the fall guy.

'You say you have him in the station now?'

'Yes, sir. As much for his own protection as anything. The villagers aren't happy about what has happened. The Cox family has been here for generations, and they're respected people. We can charge him with disturbing the peace, possibly with assault, if we have to, just to keep him in custody.'

'Do that. We can drop the charges later, if we think it's appropriate. It might even get the press off our backs for a while. Nothing like "Police said last night that a man has been charged . . ." to finish off a story.'

Williams nodded, looking at Lambert for the first time, like a man trying his first tentative steps after an operation. 'Do you want to see him, sir?' It was a genuine inquiry; only when it had been spoken did he realize that it also passed the buck firmly upwards.

Lambert thought for a moment. There were a lot of other things he needed to do, and he was confident now that Williams had given him a good summary of the situation. But sometimes one had to trust to instinct. 'Bring him up to an Interview Room in twenty minutes. I'll see him with Bert Hook. Neither of us has met him previously.' Williams wondered if this tight-lipped reminder was the nearest he would come to an official rebuke.

Johnny Pickering was like a nervous animal in the small room. It took them a full minute even to persuade him to sit down properly on the canvas chair on the far side of the square table. Lambert spoke softly into the microphone to announce the commencement of an interview with Superintendent Lambert and DS Hook, expecting the man to be further disturbed by the move. Curiously enough, Pickering seemed to be calmed rather than threatened by the recording. He was as fascinated as a small boy by the technology, watching the silently turning cassette as if it were some absorbing new toy.

It was Hook who put his finger on it when he said, 'You're important enough for us to want to keep a record of what you say, see, Johnny.' The man giggled delightedly; the laughter was an outlet for his nervousness. Looking at his face at that moment, it was difficult to see him as either forty-three years old or a serious threat to women of any age. Lambert went to the door and conveyed a low-spoken request to Williams in the office beyond it. Then he sat down beside Hook and looked without speaking at the man they had come here to see.

Pickering looked his age when his face was in repose. He had lines across his brow, and two deeper furrows ran down from the edges of his chapped lips. His face was the shiny red of a child who has been out in cold weather for too long. Above it, his grey hair was greasy and knotted, as though it had not seen a comb for weeks. His ancient cardigan had a button missing, and was spotted with food stains. The shirt beneath it had its collar torn half away on one side. He was wearing only one sock; beneath the table, the outside of his naked left foot winked persistently from the point where the battered upper of its shoe was parting company with the sole. He smelled of old clothes and dried sweat.

'You the boss sergeant?' he said to Lambert.

'Sort of.' Lambert gave him a small, encouraging smile.

'Can I have Foxy back?'

Hook said, 'He means the mask, sir. The men who picked him up brought it in. And he seems to call everyone in uniform Sergeant.'

Johnny Pickering did not mind them talking about him as if he was not there. Officialdom had always treated him like that. He wondered what it had in store for him next. He was dimly aware that his life would not go on as it had for the last two years, though he was not quite sure why. He said, 'Foxy's my mate. Like Bonzo used to be.' He grinned happily at the memory of some childhood stuffed toy.

Hook said, 'You did silly things with Foxy, Johnny. Frightened someone, didn't you? Badly.'

Johnny allowed a secret grin to steal across his red face, twisting the broad nose, narrowing the blue eyes, making the whole of his lower face into lips and teeth. 'Scared 'er good an' proper, didn' I? Should 'ave 'eard 'er screaming! Silly great girl!' He chuckled then, the secret chuckle Mary had heard following her along the hedge, full of his own cleverness. It was not often Johnny outwitted anyone. His merriment lapsed eventually into great hee-hawing guffaws, accentuated horribly in the tiny, stifling room. Presently, he seemed near to choking hysteria, and Hook was contemplating springing round the table to thump his back.

But when he saw that these serious men who he had hoped were his allies were not joining in his laughter, it stopped as though someone had turned off a tap. His face turned abruptly surly; he dropped his eyes from their faces and began to scratch his left ribcage furiously. 'Weren't no 'arm in it,' he grumbled, to himself as much as to them.

'There was, Johnny,' said Hook firmly. 'You're a man, you know, now, and you can't go round frightening women.'

'Girls,' said Pickering, spitting the word as though it were a curse. 'They did always make fun of I.'

'When was that, Johnny?'

'School, o' course. They did put I up on a table, and danced round I.'

The men opposite him were silent. Lambert had an awful vision of himself at five years old in a school playground at the end of the war, dancing round a boy with a head too big for his body and a tongue too big for his head, chanting horrible, unrepeatable things. And enjoying it. Enjoying being part of the mob, baiting that helpless, terrified child as part of an appalling collective pleasure. That image was vivid for him still. How much more vivid it must be for that boy in a man's body on the other side of the table, who had suffered not once but many times, until it had become a part of his life.

Lambert said ineffectively, 'That was a long time ago, Johnny. You're a man now, not a boy.'

Pickering's blue eyes widened. 'No. Not a boy,' he repeated. They could not be sure at first whether that incomplete mind was pleased or depressed by the idea. 'I live on my own now,' he said proudly. 'Don't need anyone to help I. I manage, see.' His lower lip stuck out, and they could see the stubbornness which had defeated the social worker who wanted to move him from his cottage.

There was a gentle knock at the door. For once during an interview, Lambert was glad of the interruption. He went to the door and took the shotgun which Williams handed in to him. He shut the door and put the weapon on the table between him and Pickering. 'Do you know what this is, Johnny?'

''Course I do, Sergeant. It's a gun.' At a nod from the Superintendent, he picked up the shotgun eagerly, examining it as gently as if it had been some small, vulnerable animal—a kitten perhaps. He ran his hands lovingly over the dark, shining barrels. Bert Hook was reminded by the angle of the bowed head in front of him of his own boys, as he had watched them a few days earlier cradling their long-waited Christmas toys.

Pickering held the shotgun like the men he had seen on stagecoaches in the Saturday morning film shows which were still the highlight of his life. 'Bang!' he said experimentally. He put it for a moment upon his shoulder, like a soldier on the march. 'Like Sergeant York,' he explained, recalling a long-dead film as though they would be immediately aware of it. Perhaps that was where his habit of calling all officers Sergeant came from.

Then, turning the barrels towards Lambert so that the dark holes at the muzzle pointed straight at his chest, he said more loudly, 'Bang! Bang!' His face shone with pleasure.

Lambert said gently, 'Load it, Johnny. Load it for me, can you?' He pushed a dummy cartridge across the table into the eager fingers.

The child's face became a man's again as it furrowed with concentration. The hands roved over wood and metal, searching for a solution to the puzzle they had been set. Finally, Pickering tried to push the dummy cylinder down the muzzle of the gun, looking interrogatively and hopefully at Lambert as he saw it disappear.

The two men opposite him were smiling with relief, and Johnny's face lit up with pleasure at the thought that he had done something clever. As he had, in a way: the sharpest villain could not have given them so convincing a demonstration of his innocence of the shootings.

Lambert said, 'Listen, Johnny. School was a long time ago, and you must forget about being teased. You're a man now, and when you frighten girls and ladies it's more serious than if you were a child.'

Pickering looked at them seriously for a long moment, then nodded vigorously. Hook thought that it was not the first time he had been told such things. Whether he understood them or was merely anxious to please was not clear.

Lambert took the shotgun gently from the man's hands and said, 'Listen, Johnny, you might be able to help us. You go into the woods sometimes, don't you?'

Pickering looked at them carefully for a moment, as if he suspected he might be chastised if he admitted it. Eventually he said, 'I do sometimes, yes. Not since The Fox, though.' He shivered suddenly, and they realized he was probably as frightened by the killings as anyone in the village. Lambert wondered which irresponsible resident had retailed the tabloid details to inflame his imagination; he was pretty sure Pickering could not have read them for himself.

Lambert said, 'And have you seen anyone in the forest with one of these?'

Pickering thought again, his face once more as transparent as a child's. After a while he nodded, though he still looked uncertain. 'Not now.'

'No. A while ago. How long ago?' Lambert tried hard not to sound excited. Innocent people as well as murderers carried shotguns. And he knew he could never put up Johnny Pickering as a witness in court.

'I seen Tommy Farr. And Charlie Webb. And Joey Jenkins. And—'

'Yes, I see, Johnny. Good.' Pickering was counting carefully on his fingers; no doubt in due course he would list most of the owners of the shotguns the police had brought in for checking after the murders. The problem was to pinpoint particular times with a man who had only the haziest sense of the passing weeks. Lambert leaned forward and said, 'Do you remember the vicar, Mr Barton, Johnny?'

'Yes. Peter. He said I was to call him Peter.' Johnny's face was suffused with pure pleasure for a moment. 'He brought me food. Let me work at his house sometimes. He said I was to call him Peter, honest, Sergeant.' In the recollection of those golden hours, Pickering suddenly found his syntax and sounded some of his aitches, as though in homage to his patron. Some long-dead teacher was revived for an instant in the habit.

'Yes, I'm sure he did, Johnny. Do you remember what happened to Peter?'

The man's revealing visage clouded as quickly as if someone had put up a new slide on a projector. 'Fox got him. Shot him.'

The big, life-worn face became that of a child again, crumpling towards tears. Hook came in hastily to say, 'Yes, he was shot, Johnny. With a gun like this one. That's why you might be able to help us find the man who did it, you see. Can you remember seeing anyone with a shotgun at around the time when he was killed?' He just avoided the temptation of reminding the man that it was before Christmas. He had a searing vision of the kind of festive season Johnny had endured. Peter Barton might have alleviated that.

Pickering frowned. 'Gummidge was here then. He had a gun.'

For a moment, Hook was at a loss, searching in his mind through a list of village names. Then his children came to his rescue again. 'Worzel Gummidge? You mean the tramp?'

Johnny nodded, surprised his questioners should be in any doubt. 'Gummidge. There for a while 'e was, afore Christmas. 'E's moved on now. Don't see 'im, not no more.' Evidently he had not realized what had happened to Ian Sharpe.

Lambert said, 'Did you talk with Gummidge much, Johnny.'

'No. He moved me on, didn' 'e, Sergeant? Didn't want to talk with the likes of I.' Johnny said it without resentment, as though he considered rejection the most natural thing in the world.

'But you didn't see Gummidge with a gun like this, did you?'

'Did, Sergeant. I saw 'im.' Pickering's lips set stubbornly, like a child's when he knows he is going to be disbelieved. He folded his arms and rocked to and fro a little, resolutely refusing to meet the challenge of Lambert's gaze. He had not once called Hook Sergeant, almost as if some perverse programming within him told him that he would be spoiling his effect by awarding the right rank.

Hook took over and tried to shake him, but he stuck to his view that he had seen the tramp with a shotgun, though they could not get any precise idea when. They thought he was probably mistaken, perhaps confusing Sharpe with one of the others he had seen with shotguns in the wood. Certainly no shotgun had been found anywhere near Sharpe's body. Nor had the earlier search of the area, conducted whilst he was in custody after Barton's murder, revealed any weapon near his camp.

Johnny was getting tired. His attention span was that of his mental age, not an adult's. Lambert said, 'Do you know there's been a second killing in the woods since Peter Barton?'

Pickering nodded. 'Fox got 'im.'

'And have you seen anyone with a shotgun in the forest in the last few days, Johnny?'

Pickering looked automatically over his shoulder at the wall behind him before he spoke. 'I seen the Sergeant with a gun.' He spoke with a knowing grin, as though this was a trick question which he had seen through with ease.

Lambert was defeated for a moment. Then he realized Pickering must have seen policemen with shotguns, collecting them from the village for examination. He said, 'Sergeants, yes, I see Johnny. But did you see anyone else?'

Pickering looked a little disappointed, as though his answer should have had more praise. 'Ain't seen no one else. Well, I don't go there much now, do I? Fox ain't going to get I.'

Lambert pushed back his chair. 'We'll have to keep you here for a while, Johnny. You'll be warm, and we'll get you some good grub.'

'Want to go to my 'ouse.' The lips set sullenly again and he stared straight ahead, refusing to rise from the table.

'Can't let you, I'm afraid. Not yet, old lad.'

Pickering looked up at the Superintendent them, possibly recognizing the jollying tone he had met before in his strange life. His features took on a look of cunning complicity. 'Can I 'ave my Foxy back with me? I won't be lonely with 'im with me, see?'

Lambert nodded to Williams at the door. 'Put the thing in his cell with him.' There was no chance of the press photographers who would love that picture getting in here. And the psychiatrist they needed might start from there. For once, he would be a welcome visitor to the cells. Johnny Pickering needed protection, not policing.

As he was led away, Lambert said, searching desperately for some consolation, 'We'll get the man who killed Peter Barton, Johnny. Don't worry about that.'

Pickering turned in the narrow passage which led down

to the cells. 'I 'ope you do, Sergeant. He was good to me, was Peter. He was the best.'

His tears gave him a dignity he had not been allowed for years.

CHAPTER 27

The faxes on Ian Sharpe made interesting reading as they accumulated. With the assistance of the complete set of prints the fingerprint officer had taken from the man he had known as Douglas Robertson, a profile of the dead man emerged which was far more accurate than anything that had been achieved while he was alive.

Sharpe had operated under different names in various parts of the country. He was almost certainly the man wanted for questioning in connection with three deaths, all of them underworld killings. He was a hard man, and a clever man. It appeared from the manner of the deaths that he killed people he had not even spoken to, then disappeared from the area immediately. The victims were known villains, so that their deaths were considerably mitigated evils as far as the respective police forces were concerned.

Because he was ruthless and elusive, Sharpe had not even been questioned about these deaths, though he was still being sought under various names at the time of his death. No doubt his knowledge of police procedures from his own days in the force, and particularly his awareness of that old policing weakness, the geographic delineations between areas of jurisdiction, had been useful to him. His criminal profile had all the marks of that baleful transatlantic import, the contract killer.

This interesting but inconclusive information presented the team investigating the killings in Gloucestershire with as many problems as it removed. With the traditional mugs of steaming tea at hand, John Lambert mulled over the contents of the telex with the expectant Rushton and Hook. He said, 'Let's assume for the moment that the boys in London are right and Sharpe was a contract killer. What light does that throw on what's happened here?'

Because Rushton still felt his inspector's rank new upon him, even after two years, he felt ideas were expected from him, even as Bert Hook shook his head. 'Obviously he was lying low for a while, using his tramp's character and his alias of Douglas Robertson. If he'd been taking money for gangland killings, he'd have had plenty of enemies. It's possible some of those choice characters followed him down here and exterminated him.'

'Quite possible, Chris. Bit sophisticated for them to copy the method of a killing in the same place four days earlier, though. And if we assume you're right, what is the connection with the murder of Peter Barton four days earlier? Country vicars are unlikely victims for underworld hit men.'

Hook said, 'One of our greatest difficulties is that it's difficult to see why anyone should want to kill Peter Barton. We've turned up a lot of people with the means and the opportunity, but almost no one so far who seems to benefit from his death. His wife and Michael Crawley are possibilities. I haven't seen Crawley; you two have.'

Rushton said, 'The hotel has confirmed that the two of them were there at the time of the murder, as they claimed. They certainly haven't seen each other since the death, but then if they were sensible, they wouldn't. They would have had to employ a third party to kill the husband who was in their way.' Rushton brightened as a few pieces of the jigsaw flashed a picture before him. 'They could have brought in Sharpe to do the job, then eliminated him in turn, I suppose.'

Lambert said, 'But don't forget your own researches into Crawley, Chris. No sizeable outgoings from his bank account in the last few months. If you're suggesting he got rid of Sharpe to avoid paying him, we know that contract killers invariably demand a sizeable advance payment. And

Crawley appears to have been at home at the time when Sharpe was killed; certainly there were no sightings of him near the forest.'

Rushton nodded glumly. Then he said wryly, 'I know we spend half our time telling our juniors not to be amateur psychiatrists, but I didn't see Crawley as a man with the nerve to organize this, still less as a man with the bottle to seek out and shoot a professional killer in the forest.'

Lambert smiled. 'Having seen both Crawley and Clare Barton, their affair doesn't strike me as the kind of grand passion which leads to murder. But the problem is, as Bert says, that although that pair don't seem convincing killers, we haven't found a motive at all for anyone else.'

Rushton said, 'You two have been around Woodford far more than I have during this investigation. Let me ask you, within the privacy of these walls: do you think there's anything at all in this Fox business that the papers are playing for all it's worth? At least it would explain the absence of a motive in Barton's case. And Sharpe's murder could then be just another random killing, unconnected with his previous career.'

Lambert was happy to prolong the discussion. It was useful enough in its own right, but he was pleased to see Rushton and Hook, who did not much like each other, exchanging views dispassionately like this. Rushton, because he was younger than Hook but now an inspector, seemed to regard Bert's occasional insights and his relationship with Lambert as threatening, which they were patently not. Hook had refused promotion for his own reasons, knowing at the time that younger men would pass him by. But most of his CID colleagues knew that, and his scorning of the ladder most of them were earnestly attempting to scale made them vaguely resent him. Integrity has its own power, especially when it makes men question their individual mores.

Lambert's own relationship with Rushton was brittle enough for him to welcome unforced exchanges. He realized now that the difficulties of this investigation were driving the three men closer together, fostering the teamwork which is nowadays the most important element in the investigation of serious crime. With luck, similar things were happening elsewhere among the sixty officers now involved in greater or lesser measure in the investigation of the murders in the forest.

Lambert said, 'I don't accept the idea of a maniac at large: I never have. If I'm wrong, we're going to have another killing on our hands before we make much progress, because we haven't found anyone in the area who remotely fits the profile. And we've checked out all the likely candidates with histories of violence over quite a wide area now.'

Rushton said, 'In that case, it would be a good idea to go over the information we've acquired about the people who have connections with either of the dead men. Not that anyone so far has admitted to any dealings with Ian Sharpe; but we do know of several people who were at least in the vicinity at the time of his death.'

Lambert said, 'Right. I have my own views on some of them, but let's confine ourselves largely to facts, in case we have overlooked anything which is significant. Michael Crawley and Clare Barton we've already dealt with. I take it none of us thinks either of them would be acting alone in this? If they're involved at all, they're in it together. They're the only ones so far with a motive for getting rid of the vicar, so we must keep them in the frame. Agreed?'

The others nodded. It was Hook who then said, 'Tommy Farr is the person with the easiest access to the scenes of both killings. He lives near the forest, he admits he goes there regularly, even since the two murders happened, and he has a shotgun. He knows all the tracks in the woods, even the minor ones, because of his walks with Kelly.'

Rushton raised an interrogative eyebrow and Lambert said with a small smile, 'Kelly's his dog. A Doberman, and not to be trifled with when Tommy Farr's around. Farr's a candidate, undoubtedly. He carries an aura of latent violence about with him, and unlike most villagers he wasn't particularly fond of Barton. He gives the impression that that was simply because he had no time for the Anglican Church, but that could be a useful front to hide some more personal hostility.'

Rushton looked at his file. 'No confirmation of his whereabouts at the time of either of the killings.'

Hook said, 'But he lives alone, of course. It's quite natural that there should be no one to corroborate his account. Mind you, it's true that both murders could have been committed when his store was closed, and that could well be significant. Village shops are open for a high proportion of the day.'

Rushton said, 'What do you make of Charlie Webb?' and Lambert sensed Hook becoming defensive. Bert's own Barnardo's boy upbringing made him sympathetic to lads with backgrounds like Charlie's; sometimes, but not often, it affected his judgement.

Lambert said quickly, 'He had the opportunity, for both killings. He left his work, ostensibly to meet a girl, at around the time we know Barton died. We know he did in fact meet the girl, as he claimed, but he had time to get to the scene of the death and back before he saw her. He was used to taking the motorbike into the forest, and we found tyre tracks from it near Barton's body. As far as we've been able to check, he's the last person known to have seen Ian Sharpe alive. He has a shotgun, which he denies using at the time of either of the killings. But forensic say that it was fired at around the time of Sharpe's death.'

He enumerated each of the points without emphasis, conscious of Hook's discomfort on his left. Rather to his surprise, the Sergeant, who was staring hard at his notebook, said nothing. It was Rushton who said, 'A strong candidate, but only if we assume he's unbalanced in some way, perhaps. I can't see what he's gained by the deaths. We'd have to assume he had endured some real or imaginary insult from these two very different men.'

He was being consciously fair; Lambert knew that he now fancied Webb for their murderer. And he was right about the unbalance: mentally disturbed young men of Webb's age were capable of the most absurd over-reactions to insults when their external behaviour seemed perfectly normal. It struck him for the first time that no one knew Charlie Webb really well, apart from his grandmother, whose own mind was faltering alarmingly.

Hook contented himself with saying, 'There's no previous history of violence.' Then, as if issuing a challenge of social class, he said, 'What about Colonel Davidson and the other two people we've seen at the Old Vicarage?'

Lambert smiled. 'Colonel Davidson appears to be in the clear for the murder of Peter Barton. He was at home at the time of the murder, on the evidence of other people as well as his wife. He could have hired Sharpe to kill Barton, as you suggested that Crawley and Clare Barton might have done. But he hasn't any reason at all that we've been able to come up with for the murder of the vicar.'

Hook said obstinately, 'But he was out in the car on his own at the time of Sharpe's death. He says he was in Gloucester, but we haven't been able to come up with any more sightings of him there, have we?'

He was looking inquiringly at Rushton, who now said, 'No, but the place was crowded, as he said. We know he was there for part of the morning, at least. The gardening shop where he bought a propagator remembers selling it to him, but cannot be at all precise about time. It may be more significant in a negative way that we've thrown up no sightings of him around the forest at the time of Sharpe's death.'

Lambert said, 'There is at least one shotgun around at the Old Vicarage, but no evidence that it has been fired recently. But then if I'd committed a murder, I'd have made sure that if I was retaining the weapon it was thoroughly cleaned afterwards. Colonel Harry Davidson seems to have had the opportunity and the means to commit only one of the murders, and no discernible motive for either of them. Which is exactly the situation with several other of our candidates.'

'Including, as far as I can see, Mrs Davidson,' said Rushton heavily. 'She is as clear as her husband as far as Barton's murder goes—she was at home with her husband, and both Mrs Jenkins and the maid, Mary Cox, have vouched for that. At the time of the second murder, her husband was out and Mary Cox says she left the house for at least part of the morning. There is a good hour and a half unaccounted for, and we compute that she could have walked to the forest, killed Sharpe and been back in thirty to forty minutes. Why on earth she should wish to do such a thing, of course, is quite obscure, but as you say, sir, the same thing applies to most of our suspects. I'm not sure we can even call them that—the more I look at the evidence, the more I'm inclined to the idea of some person we aren't even aware of yet.'

It was a melancholy, even a desperate thought, for a senior policeman aware of the work that had already gone into the case. Lambert said, 'I still think we need a new way of interpreting the facts at our disposal. I don't think we're going to come up with many new ones. But we've got to connect the two deaths in some way. We still haven't got satisfactory answers to two big questions: why on earth should anyone want to kill Peter Barton, and what is Ian Sharpe's function in the whole business.'

No one felt like answering those questions. Rushton, thumbing through his file, eventually said, 'One of the people who had opportunity to commit both murders, like Farr and Webb, seems to be Arthur Comstock, Davidson's chauffeur-handyman. Barton had his phone number in the pocket of his anorak when he was killed. And he drove away and left Peter Barton to walk home alone through the forest in darkness. It must have struck you that we've only his word for it that it was Barton who invited him to do just that. I know we've checked that he did in fact pick up his sister in Cheltenham, but he could easily have returned to the woods by the time Barton was shot.'

Lambert looked at his watch. 'Bert and I are going to see both Mrs Davidson and Comstock very shortly. We'll see what his reaction is to that notion. He still isn't cleared for Sharpe's murder, is he?'

'No. He says he was in his service cottage at the time, busy with his own affairs, but there is no one to vouch for him at around the time of Barton's death. Like Farr, he lives alone, so there's really no reason why there should be. He'd have had to walk to the forest of course, but there was plenty of time for him to do that, as there was for Mrs Davidson. Come to think of it, he has a bicycle at the back of his cottage, which would have cut down the time still further. And the route from the Old Vicarage doesn't pass other houses, so it's unlikely either he or Rachel Davidson would have been seen.'

Hook said, 'Comstock is an ex-serviceman. Have we turned up any previous connection with Sharpe?'

Rushton said, 'No. We're still waiting for some of the information you asked for from military records. They had to get security clearance, and the holiday period delayed things as usual. Comstock's service seems straightforward enough, though we should get the full details in the next twenty-four hours. Sharpe's past is pretty murky, though, with his aliases and the kind of dubious activity he was involved in. I suppose it's not impossible they could have met before.'

Lambert said, 'Chris, you've been filing all the documentation on this case. What about the house-to-house inquiries? Have you thrown up anyone else, whether from the area or outside, that you would put in the frame for either of the killings?'

Rushton was immediate and definite. 'No. We've checked out several that looked likely, but eliminated each one in turn. We didn't find anyone beyond the people we've been discussing who was in the woods at around the time of Barton's murder. Those who weren't still at work were generally speaking at home with their families, so we'd have to assume conspiracies in unlikely places. On the morning when Sharpe died, we found two men who were at least in the vicinity of the woods at the right time, but we've interrogated them and we're satisfied they had nothing to do with it.'

Lambert said, 'Right, we'll be off and see what we can get from Rachel Davidson and Arthur Comstock. By the way, Chris, you might like to listen to the tape of the interview we recorded with Johnny Pickering before you came in today. He should patently be under supervision, but you'll find he had nothing to do with these killings. But I've a feeling I can't pin down which says he has something to tell us about the case; I'm going to listen to what he said again myself later.'

As they buttoned up their coats and made ready for the freezing world outside, Rushton said a little desperately, 'Any other thoughts before you go?'

Lambert paused in the doorway. 'Just one. Not from me, but from the admirable Sergeant Hook.' Modest Bert looked suitably surprised. 'It was Bert who suggested when we last exchanged notes that these killings might not be by the same person. It's an interesting thought.'

CHAPTER 28

The service cottage where Arthur Comstock lived was spotlessly clean and almost excessively tidy.

Comstock was sawing logs in the small yard at the rear of the place when Lambert and Hook arrived. He directed them indoors and stood framed against the daylight in the rear doorway for a moment, his tall frame stooping a little to pass beneath the lintel. He inspected his dress, picked a few stray fragments of sawdust from his navy anorak, and dropped them on the flags outside; the habits of neatness built in over twenty-two years of service life were second nature to him now.

He did not offer them tea, and for a minute or so they all remained standing. He was not used to visitors, whether on business or pleasure. They observed his bearing, as their training had taught them to do. This man was stiff, watchful, cautious. But perhaps that was his normal attitude: they had not seen him in other situations, and were not likely to.

He did not inquire as most people did about the progress of the case. They wondered if he knew rather than surmised that they could not have made much headway; that might be significant. Belatedly, he asked them to sit down, and the two large men perched themselves side by side on the two-seater settee of the cottage suite, in front of the single long, low window of the room.

Before he sat down, Comstock looked round the small parlour, with its two neatly framed prints and its few carefully placed china ornaments, as if checking that all was in order. His dark hair was slicked straight back in the manner of an earlier generation, his small black moustache looked as if it had just been trimmed. It was bitterly cold in the room, but he did not seem to notice; after his exertions with the saw, he was warm enough, though he did not take off his anorak. All his behaviour implied that this need not take long, if they all behaved as sensible men.

Lambert said conventionally, 'I know that you have been asked about these things before, but we need to go over some details again, now that we have a fuller picture of everyone's movements at the time of the two murders.' Comstock nodded curtly, but made no other rejoinder. He did not appear particularly nervous. Perhaps he was a man without small talk; Lambert warmed to him a little as a kindred spirit. Then he nodded to Hook, who had his notebook open on his knee.

Bert said, 'We want to check the details of your movements at the time of the Reverend Barton's murder first of all. You said that you dropped him off in Ashbridge, drove to Cheltenham to pick up your sister, and returned here. Did you then remain in this house for the rest of the evening?'

Comstock looked at him as if he were trying to set a trap. 'No. I went out again, briefly. I drove down to the village stores to pick up an order that Tommy Farr had made up ready for me. I've told your people that.'

Hook said, 'Could you tell us exactly when this was?'

Comstock looked a little nettled, for the first time. 'No, I couldn't. I suppose it must have been some time around half past five. I thought Tommy might be closed, but I knew he'd open up for me. Is it important?'

Lambert said, 'It could be. Peter Barton was killed at about that time.'

Arthur Comstock looked genuinely shocked at the implication. He said, 'But I thought you'd decided that—' He stopped abruptly, making no attempt to complete his sentence even in the painfully prolonged pause which they allowed to follow.

'Decided what, Mr Comstock?'

'Nothing. I must have been mistaken.'

Had he been under arrest, they would never have let it go that easily. As it was, he was merely voluntarily helping the police with their inquiries, so that they could not risk him refusing to cooperate. Lambert said, 'The fact that you drove to the village store is also important. To put it bluntly, it means that you would have had time to reach the spot in the wood where the vicar was killed and return home afterwards without being away from here for more than twenty to thirty minutes. That is about the length of time your sister says that you were away.'

Comstock did not look as shocked at the fact that his sister had been questioned up in Yorkshire as Lambert had hoped. Probably she had been in touch with her brother by phone since yesterday and told him about it. Almost everyone had access to phones now: that was one of the differences from when he had started as a constable on the beat. It made it more difficult to surprise them with information like this. He said, 'Your employer tells us that your instructions on that day were to leave the car with the vicar in Ashbridge and walk home through the woods yourself.'

Comstock looked thunderous at the mention of his employer, as if he fancied that Harry Davidson might have been trying to implicate him in this death. But he carefully avoided any mention of the Colonel as he said stiffly, 'That is correct. It was the vicar who suggested the rearrangement.' He sounded like the NCO he had once been, making his report to the Orderly Officer.

Lambert nodded. 'You realize that we have only your word for that? I'm not saying we don't believe you. I'm saying that as policemen it is our job to check every statement we have against the accounts of other people, whenever that is possible. That is how we proceed: when discrepancies arise, they are often significant, you see.'

Comstock nodded, stretching his long forearms towards them as he closed his fingers over the wooden arms of the chair. 'Nevertheless, that is what happened. I argued quite hard with the vicar, but once he found that I had been planning to pick up my sister from the bus station, he was quite insistent. He was very good about things like that, the Reverend Barton. He said he had intended walking both ways to Ashbridge at the beginning of the afternoon, so that I had already saved him one journey.' He sounded as if he had already been over their conversation many times, as a conscientious man might in the light of the death which had followed.

'Quite. And nothing has occurred to you in the days which have passed since to suggest who might have killed Peter Barton?'

'I thought you—' Again he stopped. This time he said quickly, 'It doesn't matter. You know more about it than I do, with the number of men you have working on it.'

Lambert said gently, 'It might be useful to us to hear your ideas. It might even be your duty as a citizen to share your thoughts with us, Mr Comstock. Two men have died. There may be more to come.'

He looked up at them abruptly with the suggestion that there might be more killing yet, searching their faces for what they knew. Hook felt ridiculous on the small sofa, sitting up against his chief, like a fowl perched close to its neighbour for warmth; the small room had the temperature of a fridge. Comstock was too agitated to see anything ludicrous in the picture. He said, 'It's just—well, I thought—I thought the man in the woods might have killed the vicar. The man who was killed himself a few days later.'

'The tramp, you mean. You think a tramp might have killed Peter Barton?' Lambert was at his blandest.

'Not if that's all he was. I thought . . . he might be something more than that. Perhaps I was mistaken.' Comstock looked as though he bitterly regretted getting into this, but could see no way out of it. He was no expert in bending words to his own purposes, having spent most of his adult life in a system too rigidly defined to leave much room for flexibility of that kind.

Lambert leaned forward, studying the gaunt, troubled face intently. 'You were not mistaken. The man in the forest was not a simple tramp. He was a professional killer. We know that now, because of information stored in police computers all over the country. What interests me, Mr Comstock, is how you managed to deduce that for yourself, without any of our advantages.'

'I—I don't know. It's just that he was the only man around at the time, as far as I could tell, so I thought he might be involved.'

'It's a big step from thinking he was the only man around—which he patently wasn't, by the way—to deducing that he was a trained killer.'

Comstock hadn't deduced anything like as much as that, but he did not trouble to defend himself against the charge. He might have said that he knew the police had taken the man in for questioning after the murder of Barton: that at any rate must have been common knowledge around the village. Instead, he said wretchedly, 'I must have read things in the papers, put two and two together, I suppose.'

'There has been nothing in any of the papers to suggest that Ian Sharpe was anything other than a simple tramp. We've taken care to see that there wasn't.' Lambert thought he got a reaction when he threw in the name, but Comstock committed himself to no more words. He gave a slight, helpless shrug of his square shoulders and stared at the carpet.

'It's interesting to us that you should have assumed that a man who was apparently a tramp should have shot Peter Barton. There were other people around at the time who had the opportunity to kill him, despite what you said a moment ago. You, for one.'

'I didn't kill him, whatever you think,' he said sullenly.

'But he was found with your telephone number in his pocket.'

'I've already explained how that came to be there. I gave it to the vicar in case he changed his mind about walking home from Ashbridge.'

Lambert regarded him evenly. 'What clothes were you wearing that day, Mr Comstock?'

He looked from one impassive face to the other with real fear for a moment. Perhaps he thought they were closing the net upon him. 'It was cold. I think I was wearing this anorak. I don't have many clothes.' The last sentence fell almost comically into this serious context, and he gave a half-smile of apology, though he was not quite sure why.

'I see. Where were you at the time when Ian Sharpe was killed, Mr Comstock?'

It was another abrupt change of gear, and like his previous ones it threw his man for a moment. 'I don't know just when he was killed,' he said cautiously; again he spoke as though he was negotiating a trap.

'Oh, I think you do, Mr Comstock. But I'll rephrase the question, if you like. Let us ask where you were on the morning of 27th December?'

'I was here. I told your people that, already.'

'Here for the whole of the morning?'

In the pause which followed the question, a tabby cat came and stood for a moment in the doorway and inspected these rare visitors to its house with baleful yellow eyes. Apparently it did not approve of them, for it gave a leisurely swish of its tail, then disappeared as silently as it had come.

Comstock said, 'I think I was here for the whole of the morning, yes.'

Hook looked up from his notebook to say, 'That is what you said originally. We thought you might perhaps have remembered some excursion during the morning.'

'No. I didn't go out.' After his momentary uncertainty, his denial now was vehement enough to sound suspicious. Perhaps even he thought so, for he shifted his feet upon the patterned carpet. They almost touched Bert Hook's substantial black toecaps, so close were the three men to each other in the tiny room.

Lambert said, 'Is there anyone who could confirm to us that you were here for the whole or part of that morning?'

This time Comstock answered not too quickly but too slowly, so that they were made acutely aware of the deliberation which preceded his reply. Eventually, looking over their heads to where a robin hopped along a branch of the cherry tree in his garden, he said, 'No. I didn't see anyone.'

He could hardly see them with their heads against the only light coming into the low room, but they could study the strain on his gaunt face as he looked beyond them, his brown eyes fixing unblinkingly on the world outside. Lambert said, his tone now that of counsellor rather than inquisitor, 'It is in your interest to be perfectly frank with us, Mr Comstock. You are one of the few people we have questioned who had the opportunity to commit both these brutal crimes.'

He looked at them now, and there was consternation in his face. For a moment, he looked as though he might suggest some other name to them. Then he looked down at the carpet again and said, 'Mrs Davidson came across here on that morning.'

He sounded as though he was breaking a confidence. Bert Hook as he noted the statement wondered if they were uncovering an unlikely affair between the lady of that imposing edifice a hundred yards south of them and the chauffeur-handyman in the service cottage, the stuff of a hundred leery music hall jokes. He said in a carefully neutral voice, without looking up, 'At what time was this?'

'I'm not absolutely sure. I think about ten o'clock.'

'And how long did Mrs Davidson spend here?'

'I suppose about twenty minutes.' Comstock sounded as though they were drawing teeth.

Lambert said, 'That would account for at least part of the morning.' For two people, he was thinking. Whatever they were doing. 'What was the purpose of this meeting, Mr Comstock?'

'Purpose?' He looked at them for a moment as though he did not comprehend.

'Yes. What did you talk about?'

The lean face set obstinately. 'I don't wish to talk about that. It—it hadn't anything to do with these killings.'

Lambert thought quickly. They would get it out of him if they had to, in due course. And they were going to interview Rachel Davidson, very shortly. It would be interesting to see what she had to say about his meeting, if meeting there had been. He said, 'You didn't have transport that morning, did you?'

'No. Colonel Davidson took the Rover into Gloucester to take his aunts to the railway station.' There was a flash of animation from him on this, but it might have been merely relief that they had let him off so easily about his meeting with the Colonel's wife.

'Except, of course, for the bicycle you keep in the old stable behind this cottage.' Lambert threw away the line like an actor knowing its impact, and was rewarded as he moved on by Comstock's startled expression. 'Colonel Davidson tells us that he was in Gloucester at the time when we think the murder of Ian Sharpe took place. I don't suppose you can tell us anything to confirm that?'

They were standing now, ready to go; it was an old ploy of Lambert's to throw a final thought in just as the subject relaxed vigilance in the belief that the interview was over. Comstock said, 'No, I can't help you, I'm afraid. He certainly wasn't back here until late morning.'

The tactic had worked, as it had before. Comstock was

scarcely aware that he had dropped his guard. But his satisfaction as he denied his employer an alibi was quite unmistakable.

CHAPTER 29

The Old Vicarage was as warm and welcoming as its service cottage had been cold and unfriendly. Rachel Davidson received them in the big drawing-room. There was no sign of her husband, and Lambert wondered which of the pair had ensured his absence.

It was a gracious, civilized room, as far removed from a world where people blasted each other apart with shotguns as could be imagined. Hook wondered whether that was perhaps the effect intended: prolonged contact with serious criminals tends to make a man cynical. There were skilfully lit paintings of ancient cities on the walls, a bookcase with volumes which looked as though they were actually taken down and read, pieces of silverware gleaming on the surfaces of mahogany that had the patina which comes only from a century of polishing. A Steinway grand in the corner of the room accommodated an arrangement of winter flowers that contrived to be at once opulent and discreet. The scent of freesias emanated from tiny vases on each of the window-sills.

They had an appointment, and they came precisely as arranged, as their subject acknowledged with a small, composed smile. Effortlessly exotic and foreign, cosmopolitan and cultured, she could hardly have made a greater contrast to the taut, scarcely articulate man they had just left. Bert Hook found himself speculating again on the possibilities of a liaison between such an unlikely pair.

Rachel Davidson behaved like a hostess, rather than a key figure in a murder investigation. As they perched a little awkwardly on the edges of their velvet-covered Victorian armchairs, Mary Cox brought in a large tray, with gold-rimmed coffee cups and a plate of gingerbread slices. Watching the coffee pouring in a smooth dark stream from the Royal Worcester coffee pot, Bert Hook decided that there were perks after all in CID work, some of them more agreeable even than the boot allowance he had long ago relinquished.

If Rachel Davidson had been aiming at a deliberate effect, she did not carry it through into her own dress, which was as modern as the room was graciously period. She wore a black cotton top, which was slim-fitting enough to emphasize her small, shapely breasts. A slim gold chain was visible at her neck, but disappeared beneath the cotton, and her long fingers carried only engagement and wedding rings. The tight-fitting dark grey cord trousers emphasized how youthful her figure still was, as she moved lithely across the big room in her simple, low-heeled shoes.

It was as though she had dressed in deliberate contrast to the formality of the clothes she had worn at the funeral of Peter Barton. Yet as she subsided gracefully into a chair opposite the two large men, she was as effortlessly elegant as they were awkward. She crossed her legs and picked off the two tiny specks of mud she noticed on the dark corduroy. 'I've been walking our springer spaniel,' she explained, as though claiming a peculiarly English habit. The smile on her wide, expressive mouth softened features which in repose looked perhaps a little too grave and serious.

Hook reminded himself conscientiously that the possession of a dog gave her an excuse to go regularly into the forest, and probably a knowledge of its intricacies. He had been ribbed too often about his vulnerability to female charms not to be a little wary. And his experience of wealthy ladies thirty years ago, when he was taking his first tentative steps into the great world outside Barnardo's, made him still suspicious of the species.

Lambert took her quickly through the details she had given earlier of her whereabouts and those of others at the time of Barton's death. It was all low-key, urbane; a necessary, even a boring, ritual on both sides. Then, after a tiny pause, he shot at her, 'Who do you think killed your vicar, Mrs Davidson?'

If she was ruffled for a moment, she recognized it as the tactic it was. Her face creased momentarily into that smile which lit up its whole surface; then she banished it, in acknowledgement of the seriousness of the matter. 'If I knew that, Superintendent, I should have told you long ago.'

'I'm sure you would. But I said "think", not "know". You must realize from the fact that we haven't made an arrest that we are not yet certain ourselves.' His slight, ironic smile and her answering one registered the understatement. 'Frankly, I'm inviting you to speculate. We shall respect your confidence, of course, but you've been in this locality for some years and often—'

'The locality is more foreign to me than to you or your men.' For the first time, they could detect her Swiss accent, particularly on the word 'locality', in which she pronounced each syllable carefully and distinctly. Her vehemence must have shocked herself as much as it did them, for she stopped abruptly. Then she attempted to recover her more relaxed delivery as she said, 'Remember that I am in a foreign country, and in a rural area of that country. In Woodford, many of the families have been here for a long time—for centuries in some cases. We Jewish people are not used to such permanence.' This time the smile was wry, even grave, but the white brow beneath the austerely controlled black hair lost its furrows just the same.

Lambert said, 'I am sure you are a valuable addition to the local community, Mrs Davidson.' He meant it; he was thinking of the moment after the interment of Barton's body on the previous day, when she had taken Clare Barton's hand between hers. It would have been a sentimental intrusion more often than not; yesterday, it had been the most natural conclusion in the world, subsuming the widow's personal grief into a wider sense of human tragedy as effectively as some great Renaissance *pietà*.

She looked at him to check whether this was a hollow reassurance he offered. Then she said stiffly, 'I really have no idea who killed young Peter Barton. I presume from your question that you haven't either.' She stared steadily out of the window. But in the pause he now allowed himself, he was surprised to catch her darting a quick glance at his face to check his reaction. He realized in that moment that she wanted to know whether they were contemplating an arrest. Was she anxious for herself, or on behalf of someone else?

'Mrs Davidson, you say you have only lived in this country for a few years. Since your marriage, in fact. Did you spend all your previous life in Switzerland?'

She looked him full in the face then, testing his inscrutability to the full. 'No, Mr Lambert. Like many European Jews, our family felt it owed support, financial and otherwise, to the state of Israel. I was born in 1941. I cannot remember much of the War, nor of the holocaust, but my earliest memories are of the fear and the grief in my family. And I certainly remember as a child the enthusiasm all Jews felt for the new state in 1948. I spent six years in Israel as a young woman.'

'I see. And perhaps at that time you had some sort of training in the use of arms?'

'I undertook compulsory military service. I was proud to do so, just as I was proud to live in a kibbutz. Israel does not distinguish between its young men and its young women in the way the countries of Western Europe do.' This time the smile was proud, the head held high, the gaze trained on a point far out beyond the boundaries of the Old Vicarage. They had a momentary glimpse of that fervent religious nationalism which the nineteenth century found so admirable and the twentieth one finds so threatening as it moves towards its end.

Lambert said quietly, 'So you are proficient in the use of weapons, Mrs Davidson.'

She turned back to him like one being recalled from a trance. 'I am, as you say, "proficient". Perhaps even a little more than that; in our dining-room, there are cups I won for rifle-shooting. A long time ago, now.' She looked down reminiscently at the fingers which seemed far too delicate for military ambitions.

'I think you also have some more recent trophies. For clay pigeon shooting, I believe.' Lambert's inquiries around the village threw up some fascinating sidelights upon its occupants. The activities of the well-heeled were always of interest to the less fortunate, especially when an exotic foreign lady turned out to be better than the men in what they had thought of as one of their preserves.

'For clay pigeon shooting, yes.' She looked at Lambert steadily. 'With a shotgun. You could simply have asked me whether I was experienced and proficient in the use of shotguns, Superintendent.' It was impossible to tell from her tone whether their researches had made her impressed, amused or furious.

Now it was Lambert who smiled. 'I could have done that, I suppose. I find that when I lead people logically, they tell me fewer lies, which is less embarrassing for both sides. So you are used to handling a twelve-bore shotgun, and have done so recently.'

'Not recently enough for your purposes, Mr Lambert. I haven't touched a shotgun in the last month. But for your records, you will probably want to confirm that I am quite efficient with a twelve-bore. I should certainly have hit a man's heart at five paces, had I had occasion to do so.'

There was no doubt this time that she was exasperated. The colour had risen in her sallow face, her lips had tightened, her delivery had become ominously precise. And perhaps emotion had led her into an indiscretion, as often happened.

Lambert said, 'Five paces? You seem to have an extremely accurate knowledge of the distance from which the fatal cartridges were fired, Mrs Davidson. I don't think there has been any discussion of such distances in the press. And we have certainly never released that information.'

She was physically totally calm. Even the hands which

she felt had just been accused remained folded on her lap. There was perhaps a little tenseness about her shoulders and the slim neck which rose above the cotton shirt, but that had probably been there all through their exchanges. Only her eyes, narrowed and darkly glittering, gave away the anger which burned behind them.

There was no doubt now that she had to struggle for the control of her voice as she said in measured tones, 'I am not sure where I gathered the information, Superintendent. Perhaps I heard it around the village; the children who discovered Peter's body lived locally, you know. Perhaps I deduced it from what we have heard about the wounds. Perhaps I know how close a person would have to be to the victim to discharge a shotgun with the certainty of killing a man: it is not the most accurate of weapons from any great distance, as you are no doubt aware.'

Lambert acknowledged her thoughts with a little bow of his grizzled head. It was a rational enough explanation, but he was not going to let her know whether or not it convinced him. He said, 'May I ask how long you have been married, Mrs Davidson?'

Perhaps she was relieved to have him leave the questioning about shotguns. She said tersely, 'Five years. Is it relevant?'

'It might be. It is very difficult to say what is relevant to an inquiry like this. To put it bluntly, a woman who has been married for thirty years generally knows more about her husband's past than one who has been married for five. And he about hers, of course. I should not like to give the impression that we were interested exclusively in your husband.'

She looked at him evenly, trying to calculate what was in his mind. He had played these games for far too long for her to discover anything. 'I intended at one time to settle in Israel, Superintendent. The man I was planning to marry was an army officer. He was killed during the Six Day War in 1967. I left Israel shortly afterwards and lived in Switzerland until my marriage to Harry five years ago.

I met him while I was on a long visit to my sister in Buckinghamshire. He was on his demobilization leave at the end of his service at the time.'

She delivered the information in a monotone which was itself a protest, but Lambert was too professional to let that ruffle him. 'I believe your husband served with distinction in the Falklands War.'

'Yes, I believe so. It was before I knew him, and he is not a boastful man. If you wish to know about something which can have no bearing on this case, no doubt you will ask him about it.' She made as if to rise, but the two men did not cooperate. They had not finished yet.

She saw no sign pass between them, but it was Hook who now said, 'Probably you have discussed the time of the second murder with your husband. You are no doubt aware that he says he was shopping in Gloucester at the time of the killing. We have not been able to find anyone so far to confirm that. Can you offer us anything, or suggest anyone who might be able to substantiate his story? I should emphasize that we are merely trying to eliminate him from our inquiries, as we have been able to eliminate several others.'

She looked at him for a moment, which seemed to Bert very long and very quiet. 'What possible reason could my husband have to kill a tramp in the forest, Sergeant Hook?' Through his discomfiture, Bert was still flattered that she had remembered his name from the formalities of Lambert's introduction: most people remembered the chief, but forgot the details of his side-kick straight away.

Lambert said, 'It appears he was not simply a tramp, Mrs Davidson. He may well have been a professional killer.'

Her dark eyes widened now. He wished they were the cornflower blue of Clare Barton's; that seemed to him to be a much more revealing colour. She might have been acting surprise, of course: detectives had always to be aware of that. She might have been shocked at the notion. What he thought he had seen was a flash of fear, but he could not be certain. She said, 'And what was he doing here?'

'If we knew that, Mrs Davidson, we might be close to an arrest. Have *you* any idea why such a man might be in the area? Unless he was just hiding in the woods, you see, it is probable that someone had paid him to come here.'

'Had hired his professional services, you mean. No, I cannot think that anyone in this area had use for such a man. I find it inconceivable.'

Hook said, 'We had better have the details of your own movements on that morning, Mrs Davidson.'

'For your elimination, yes.' Again she pronounced every syllable of the long word with deliberation, giving it a ring of irony. 'I was here for most of the morning, I think. I probably went out for a walk with Sheba at some time—that's our spaniel. It's difficult to be precise about times: I wasn't expecting to be questioned about the morning by senior policemen, you see.' It was thrown at them carelessly, even defiantly. Yet it was a front: she had been questioned in some detail about this already.

Hook said, 'So there is no witness to your movements on the morning of 27th December, any more than there is to your husband's.'

She turned and looked at him coldly. 'Probably not. I should have thought Mary could confirm that I was here for most of the morning, but no doubt you have already questioned her.'

Lambert said, 'We have already questioned everyone in the village, and about fifty other people from further afield, about that morning, Mrs Davidson. As Sergeant Hook implies, we have been able to eliminate most of them from the investigation.'

Both of them wondered as they rose why she had not chosen to mention her visit to Arthur Comstock and the service cottage on the morning of Sharpe's murder. That meeting would account for an important part of the morning for both of them. Assuming, that is, that it had actually taken place.

Mary Cox came into the warm room as they were

buttoning their coats. 'There is an urgent phone call for Superintendent Lambert,' she said.

It was Rushton, as he knew it must be. 'We've got the full information in from military records,' he said. 'There's some interesting stuff about both Arthur Comstock and Harry Davidson.'

CHAPTER 30

In the Murder Room at Oldford police station, Rushton had already added the information from Army Records to his burgeoning files. It did not seem to him particularly significant, but he was a natural bureaucrat, welcoming anything which made his files more complete. If the case was not solved in the next day or two, the Regional Crime Squad would be brought in. The senior officers involved would find Detective-Inspector Christopher Rushton's records both comprehensive and beautifully presented.

In the meantime, he had his summary of the faxes ready for Lambert. 'Arthur Comstock began military life as a driver in the RASC. Drove all kinds of vehicles; served in various overseas stations; was in charge of an armoured vehicles unit in Northern Ireland from 1986 to 1988. Active Service Medal for the Falklands campaign—apparently he went because he had a Special Proficiency Certificate for amphibious vehicles. He held the substantive rank of sergeant for the last eight years of his service. He took a voluntary discharge after twenty-two years in 1989.'

'Any blemishes on his record?' asked Lambert. Fallibility was always more interesting than virtue to those engaged in detection.

'Not much, sir. He was busted from corporal to the ranks for a fight with another NCO in Germany in 1980. Made up again a year later. He was married, without children, but his marriage packed up many years ago. That conforms with what we got from him about his background in our own initial interviews. He seems to have been a hard man and a bit of a loner in his army days.' Rushton produced the last sentence with some diffidence: these were the very phrases one of the national dailies had come up with when they were encouraging local people to search out The Fox.

Lambert did not react. 'Any details of his service in the Falklands?'

'No, sir. But there is one interesting sidelight. There's a handwritten note on Arthur Comstock's Army file to record the death of his brother-in-law in the Falklands. No more details, because he was in the Navy, not the Army. He was killed when HMS *Sheffield* went down in May 1982.'

There was a little pause as they digested this, almost as though it was a tribute to a man they had not even known existed until now. Then Lambert asked 'Have you found any connection between Comstock and Ian Sharpe?'

'No, sir. They certainly didn't serve together. But any other connection would be unlikely to show up in Army records, of course. Indeed, Sharpe seems never to have enlisted in the armed forces, as far as we know, though he was almost certainly a mercenary in the period after he was kicked out of the police. If they had contact, it would probably be after Comstock finished his Army service. According to what he told us himself, he didn't find it easy to get employment, at first.'

Hook said, 'He must have been grateful to be taken to here by Colonel Davidson. I expect the ex-Army connection helped; they must have come out of the forces at about the same time.' Bert, who had had to make his way in life without such help, occasionally exaggerated the importance of 'connections' of this sort.

Rushton said nothing, conscious that he had something curious to report in a few moments on Colonel Davidson. Lambert for his part was thinking about Comstock's assumption that Sharpe had been more than a tramp; about his refusal to talk about his meeting with Rachel Davidson; about his satisfaction when he had been unable to alibi his employer for the murder of Sharpe. The chauffeur-handyman did not seem unduly burdened with gratitude for the employment he had been offered.

Rushton said, 'There does seem from our own surveillance of the village to be some connection between Arthur Comstock and Tommy Farr. Maybe no more than friendship, of course. Two men who have been deserted by their wives; two hard men who are happiest in their own company. But they've been seen together quite a lot in the last week. By Charlie Webb, among others.'

Lambert said sharply, 'Your man did check that Webb had got that gun secure in the house now?'

'Yes, sir. In his bedroom. Much to Granny Webb's disgust, apparently.'

Lambert smiled. 'Charlie should be grateful to his grandmother, for all kinds of reasons. Not least that she helped to convince Bert and me that Charlie hadn't killed Sharpe, when we knew his shotgun had been fired at about the right time.'

Bert, who had been in this situation before, put on what he thought of as his suitably knowing look. To the others in the Murder Room, he looked ineffably smug. It was left to Rushton to say glumly, 'You've eliminated Webb from our suspects, then?' He had rather fancied Webb as their murderer since the early days of the investigation, and when Webb's neighbour, Mrs Baker, had seen Charlie going into the woods on the morning of Sharpe's death, he had thought they had their man.

Lambert said, 'What is the first thing you would do, Chris, if you shot a man?'

Rushton said promptly, 'Get rid of the weapon. In the deepest piece of water that was convenient, I should think.'

Lambert grinned ruefully at this departure from his script. 'All right. You're an experienced CID man, so you know how often we get a conviction by following up the weapon. But suppose the weapon was a prized possession, and you wanted to keep it. Perhaps you even knew that shotguns, unlike rifles, couldn't easily be pinned to a particular shooting. Perhaps you realized, indeed, that even the absence of a weapon people knew you should have would itself be suspicious.'

Rushton thought hard, then shook his head in puzzlement. 'I don't know. I suppose I'd clean it up in the normal way. After that, no one would be able to prove that it was my shotgun that had discharged the murder cartridges.'

'Precisely. Sam Johnson from forensic asked us exactly the right question when he brought us his report on the shotguns: "Is Webb the sort of chap who would normally be careless about cleaning his shotgun?" That is one of the key things Bert and I had to sort out when we went to see Charlie and his grandmother. Mrs Webb's mind is not as steady as it used to be. But minds which are off balance are sometimes more reliable than sound ones: they do not normally set out to deceive, for one thing.'

Bert Hook, who had been wrestling that morning with an abstruse article on the Fool in Shakespeare for his Open University studies, found this practical demonstration easier to follow than the convoluted theory he had fought with on paper. He saw as he turned to his notebook the point of the words he had recorded when the old lady used them. He said, 'Old Mrs Webb told us that she didn't let Charlie keep his shotgun in the house.'

'Precisely. So the twelve-bore was in the shed at the bottom of their garden. Which was unlocked, and not five yards from the footpath running behind the houses. And whence the gun could be easily removed by those with malice aforethought. But we asked Mrs Webb about whether Charlie cleaned the shotgun regularly, as Sam Johnson had indicated we should.'

Bert had the answer ready. 'She said, "Always at it, he is. Takes it to pieces on the kitchen table. Oils it and polishes it."'

Lambert smiled. 'Not a lad who would leave a shotgun uncleaned after use in ordinary circumstances, Charlie. Still less, then, when he had killed a man with it. Someone else used that gun, not Charlie Webb. The most we could charge Charlie with is not keeping a shotgun under lock and key.'

Rushton nodded, accepting the logic and reluctantly discarding his candidate. He said, 'We have the information from Army records on Harry Davidson, as well, sir.'

'Let's have it, Chris. Cut the routine stuff and let us know about any discrepancies.'

Rushton, who had been planning to build to the interesting information through a scaffolding of routine entries, said with a grin, 'All right, sir. He had what I take to be a normal career for an infantry officer in peacetime. Commissioned after the normal selection boards and training at Sandhurst. Full Lieutenant two years later, acting Captain, then substantive Captain, then Major. Where he seems to have stuck.'

Rushton delivered his little bombshell effectively enough. There was a small, shocked silence around the table. Then Lambert said, 'He wasn't made up to Colonel and then reduced because he blotted his copybook?'

'No trace of that on his Army file, sir. And he certainly left the Army as a Major. The details of his pension are recorded.'

'No record of his having held even the acting rank for a period? In the Falklands, perhaps?'

'No, sir. In fact, that's the other thing. There's no trace that he was ever in the Falklands. He seems to have spent the campaign at the Regimental Depot in England. Mind you, it's difficult to see any connection between that and two murders ten years later.'

'Except that that kind of lie can be more important to the man who used it than to anyone else.' Lambert became suddenly urgent. He was on his feet by the time he said to Hook, 'Let's go and see Harry Davidson.'

It was a cold, crisp day, rising above freezing point only for a few hours around noon, and that in the sun. That sun was shining on the long windows of the Old Vicarage as they drove up the wide gravel drive in Lambert's old Vauxhall. For an instant, its reflection was a red disc of fire in the glass, belying the temperature around the house.

Mary Cox opened the door to them, but her mistress was immediately visible in the hall behind her. Her dark hair was as impeccably groomed as ever, held straight and severe above her forehead by a single wide slide. Her face was white and strained as she came forward to speak to them; perhaps some of Lambert's gravity had communicated itself to her.

'Harry isn't here,' she said in response to Hook's inquiry.

'Where is he, Mrs Davidson?' asked Lambert. His tone was a warning against deception or prevarication.

'He went out. On foot, about half an hour ago, I think.' It was as though she divined their questions without their being asked.

'Mrs Davidson, can you tell us anything about his service in the Falklands?'

She controlled herself well. Only the tightening of her hand on the curved back of a chair showed that the query had struck home. She said in a low voice, 'I can't tell you because he wasn't there, Superintendent. I presume from your question you know that.'

He said harshly, 'Who else knows?' She looked down at the seat of the chair, refusing to meet his eyes. He had to say, 'Please, Mrs Davidson, it's vital that we know.'

'Only Arthur Comstock.' She stared miserably at the carpet, as though she had betrayed someone by her replies. Whether it was Harry Davidson or Arthur Comstock was not clear.

'Have you any idea where your husband might have gone?'

'No.' Now at last her wide black eyes rose to meet Lambert's. They filled with sudden apprehension in the face of his gravity. 'Is it important?'

'It could be. If he comes in, please phone Detective-Inspector Rushton at Oldford immediately, and keep him here until we arrive. Do you know if Mr Comstock is in his cottage?'

'I should think so. He certainly wasn't driving Harry today.'

The cottage was only eighty yards from the house, though it was almost hidden by the leafless winter tracery of the large oaks. They had rapped twice at the door when they saw Mary Cox hurrying across the cobbled yard from the house, looking anxiously over her shoulder to see if she was observed.

'He's out,' she said breathlessly. 'Arthur, I mean. He left about ten minutes ago. You'd have seen him if you'd come from the village.'

'Do you know where he went?'

She shook her head. Her young eyes were wide, inquisitive, intelligent. With her head inclined a little to one side, she looked to Hook like an alert young dog which was anxious to be involved in its master's business. As if she were loath to detach herself from what she sensed must be dramatic events, she said, 'He was on his bicycle. He might have gone to the village store. His bike has a basket on, see, so he can carry—'

But Lambert was already out of earshot, racing on long, rather stiff legs towards the old Vauxhall. It threw up a little spray of gravel as it swung round and headed off down the drive, such was the unwonted urgency of his driving. Mary stood and watched it go without resentment, stirred to be involved even on the periphery of happenings that would be retailed in the village for half a century and more.

From the high windows of the drawing-room, Rachel Davidson also watched the policemen's departure. She felt the terror and the pity of life, as she had felt it in her childhood when her parents wept over the loss of the relatives she had never seen; as she had felt it in her young womanhood when the man she was to marry was killed in a successful war, leaving her in tears while those around her rejoiced.

The fear she thought she had defeated for ever confronted her now like an old enemy come for a reckoning.

CHAPTER 31

Mary Cox was right. When they pulled up at the village store, they saw Comstock's bicycle leaning against the side of the stone house. It was half past one now; the door of the store was closed for lunch, and knocking brought no response. Either Farr was out or he did not care to have his lunch-hour disturbed.

Hook, who was braver about large dogs than Lambert, went to the rear of the building and called 'Kelly?' Rather to his relief, there was no growl or bark to answer him. At a nod from Lambert, he went cautiously to the old wooden rear door and tried the latch. As he had expected, it was not locked; people with Dobermans were a little careless about these things, whatever the police advised about security precautions.

They looked inside the small rear scullery like thieves, poking their heads forward and bending their torsos to the right, as if by keeping their feet only on the borders of the property they respected the owner's rights to privacy. They saw all they needed to see. The hook where Kelly's lead hung was bare. So was the small niche beyond it where Farr kept his twelve-bore.

It did not take more than two minutes to drive the Vauxhall to the nearest entrance to the wood. It was long enough for Hook to contact Rushton, who detailed a police car to attend at the other side of the long tongue of forest they were entering.

As they left the sun and hurried under the long nave of arching trees, the cold hit them as suddenly as if they had walked into a butcher's freezer room. Lambert hesitated a moment when they came to a choice of paths, then turned on to the larger of the two, which led towards the spot where Ian Sharpe had been killed. Their steps rang loud in the silence upon the frosted flints of the path. Then, as it narrowed and was submerged under an inch of decaying leaves, the sounds of their movements were deadened. At the same time, as though they were taking a cue from this, they slowed their pace and trod more warily, listening for any sound which would tell them of another presence in this frozen place.

They passed the spot where Sharpe had fallen. A short length of the cord which the Scene of Crime team had used to isolate the area of their detailed search lay still trapped at the base of a gorse bush. Beyond here, they moved into a stretch of tall evergreens, which shut out most of the little light they had enjoyed and turned a bright day outside the woods into a twilight world within them.

They almost missed Comstock. He was fifty yards ahead of them, with his back to them, moving warily along the edge of the path, wearing the navy anorak he had worn on the day of Peter Barton's death. Hook remembered his bleak little statement, 'I don't have many clothes.'

And at that moment, things happened very fast, though the watchers experienced the slow-motion effect of a car accident. Harry Davidson appeared ten yards beyond Comstock. He had a twelve-bore tucked hard into his shoulder, trained upon Comstock's breast. There was a harsh, urgent command from the woods on the left, and as Comstock threw himself sideways, a black force launched itself at Davidson's throat, bowling him inexorably backwards.

For a moment, Hook thought it was some wild, nightmare creature of the forest. Then, as they ran forward, his brain as well as his senses reasserted themselves. By the time they reached Davidson, he was sitting up, watching the dog's brown eyes fearfully from no more than eighteen inches. Tommy Farr kicked away the shotgun which had been levelled at Comstock. Farr's own twelve-bore hung loose in his left hand, pointing at the ground. There was no need for that, with the dog there. 'Easy, Kelly,' said Farr, as Davidson clutched his left elbow and a warning growl rumbled deep in the dog's throat. Somewhere in front of them, they heard the sound of the police siren as the car stopped at the edge of the forest.

'Stay right where you are, Major Davidson,' said Lambert. The man on the ground had not even known they were there until he spoke, but it was the use of the rank which announced to him that all was lost. He remained motionless on the ground while Hook pronounced the words of the caution, then slipped a handcuff on to his right wrist. Hook had to help his prisoner to his feet; he looked dazedly at the steel, as though the wrist it encircled belonged to someone else.

Comstock had risen with him from the shallow ditch into which he had thrown himself at the sight of the shotgun. For a moment, the two men confronted each other, both breathing hard in great snorts of white vapour. The mutual hatred of employer and employee was manifest in their every movement.

'I should have got you myself, in the first place,' said Davidson.

'Instead of which, you killed a man who never hurt anyone!' Comstock's contempt turned the words into a snarl.

'Barton was too bloody good to be true. If you'd only done as I told you and left him with the car, it would have been you whom Sharpe killed in the woods. And he'd have been away that night, with no one any the wiser.'

Lambert had an uncomfortable feeling that that might be true. He heard the cautious tread of large feet in the woods behind Davidson, and called the officer forward to take charge of the prisoner. He said as Hook passed over the manacle, 'What happened to the radio telephone?'

Davidson was the only one not surprised by the question. He said, 'I took it away when I disposed of Sharpe. He'd hidden it after he'd killed Barton. He was a professional, you see; he knew you'd be taking him in and searching his camp.' He sounded as though he was explaining some military procedure to those without experience.

Lambert, happy to get him talking while his senses still reeled, said 'Why did you kill him?'

Davidson shrugged; all moral sense had now departed him. 'He was threatening to split on me if you got any closer. And he wanted more money, even though he hadn't fulfilled his contract.'

'You used Charlie Webb's shotgun.'

'It was used for both the killings, yes. But it was returned each time. I'd seen young Webb putting it away in the shed in the garden, and it seemed an obvious strategy, careless young beggar! Sharpe liked the idea: he knew the police would be searching for the murder weapon. It was easy enough to remove it under cover of darkness, and if anyone had seen me, remember I'm a JP, merely detecting a dangerous weapon improperly kept.'

There was no sign of his stammer now. He smiled a little at the recollection of his own cleverness: for a moment, with the reference to strategy, he was twenty years back on Salisbury Plain, showing his initiative in the plans he made as a young platoon officer.

'Take him away!' said Lambert abruptly. After a working lifetime of crime, he could still be revolted when a man guilty of the greatest one of all showed no sign of remorse.

The officers who had appeared from the woods behind Davidson moved in and led him away. The young policeman among them, Bill Evans, was aghast to recognize as the prisoner in his charge the Chairman of the Parish Council, the magistrate who had been on the bench when he first appeared as a prosecution witness in court. Evans was young enough never to have been handcuffed to a prisoner before. He departed from their sight like a comic soldier, watching Harry Davidson's feet and trying hard to get in step with him.

Comstock watched the group until it disappeared before he said, as though he still could not quite believe it, 'He would have killed me.'

'Today he would, yes. You would have died on the 22nd December, if you hadn't changed his arrangements. He brought in a professional to achieve just that. Why?'

Comstock paused for a moment, as though he might deny

all knowledge of the matter. Then he said, 'Because I had a hold over him, I suppose.'

'You knew he had never been a colonel, the rank he had used as he took his position in the local community.'

'Oh, I knew that, yes.' Comstock brushed away the thought as if it were no more than a troublesome fly. 'But I knew he'd never been in the Falklands, when he'd told people here he had. Even told his wife, when he was getting ready to marry her!' Comstock who had no wife himself now, spat the thought as though it were the ultimate marital deception.

Lambert let the man's anger run, and his next words explained his fury. 'My brother-in-law was blown to bits in that war, which we're now told need never have been fought. I saw men burned and maimed for life. And that sod claimed he'd been there, when he'd never seen active service, even once.' For the first time, the watchers saw how Davidson might have killed him, to suppress a knowledge which had seemed too trivial to warrant murder. Bitterness such as Comstock felt was never permanently silent, however expensively it was bought off.

It was Hook who said, 'His lies were useful enough to you. You made him give you a job.'

'Yes. In a recession, it was all I could get. I heard from Tommy here that the richest man in the area was a Colonel Davidson, who had fought in the Falklands. So I took myself round to his house, hoping for employment for old times' sake. I quickly twigged he'd never been in the Falklands. Later I checked with a pal in his regiment and found out about his rank. I expect you wondered why a man who had only one car and had driven himself until I came needed a chauffeur.'

His resentfulness seemed now to be directed against himself as much as the other figure in this bizarre charade. 'We called it "chauffeur-handyman", and I managed to find plenty to do about the place. I was quite sorry for his wife sometimes. She obviously didn't know what I knew about the sod.'

Lambert suppressed the thought that Davidson might also have been a thoughtful, even a loving husband. People played many roles in life, and murderers in his experience kept stricter divisions between them than most. He said gently, 'Was that what Rachel Davidson came to see you about on the morning of Sharpe's murder?'

Comstock nodded. 'She asked about the Falklands and her husband's service there. She seemed to know already that he had only been a major. I tried to keep it from her, but I don't think I convinced her.'

That was almost certainly true. The taciturn, almost inarticulate ex-sergeant would be no match for the intelligent cross-examination of that subtle woman. Lambert said, 'Why on earth didn't you come to us earlier?'

'I didn't think I was in any danger. I was as puzzled as anyone else about poor Peter Barton's death—I didn't know it should have been me.'

Lambert said, 'Peter Barton was a generous man, as everyone knows. His last unselfish thought cost him his life. When he insisted on your going to collect your sister in the Rover, he took your place as a murder victim. He was wearing a similar navy anorak, and his killer had not seen either of you before. When Davidson contacted him on the radio telephone to tell him you would be walking home through the forest, he couldn't have expected anyone else to arrive in the darkness—by that time his victim was already late.'

Comstock nodded dolefully. 'It wasn't until after the second murder that Tommy and I began to work out what had happened. We presumed like everyone else that the same person had killed both people at first, especially with all the papers talking about serial killings and The Fox. Then Tommy saw Granny Webb in her garden and she said Davidson had been snooping around.'

Farr glared at him from beneath black Welsh brows, recalling to them his earlier resolution to have no dealings with the police. He growled, 'I didn't think the old girl was in her right mind, see?' without looking at Lambert or

Hook. 'Arthur and I met in the forest to exchange notes about Davidson's movements.'

Farr was a natural vigilante, thought Lambert, looking at the Doberman by his side and the shotgun hanging loose in his hand. No doubt he had enjoyed a little cloak-and-dagger secrecy, even perhaps the frisson of danger. He had not killed Davidson just now, when many wild men would have done so rather than use the dog. But he would like to have brought in Davidson without police help, even when it meant risking injury to himself or Comstock.

Lambert said, 'Always listen to people like Granny Webb when you think they may not be in their right minds. They are less devious than many allegedly normal people—village storekeepers, for instance, who choose to withhold evidence. It was poor Johnny Pickering, you see, who told us that Davidson had been in the forest on the morning of the second shooting. He'd seen "the Sergeant", he said. But he called everyone with a rank Sergeant, including me. Since Davidson was the only one around the village who had chosen to carry a military rank into later life, the likelihood was that he was the man whom Johnny had seen.'

Farr said with reluctant admiration, 'It was a pretty thin deduction to pin a murder on the man.'

'Of course it was. Alone, it would have been useless. But our function is to put together various pieces of information until we see a pattern. There were other things, you see. Davidson lied to us about having to be in Tewkesbury at the time of Barton's funeral: his chauffeur here was driving the Rover he said he was using at the time, so he couldn't possibly have used it. My guess is that he couldn't face acting a prominent part in the last rites for the man he had virtually executed. He also seemed to recognize Ian Sharpe's name as soon as I mentioned it, even though it had never been made public. These are significant details, no more: a long way from a case which would stand up in court. But had you two not withheld your thoughts from us, the pattern might have been apparent earlier.'

They had been walking slowly to the edge of the forest

as they spoke. Now they left it, and Farr and Comstock quickened their pace, moving towards the village store as though it were a haven from interrogation. If Lambert suspected they had kept silent because they hoped to wring money or other concessions from Davidson at the meeting which had nearly cost a life, he held his peace. There was little chance now of such revelations.

Lambert and Hook, each busy with his own thoughts, exchanged not a word as they drove slowly through the village. There was a furniture van outside the red brick of the New Vicarage. Clare Barton was moving out. There would be a new vicar soon in the old church: he would have much to live up to if he was to emulate the much-loved Peter Barton. Behind the high wrought-iron gates of the Old Vicarage, Rachel Davidson had yet to learn the details of this new horror in her life. No doubt she too would move out, leaving the country as well as the house where her new life had been so abruptly shattered.

Both the New Vicarage and the Old would be shadowed by these events for generations. Only the forest would shrug off these human tragedies quickly, absorbing them alongside the thousands of smaller deaths it accepted each year.

THE RULE OF LAW
IN INTERNATIONAL AFFA

THE RULE OF LAW IN INTERNATIONAL AFFAIRS

International Law at the Fiftieth Anniversary of the United Nations

by

IAN BROWNLIE
Chichele Professor of Public International Law,
University of Oxford

MARTINUS NIJHOFF PUBLISHERS
THE HAGUE / LONDON / BOSTON

A C.I.P. Catalogue record for this book is available from the Library of Congress.

ISBN 90-411-1068-2

Published by Kluwer Law International,
P.O. Box 85889, 2508 CN The Hague, The Netherlands.

Sold and distributed in North, Central and South America
by Kluwer Law International,
675 Massachusetts Avenue, Cambridge, MA 02139, U.S.A.

In all other countries, sold and distributed
by Kluwer Law International, Distribution Centre,
P.O. Box 322, 3300 AH Dordrecht, The Netherlands.

Printed on acid-free paper

Printed in the Netherlands

FOREWORD

World renowned as a centre of teaching, the Hague Academy of International Law is also an important centre of research; one notes with some satisfaction that its publications, reflecting this scientific vitality, have developed as its activities have diversified. The Academy's publishing role has been facilitated by the excellent relations which have always existed between it and Martinus Nijhoff Publishers, now part of Kluwer Law International.

Obviously since the beginning of the Courses in 1923, the keystone of the Academy's publishing programme has remained the prestigious *Collected Courses* (*Recueil des Cours*), which the much-missed Professor Dupuy justifiably described as the "backbone"[1] of the Academy. Since 1985, the Academy has also published, annually, the reports of the two Directors, anglophone and francophone, of the Academy's Centre for Studies and Research in International Law and International Relations. The Centre's work is a particularly stimulating source of study in depth of a selected aspect of international law.

In addition to its regular publications, the Academy publishes several other series. Since 1968, the proceedings of the Academy's 14 Workshops have been published, each looking at future-oriented topics in international law. Likewise, the Academy has started a new collection of fundamental books, "The Law Books of the Academy"; two collective works opened this series: the *Handbook on International Organizations*[2] and *A*

1. "La contribution de l'Académie au développement du droit international", *Recueil des cours*, Vol. 138 (1973), p. 53. The *Recueil* today consists of more than 260 volumes, reproducing the lectures in the language in which they were given, i.e. in English or French.

2. Edited by R.-J Dupuy (1st ed., 1988, 714 pages; 2nd ed. 1998).

Handbook on the New Law of the Sea[3]. More recently, if the Centre for Studies and Research attains an exceptionally high standard, a single volume containing the reports of the Directors and the best contributions from the participants is published: such was the case in 1992, when the Centre dealt with the external debt[4]. This series will soon be augmented by several new titles[5].

Mindful of its aim to disseminate knowledge to the greatest extent possible, the Academy, in common accord with Kluwer Law International, has decided to start the present new series, conceived for all those who, greatly interested in a subject already expounded in the lecture hall of the Academy, wish to be able to consult the lectures in a separate publication. Some of the lectures delivered during the summer courses, and published in the *Recueil des cours*, do indeed merit such separate publication. The Curatorium has accepted that this will, exceptionally, be the case, and it is a pleasure to see that this series is now being inaugurated by the General Course given in 1995 by Professor Ian Brownlie, of the University of Oxford, during the session on public international law[6], under the title "International Law at the Fiftieth Anniversary of the United Nations". Professor Brownlie's course now appears in the present work enhanced by a preface and an index.

This new series of Academy publications will further extend the dissemination of some of the great syntheses which punctuate the story of juridical thought in the field of public international law, as well as that of private international law, and which have been presented to the attenders of the Academy. The writer of these lines is convinced that Professor Brownlie's work will be followed, in the years to come, by publications of a similar quality, in both English and French.

Daniel Bardonnet

---

3. Edited by R.-J. Dupuy and D. Vignes, 2 vols., 1991, 900 and 882 pages.
4. *The External Debt*, edited by D. Carreau and M. Shaw, 1995, 750 pages.
5. Next to appear are the works of the Centre held in 1994 on the environment, in 1995 on the international aspects of natural and industrial catastrophes, and in 1996 on state succession.
6. *Recueil des cours*, Vol. 255 (1995), pp. 9-228.

PREFACE

This book consists of a carefully edited version of the General Course on Public International Law delivered at the Hague Academy of International Law in 1995. The formal title of the lectures was 'International Law at the Fiftieth Anniversary of the United Nations'. The lectures were to have been given by José Maria Ruda, Judge of the International Court 1973 to 1991, and President in the years 1988 to 1991. His untimely death cut short the career of a distinguished Argentinian jurist whose professional expertise and personal qualities were widely recognised.

It is the custom to provide a General Course with a theme or particular flavour. My preference was the Rule of Law in international affairs. This topic seemed appropriate at the fiftieth anniversary of the United Nations and was, in my opinion, compatible with the concerns of Judge Ruda. It is also a theme which coincides fittingly with the United Nations Decade of International Law.

The Rule of Law in international affairs is a question of perennial concern but it is of greater moment these days for a number of reasons. The active agenda of the Security Council and its relative solidarity creates a paradox. Its increased political power is a source of hope but the modalities of the exercise of power present problems of principle and of legal control. Another area of concern is the International Court, which has had a successful record since the early eighties and provides one of the guarantees of the maintenance of legality. Recent successes of the Court include the effective resolution of the territorial dispute between Chad and Libya. The general level of compliance by States with its decisions is impressive. Yet its success is matched not by encouragement and enhancement of its facilities but by

United Nations financial constraints which hinder its work and, ultimately, may threaten its independence in relation to the political organs of the United Nations.

I would offer my thanks to my wife, Christine, for her helpful comments on matters both of form and substance. I am also beholden to the staff of the Hague Academy and, in particular, to Professor Daniel Bardonnet and Madame M. Croese for their kindness during my stay in The Hague. Finally, I owe a considerable debt of gratitude to Susan Prior and Deborah McGovern for their secretarial assistance.

All Souls College
Oxford
9 May 1997

IAN BROWNLIE

TABLE OF CONTENTS

CHAPTER III.

THE SUBJECTS OF INTERNATIONAL LAW

CHAPTER IV.

THE MECHANISMS OF PUBLIC ORDER

Chapter V.

THE PROTECTION OF HUMAN RIGHTS

Chapter VI.

THE CONCEPT OF STATE RESPONSIBILITY

Chapter VII.

THE CONDITIONS FOR THE MAKING OF INTERNATIONAL CLAIMS

CHAPTER X.

CONTROL OF MAJOR NATURAL RESOURCE

CHAPTER XI.

TITLE TO TERRITORY (ACQUISITION AND LOSS OF TERRITORY)

CHAPTER XIII.

THE PROTECTION OF THE TERRITORIAL INTEGRITY AND THE ENVIRONMENT OF STATES

CHAPTER XIV.

THE USE OF FORCE BY STATES

CHAPTER XV.

THE ROLE OF THE SECURITY COUNCIL AND THE RULE OF LAW

BIOGRAPHICAL NOTE

Ian Brownlie, born 19 September 1932, Liverpool.

Educated at the Alsop High School, Liverpool; Hertford College (Oxford); King's College (Cambridge); Humanitarian Trust Student (Cambridge) (1955-1956); B.A. (Oxon) (1953); D.Phil. (Oxon) (1961); D.C.L. (Oxon) (1976).

Lecturer, University of Nottingham (1957-1963); Fellow of Wadham College, Oxford, and University Lecturer (1963-1976); Professor of International Law in the University of London (London School of Economics) (1976-1980); Chichele Professor of Public International Law, University of Oxford (since 1980); Fellow of All Souls College (since 1980).

Associé de l'Institut de droit international (1977-1985); Membre (since 1985); Fellow of the British Academy (since 1979); Director of Studies, International Law Association (1982-1991); Joint Editor, *British Year Book of International Law* (1973-1982); Senior Editor (since 1982); General Editor, *Oxford Monographs on International Law* (1985).

Certificate of Merit of the American Society of International Law for *Principles of International Law* (2nd ed., 1973); C.B.E. for services to International Law (Queen's Birthday Honours, 1993); Commander of the Order of Merit of the Norwegian Crown (1993) (for services in the International Court).

Member of the English Bar (in practice since 1967); Queen's Counsel (1979); Bencher of Gray's Inn (1988); Member of Panel of Arbitrators and Panel of Conciliators, International Centre for the Settlement of Investment Disputes (of the World Bank) (since 1988); counsel in 21 proceedings in the International Court of Justice.

PRINCIPAL PUBLICATIONS

BOOKS

International Law and the Use of Force by States, Oxford, Clarendon Press, 1963.

African Boundaries: A Legal and Diplomatic Encyclopedia, London, Hurst, 1979.

System of the Law of Nations: State Responsibility, Part I, Oxford, Clarendon Press, 1983.

Liber Amicorum for Lord Wilberforce (ed., with Maarten Bos), Oxford, Clarendon Press, 1987.

Principles of Public International Law, 4th ed., Oxford, Clarendon Press, 1990; Russian ed. of 2nd ed., 1977; Japanese ed. of 3rd ed., 1989; Portuguese ed. in preparation.

Basic Documents on Human Rights, 3rd ed., Oxford, Clarendon Press, 1992.

Treaties and Indigenous Peoples: The Robb Lectures 1991 (ed. by F. M. Brookfield), Oxford, Clarendon Press, 1992.

Basic Documents in International Law, 4th ed., Oxford, Clarendon Press, 1995.

ARTICLES

"The Individual before Tribunals Exercising International Jurisdiction", *International and Comparative Law Quarterly*, Vol. II (1962), pp. 701-720.

"The Relations of Nationality in Public International Law", *British Year Book of International Law*, Vol. 39 (1963), pp. 284-364.

"The Justiciability of Disputes and Issues in International Relations", *British Year Book of International Law*, Vol. 42 (1967), pp. 123-144.

"A Survey of International Customary Rules of Environmental Protection", in Ludwik A. Teclaff and Albert E. Utton (eds.), *International Environmental Law*, New York, Praeger, 1974, pp. 1-11.

"Recognition in Theory and Practice", *British Year Book of International Law*, Vol. 53 (1982), pp. 197-212.

"The Calling of the International Lawyer: Sir Humphrey Waldock and His Work", *British Year Book of International Law*, Vol. 54 (1983), pp. 7-74.

CHAPTER I

THE FUNCTION OF LAW IN THE INTERNATIONAL COMMUNITY

(A) Introduction

The Hague Academy has given me the considerable honour of delivering the General Course to celebrate the fiftieth anniversary of the United Nations.

The political agency behind the formation of the United Nations was the Second World War and the associated history of barbarism. The moral purpose of the United Nations was the promotion of the Rule of Law in international relations, and it is therefore fitting that the framework of this course should be the elements of international public order and of the Rule of Law. It follows that the approach must involve a standing back and an evaluation of the institutions of international law. This follows because the Rule of Law is much more than the application of the existing legal norms, but must involve an assessment of the quality of the legal norms.

The presentation of the General Course constitutes something of a juncture in the life of an international lawyer and I would like to acknowledge those who helped me on my way in learning law. The foundations were provided by my Oxford teachers, Cecil Fifoot and Peter Carter. The development of my knowledge of public international law involves substantial intellectual debts to Sir Humphrey Waldock and Sir Robert Jennings, both of whom supervised my doctoral thesis some forty years ago. I also owe a great deal to the analytical expertise of Sir Gerald Fitzmaurice in his substantial publications.

My general outlook is that of the objective positivist, that is to say, I make the effort to take into account the views of States generally. However, my positivism is supplemented by an awareness of the significant role of international tribunals in making law.

My approach is also influenced by the fact that I see the law from the standpoint of a practitioner, as a functioning system, flawed no doubt, but a part of reality. Thus I have worked on a professional basis, that is, as a member of the English Bar, for 35 States, along with other types of client, and in this capacity I have been involved in 21 separate proceedings in the International Court. In this context I act in accordance with the ethics of the English Bar, the rules of which oblige members to accept clients requiring assistance within the lawyer's area of expertise. In this way legal assistance is available to all clients on an equal basis. This surely accords with Rule of Law principles.

As to the content of this course, after three preliminary topics, the content consists of two principal divisions.

The first of these concerns the mechanisms of public order, that is to say:

(1) The State as a public order system.
(2) The United Nations as a public order system.
(3) The protection of human rights.
(4) The concept of State responsibility.
(5) The process of making international claims.
(6) The peaceful settlement of international disputes.
(7) Remedies for breaches of obligations.

The second principal group of topics consists of areas of substantive law especially related to contemporary issues of public order, including boundary questions and title to territory.

Finally, certain questions of immediate relevance to the Rule of Law will be addressed, including the role of the Security Council in the context of Rule of Law principles.

I can now turn to my first preliminary topic: the function of law in the international community from a theoretical standpoint. This subject is important because it is the theories of law which are one of the principal causes of low morale among students of international law. My first task will be to examine the ideas of three leading theorists. My second task will be to ask whether theory provides *any* useful answers to the critical questions. Finally, I shall offer some views on the nature of international law.

(i) *Hart's concept of law and the insistence on the definition of "law"*

It is reasonable to look first at Herbert Hart's influential work, *The Concept of Law*, first published in 1961 [1], of which more than 100,000 copies have been sold. Hart has made a very considerable contribution to the debate about the nature of law. His positive contribution has included an insistence on the need to explain the difference between a legal order and the role of the gunman carrying out a bank robbery: both are coercive orders but what are the specific qualities of a *legal* order? Moreover, Hart seeks to avoid a focus upon the "definition of law" in monolithic form and uses the more sophisticated framework of the "concept of law".

Hart gives two specific qualities of the concept:

(1) The existence of both primary and secondary rules; the former type are laws concerning human actions of the usual kind, the latter are concerned with the conferring of powers and the identification of those competent to make, and change, the primary rules.

(2) The existence of an ultimate *rule of recognition* which provides the particular system of rules with its criteria of validity, in other words, a rule which specifies the sources of valid rules.

This approach is more empirical and more fruitful than the search for a "definition" and yet the methodology is not dramatically different. The basic assumption is that *the* concept of law awaits identification if only the incorrect views of the Austinians are discarded. Law is presented as a concept which has some special qualities and its own integrity. This assumption seems to me to be in its own way as restrictive as the prescribing of some neat definition. It tends to inhibit examination of the enormous number of social roles which quantities called "law" have in fact

1. H. L. A. Hart, *The Concept of Law*, 2nd ed., Oxford, Clarendon Press, 1994.

played. The study of law as a phenomenon is presented as a search for a species of butterfly which, it is believed, has certain characteristics, though it has not yet been found. Butterflies noticed during the search are ignored as not corresponding to the model searched for. When a butterfly is found which for a while is thought to correspond to the model then others noticed are *ex hypothesi* of no account.

In other words, the Hart approach is an example of *a priorism* and over-simplification, all the more influential because it refers to a *concept* of law and proceeds from a writer of authority and sophistication. So in his opening chapter Hart is already referring to the "clear standard cases" constituted by the legal systems of "modern states"[2], which are contrasted with the "doubtful cases" exemplified by "primitive law" and international law. In this way he partitions his material at the outset of his study and, it would seem, decides to rely on a certain type of political framework as offering the evidence for conclusions on law in general.

Hart offers views related primarily to the way things are ordered in the more developed modern States. In adopting this type of presentation, and in coming to the conclusions about law referred to earlier, Hart relies on conceptions which do not derive from an empirical study of the evidence. In a university setting the highly generalized study of law within a jurisprudence syllabus leads easily to the assumption that one is dealing with a concept, a logical whole, a system of norms and so on. Moreover, the analyst and philosopher, eager to make law respectable in terms of other disciplines, and to make it fit into his particular intellectual system, is inevitably drawn to the abstract presentation. But, socially and politically, it is difficult to believe that those in charge of even the more organized societies of recent times have been very conscious of law as a unitary concept or system, and as a system consisting of primary and secondary rules.

The elements of the abstract model of law offered by Hart are inextricably bound up with political and social quantities which

---

2. *Op. cit.*, pp. 3-4. These criticisms of Hart's views appeared first of all in the *British Year Book of International Law* (hereafter *British Year Book*), Vol. 52 (1981), p. 1 at pp. 5-8.

have to be caricatured by him and others in order to be accommodated to the abstract model. Thus in a system in which rules by convention stand with other kinds of rules, both common law and statute, as in the British Constitution, there is no neat "ultimate rule of recognition" which provides an intellectual basis for a system of rules, but a complex state of political fact referred to compendiously as the law and custom of the constitution. Moreover, in many societies there is nothing which approximates to a single rule of recognition as a guide to the law-determining agencies. The rules of recognition may vary. Thus in Turkey and Iran modern city-based code law has at times marched alongside adherence to local custom and Koranic law by the peasant peoples of the provinces and the nomadic groups. Lack of social cohesion often cuts across any notion of a unity of legal rules based on a system both known and accepted throughout the country concerned.

The highly political provenance of the secondary rules in the Hart model, that is, the basic principles of the constitution detailing the competent law makers, means that to describe them as "secondary rules" is to adopt a level of abstraction which is unhelpful. Thus some secondary rules, for example the principle of parliamentary sovereignty in the United Kingdom, may be much more significant than others similarly classified.

Of especial importance is the fact that the operation of the secondary rules may break down without affecting the operation of the primary rules to any great extent, or at all. Civil strife may place the secondary rules in jeopardy and possibly change them, yet during the time when the political foundations are being remade there is generally no legal vacuum — acts in the law of the ordinary sort are valid; there is no moratorium for crime and even after a change of sovereignty there is no moratorium on ordinary crime as opposed to political crime committed in the territory prior to the change.

The work of Hart and others avoids the cruder aspects of the notion that legal rules operate as coercive orders from particular human beings received and obeyed by the population at large.

However, the intellectual conception of law with its emphasis on rules of recognition shares some of the mechanical oddities of the notion of coercive orders, since it assumes that law operates in a community of well-tutored individuals receptive to a particular system of norms. Yet it is obvious that populations do not see law in this way and it is a fact that a large section of a population may take note of secondary rules, and thus primary rules as well, laid down by rival authorities, for example a separatist movement, a militant religious body at odds with the civil authority, or rival customary law which runs contrary to the code of law of the central administration. Law is relative to the social order of things, and the reasons for its effectiveness are not to be referred to a single notion of obedience or of appreciation of the validity of norms according to a central principle.

The general emphasis on secondary rules and reference to the compulsory jurisdiction of courts, a legislature as the normal marks of a legal system, and centrally organized sanctions, lead Hart to give a low, or at any rate abnormal, status to public international law[3]. Hart, consistently with his flexible approach *via* a concept and not a definition, avoids the conclusion that international law is not "binding" and so not worth the title "law". At the same time, the intellectual segregation which he imposes on international law is unfortunate and Hart remains too heavily influenced by the paradigm of municipal law. And in this context Hart probably exaggerates the role of secondary rules in municipal systems in maintaining the more basic forms of legality.

It is time to turn to an examination of the ideas of the great legal philosopher Hans Kelsen.

(ii) *Hans Kelsen and the international legal order*

Legal theorists fall into roughly three categories. First, general theorists who fit international law into their theories but do so from a position of relative ignorance and non-involvement in for-

3. *Op. cit.*, pp. 213-237.

eign affairs. Herbert Hart is an example of this type. Secondly, theorists such as Professor Reisman, who are primarily experts in international law but who propose a theoretical perspective of international law. Finally, there is the small number of *general* theorists who also have substantial expertise in international law. Hans Kelsen is the best representative of this group.

Kelsen's approach is very helpful to the morale of the international lawyer. On the one hand, he offers a highly developed theoretical structure. In particular, he tries to identify the elements which distinguish law from other normative systems. On the other hand, Kelsen avoids a starting point which involves the acceptance of *national* legal systems as the paradigm to which international law has to be adjusted, on the basis that it is in some way eccentric.

Kelsen emphasized that the State was a centralized legal order, whilst international law is marked by a "wide-ranging decentralization" [4]. At the same time Kelsen did not construct his theory in a way which conferred an a priori inferiority upon international law. In his view, in spite of the fact that self-help by individual States provided the sanctions, international law constituted a coercive order and therefore qualified as a legal order[5]. Kelsen also provided an intellectual construct which treated international and municipal law as part of the same system of norms, receiving their validity and content from the same basic norm. The basic norm he formulated as follows: "The States ought to behave as they have customarily behaved." [6] The construction of a unified system of norms then proceeds as follows: when the basic norm

4. H. Kelsen, *Introduction to the Problems of Legal Theory* (1934), translated by B. L. and S. L. Paulson, Oxford, Clarendon Press, 1992, pp. 107-108. See also Kelsen, *The General Theory of Law and State*, New York, Russell and Russell, 1945, pp. 325-327.

5. H. Kelsen, *Principles of International Law*, New York, Rinehart, 1952, p. 20; 2nd ed. by Robert W. Tucker, New York, Holt, Rinehart and Winston, 1967, p. 18. See also Kelsen, *The General Theory of Law and State*, *supra* footnote 4, pp. 328-341.

6. *Principles of International Law*, 1952, pp. 417-418; 2nd ed., 1967, p. 564. See also H. Kelsen, *The General Theory of Law and State*, *supra* footnote 4, p. 369.

came to support a system of international law, the principle of effectiveness contained therein, which allows revolution to be a law-creating fact, and accepts the first legislators of a State, provided the basic norm of national legal orders, that is, the effectiveness of the new internal legal orders established on the basis of acts which may be contrary to the previous constitution. Consequently:

> "Since the basic norms of the national legal orders are determined by a norm of international law, they are basic norms only in a relative sense. It is the basic norm of the international legal order which is the ultimate reason of validity of the national legal orders, too." [7]

(iii) *Myres S. McDougal and Michael Reisman: international law in a policy-orientated perspective*

It is necessary to turn now to a type of legal theory propounded by thinkers who are primarily experts in public international law. I refer to the influential views of Myres McDougal and Michael Reisman of the Yale Law School. It would be impossible in a short space to do justice to the views of the Yale School. However, it is possible to indicate certain important distinguishing elements in the Yale approach [8].

First: it is a given quantity that there is a world community and that this embraces the whole arena of earth and space.

Secondly: it is also a *datum* that there is a world community process which is "a process of effective power in the sense that

7. *Principles of International Law*, 1952, p. 415; 2nd ed., 1967, p. 562; *Recueil des cours*, Vol. 84 (1953-III), p. 196. See further H. L. A. Hart, "Kelsen's Doctrine of the Unity of Law", in *Ethics and Social Justice*, Albany, 1968, p. 171.

8. The principal sources of this approach are as follows: Myres S. McDougal, Harold D. Lasswell and W. Michael Reisman, "The World Constitutive Process of Authoritative Decision", *Journal of Legal Education*, Vol. 19 (1967), pp. 253-437; McDougal and Reisman, in R. St. J. Macdonald and Douglas M. Johnston (eds.), *The Structure and Process of International Law*, The Hague, Martinus Nijhoff, 1983, pp. 103-129.

decisions are in fact taken and enforced, by severe deprivations or high indulgences, which are inclusive in their reach and effects"[9].

Thirdly: there is a process of authoritative and controlling decision that is global in its reach.

These broad formulations are thought-provoking but they tend to confuse normative prescription with factual assumptions. It is more enlightening to examine what the proponents of the Yale School have to say about the views of *other* writers about international law.

The key Yale positions appear to be as follows:

(1) The perception of law as "rules" is rejected. In the first place this rejection rests on the view that legal principles are very varied in content and in the roles they play and that international law is a continuing process of authoritative decisions. This view makes good sense and the variety of legal norms is readily apparent to the student of both municipal and international law.

(2) The second Yale prescription is much more problematical. According to McDougal and Reisman a theory about international law must be focused upon policy and all decisions must be "policy-orientated". Thus:

> "For every inquirer about international law, the most insistent question must be that of what basic policy goals he, as a responsible citizen of the larger community of human kind and of its various component communities, is willing to recommend to other similarly responsible citizens as the primary postulates of world public order."[10]

It is, of course, important to evaluate rules and decisions in terms of policy and this process can be carried out in the absence of a special theory. It has long been recognized that judicial

9. Myres S. McDougal and W. Michael Reisman, *supra* footnote 8, p. 119.

10. Myres S. McDougal and W. Michael Riesman, in R. St. J. Macdonald and Douglas M. Johnston (eds.), *The Structure and Process of International Law*, *supra* footnote 8, p. 122.

activity involves law-making and a range of choices beyond a simple model of law-finding.

The real difficulty with the Yale approach is that the balance of policy-orientation and legal criteria, however flexible such criteria may be, is not spelled out. On occasion one receives the impression that for the Yale theorist the legality of a given action depends on the identity of the actors. Thus (in the 1950s) nuclear weapons testing by State A would be lawful whilst the same activity by State B would be unlawful. A necessary corrective is the assertion that the policy-science approach cannot be used "to find every means possible if the end is desirable" [11]. The problem which remains is to what extent policy-orientation can be allowed to override the existing legal principles, which constitute, after all, the best evidence of the community values to which the Yale School attaches great significance.

The further difficulty with the policy-orientated approach is the way in which its exponents apply the theory to specific situations. A striking example of this appears in a recent publication of Professor Reisman. Thus, with particular reference to the *Nicaragua* case [12] Professor Reisman expresses both surprise and irritation that the editors of the ninth edition of Volume I of Oppenheim's general treatise [13] should view judgments of the International Court as filling gaps in the law [14]. This is a super-positivist attitude. If the Court is not an authoritative decision-maker expressing community values, what is?

It is a weakness of the policy-orientated approach that the concept of "the authoritative decision-maker" is not presented with clarity. It appears to be related to "power" and it appears to allow individual powerful States to stand in as proxies for community values. Multilateral expressions of decision-making, for example

---

11. R. Higgins, *Problems and Process*, Oxford, Clarendon Press, 1994, p. 6, and see generally at pp. 2-8.

12. Case concerning *Military and Paramilitary Activities in and against Nicaragua (Nicaragua* v. *United States of America)*, *ICJ Reports 1986*, p. 14.

13. *Oppenheim's International Law*, 9th ed., Vol. I, *Peace*; ed. by Sir Robert Jennings and Sir Arthur Watts, London, Longman, 1992.

14. *Yale Journal of International Law*, Vol. 19 (1994), p. 255 at p. 273.

by the General Assembly, are not accorded much respect. The process of authoritative decision-making is "an integral part of the more comprehensive processes of effective power . . ."[15]. The problem is that in terms of "effective power" the exponents of the Yale approach consistently appear to envisage the Government of a single member of the Security Council rather than other expressions of power, such as the power which coalitions of States may represent either in the General Assembly or in regional organizations.

(iv) *The validity and effectiveness of a legal order must be determined ultimately by extra-legal criteria*

Thus far the purpose has been to provide a substantial sample of the more sophisticated theories of law available in the intellectual market place. It is now necessary to move on to my second task which is to ask whether theory can provide any useful answers to the critical questions concerning the ultimate source of the binding force of law.

It is at this point that I can show my hand. In spite of considerable exposure to theory, and some experience in teaching jurisprudence, my ultimate position has been that, with one exception, theory provides no real benefits and frequently obscures the more interesting questions. The exception is produced by the fact that it is often practically useful to understand the theories which have influenced a particular individual or group of decision-makers.

This denial of the value of theory can itself be provided with a theoretical basis. This consists of the logical demonstration that the ultimate source of the binding force of law can only be found outside the law. This was essentially the position of Kelsen. Whilst individual norms did not have to satisfy a criterion of effectiveness, the legal system *as a whole* had to be efficacious to count as such, and the criteria of efficacy were pre-legal matters of fact.

---

15. Myres S. McDougal and W. Michael Reisman, in R. St. J. Macdonald and Douglas M. Johnston (eds.), *op. cit., supra* footnote 8, p. 120.

A distinguished exponent of this view was Sir Gerald Fitzmaurice, Legal Adviser to the British Foreign Office until elected to the International Court in 1960. Sir Gerald did not hold himself out as a theoretician but, whilst still Legal Adviser, he set forth his views in the course of his lectures to the Hague Academy in 1957 [16]. Fitzmaurice poses the question: what is the ultimate source of the power of the law-giver on the plane of domestic law? His answer is as follows:

> "What is it that imposes a legal duty on the population to obey the law-giver, as opposed to a merely factual necessity to do so arising from superior force? To say that it is the law-giver himself is either merely tautologous, or else raises the same question again as to the source from which the law-giver derives his own legal right. This question cannot be answered satisfactorily by saying that the law-giver has the right because he has the power. Right and power may coincide, but they may not: they are in any case distinct concepts. People do not obey the laws of their countries merely because they know or believe that they will, if necessary, be made to do so. They obey them also, and chiefly, because they regard them as the law — for the law is not obligatory because it is enforced: it is enforced because it is already obligatory; and enforcement would otherwise be illegal. The fact is, that reliance on the figure of the law-giver does not, even in the domestic field, get rid of the problem of the source of legal obligation: it only puts it a stage further back. The law-giver may be the proximate source of the obligation, if he prescribes that the law he has formulated is to be obeyed. But unless the law-giver's own authority and right can be accounted for, so as to show why anyone should obey his prescriptions, the enquirer is no nearer to discovering the true source of the obligation. Further investigation shows that this source is in the ultimate sense undiscoverable; for logically and in the last analysis, the validity of any criterion, or of any source of right can only be discussed and established by reference to something outside itself — *i.e.* in terms of an antecedent criterion or source. In the last analysis therefore, there can be no finality. Cer-

16. *Recueil des cours*, Vol. 92 (1957-II), pp. 36-47; and see also "The Foundations of the Authority of International Law and the Problem of Enforcement", *Modern Law Review*, Vol. 19 (1956), p. 1 at pp. 8-13.

tainly there can be no ultimately final explanation in terms of law itself, or there would be nothing to explain." [17]

This point may seem rather obvious but it is too often ignored in the literature. It is also to be appreciated that such realism — that a legal order must rest upon extra-legal foundations — avoids the condescension of attempts to "validate" international law in terms of legal science, and especially legal science based upon the paradigm of domestic law.

(v) *The nature of international law: some conclusions*

Some conclusions can now be offered on the nature of international law and, in particular, some comparisons between international law and public law within national legal systems.

First of all, the reality of international law, that is to say, the actual use of rules described as rules of international law by Governments, is not to be questioned. All normal Governments employ experts to provide routine and other advice on matters of international law and constantly define their relations with other States in terms of international law. Governments and their officials routinely use rules which they have for a very long time called the "law of nations" or "international law". The evidence is that reference to international law has been a part of the normal process of decision-making. Some of the evidence is to be seen in the volumes of the *British Digest of International Law* which relate to the period 1860-1914. There are to be seen there the confidential opinions of the Law Officers of the Crown.

The law delimits the competence of States. No journey by air could take place in reasonable conditions if it were not for a network of legal structures involving the jurisdiction of States, the agreements of States and various ICAO procedures and standards. The law also provides the tools for constructing institutions. Typically, what is, in effect, the *loi-cadre* of the EEC is a multilateral treaty.

17. *Op. cit.*, *supra* footnote 16, pp. 44-45.

Given the reality of international law, its actual role in the business of States, the more interesting and necessary enquiry is into the performance or efficacy of the law. As a first line of approach it may be said that international law confronts certain objective and inescapable features of the political landscape. In the first place, the addressees of the rules are normally and primarily the Governments themselves. It is too often forgotten that this feature is shared by public law within States. Like the law of the constitution, international law addresses the very agents who should apply the rules: the rules are essentially principles of self-limitation and, for Governments, they are immanent and not external.

A connected proposition would be this: on empirical grounds, given the number of civil wars, wars of secession and coups d'état since — let us say — 1945, a good case can be made out for saying that public international law is *more* efficacious than *public* law within States. At any rate, whether or not such a judgment is sustainable, those who would judge international law would do well, on grounds of logical consistency, to start out by taking a hard look at the performance of *national* legal systems. It is a striking fact that in discussion of the efficacy of sanctions directed at the Smith régime in Rhodesia after the unilateral declaration of independence it was common for reference to be made to the "ineffectiveness" of United Nations resolutions. In this context it was unusual to hear reference to the efficacy of the Southern Rhodesia Act of 1965 and the law of treason as applicable in Rhodesia and yet logically the Westminster *grundnorm* was as much in issue as the the New York *grundnorm.*

Indeed, within States a fair degree of common sense prevails in assessing the performance of law. It does not seem sensible to say, for example, that because the rule of law is weak in a particular region and murders common, we can conclude that the law of the United Kingdom is not a reality. That kind of logic involves saying that if an ideal score of one hundred is not achieved any other lesser score is not to be counted.

There is a second inescapable feature of the political landscape. International law is essentially a law *between* States and this remains true in spite of the appearance of various international organizations and the significance of human rights standards. There is no world State. Thus even if the assumption be made that a world federal State or whatever is a desirable goal, since State law will be more effective, then the whole question of the efficacy of international law would become moot if such a global State were formed. In other words, the Austinian "command theorist" can only be satisfied on the terms that the experiment is set aside.

The general problem has other facets. Perhaps the key to the whole discussion is the proposition that legality is indivisible. The episodes which we usually describe as "serious breaches of international law" — genocide, hostage-taking, various other breaches of human rights — are the product of government policies as such. The Watergate affair involved a decision to use methods, previously employed against foreign political targets, against political groups at home. At the less dramatic level the dumping of oil at sea in breach of treaty standards is the consequence of the relative inefficacy of domestic law in enforcing those treaty standards. The protection of the environment and much of the protection of human rights depend upon the application of standards *within the national legal and administrative systems*. Probably the biggest single obstacle to treaty enforcement is the inability of national administrations in many countries to cope with even a minimal burden.

Both legal systems, international and domestic, exhibit cases of what may be called the discretion not to prosecute. Within the United Kingdom the more striking examples include the non-prosecution of the Ulster conspiracy in 1912-1913, the readiness to negotiate with Ian Smith and his fellow conspirators, and the aftermath of the revelations of breaches of Rhodesian sanctions contained in the Bingham Report. It is a delicate matter to provide parallel cases in international relations. The failure to condemn the Indian intervention at the time of the independence of Bangladesh or the Tanzanian intervention to overthrow Idi Amin may be appropriate as examples, and some would instance the attitude of most Governments to the Entebbe operation by Israeli forces.

The fact is that legal and political systems from time to time face situations in which the positive way forward involves amnesty and a healing of social wounds rather than the inflexible application of the law. The example of the policy of the Nigerian Government after the defeat of the Biafrans deserves notice as a model of peaceful reconciliation and the avoidance of revenge.

In national life the law is not expected to cover all events; by a paradox in international relations almost every event, including large areas of administrative activity, is considered to be classifiable as lawful or unlawful. Much of what is considered to be a "part of international law" — the constitutions of international organizations, the standards and recommendations of such organizations — is in reality to an extent the functional counterpart of administration in national systems. Many treaties are concerned with the statement of agreed policies and programmes or constitute promises of particular performances: they are part of a process of dealing and not much more. A major source of confusion in international law lies in the overlap between the concept of State responsibility (or the concept of delict) and the notion of the *ultra vires* act. In other words, many cases of illegal behaviour on the part of States are really the equivalent of the *ultra vires* act by a public body or minister which is not also a tort. The constant outcome is an inflation of the concept and incidence of illegality in international life.

A persistent feature of the debate about the effectiveness of international law is the tendency to pursue the argument in terms of jurisprudence, or otherwise in more or less abstract terms. The professional legal theorists have to an extent dictated the terms of the debate and this is unfortunate for a number of reasons. The legal philosophers, with few exceptions, are unacquainted with international law. Certainly they lack knowledge of its practical applications. Thus there is much theorizing, usually on the basis of testing the law of nations against criteria which are thought to be characteristic of domestic legal systems, and not enough examination of the vast array of evidence of the actual role of international law, both in the routine stewardship of State affairs and also in more strenuous political circumstances. As it has been suggested above, if a government official considers that the legal aspects much be carefully taken into account in the process of decision-making, then to an important extent, the law has a significant role and is thus "effective".

CHAPTER II

THE FORMATION OF GENERAL INTERNATIONAL LAW

(A) General International Law

The theme of the sources of international law has several significant points of contact with the theme of the Rule of Law, and is the subject of the second preliminary chapter.

First of all, the rules applicable should be reasonably ascertainable and reflect the normal expectations of States.

Secondly, the rule-making should allow for special relations based upon considerations of good faith.

Thirdly, there is the problem concerning the relations between treaties and general international law.

And finally, there is the set of questions involving what may be called, for the sake of convenience, the politics of the sources of international law. Thus the formation of customary law and the operation of other sources may be in tension with the hegemonial approach to the sources, in which equality of application of the law is to be subordinated to the power ratio of the States in dispute.

(i) *Custom*

It is necessary to examine the constituent elements of custom, but before that is done it will be useful to deal candidly with some misconceptions about the subject. First of all, customary international law is not a special department or area of public international law: it *is* international law. Whilst there are some points of possible distinction, customary law and general international law are for practical purposes identical. Secondly, it is sometimes wrongly assumed, especially in anglophone contexts, that custom is ancient, retrogressive and difficult to change. Such assumptions are based on cultural or national prejudices about custom and customary law. In the case of international law it is well established that long duration is not a condition for the existence of customary rule. It is certainly true that certain areas of customary law, for example the principles governing the status of the high seas, are ancient. But there are many examples of new rules emerging within a relatively short time span. Provided the practice shows sufficient generality and consistency, no particular duration is required.

The principles governing the legal régime of the continental shelf emerged from the practice of States within a period of 20 years or less. In the *North Sea Continental Shelf* cases[18] the International Court accepted in 1969 that the first three Articles of the Continental Shelf Convention of 1958 were declaratory of customary law. In fact the practice of States in this sphere had only started in 1945 and remained sporadic until the early 1950s. The reality is that customary law can develop rapidly when the need arises. New custom depends upon the emergence of the practice of States which exhibits a substantial uniformity. The International Court has emphasized the complementary factors of generality and consistency[19].

The evidence of State practice consists of a variety of material sources, including diplomatic correspondence, policy statements, press releases, the published opinions of government legal advisers, manuals of military law, executive decisions and practices, recitals in treaties, and so forth[20].

The process of synthesizing State practice is assisted by several mechanisms. First, the resolutions of the General Assembly of the

18. *ICJ Reports 1969*, p. 3 at p. 39, para. 63.

19. *Asylum* case, *ICJ Reports 1950*, p. 266 at pp. 276-277 ; *North Sea Continental Shelf* cases, *ICJ Reports 1969*, p. 3 at p. 43, para. 74; *Nicaragua* v. *United States (Merits)*, *ICJ Reports 1986*, p. 14 at p. 98, para. 186. See further H. W. A. Thirlway, *British Year Book*, Vol. 61 (1990), pp. 54-75.

20. See K. Zemanek, "What is 'State Practice' and Who Makes It ?", *Festschrift für Rudolf Bernhardt*, Berlin, Springer-Verlag, 1995, p. 289.

United Nations, when they touch upon legal matters, constitute evidence of State practice. So also do resolutions of Conferences of Heads of States such as the Cairo Conference of 1964[21]. Similarly, the judgments of the International Court and other international tribunals have a role in the recognition and authentication of rules of customary law. Finally, the process of the making of international claims by one State against another constitutes an act of State practice[22]. The identification of what is practice for this purpose is not free from controversy. Hugh Thirlway, a thoughtful writer on customary law, has asserted that "the occasion of an act of State practice contributing to the formation of custom must always be some specific dispute or potential dispute"[23]. According to this view, statements of principle by States at codification conferences, or as comments on drafts prepared by rapporteurs of the International Law Commission, will not count as evidence of State practice for the purpose of assessing the generality of State practice.

The distinction on which Thirlway insists is not, in the ultimate analysis, convincing. The so-called "abstract" statements are often given more careful preparation than speedily drafted protest notes. The expressions of the views of Governments on legal questions are very varied in form and each form of evidence should be weighed on its particular merits. Indeed, Thirlway concedes that the so-called "assertions in the abstract" can be relied on as supplementary evidence[24].

The requirement of a pattern of State practice which exhibits a substantial uniformity is accompanied by a more complex criterion which insists that the State practice is accompanied by an *opinio juris*. Hudson described this as a "conception that the practice is

---

21. Case concerning the *Frontier Dispute (Burkina Faso/Republic of Mali)*, *ICJ Reports 1986*, p. 554 at pp. 565-566, para. 22.

22. See H. W. A. Thirlway, *British Year Book*, Vol. 61 (1990), p. 41.

23. H. W. A. Thirlway, *International Customary Law and Codification*, Leiden, A. W. Sijthoff, 1972, p. 58. See also Thirlway, *British Year Book*, Vol. 61 (1990), pp. 54-56.

24. *International Customary Law and Codification*, p. 58.

required by, or consistent with, prevailing international law". The Statute of the International Court of Justice refers to "international custom, as evidence of a general practice *accepted as law*" (Art. 38 (1) *(b)*)[25].

The element of *opinio juris* presents peculiar difficulties. If its presence were insisted on rigorously, no new custom could appear or, having appeared, achieve further elaboration. However, in practice the question of proof does not present as much difficulty as the writers have anticipated. In the first place, international tribunals recognize early developments in State practice without much fuss. Thus in the *North Sea* cases the Court referred to "emergent rules of customary international law"[26], a formulation which indicates a flexible approach to the criterion of *opinio juris*. In general the Court appears to be willing to assume the existence of an *opinio juris* on the basis of evidence of a general practice, or a consensus in the literature, or the previous decisions of the Court or other international tribunals.

However, there are certain situations in which the Court has applied a certain stringency in the matter of *opinio juris*. Two examples of this occasional rigour may be recalled. The first concerns the analysis by the Court in the *North Sea Continental Shelf* cases of the practice relating to the use of the equidistance method in continental shelf delimitation. The Court held that practice by States parties to the Geneva Convention could not count as evidence of custom:

> "To begin with, over half the States concerned, whether acting unilaterally or conjointly, were or shortly became parties to the Geneva Convention, and were therefore presumably, so far as they were concerned, acting actually or potentially in the application of the Convention. From their action no inference could legitimately be drawn as to the existence of a rule of customary international law in favour of the equidistance principle."[27]

---

25. H. W. A. Thirlway, *British Year Book*, Vol. 61 (1990), pp. 42-54.
26. *ICJ Reports 1969*, p. 39, para. 63 ; and p. 40, para. 66.
27. *Ibid.*, p. 43, para. 76.

The second example is the case of *Nicaragua* v. *United States*[28]. In that case the Court had (at the preliminary objections stage) postponed consideration of the multilateral treaty reservation in the United States acceptance of the compulsory jurisdiction of the Court by virtue of Article 36 (2) of the Statute. Nicaragua had relied on causes of action relating to the use of force by States based upon customary international law. It had also relied upon the relevant provisions of the United Nations Charter in this respect. The critical question then was: did the causes of action based upon custom escape the multilateral treaty reservation in spite of the fairly close relationship between the customary law and the relevant Charter provisions on this subject? The Court took the view that the reservation, which clearly applied to the United Nations Charter (as a multilateral treaty) did not extend to the customary law causes of action.

In the *Nicaragua* case the Court accepted the position argued for on behalf of Nicaragua that the Charter principles and the customary law principles were distinct and existed simultaneously, even although they had a close relationship both as to content and historical developments[29]. In this context it has been suggested by Thirlway[30] that the decision in the *Nicaragua* case was inconsistent with the earlier decision in the *North Sea Continental Shelf* cases. However, the latter was related to an area of law in which new rules were emerging and the relevance of *opinio juris* was placed in a significantly different milieu.

The other aspect of the decision of the Court in the Merits phase of the *Nicaragua* case which calls for attention is the way in which the Court applied the criterion of *opinio juris*. The Court took the unprecedented course of insisting on evidence that the particular formulations concerning the use of force and non-intervention must have been expressly consented to *by the two parties* in the form of votes at diplomatic conferences or in the General

28. *ICJ Reports 1986*, p. 14.
29. *Ibid.*, pp. 92-97, paras. 172-182.
30. *British Year Book*, Vol. 61 (1990), pp. 46-49.

Assembly of the United Nations[31]. It is sometimes suggested that the Court went out of its way to help the claimant State in the *Nicaragua* case. As counsel for Nicaragua, the lecturer finds such views difficult to accept. Thus in relation to the question of proof of *opinio juris* the Court's requirement of evidence of express consent to the relevant norms appears to have been unusually rigorous.

(ii) *General principles of law recognized by civilized nations*

This source is given express recognition in the Statute of the International Court and of its predecessor, the Permanent Court. In spite of this the source has not provided the explicit basis for any single decision of either the present Court or its predecessor[32]. The relevance of general principles of law varies considerably from one area of public international law to another. Thus, attempts to infuse general principles into the law of maritime delimitation have not received encouragement from the International Court. On the other hand, international tribunals have invoked municipal law concepts concerning evidence and procedure, areas in which it could not be expected to find assistance from State practice.

Whilst it is difficult to find decisions of international tribunals expressly based upon general principles of law, such principles often play a significant role as part of the legal reasoning in decisions. This was true, for example, of the decision in the *Barcelona Traction, Light and Power Company, Limited* case in the context of the legal personality of corporations and the position of shareholders[33]. In this context there may be considerable difficulty in the choice of the "correct" or "most relevant" legal analogy. In the *Corfu Channel* case (Merits)[34] an important element in the differ-

31. *ICJ Reports 1986*, pp. 98-101, paras. 187-190; pp. 106-107, paras. 202-204.

32. See the survey presented by H. W. A. Thirlway, *British Year Book*, Vol. 61 (1990), pp. 110-126.

33. *ICJ Reports 1970*, p. 4 at pp. 33-41, paras. 37-68.

34. *ICJ Reports 1949*, p. 4.

ences of approach among the Judges was the distinction between reliance upon fault liability *(culpa)* and objective responsibility[35]. There is, of course, a danger that decision-makers will fail to appreciate that the most relevant analogy is vicarious responsibility for the acts of employees or other agents, because the State, being a legal person, can only act through others. On this analogy the correct general approach is by way of the *relatively* strict form known as objective responsibility.

(iii) *Doctrine*

In the drafting of the majority judgments in collegiate courts, such as the International Court of Justice, references to specific doctrinal sources do not appear. But doctrine does play a role both in pleadings and also in the formation of judicial opinion. Thus the International Court will sometimes refer compendiously to "the writings of publicists"[36], and references will often be seen in the individual opinions of judges. National courts rely on textbooks to a greater extent than international tribunals, and there are practical reasons for this tendency.

(B) SPECIAL RELATIONS

The role of custom and the presumption that all States are bound by rules of customary law produce a generalized and majoritarian régime which, without some degree of flexibility, would produce an unacceptable uniformity and rigidity.

It therefore comes as no surprise that the law countenances the existence of various exceptions and variations, within appropriate limits, in the form of various special relations. These exceptions are based on various moral and policy considerations each of which is essentially compatible with the Rule of Law.

35. See the emphasis on the requirement of fault in some of the dissenting opinions: *ibid.*, p. 65 (Badawi Pasha), pp. 71-72 (Krylov), pp. 82-96 (Azevedo), pp. 127-128 (Ecer).

36. As in the *Nottebohm* case (Second Phase), *ICJ Reports 1955*, p. 4 at p. 22.

(i) *The persistent objector*

The Judgment of the Court in the *Anglo-Norwegian Fisheries* case provides the source, if not the phraseology, of the principle of the "persistent objector", that is, the State which continues to object to a new customary rule which is in the process of formation. In the relevant passage the Court said:

> "In any event, the ten-mile rule would appear to be inapplicable as against Norway, inasmuch as she has always opposed any attempt to apply it to the Norwegian coast." [37]

This mild qualification of the majoritarian principle has been recorded without much criticism by leading publicists [38]. The principle is well recognized by international tribunals and in the practice of States. The principle was applied, with considerable success, by the Government of Japan, in relation to new developments in the law of the sea concerning certain aspects of continental shelf and fisheries zones, in the period 1945 to 1977 [39].

(ii) *Recognition, acquiescence and opposability*

International tribunals have accepted and applied a group of concepts, based upon principles of good faith and equity, which include recognition, acquiescence and opposability. Perhaps the most basic of these is opposability. The literature of the law has not provided much intellectual elaboration of this concept but it has nevertheless found favour with tribunals. The idea behind opposability is that of good faith. The operation of opposability depends upon the existence of a status quo known to the claimant

---

37. *ICJ Reports 1951*, p. 116 at p. 131.

38. See the views of G. G. Fitzmaurice, *Recueil des cours*, Vol. 92 (1957-II), pp. 99-101; C. H. M. Waldock, *ibid.*, Vol. 106 (1962-II), pp. 49-50; M. Sørensen, *ibid.*, Vol. 101 (1960-III), pp. 43-44; M. Akehurst, *British Year Book*, Vol. 47 (1974-1975), pp. 24-27; and E. Jiménez de Aréchaga, *Recueil des cours*, Vol. 159 (1978-I), p. 30. For a more sceptical view, see J. I. Charney, *British Year Book*, Vol. 56 (1985), p. 1.

39. See Shigeru Oda and Hisashi Owada, *Japanese Journal of International Law*, Vol. 28 (1985), pp. 94-122.

which the claimant appears to accept by avoiding protest or other inconsistent conduct.

The essence of the matter is a level of tacit or apparent recognition by conduct which leads to the status quo thus recognized becoming opposable to the claimant or proponent State. The principle was applied by the Court in the *Anglo-Norwegian Fisheries* case thus:

> "The United Kingdom Government has argued that the Norwegian system of delimitation was not known to it and that the system therefore lacked the notoriety essential to provide the basis of an historical title enforceable against it. The Court is unable to accept this view. As a coastal State on the North Sea, greatly interested in the fisheries in this area, as a maritime Power traditionally concerned with the law of the seas, *the United Kingdom could not have been ignorant of the Decree of 1869 which had at once provoked a request for explanations by the French Government*. Nor, knowing of it, could it have been under any misapprehensions as to the significance of its terms, which clearly described it as constituting the application of a system. The same observation applies *a fortiori* to the Decree of 1889 relating to the delimitation of Romsdal and Nordmore which must have appeared to the United Kingdom as a reiterated manifestation of the Norwegian practice.
>
> The Court notes that in respect of a situation which could only be strengthened with the passage of time, the United Kingdom Government refrained from formulating reservations.
>
> The notoriety of the facts, the general toleration of the international community, Great Britain's position in the North Sea, her own interest in the question, and her prolonged abstention would in any case warrant Norway's enforcement of her system against the United Kingdom."[40]

Essentially similar elements appear in the Judgments in the case concerning the *Arbitral Award Made by the King of Spain on 23 December 1906* and in the *Temple of Preah Vihear* case (Merits). In the *Arbitral Award* case the Court stated emphatically that "it is no longer open to Nicaragua to go back upon that recognition and to challenge the validity of the Award"[41], and in the *Temple* case the

40. *ICJ Reports 1951*, pp. 138-139, emphasis added.

41. *ICJ Reports 1960*, p. 213.

Court observed that "it is not now open to Thailand . . . to deny that she was ever a consenting party to [the settlement]"[42].

(iii) *Estoppel or preclusion*

The principle of estoppel (or preclusion) is similar to acquiescence and therefore a clear and consistent acceptance is required. However, estoppel *stricto sensu* is distinguished from acquiescence by the element of detriment or prejudice caused by a State's attitude: see the views of the Court in the *North Sea* cases[43] and the views of the Chamber in the *Gulf of Maine* case[44].

(iv) *Local custom*

The bilateral relations of States may be determined to some extent by the existence of a local custom. In the *Right of Passage* case[45], the issue raised concerned the existence of a local custom establishing a right of passage over Indian territory between territorial enclaves of Portugal inland from the Portuguese port of Daman. In this type of case the general law is to be varied and the claimant of the special right must provide affirmative proof of a sense of legal obligation on the part of the territorial sovereign.

(C) THE RELATION OF TREATIES TO GENERAL INTERNATIONAL LAW

A recurring problem is the relationship of multilateral conventions and customary international law. The impact of multilateral treaties on the content of customary law varies but is undeniable[46].

---

42. *ICJ Reports 1962*, p. 32.

43. *ICJ Reports 1969*, p. 26, para. 30.

44. *Delimitation of the Maritime Boundary in the Gulf of Maine Area, ICJ Reports 1984*, p. 309, para. 145.

45. Case concerning the *Right of Passage over Indian Territory, ICJ Reports 1960*, p. 6.

46. See the valuable discussion by H. W. A. Thirlway, *British Year Book*, Vol. 61 (1990), pp. 87-102.

Three situations may be envisaged. First, a multilateral treaty may be a more or less straightforward codification of the customary law in a given field. A standard example is the High Seas Convention of 1958 in which the preamble states that it was adopted as "generally declaratory of established principles of international law". Moreover, in the case concerning *United States Diplomatic and Consular Staff in Tehran*[47], the Court treated the Vienna Conventions on Diplomatic and Consular Relations as codifications of pre-existing obligations under general international law.

Secondly, a multilateral standard-setting treaty may contradict existing principles of customary law. Such a treaty may nevertheless provide the basis for new directions in State practice and a change in the customary law.

Thirdly, a multilateral treaty may appear in temporal terms as part of a process of development in customary law which is incomplete. This was essentially the situation in the *North Sea Continental Shelf* cases, in which the Court recognized that the first three Articles of the Continental Shelf Convention of 1958 reflected "received or at least emergent rules of customary international law"[48], whilst regarding Article 6 (on delimitation) as "a purely conventional rule"[49], which had not been confirmed sufficiently by subsequent practice as a customary rule[50].

(D) JUDICIAL REASONING AND JUDICIAL LEGISLATION

In any formal description of the sources of international law "judicial legislation" would not figure, and yet important sectors of the law, and especially the law of the sea, have been affected by what was, in effect, judicial legislation. In the *Anglo-Norwegian Fisheries* case[51] the Court applied the existing principle of the low-

---

47. *ICJ Reports 1980*, p. 3 at p. 31, para. 62.
48. *ICJ Reports 1969*, p. 39, para. 63.
49. *Ibid.*, pp. 37-41, paras. 60-69.
50. *Ibid.*, pp. 41-46, paras. 60-82.
51. *ICJ Reports 1951*, p. 116.

water mark as the basis for delimitation of the territorial sea, but accepted the legality of the Norwegian system of straight baselines. In so doing the Court rejected the view that Norway was claiming recognition of an exceptional case: "all that the Court can see therein is the application of general international law to a specific case".[52] It is clear that what was involved was a process of creative judicial reasoning which amounted to "judicial legislation". The proof of this includes the evident desire of the Court to demonstrate that other North Sea States had accepted the Norwegian system[53].

A much more radical example of judicial legislation is provided by the *North Sea Continental Shelf* cases[54]. Before this decision there had been some indeterminate references to "equitable principles" in State practice[55], and the famous progenitor, the Truman Proclamation of 1945, had stated that:

> "In cases where the continental shelf extends to the shores of another State, or is shared with an adjacent State, the boundary shall be determined by the United States and the State concerned in accordance with equitable principles."

The decision in the *North Sea* cases does not purport to reflect pre-existing principles or a pattern of State practice, although the Court makes a certain claim to a reflection of "the *opinio juris* in the matter of delimitation". The key paragraph in the Judgment is as follows:

> "It emerges from the history of the development of the legal régime of the continental shelf, which has been reviewed earlier, that the essential reason why the equidistance method is not to be regarded as a rule of law is that, if it were to be compul-

52. *ICJ Reports 1951*, p. 131.

53. *Ibid.*, pp. 136-139. See further G. G. Fitzmaurice, *British Year Book*, Vol. 30 (1953), pp. 8-26.

54. *ICJ Reports 1969*, p. 4.

55. See, for example, the "Truman" Proclamation, 1945, *American Journal of International Law*, Vol. 40 (1946), p. 4; the Saudi Arabian Royal Proclamation of 28 May 1949, *British and Foreign State Papers*, Vol. 155, p. 866; and the Bahrain Proclamation of 5 June 1949, *American Journal of International Law*, Vol. 43 (1949), Suppl., p. 185.

sorily applied in all situations, this would not be consonant with certain basic legal notions which, as has been observed in paragraphs 48 and 55, have from the beginning reflected the *opinio juris* in the matter of delimitation; those principles being that delimitation must be the object of agreement between the States concerned, and that such agreement must be arrived at in accordance with equitable principles. On a foundation of very general precepts of justice and good faith, actual rules of law are here involved which govern the delimitation of adjacent continental shelves — that is to say, rules binding upon States for all delimitations; — in short, it is not a question of applying equity simply as a matter of abstract justice, but of applying a rule of law which itself requires the application of equitable principles, in accordance with the ideas which have always underlined the development of the legal régime of the continental shelf in this field, namely:

(a) the parties are under an obligation to enter into negotiations with a view to arriving at an agreement, and not merely to go through a formal process of negotiation as a sort of prior condition for the automatic application of a certain method of delimitation in the absence of agreement; they are under an obligation so to conduct themselves that the negotiations are meaningful, which will not be the case when either of them insists upon its own position without contemplating any modification of it;

(b) the parties are under an obligation to act in such a way that, in the particular case, and taking all the circumstances into account, equitable principles are applied, — for this purpose the equidistance method can be used, but other methods exist and may be employed, alone or in combination, according to the areas involved;

(c) for the reasons given in paragraphs 43 and 44, the continental shelf of any State must be the natural prolongation of its land territory and must not encroach upon what is the natural prolongation of the territory of another State." [56]

This is, by any standards, a remarkable exercise in law-making. The Court relies upon "certain basic legal notions" rather than a

56. *ICJ Reports 1969*, pp. 46-67, para. 85; and see also p. 46, para. 83.

survey of actual practice, and it is essentially a process of judicial reasoning which leads to the rejection of "the equidistance principle" in favour of the "equitable principles". And the latter are described as the consequence "of applying a rule of law" [57]. Whilst the development of a viable régime of equitable principles *infra legem* is still proceeding, few lawyers have sought to challenge the general approach adopted by the Court in the *North Sea* cases.

The work of the International Court demonstrates very clearly the extent to which legal reasoning can be used to regulate and to channel principles already accepted as a part of customary law. The decision in the *North Sea* cases, like that in the *Anglo-Norwegian Fisheries* case, shows to what extent judicial reasoning provides the necessary refinement of positivist materials. It is in this general setting that the Court in the *North Sea* cases affirmed by implication that a concept, in this case that of the continental shelf, may crystallize in a first stage, even although the basic elements thus recognized need a consequential apparatus of rules dealing with related problems, such as delimitation of the shelf areas of opposite or adjacent States.

It is well recognized that the law of the sea provides the experience which contradicts the assumption that customary law is a conservative force. As the jurisprudence indicates, the Court has been prepared to act as patron to *débutant* or "emergent" rules of customary law [58].

Given the significance of developments in customary law since 1945, it was inevitable that the Court had to face the situation in which the issues raised by an Application were related to an area of general international law in a period of rapid change. This was the background to the *Fisheries Jurisdiction (United Kingdom* v. *Iceland)* case [59]. In these proceedings the United Kingdom asked

57. See also *ICJ Reports 1969*, p. 48, para. 88.

58. See the Judgments in the *North Sea* cases, *ICJ Reports 1969*, pp. 38-39, para. 63; and the *Fisheries Jurisdiction* case *(United Kingdom* v. *Iceland)*, *ICJ Reports 1974*, pp. 22-27, paras. 49-60 (and see also the *Fisheries Jurisdiction* case *(Federal Republic of Germany* v. *Iceland)*, *ibid.*, pp. 191-196, paras. 41-52).

59. *ICJ Reports 1974*, p. 3.

for a declaration that the Icelandic claim to extend its fisheries jurisdiction, by establishing a zone extending to 50 nautical miles from the base-lines, had no foundation in international law. Already in this period a number of States had similar claims. The Court could not afford to declare a *non liquet* on the basis of the uncertainty of the customary law, and, in any case, the Court rested its decision on the Exchange of Notes of 1961 and thus held that the Icelandic extension of fishing rights was "not opposable to the Government of the United Kingdom" [60].

This finding did not, however, avoid some elements of confusion in the Court's treatment of general international law. On the one hand the Judgment affirmed that the extension of a fishery zone up to a 12-mile limit "appears now to be generally accepted" [61], and insisted that the Court could not anticipate possible future developments [62]. But, on the other hand, the Court avoided finding that the Icelandic claim had no foundation in customary law and introduced elements in the *dispositif* akin to an exercise in conciliation. The result was a legal twilight. Judge Onyeama pointed out that the Court's finding in favour of a 12-mile limit for a fishery zone indicated a conclusion that the Icelandic claim was contrary to general international law [63]. The form of the *dispositif* caused no little confusion in the public forum and Sir Gerald Fitzmaurice, in a letter to the press, expressed the view that "the Court failed to find in any definite terms that Iceland's 50-mile claim either was or was not contrary to general international law . . ." [64].

(E) THE POLITICS OF THE SOURCES OF INTERNATIONAL LAW

The standard principles relating to the sources of general international law conceal some political questions. The *modus operandi* for the formation of customary law supposes an equality of States

60. *ICJ Reports 1974*, pp. 22-29, and see in particular at p. 29, para. 68.

61. *Ibid.*, p. 23, para. 52.

62. *Ibid.*, pp. 23-24, para. 53.

63. *ICJ Reports 1974*, p. 171, para. 17. See also the dissenting opinion of Judge Gros, *ibid.*, p. 135, para. 15.

64. *The Times*, 13 September 1974.

and also a principle of majoritarianism. A certain amount of contracting out is possible but the generality of States are permitted by their conduct to develop customary rules. On the same basis, more or less, new States and new régimes, like the Soviet Government of 1917, are subjected to existing rules of general international law.

This approach to international law creates problems for those who hold that inequalities of power between States should be reflected in the way in which the law is made and applied, and this involves what may be called the hegemonial approach to law-making. The hegemonial approach to international relations may be defined as an approach to the sources which facilitates the translation of the difference in power between States into specific advantages for the more powerful actor. The hegemonial approach to the sources involves maximizing the occasions when the powerful actor will obtain "legal approval" for its actions and minimizing the occasions when such approach may be conspicuously withheld.

The hegemonial approach will necessarily favour the decisions of the Security Council, especially in the present constellation of world politics. It will tend not to favour institutions like the International Court, which cannot be controlled by a small group of States as in the new "trilateral Security Council". In this hegemonial framework the resolutions of the General Assembly, however broadly supported, count for little or nothing. Positivism, which favours the majoritarian approach to the formation of custom, is replaced by a new form of natural law. This natural law depends upon reference to political "context", and the seeking out of "legal formulations that are attended by the requisite political force to make them effective". These revolutionary criteria appear in the review by Professor Reisman [65] of the ninth edition of *Oppenheim's Inter-*

65. *Yale Journal of International Law*, Vol. 19 (1994), p. 255 at pp. 273-274. See also W. Michael Reisman, *European Journal of International Law*, Vol. 5 (1994), p. 120 at pp. 122-123.

national Law (Vol. 1, *Peace*) [66]. On the basis of such normative alchemy it becomes relatively easy to explain discrimination between one State and another in the application of the law. It is the "context" which makes the difference and this includes elements which, it is to be supposed, justify the discrimination.

A special department of the hegemonial approach is that the primary instruments of hegemony — the use of threat or armed force — should not be subjected to judicial scrutiny. In short, they are not justiciable [67]. The recent work of the International Law Commission concerning countermeasures raised the same issue: the Draft Articles involve the decisions of the Security Council in the allocation of responsibility [68].

After these gloomy asides, it is as well to end this passage on sources by reference to the positive role which general international law plays in the process of dispute settlement. This positive role is particularly prominent in the law of the sea and the resolution of issues relating to title to territory. Customary (or general) international law remains the only universal cement of the system.

66. See footnote 13, *supra.*

67. See W. Michael Reisman, *Yale Journal of International Law*, Vol. 19 (1994), pp. 273, 278. It is not a view widely shared by other publicists. But it was the view of the United States Department of State in 1985 relating to the *Nicaragua* case: see the Statement of 18 January 1985, *International Legal Materials*, Vol. 24 (1985), pp. 261-263.

68. See D. W. Bowett, *European Journal of International Law*, Vol. 5 (1994), p. 89 at p. 98.

CHAPTER III

THE SUBJECTS OF INTERNATIONAL LAW

The third and final preliminary topic is concerned with the subjects of international law.

(A) INTRODUCTION

The classical definition of a subject of the law is that it is an entity capable of possessing rights and duties under international law and having the capacity to maintain its rights by making international claims. This definition is unfortunately circular because the indicia referred to depend on the existence of a legal person. Broadly speaking, there are two situations to be distinguished. First, customary law recognizes certain entities as *capable* of possessing rights and duties, and of making international claims, and the legal personality will automatically confer the apparatus of rights and duties. States, and, in certain circumstances, units of self-determination, are the only types of person falling within this class.

The second type of situation covers entities not qualified by customary law as within the first class of entity, but which have legal personality of a restricted kind, dependent upon the agreement or acquiescence of recognized legal persons from the first class and opposable on the international plane only to those agreeing or acquiescent. An example of this situation is provided by the readiness of non-Member States to grant legal privileges and immunities to international organizations of which they are not members.

In any event there is a variety of subjects of international law and a list of types will provide a helpful reminder. Established legal persons have in the course of the twentieth century included the following:

(1) States, and political entities legally proximate to States, like the Free City of Danzig.
(2) Condominia, such as the Anglo-French condominium in respect of the New Hebrides.
(3) Intergovernmental organizations, including the United Nations, the Organization of American States, and the Organization of African Unity.
(4) Units of self-determination, that is, non-self-governing peoples.

(i) *The indicia of legal personality*

The indicia of legal personality are generally recognized as including

First: a capacity to make treaties.

Secondly: a capacity to present international claims by diplomatic procedures or in other available forms.

Thirdly: a liability for the consequences of breaches of international law.

Fourthly: privileges and immunities in relation to the national jurisdictions of States.

It is not necessary, of course, that an entity should bear all these indicia.

(ii) *The paradigm is the State itself*

The standard type of legal person in international law remains the State itself and it is therefore logical that it is the State which provides the legal paradigm against which other legal persons are measured. Aspiring liberation movements and governments in exile adopt the goal of statehood. The existence of hybrid models, including federal unions and economic communities, does not appear to make any substantial change in the picture.

(B) THE STATE

(i) *The historical role of statehood*

There is currently a theoretical assault on sovereignty as a political and legal concept and an aspect of this involves an attack on the concept of statehood. During the 88th Annual Meeting of the American Society one of the Theme Panels was devoted to the topic: "The End of Sovereignty?" Much of the discussion consisted of criticism of the role of States in human affairs[69].

The problem with this is, quite simply, that for the foreseeable future the State is the only available public order system. Like the motor car, the State can be the agency for the commission of crimes but this is not really a good reason for discarding the State in the absence of some alternative working model. It is relevant to recall that some of the world's examples of human rights abuses and refugee flows in the recent past have involved the *collapse* of States.

The criticisms of statehood to be found in recent debates are by no means impressive. It is said, for example, that States do not give adequate recognition to the rights of women or the status of indigenous peoples. This is probably true but the collapse of State authority is highly unlikely to enhance the rights of any class of person, however defined. The debate, in my view, should focus upon the *conditions* in which State power is exercised, in other words the Rule of Law.

(ii) *Criteria of statehood*

What are the criteria of statehood, the conditions of its legal existence? The question is one of mixed fact and law. In the first place a State consists of a community of citizens with a stable territorial base. But it is well established that the frontiers do not have to be determined provided there *is* a stable territorial base.

---

69. American Society of International Law, *Proceedings of the 88th Annual Meeting*, Washington, 1994, pp. 71-87.

The recognition of the reconstituted Poland in 1918 provides a good example and there are many States whose existence is undoubted in spite of substantial disputes relating to their boundaries.

Secondly, it is axiomatic that a State has a population, however small. Thirdly, the State must have an effective government. Finally, the entity claiming statehood must be independent. This last criterion is the most important but involves substantial difficulties of application. In practice certain conventions have been observed and high levels of foreign influence have commonly been ignored provided that no actual annexation had taken place. Good examples of this policy are the status of the States of Eastern Europe within the former Soviet bloc. With the sole exception of East Germany such States were accorded recognition by, for example, the Member States of NATO.

In this recital of criteria the question of recognition has been left on one side, and it must be recalled that illegal usurpation of power as a result of foreign invasion will not cause the demise of a State, although it will compromise its enjoyment of the incidents of statehood within a part or the whole of its own territory.

The application of the criteria involves certain modalities based upon sound legal policy. These modalities are as follows:

(1) Once established, a State is presumed to continue in existence (cf. the Congo, as it then was, in 1960-1964).

(2) Statehood cannot be founded upon the illegal use or threat of force (cf. the cases of "Manchoukuo", 1932 (created under Japanese auspices); "Croatia", 1941 (created under German auspices); and the "Turkish Republic of Northern Cyprus", 1983 (created under Turkish auspices).

    This prescription results from independent considerations of international public order.

(3) Statehood cannot be terminated by the illegal use or threat of force (cf. Estonia, 1940; Poland, 1939; and Kuwait, 1990).

There are, however, some difficult problems when reinstatement of independence occurs a considerable time after the original intervention.

(iii) *The bases of statehood*

It is useful next to look briefly at the very varied factual and political *sources* of statehood. It is impossible to provide a complete catalogue but the following list is representative:

(1) Forcible secession, as in the case of Texas in 1840, or Israel in 1948.
(2) Peaceful secession or decolonization with the agreement of the former sovereign.
(3) A process of multilateral decision-making, for example by the Allied and Associated Powers at the end of the First World War. The results were contained in the Peace Treaties of 1919-1920.
(4) A voluntary union of States, as in the case of the United Arab Republic in 1958-1961.
(5) Dissolution of a union by agreement, as in the recent case of Czechoslovakia.
(6) United Nations action in supervising the process of self-determination, particularly in relation to Trusteeships as, for example, in the case of Tanganyika (1961) and Nauru (1968). In the case of Libyan independence (1951) the United Nations General Assembly acted for the most part by virtue of powers delegated to it in the provisions of the Italian Peace Treaty[70].
(7) A process of gradual political transition, as in the case of Egypt in the period 1922 to 1954, which was a product of a complex political history[71].

(C) PEOPLES AND UNITS OF SELF-DETERMINATION

Having examined the State as a legal person it is necessary to move on to the legal personality of peoples as units of self-deter-

---

70. Marjorie M. Whiteman, *Digest*, Vol. II, Washington, USGPO, 1963, pp. 198-200; J. Crawford, *The Creation of States in International Law*, Oxford, Clarendon Press, 1979, pp. 325-326, 330-332.

71. See L. Oppenheim, *International Law*, Vol. I, *Peace*, 8th ed. by H. Lauterpacht, London, 1955, p. 189; P. J. Vatikiotis, *The History of Modern Egypt*, 4th ed., London, 1991.

mination. The principle of nationalities, the earlier version of the principle of self-determination, is a political and moral principle going back to the eighteenth century. It featured prominently in the history of nineteenth-century Europe and was deployed extensively by the Allied Powers in 1918 as a basis for the demolition of the Austro-Hungarian and Ottoman Empires. Whilst this deployment was not very consistent, it gave self-determination an ineradicable prominence on the political landscape.

Until recently, and with some justification, lawyers in the West assumed that the principle of self-determination had no *legal* content. Developments in the era of the United Nations Charter have changed the picture considerably and it is now anachronistic to assert that self-determination is no longer recognized in general international law[72]. The United Nations Charter gave a somewhat generalized recognition to "the principle of equal rights and self-determination of peoples" as one of the purposes of the United Nations, but did not establish an unambiguous link between the principle and a right of secession and independence.

However, in the practice of the United Nations General Assembly, and therefore of the majority of the Member States, it has been recognized that the principle of self-determination applies to "all peoples and nations".

Two major developments may be recalled in this connection. In 1960 the General Assembly adopted the Declaration on the Granting of Independence to Colonial Countries and Peoples (resolution 1514 (XV))[73]. The resolution, if its language be carefully examined, is not confined to colonial situations, and applies to all dependent peoples[74]. It is thus not surprising that the General Assembly resolutions confirming the right of the Palestinian people to self-determination refer to resolution 1514 (XV)[75], or that the United Kingdom recognizes that the principle applies to

72. See Antonio Cassese, *Self-determination of Peoples*, Cambridge University Press, 1995, pp. 126-127.

73. Marjorie M. Whiteman, *Digest*, Vol. XIII, Washington, USGPO, 1968, pp. 701-768.

74. For a different construction see Antonio Cassesse, *op. cit.*, pp. 71-74.

75. See General Assembly resolution 2787 (XXVI), 6 December 1971.

the situation in Northern Ireland. The Declaration regards the principle of self-determination as a part of the obligations deriving from the United Nations Charter. Moreover, it is not a "recommendation" but is expressed in the form of an authoritative interpretation of the Charter[76].

The second major development was the appearance of a common provision in the two International Covenants on Human Rights adopted by the General Assembly on 16 December 1966. Article 1, paragraph 1, of each Covenant provides as follows:

> "All peoples have the right to self-determination. By virtue of that right they freely determine their political status and freely pursue their economic, social and cultural development."

The principle has now been accepted by a majority of States, including the United Kingdom[77].

It is against this background that the Advisory Opinion of the International Court relating to the *Western Sahara* confirmed "the validity of the principle of self-determination" in the context of general international law[78]. The principle also receives affirmation in the *Namibia* Opinion of 1971[79], and in the Judgment in the *East Timor* case[80].

(i) *Problems of application*

The general recognition of the principle of self-determination is one thing, its implementation is another. A considerable agenda of problems remains open. The first problem is that of identifying peoples as units of self-determination. There is no agreement on the precise criteria to be employed in the process of identification.

---

76. See the authoritative view of C. H. M. Waldock, *Recueil des cours*, Vol. 106 (1962-II), p. 33.

77. See, for example, G. Marston, *British Year Book*, Vol. 52 (1981), pp. 386-388 (*in re* the Falkland Islands and the Palestinians).

78. *ICJ Reports 1975*, p. 12 at pp. 31-33, paras. 54-59.

79. *Legal Consequences for States of the Continued Presence of South Africa in Namibia (South West Africa) notwithstanding Security Council Resolution 276 (1970)*, *ICJ Reports 1971*, p. 16 at pp. 31-32, paras. 52-53.

80. *ICJ Reports 1995*, p. 90 at p. 102, para. 29.

However, there has been a long catalogue of situations in which the majority of States had no difficulty in identifying the relevant unit of self-determination. The case of the independence of Namibia provides an illustration of the process. In this context it is to be noted that the procedure of recognition, and, in particular, collective recognition in the form of resolutions by the political organs of the United Nations, has had a major role to play[81]. In other cases, such as the independence of Bangladesh in 1971, the collective recognition of States, acting individually, has legitimated the political change. Thus in practice the problems of implementation are solved without too much difficulty. At the same time there can be no doubt that serious problems of implementation remain. The territory of the former Yugoslavia and also that of the new Russia present the major problems resulting from the disintegration of multi-national federations. Neither international law nor municipal law provides a procedure for peaceful disintegration when national groups within a federal State find themselves as minorities, unrecognized as such within the succession States.

In the procedural context of litigation, even the *erga omnes* character of the principle of self-determination will not help it to overcome the limitations of jurisdiction on the basis of consent. As the International Court explained in its Judgment in the *East Timor* case:

> "In the Court's view, Portugal's assertion that the right of peoples to self-determination, as it evolved from the Charter and from United Nations practice, has an *erga omnes* character, is irreproachable. The principle of self-determination of peoples has been recognized by the United Nations Charter and in the jurisprudence of the Court . . .; it is one of the essential principles of contemporary international law. However, the Court considers that the *erga omnes* character of a norm and the rule of consent to jurisdiction are two different things. Whatever the nature of the obligations invoked, the Court could not rule on the lawfulness of the conduct of a State when its judgment would imply an evalua-

---

81. See John Dugard, *Recognition and the United Nations*, Cambridge, Grotius, 1987.

tion of the lawfulness of the conduct of another State which is not a party to the case. Where this is so, the Court cannot act, even if the right in question is *erga omnes*." [82]

In another procedural context, the United Nations Human Rights Committee, the claim of self-determination was denied to an individual. The Communication concerned was *Ominayak and the Lubicon Lake Band* v. *Canada* [83]. This case was submitted by Chief Ominayak as the leader of the Lubicon Lake Band, a band of Cree Indians. The HRC described the band as a "self-identified, relatively autonomous, socio-cultural and economic group", whose "members have continuously inhabited, hunted, trapped and fished in a large area encompassing approximately 10,000 square kilometres in northern Alberta since time immemorial".

The communication complained of violations of Article 1 of the Covenant in the denial of the right of self-determination and the right of members of the band to dispose freely of their natural wealth and resources.

In its decision on the admissibility of the claim the HRC stated:

"that the author, as an individual, could not claim under the Optional Protocol to be a victim of a violation of the right of self-determination enshrined in Article 1 of the Covenant, which deals with the rights conferred on peoples, as such".

A further question concerns a debate arising from the insistence by certain jurists that the principle of self-determination is confined to the "colonial agenda" and is inapplicable otherwise [84]. An exponent of a related standpoint is Professor Thomas Franck [85].

Professor Franck underestimates the general impact of the

82. *ICJ Reports 1995*, p. 102, para. 29.

83. 26 March 1990, *International Law Reports*, Vol. 96, p. 667.

84. For this viewpoint see M. Shaw, *Title to Territory in Africa*, Oxford, Clarendon Press, 1986, pp. 59-144; R. Higgins, *Problems and Process*, Oxford, Clarendon Press, 1994, pp. 111-128.

85. *Recueil des cours*, Vol. 240 (1993-III), pp. 129-149. See also Thomas M. Franck, *Fairness in International Law and Institutions*, Oxford, Clarendon Press, 1995, pp. 149-169.

practice of the political organs of the United Nations (and therefore of States generally) in matters of self-determination. However, he reformulates the issue in the following way:

> "At stake is *not* whether a right of self-determination has survived the end of the era of decolonization. The clear textual evidence of the Covenants and the Helsinki Accord places that beyond serious dispute. Less clear, however, is whether self-determination in the new post-colonial context continues to validate a right of secession . . ." [86]

Professor Franck's answer to this question is that there is no such right of secession for what he calls "minorities". But the evidence he adduces for this view is very thin. Professor Franck also argues that the principle of self-determination is at least to some extent in tension with the principle of *uti possidetis*. This reasoning is not easy to follow. The principle of *uti possidetis* is very specialized in its function. It provides simply that a succession of States, in the form of decolonization or otherwise, does not *as such* affect the boundaries of the political units involved in the process of change. The principle is without prejudice to the principle of self-determination, and is neutral in relation to it.

At the end of the day it seems odd to assert, as some colleagues do, that there is a high quality and on-going right to "democratic governance" but no right to secession. It is very clear that the right to self-determination in relation to colonialism involved a right of secession in nearly all cases. Does it not seem very inconsistent to accord such a right to the people of India or Zimbabwe, but not to Kurds or Palestinians or the peoples of the former Yugoslavia, simply because, according to a conventional and transient political vocabulary, these groups are not "colonial peoples"?

At this point it is necessary to address an issue which is ignored by many of the recent discussions of self-determination. The principle confers a right which remains amorphous until there is an entitlement, and the link between the two is the "unit of self-determination". This depends, as in the case of statehood, upon a

86. *Recueil des cours*, *supra* footnote 85, p. 140; *Fairness in International Law and Institutions*, p. 158.

mixture of essence and of acceptance by existing legal persons. The essence is the existence of a population attached by residence and cultural history to a finite territorial area. If the population claims self-determination and is recognized as a unit of self-determination by States, acting individually or collectively, then the *right* of self-determination is to that extent certified, even if the territorial sovereign is reluctant to implement the right.

The process of recognition and certification involves procedures similar to those employed in relation to the creation of States and, indeed, in many cases is closely related to the creation of new States. The following processes have been commonly employed since the inception of the United Nations:

(1) Collective recognition in the form of affirmative votes for General Assembly resolutions recognizing a unit of self-determination.
(2) Collective recognition in the form of a plurilateral treaty which stipulates that a territory is to be regarded as a unit of self-determination, followed by the acquiescence of States not parties to the original treaty. The Treaty of Peace with Italy which fostered the independence of Libya (in 1951)[87] and the package of Treaties out of which emerged the Republic of Cyprus (in 1960) provide useful examples of this process[88].
(3) A forcible secession may acquire *ex post facto* recognition as a unit of self-determination in the form of multiple (but unilateral) acts of recognition from existing States, as in the cases of Indonesia (1949), Vietnam (1948), Bangladesh (1971), and Guinea-Bissau (1973)[89]. The case of Bangladesh is particularly instructive because the evident legitimacy of East Bengal as a unit of self-determination was generally accepted in spite of the intervention by Indian forces.

---

87. Marjorie M. Whiteman, Vol. II, Washington, USGPO, 1963, pp. 198-200; J. Crawford, *The Creation of States in International Law*, Oxford, Clarendon Press, pp. 325-326, 330-332.

88. Marjorie M. Whiteman, *op. cit., supra* footnote 87, pp. 149-151.

89. See generally J. Crawford, *op. cit., supra* footnote 87, pp. 247-266.

(4) Conversely, the process of collective recognition may operate to deny recognition and certification to entities proposed as units of self-determination which lack authenticity as a result of foreign intervention or their association with a process of "ethnic cleansing". Such recognition was accordingly denied to the so-called "Bantustans" created by South Africa [90] and to the "Turkish Republic of Northern Cyprus" [91].

(5) Recognition or confirmation of the validity of a unit of self-determination may be granted by the International Court of Justice. Whilst it did not form part of the task given to the Court by the General Assembly, in the *Western Sahara* Advisory Opinion the International Court examined the process by which the Assembly had administered the right of the people of Western Sahara to self-determination [92]. Again, in its Judgment in the *East Timor* case, the Court confirmed the status of East Timor as a non-self-governing territory, the people of which "has the right to self-determination" [93].

In the final analysis it is the process by which units of self-determination are validated which is all-important. There can be no question that the right of self-determination is not confined to the so-called colonial agenda. The right inheres in "all peoples" [94]. The problem of definition is in most cases solved by a procedure of recognition and validation. This factor reduces the likelihood of instability and the operation of the principle of self-determination overlaps to a considerable degree with the normal political agenda relating to the formation of new States.

It is against this background that it can be appreciated that

90. See John Dugard, *op. cit., supra* footnote 81, pp. 98-108.

91. See Security Council resolution 541 (1983), adopted on 18 November 1983; and John Dugard, *supra* footnote 81, pp. 108-111.

92. *ICJ Reports 1975*, pp. 31-37, paras. 54-73.

93. *ICJ Reports 1995*, p. 103, para. 31.

94. This position appears to be accepted by the following sources: E. Jiménez de Aréchaga, *Recueil des cours*, Vol. 159 (1978-I), pp. 100-107; J. Crawford, *The Creation of States in International Law*, Oxford, Clarendon Press, 1979, pp. 91-102; Tomuschat, in C. Tomuschat (ed.), *Modern Law of Self-determination of Peoples*, Cambridge UP, 1995, pp. 90-99.

there is no "automatic" right of secession by ethnic or religious groups, no more than there is an "automatic" right to statehood. In this connection the alleged antithesis between territorial integrity and the right of self-determination lacks reality[95].

(D) MINORITIES

Article 27 of the International Covenant on Civil and Political Rights provides as follows:

> "In those States in which ethnic, religious or linguistic minorities exist, persons belonging to such minorities shall not be denied the right, in community with the other members of their group, to enjoy their own culture, to profess and practise their own religion, or to use their own language."

The rights of minorities[96] are generally seen as an aspect of the rights of *individuals* to certain standards of treatment. In the *Ominayak* case[97] the United Nations Human Rights Committee showed a marked reluctance to recognize group rights as such. Whilst it is clear that not all groups qualifying as "minorities" will constitute also units of self-determination, there is no reason why, in certain conditions, a minority should not simply constitute a unit of self-determination, particularly if the group are the habitual residents of a specific area.

(E) INDIGENOUS PEOPLES

Within the United Nations a Working Group has been formulating a Draft Declaration on the Rights of Indigenous Peoples[98]. The Draft formulates standards of protection specific to the con-

---

95. Cf. Antonio Cassese, *op. cit.*, *supra* footnote 72, pp. 110-111.

96. See generally Patrick Thornberry, *International Law and the Rights of Minorities*, Oxford, Clarendon Press, 1991; Warwick McKean, *Equality and Discrimination under International Law*, Oxford, Clarendon Press, 1983.

97. See footnote 83, *supra*.

98. See the Draft Declaration adopted in 1994: *International Legal Materials*, Vol. 34 (1995), p. 546.

dition of indigenous peoples. No definition is offered. Article 3 of the Draft provides, in vague terms, that indigenous peoples have the right to self-determination[99]. The endemic problem is, of course, the overlap of indigenous peoples and the concept of minorities. Moreover, not all indigenous peoples constitute units of self-determination.

(F) INDIVIDUALS

The question of individuals in the scheme of things is more appropriately considered within the framework of human rights protection. In strict analytical terms it still cannot be said that the individual *per se* is a subject of international law. The principal connection between the individual and the system of international law is still *via* the status of nationality.

By a sort of paradox, the only context in which the individual as such has full procedural capacity is within the sphere of international criminal responsibility for war crimes and crimes against humanity. It is, of course, true that the individual has rights of complaint within the European Convention of Human Rights, and to bodies such as the United Nations Human Rights Committee. But all such rights of recourse depend upon the prior consent of the State concerned and such consent is often given for quite short periods.

(G) INTERNATIONAL ORGANIZATIONS

The principles of the law of treaties, coupled with general concepts of law derived from municipal systems, provide the mechanism by which intergovernmental organizations, or organizations of States, are created. Such organizations involve a distinction between the organization and the Member States, and the organs

99. See Garth Nettheim, in J. Crawford (ed.), *The Rights of Peoples*, Oxford, Clarendon Press, 1988, pp. 107-126; I. Brownlie, *Treaties and Indigenous Peoples*, Oxford, Clarendon Press, 1992.

have powers exercisable on the international plane and not solely within the municipal legal systems of the Member States.

There are some 170 international organizations in existence with a great diversity of geographical ambit and function. Some are more or less universal in membership whilst others are localized and relate to the management of a particular river basin or the operation of a regional economic community. In principle, international organizations possess only those powers expressly conferred upon them by the constituent instrument. However, once such organizations come into operation the alchemy of legal personality supervenes and complex legal problems arise.

In the present context it will suffice to provide a succinct indication of the types of problem encountered in practice. The most common issue is that of the process of interpretation which determines the existence of "inherent" or "implied" powers. Thus the International Court has held that a capacity in the General Assembly to do justice between the Organization and its staff members "arises by necessary intendment out of the Charter" [100]. The context in which the issue of implied powers arises is that of relations between the organization and the Member States. As a result the implication has a basis in agreement deriving from the multilateral treaty which is the constituent instrument of the organization.

The more problematical context is that of relations between an organization and third States. In the *Reparation for Injuries Suffered in the Service of the United Nations* Advisory Opinion the International Court decided that the United Nations had a power to bring claims against non-Member States. The Court's reasoning, which involved an assertion of a political *datum*, was as follows:

> "the Court's opinion is that fifty States, representing the vast majority of the members of the international community, had the power, in conformity with international law, to bring into being an

100. *Effect of Awards of Compensation made by the United Nations Administrative Tribunal, Advisory Opinion, ICJ Reports 1954*, p. 47 at pp. 56-57.

entity possessing objective international personality, and not merely personality recognized by them alone, together with capacity to bring international claims" [101].

It cannot be assumed that this reasoning applies to other organizations, and the question of relations with non-Member States remains difficult. There is no question that States may, by agreement, enter into relations with international organizations of which they are not members, and it is common for non-members to grant privileges and immunities to organizations. A more delicate area concerns the question of liability for damage caused to non-members or their nationals [102].

This question of liability to third parties becomes acute when a risk creating activity is entrusted to an international organization but the constituent instrument makes no provision for the contingency of loss caused to third parties. In any event such provisions would not have the function of either establishing or limiting the position of non-members.

Three possible approaches to the question of liability may be envisaged:

(1) A liability in the Member States arising by operation of law and on the basis of the ordinary principles of State responsibility. This responsibility is contingent, in the sense that it arises only if the organization itself is not adequately empowered, but it is not appropriate to describe it as "secondary".
(2) A construction of the constituent instrument to the effect that there was no intention to exclude the liability of the Member States, and that the organization was no more than an *alter ego* or collective agent of the Member States [103].

---

101. *ICJ Reports 1949*, p. 174 at pp. 184-185.

102. See R. Higgins, "Les conséquences juridiques pour les Etats membres de l'inexécution par des organisations internationales de leurs obligations envers des tiers", *Annuaire de l'Institut de droit international*, Vol. 66, I, 1995, pp. 253-288.

103. *Westland Helicopters Ltd.* v. *Arab Organization for Industrialization*, 23 *International Legal Materials* (1984), p. 1071.

(3) A construction of the constituent instrument on the basis of a presumption that the Member States had intended to bear any burdens generated by the enterprise and, further, that the existence of a separate legal personality of the organization did not preclude a joint and several liability for debts to third parties [104].

Another area of confusion and difficulty is the question of the capacity of an international organization to sue and be sued in the domestic courts of a non-Member State. The English courts have been unwilling to recognize the legal personality of an international organization created by treaty except on the basis either of incorporation by legislation in England [105] or of legislation in a Member State of the organization in question recognizing it as a corporate body [106]. There can be little question that the recognition of legal personality should be based upon recognition by the executive (of the forum State) of the organization, and that an insistence on incorporation by legislation is unnecessary and inconvenient.

104. See the useful exposition in the dissenting judgment of Nourse L.J., in *Maclaine Watson* v. *Department of Trade* [1988] 3 All England Law Reports, 257 at pp. 332-334.

105. *J. H. Rayner (Mincing Lane) Ltd.* v. *Department of Trade and Industry* [1990] 2 AC 418.

106. *Arab Monetary Fund* v. *Hashim and Others (No. 3)*, [1991] 2 AC 114.

CHAPTER IV

THE MECHANISMS OF PUBLIC ORDER

After completion of the preliminary topics it is possible to move on to the series of principal subjects which may be described as the mechanisms of public order. The first topic in this series involves the examination of the State as a part of the public order system of international relations. This examination will be accompanied by a brief look at the United Nations as a public order system.

(A) Territorial Sovereignty and Boundaries

In the first place it is worth pointing out that in essence the international community of independent States constitutes a sort of traffic system based upon the three-dimensional boxes of territory and territorial jurisdiction of which individual States consist. In this context it is the role of boundaries which is critical in dividing the spheres of action of States and their police and security forces, and in avoiding breaches of the peace. And thus there is a series of legal concepts which correspond to political reality and which, operating jointly, provide a simple but efficacious system of international public order. These concepts are the existence of States as such, the concept of title to territory, the principle of territorial integrity, and the role of boundaries.

(B) The System of States and the Threats to Public Order Posed by the Formation of New States

The relevant concepts will be examined in a logical sequence.

(i) *States as the basis of the legal order*

As it was pointed out in the third chapter, States remain as the standard public order model. Other models encountered in experience tend to be complex and/or transitional in purpose: and the other models are confederations, trusteeships and condominia. International organizations rely for their efficacy upon the co-operation and effectiveness of their Member States, and, for present purposes, may be counted as essentially a part of the system of States.

(ii) *The concept of title to territory*

Governments have an acute sense of territorial entitlement. This is recognized by the law but is not a mere legalistic construct. Politicians and ministers have a natural sense of entitlement based on historical considerations and a sense of the role of the individual State in relation to other States. It is no coincidence that a significant proportion of disputes taken to the International Court or to arbitration are concerned with title to territory.

The principal source of title is in fact the independence of the State and its recognition as such [107]. More specific sources of title include effective occupation, acquisitive prescription, treaties of cession, adjudication, and disposition by joint decision of the major powers.

(iii) *The principle of territorial integrity and the role of boundaries*

Boundaries constitute a significant element in the system of international order. They provide the practical basis for the effective application of the principle of the territorial integrity of States, the principle of non-intervention, and the principle set forth in Article 2, paragraph 4, of the United Nations Charter:

> "All Members shall refrain in their international relations from the threat or use of force against the territorial integrity or politi-

107. R. Y. Jennings, *The Acquisition of Territory in International Law*, Manchester UP, 1963, p. 7.

cal independence of any State, or in any other manner inconsistent with the Purposes of the United Nations."

It was these principles which were affirmed and applied by the International Court in the *Corfu Channel* case [108] and in the Merits phase of the proceedings in *Nicaragua* v. *United States*[109].

It is in this context that the public order function of boundaries emerges. The international order is based upon the allocation of territory as between States. The territorial space of States can only be penetrated by consent. And threats to the peace are avoided by the physical separation of jurisdictions and the areas in which police and security forces may carry out patrolling and enforcement actions.

(iv) *The formation of new States*

The stability and efficacy of the system outlined above may be threatened by the formation of new States, and especially by situations of civil strife in which the forces unleashed may have political purposes unrelated to the dimensions of existing public law units. In the case in which the reformation of States is carried out by multilateral decision-making in which those affected acquiesce, there are no serious problems. This was the case with the reformation of the territories of the Austro-Hungarian Empire. Nor will there be serious difficulties in the case of a voluntary union of two existing States or of a peaceful secession of a discrete political unit. The difficult situations are those in which secessions take place which are incomplete or strongly opposed by significant groups within the populations of the areas concerned. Such was the case in relation to the appearance of Israel in 1948 and the secession of Croatia and other Republics from the Socialist Federal Republic of Yugoslavia.

(v) *State succession and boundaries*

In this context it is of great importance to determine what happens to international boundaries when there is a change of

108. *ICJ Reports 1949*, p. 4.
109. *ICJ Reports 1986*, p. 14.

sovereignty. In the doctrine of international law it has long been accepted that a change of sovereignty does not as such affect international boundaries[110]. This principle was assumed to apply by the International Court in the *Temple* case (Merits)[111] between Thailand and Cambodia.

However, this principle would not cover the problems arising when the former sovereign relinquished control over large areas of colonial empire. In Latin American practice the principle of *uti possidetis* was adopted in order to deal with the situation within the former colonial domains.

(c) The Principle of *Uti Possidetis*

The American jurist Hyde reported the principle in the words of two Spanish jurists:

> "When the common sovereign power was withdrawn, it became indispensably necessary to agree on a principle of demarcation, since there was a universal desire to avoid resort to force, and the principle adopted was a colonial *uti possidetis*; that is, the principle involving the preservation of the demarcations under the colonial regimes corresponding to each of the colonial entities that was constituted as a State."[112]

This principle originated as a political policy and evolved into a legal principle in Latin America. The legal principle involves an implied agreement to base territorial attributions on a rule of presumed possession by previous Spanish administrative units in 1810 (in South America) and in 1821 (in Central America). The principle has played a significant role in arbitrations involving Latin American States.

Apart from the principle of continuity, the concept has two corollaries. First, it was presumed that the dissolution of the Spanish

110. Case concerning the *Frontier Dispute (Burkina Faso/Republic of Mali)*, *ICJ Reports 1986*, p. 554 at p. 566, para. 24.

111. *ICJ Reports 1962*, p. 6.

112. C. C. Hyde, *International Law, Chiefly as Interpreted by the United States*, 2nd ed., Vol. I, Boston, Little Brown, 1947, p. 499, note 3.

Empire did not have the effect of leaving any territory as *terra nullius*. Secondly, given the difficulties of proving the precise locations of ancient administrative divisions in poorly mapped areas, the strict principle of *uti possidetis juris* was supplemented in the practice of international tribunals by *uti possidetis de facto*. Both in origin and function the principle constituted a part of Latin American regional international law, and was seen as such in the literature of the law.

(i) *Adoption in Africa*

The principle of the stability of boundaries during the process of decolonization was recognized by the Organization of African Unity in the Resolution of 21 July 1964, and a Chamber of the International Court has adopted the principle of *uti possidetis* as applicable in relation to African boundaries [113].

(ii) *Adoption in Asia*

Whilst there has been no multilateral declaration concerning *uti possidetis* in an Asian context, there can be no doubt that the principle applies in relation to Asian territorial disputes. The principle of stability of boundaries was affirmed in the *Temple* case (Merits) [114] and the essence of *uti possidetis* was recognized in the Award of the Tribunal in the *Rann of Kutch* Arbitration [115]. Moreover, the Chamber in the case concerning the *Frontier Dispute (Burkina Faso/Republic of Mali)* [116] stated that *uti possidetis* is "a principle of a general kind which is logically connected with this form of decolonization wherever it occurs".

113. Case concerning the *Frontier Dispute (Burkina Faso/Republic of Mali)*, *ICJ Reports 1986*, p. 554 at pp. 565-567, paras. 20-26; p. 568, para. 30; pp. 586-587, para. 63.

114. *ICJ Reports 1962*, p. 6 at pp. 32-35.

115. *International Law Reports*, Vol. 50, p. 2 at p. 470. See also the dissenting opinion of Judge Bebler, pp. 407-408.

116. *ICJ Reports 1986*, p. 566, para. 23.

(iii) *Adoption in Europe*

The principle has been adopted in the practice of European States in relation to the changes in Eastern Europe and in the Soviet Union. Thus the European Community and its Twelve Member States issued a Declaration on 16 December 1991 of "Guidelines on the Recognition of New States in Eastern Europe and in the Soviet Union"[117]. One of the conditions for recognition of the new States was "respect for the inviolability of all frontiers which can only be changed by peaceful means and by common agreement".

On the same date the European Community and its Twelve Member States issued the "Declaration on Yugoslavia"[118] relating to recognition of the independence of "the Yugoslav Republics". This incorporated the same Guidelines and included the following:

> "The Community and its Member States agree to recognise the independence of all the Yugoslav Republics fulfilling all the conditions set out below."

The conditions included a reference to "the above-mentioned guidelines".

On 31 December 1991 the European Community issued the following Statement:

> "The Community and its Member States welcome the assurance received from Armenia, Azerbaijan, Belarus, Kazakhstan, Moldova, Turkmenistan, Ukraine and Uzbekistan that they are prepared to fulfil the requirements contained in the 'Guidelines on the recognition of new States in Eastern Europe and the Soviet Union'. Consequently, they are ready to proceed with the recognition of these Republics.
>
> They reiterate their readiness also to recognise Kyrghyzstan and Tadzhikistan once similar assurances will have been received.
>
> Recognition shall not be taken to imply acceptance by the European Community and its Member States of the position of

117. *British Year Book*, Vol. 62 (1991), p. 559.
118. *Ibid.*, p. 560.

any of the Republics concerning territory which is the subject of a dispute between two or more Republics.

Recognition will furthermore be extended on the understanding that all Republics participating with Russia in the Commonwealth of Independent States on whose territory nuclear weapons are stationed, will adhere shortly to the Nuclear Non-Proliferation Treaty as non-nuclear weapon States." [119]

The Guidelines on Recognition were in due course applied by the Arbitration Commission of the International Conference on Yugoslavia in a series of Opinions on the recognition of the Republics of Yugoslavia, of which Opinion No. 3 recognized *uti possidetis* as a general principle [120].

In conclusion it is clear that the principle of *uti possidetis* has attained the status of a principle of general international law, and this has received ample judicial recognition. The following decisions attest to this:

(1) *Guinea-Guinea (Bissau) Maritime Delimitation* case, Award of 14 February 1985 [121].
(2) Case concerning the *Frontier Dispute (Burkina Faso/Republic of Mali)* [122].
(3) Case concerning the *Land, Island and Maritime Frontier Dispute (El Salvador/Honduras: Nicaragua intervening)* [123].

By way of clarification it is necessary to emphasize that *uti possidetis* does not freeze boundaries. It consists essentially of the single principle that the change of sovereignty does not *as such* change the status of a boundary, and thus pre-existing disputes will subsist as an aspect of the principle of continuity.

(iv) *The relation of* uti possidetis *and the principle of self-determination*

One question which arises concerns the relation of *uti possidetis*

119. *British Year Book*, Vol. 62 (1991), p. 561.
120. *International Law Reports*, Vol. 92, pp. 162-211.
121. *Ibid.*, Vol. 77, at p. 657.
122. *ICJ Reports 1986*, pp. 565-567, 586-587.
123. *ICJ Reports 1992*, pp. 390-401.

and self-determination. As a matter of policy *uti possidetis* militates in favour of territorial stability. Can it be reconciled with self-determination which, at first sight, constitutes a source of change and territorial instability? The answer is unavoidably complex and has several distinct elements.

In the first place, few writers express the opinion that a condition of the validity of a transfer of territory is the provision of opportunity for the expression of opinion concerning the transfer by the inhabitants [124]. Moreover, it must be appreciated that there is a complementarity between *uti possidetis* and the principle of self-determination. It is *uti possidetis* which creates the ambit of the putative unit of self-determination, and which in that sense has a logical priority.

This complementarity is evident in the practice of the European Community relating to the Republics of Yugoslavia. In particular, Opinion No. 4 of the Arbitral Commission of the International Conference on Yugoslavia [125] adopts the territorial unit of the Socialist Republic of Bosnia-Herzegovina as the relevant unit for the purposes of its Opinion on international recognition. On this premise the Commission applies the EC Guidelines on the recognition of new States and decides that "the will of the peoples of Bosnia-Herzegovina to constitute" Bosnia as a sovereign State "cannot be held to have been fully established".

(D) IS DEMOCRACY A CRITERION OF LAWFUL GOVERNMENT IN PUBLIC INTERNATIONAL LAW?

Leaving the problems attending the formation of new States it is necessary to turn to a trend in the literature which provides a new form of threat to international public order. This is the assertion that a Government is not lawful unless it adheres to demo-

---

124. See I. Brownlie, *Principles of Public International Law*, 4th ed., Oxford, Clarendon Press, 1990, pp. 170-171.

125. *International Law Reports*, Vol. 92, p. 173.

cratic principles[126]. In relation to the invasion of Panama in 1989 the corollary was asserted, namely, that the use of force is lawful in order to restore democracy[127].

The question of forcible intervention will be examined in Chapter XIV, and for the present the purpose is to address the general issue of democracy as a condition of lawful government.

As a preliminary it can be asserted that there can be no doubt that general international law does not recognize such a criterion[128]. Indeed, the small number of adherents to this new doctrine have not taken the trouble to adduce evidence of its existence. If the criterion has a role in present diplomatic life, it appears to be to provide the United States with a highly selective political weapon to destabilize Governments which are disliked on grounds unrelated to any issue of democratic principle. It is difficult to see even the beginnings of a new principle of customary law when the evidence of *opinio juris* is not merely thin but negative.

As an example, let us take United States policies towards the States of Central America. When the Somocista Government of Nicaragua was overthrown in 1979, Nicaragua had been ruled by successive members of the Somoza family for 45 years. The United States had close relations with the Somocista Governments. The hostility of the United States towards the new Nicaraguan Government, even after perfectly adequate elections in 1984, was premised on collateral political considerations. The attitude of the United States towards Governments in the Middle East has for 50 years been based on political preferences. When Dr. Moussadiq headed the first respectable parliamentary régime in Iran, his Government was overthrown by the joint action of

126. Adherents to this view: E. Lauterpacht, *The Times*, 23 December 1989, p. 11; R. Higgins, *Problems and Process*, Oxford, Clarendon Press, 1994, pp. 111-128.

127. *American Journal of International Law*, Vol. 84 (1990), pp. 545-549.

128. This is the position of J. Crawford, *British Year Book*, Vol. 64 (1993), pp. 113-133; and Thomas M. Franck, *Fairness in International Law and Institutions*, Oxford, Clarendon Press, pp. 83-139 (but he supports the principle *de lege ferenda*).

British and American intelligence agents in 1953 [129]. Autocratic monarchical régimes (with acceptable policies) do not even face criticism, let alone forcible intervention. Against this background it is difficult to take the new doctrine very seriously.

However, certain distinctions must be drawn. First of all, Governments can base their policies in areas of discretion upon a precondition of democratic practice. The EC Guidelines on the Recognition of New States in Eastern Europe and in the Soviet Union [130] insist on adherence to various guarantees of good government as a condition of recognition. In particular, the EC Declaration required

> "respect for the provisions of the Charter of the United Nations and the commitments subscribed to in the Final Act of Helsinki and in the Charter of Paris, especially with regard to the rule of law, democracy and human rights".

At the same time it is not clear that the EC is stating that such adherence to standards of good government is a condition of statehood. The Guidelines appear to *assume* the existence of the new States.

Secondly, it is perfectly possible for a State to enter into international commitments to organize free elections, and standard-setting treaties concerning human rights establish obligations of this type. However, it is difficult to see that breaches of such obligations can affect the legality as such of the Government concerned.

The adoption of a standard of democratic government would lead to endless intervention in the affairs of other States. The standards of democratic government are varied and open to facile controversy. Not infrequently, the complaint of autocracy is made by Western Governments precisely when a society has moved to a *relatively* democratic first stage. Thus the concern for democracy in Libya, Cuba and Nicaragua emerged only when those societies

---

129. P. Avery, G. Hambly and C. Melville (eds.), *The Cambridge History of Iran*, Vol. 7, Cambridge, 1991, pp. 440-442.

130. *British Year Book*, Vol. 62 (1991), p. 559.

had rejected pro-Western autocracy for non-aligned independence.

The standard of democracy is, of course, difficult to apply and Governments which are democratic in principle may deny self-government to large sections of the territory they control. Moreover, the cruder models of majoritarian democracy may lead to discrimination against minorities and regions.

There is a final point, which is arguably the most significant in the debate. The principle of democratic government as a condition of legality tends to carry with it the promise of external action in order to apply the principle. Such external action, whether unilateral or disguised as multilateral, may result not in democracy but in a foreign military government acting through local protégés. The results of foreign intervention on a large scale will be lasting damage to the legitimacy of local institutions. The local institutions may be flawed in operation but they have a legitimacy which itself must be taken into account in implementing the democratic principle.

(E) THE ROLE OF THE UNITED NATIONS

The question which remains is to what extent the United Nations changes or reinforces the elements of the system of public order examined earlier. In a general way the United Nations replicates the pre-war system of security but with specific improvements. Thus the following familiar elements constitute the system of public order:

(1) The recognition of the right of self-help in the form of the right of individual self-defence if an armed attack occurs (Art. 51), subject to the overall authority of the Security Council to take action in order to maintain or restore international peace and security.
(2) The right of collective self-defence on the same conditions.
(3) The role of regional arrangements subject to the authorization of the Security Council in the event that enforcement action is taken under regional arrangements.

(4) A system of collective security and sanctions based upon action by the Security Council by virtue of Chapter VII of the Charter.

The Charter embodies certain Principles, set forth in Article 2, which bind both the Organization and its Members. In the scheme of the Charter the Organization is clearly differentiated from the Member States. The United Nations is essentially an organization of States with special purposes. Whilst membership involves some erosion of sovereignty, this is true of any acceptance of treaty obligations. Similarly, although certain States have a privileged status as permanent members of the Security Council, the fundamental principle is that of "the sovereign equality of all its Members" (Art. 2 (1)). As a system of public order the United Nations has four principal characteristics.

First, there is no system of compulsory dispute settlement and the relevant part of the Charter, Chapter VI, is promotional and permissive. The Security Council only has powers of recommendation and there is no automatic reference of disputes to the International Court. The emphasis is on peace-keeping rather than the settlement of disputes in accordance with the principles of international law.

Secondly, the power to impose sanctions involves reliance on the Member States and even the forces envisaged by Article 43 would have been forces made available by individual Member States.

Thirdly, in spite of the absence of a standing armed force, the United Nations has what is in principle a monopoly of the use of force, which is the principal characteristic of a system of public order.

Fourthly, it is not the case that the United Nations is predestined to be powerless. The often alleged powerlessness of the United Nations derives essentially from the fact that, as a matter of political contingency, it was for long unlikely that action could be agreed upon in the absence of collaboration between the permanent members of the Security Council. That situation no longer obtains and the Security Council has in recent years taken many initiatives involving the use of force or economic sanctions. This increased ambition on the part of the Council has in fact raised delicate issues concerning the extent to which the actions of the Council are subject to legal controls. This issue will be revisited in Chapter XV.

CHAPTER V

THE PROTECTION OF HUMAN RIGHTS

The second subject under the general heading "The Mechanisms of Public Order" is the protection of human rights.

(A) The Rule of Law and Human Rights

It should be unnecessary to explain the connection between the Rule of Law and human rights. In any event the concepts of human rights and the institutions aimed at the monitoring and enforcement of human rights constitute what is, to a certain extent, a discrete public order system. The human rights system supplements the community of States as a public order system. At the same time, and this is paradoxical, the protection of human rights depends upon the system of States and forms part of it.

(B) The Problem of the "Applicable Law"

Human rights is a broad area of concern and the potential subject- matter ranges from the questions of torture and fair trial to the so-called third generation of rights, which includes the right to food, the right to economic development, and the right to health.

Many lawyers in academic life refer to an entity described as "International Human Rights Law" which is assumed to be a separate body of norms. While this is a convenient category of reference, it is also a source of confusion. Human rights problems occur in specific contexts. The issues may arise in domestic law, or within the framework of a standard-setting convention, or within general international law. But there must be reference to the specific and relevant applicable law. There is thus the law of a particular State, *or* the principles of the European Convention on Human Rights, *or* the relevant principles of general international law. But in the real world of practice and procedure, there is no such entity as "International Human Rights Law" and, when this concept is imposed on students, it can only be a source of confusion. Since it is not an "applicable law", it divorces learning in universities from the actual procedural contexts in which problems arise.

(c) The Historical Dimension

The concept of human rights, or the Rights of Man, is inevitably ideological and the history of human rights forms part of the history of philosophy, of religion, and of political ideas. It used to be customary for the Hague Academy to offer courses in which the lecturers made the claim that, respectively, each of the major religions had invented and nurtured human rights from early times.

In the present context, the idea of human rights must be seen empirically and historically. The type of human rights now offered as a basis of universal standards is the product of political ideas derived from eighteenth-century French political thinkers, the French revolution, and the appearance of Bills of Rights in France and the United States. The ideas involved were secular but favoured freedom of religion. They were also democratic in theory, although the practice was variable, it being regarded as acceptable to apply different standards to overseas colonies.

The appearance of human rights in the sphere of international law and organizations is often traced to the era of the League Covenant of 1919, and the Minorities Treaties and League of Nations mandated areas which were associated with the Covenant. There can be no question that the Minorities Treaties, in particular, constituted an important stage in the recognition of human rights standards and provided "an instrument of supervision in the interest alike of the individual and of international peace" [131]. Though only relatively effective, these were a much more promising beginning than the vague "guarantees" applied when the break-up of the former Yugoslavia occurred.

The emphasis upon the League Covenant and the Minorities Treaties of 1919-1920 is in fact misplaced. Neither the Mandates system nor the Minorities régimes were representative in character. The League Covenant did not contain a general minorities clause. Amongst the proposals which were discarded was the following Japanese amendment:

> "The equality of nations being a basic principle of the League of Nations, the High Contracting Parties agree to accord as soon as possible to all aliens nationals of states members of the League equal and just treatment in every respect making no distinction either in law or fact on account of their race or nationality." [132]

The Minorities Treaties at least presented a model, even if the model was applied selectively. Of significance also was the foundation of the International Labour Organisation created in 1919 as an autonomous partner of the League of Nations, and the body of International Labour Conventions which the ILO fostered. However, the idea of universal human rights awaited the wartime planning in the United States relating to postwar organization, and a draft bill of rights was prepared as early as December 1942 [133].

(d) The United Nations Charter as the Base Line

There can be no question that it was the United Nations Charter which established human rights as a major element in the

---

131. *Oppenheim's International Law*, ed. by H. Lauterpacht, Vol. I, 8th ed., 1955, pp. 715-716.

132. David Hunter Miller, *The Drafting of the League Covenant*, New York, 1928, Vol. II, p. 229 at pp. 323-325. See also Warwick McKean, *Equality and Discrimination under International Law*, Oxford, Clarendon Press, 1983, pp. 14-26.

133. Ruth B. Russell and Jeannette E. Muther, *A History of the United Nations Charter*, Washington, DC, The Brookings Institution, 1958, pp. 323-329, 777-789.

sphere of international legal obligations. Unlike the Covenant of the League of Nations, the Charter of the United Nations directly addressed the issue of human rights, insisted on the equality of peoples, and, for the first time, employed the terminology of human rights.

The provisions of the Charter provide a foundation for human rights protection but were not regarded originally as being much more than hortatory and programmatic. In the preamble the members "reaffirm faith in fundamental human rights, in the equal rights of men and women . . .". The purposes of the United Nations are stated to include co-operation "in promoting and encouraging respect for human rights . . ." (Art. 1).

Article 55 is the most important provision:

> "the United Nations shall promote:
>
> . . . .
>
> (*c*) universal respect for, and observance of, human rights and freedoms for all without distinction as to race, sex, language, or religion".

Article 56 provides that:

> "All Members pledge themselves to take joint and separate action in co-operation with the Organization for the achievement of the purposes set forth in Article 55."

(E) MULTILATERAL NON-BINDING INSTRUMENTS

It is true to say that the more or less generalized references to human rights in the Charter left much to be done and the United Nations organs embarked upon an extended programme of codification which eventually resulted in the two International Covnants and other multilateral standard-setting conventions. The importance of such multilateral treaties goes without saying but in historical sequence it was a non-binding instrument which surfaced before the International Covenants, the Universal Declaration of Human Rights adopted by the General Assembly of the United Nations on 10 December 1948. Moreover, another non-binding instrument, the Helsinki Final Act, was also to have considerable significance in practice.

The two instruments have particular interest for lawyers because they demonstrate that the normative impact of an instrument does not necessarily depend upon its formal legal status.

(i) *The Universal Declaration of Human Rights, 1948*[134]

This Declaration was adopted in the form of a General Assembly resolution. The voting was 48 for, none against, and eight abstentions. By reason of its form, and for other reasons, the Declaration was clearly not a legally binding instrument *as such*, and at the time of its adoption some of its provisions departed from the generally accepted rules. Nevertheless, the Universal Declaration has had influence in at least three different ways. First, it has had the status of an authoritative guide, produced by the General Assembly, to the interpretation of the Charter. It soon became accepted as part of the "Law of the United Nations"[135]. Secondly, some of its provisions either constitute general principles of law or represent elementary considerations of humanity. And thirdly, the Declaration has been invoked by municipal courts.

The Declaration is a good example of an informal prescription given legal significance by the actions of authoritative decision-makers, and thus it has been used as a standard reference in the Helsinki Declaration, the second of the "non-binding" instruments which have been of considerable importance in practice.

(ii) *The Helsinki Final Act, 1975*[136]

On 1 August 1975 there was adopted the Final Act of the Conference on Security and Co-operation in Europe in Helsinki. This contains a declaration of principles under the heading "Questions Relating to Security in Europe". The Final Act was signed by the

---

134. I. Brownlie (ed.), *Basic Documents on Human Rights*, 3rd ed., Oxford, Clarendon Press, 1992, p. 21.

135. C. H. M. Waldock, "General Course on Public International Law", *Recueil des cours*, Vol. 106 (1962-II), pp. 198-199.

136. I. Brownlie, *op. cit., supra* footnote 134, p. 391.

representatives of 35 States, including the United States and the USSR.

The document was obviously not in treaty form, and therefore not legally binding as such. The United States, along with other signatories, affirmed that the instrument was not legally binding[137]. At the same time the document constitutes evidence of the acceptance by the participating States of certain principles as principles of customary or general international law, including the standards of human rights.

The significance of the Helsinki Final Act was recognized by the International Court in its Judgment on the Merits in the case of *Nicaragua* v. *United States*. In the words of the Court:

> "Also significant is United States acceptance of the principle of the prohibition of the use of force which is contained in the declaration on principles governing the mutual relations of States participating in the Conference on Security and Co-operation in Europe (Helsinki, 1 August 1975), whereby the participating States undertake to 'refrain in their mutual relations, *as well as in their international relations in general*', from the threat or use of force. Acceptance of a text in these terms confirms the existence of an *opinio juris* of the participating States prohibiting the use of force in international relations."[138]

(iii) *The Paris Charter, 1990*[139]

In this Declaration the participating States in the Conference on Security and Co-operation in Europe (34 in all) reaffirmed their commitment to the principles of the Helsinki Final Act.

(F) STANDARD-SETTING BINDING MULTILATERAL CONVENTIONS

There can be no doubt that the main corpus of human rights standards consists of an accumulated code of multilateral

---

137. United States Department of State, *Digest of United States Practice in International Law*, 1975, USGPO, Washington, DC, pp. 325-327.

138. *ICJ Reports 1986*, p. 100, para. 189, emphasis added; and see also p. 133, para. 264.

139. I. Brownlie, *op. cit.*, *supra* footnote 134, p. 474.

standard-setting conventions. These fall into four general categories. First of all, the two comprehensive International Covenants on Economic, Social and Cultural Rights and on Civil and Political Rights adopted in 1966. Secondly, the comprehensive regional conventions: the European Convention on Human Rights of 1950, the American Convention on Human Rights of 1969, and the African Charter on Human and Peoples' Rights of 1981. Thirdly, the conventions dealing with specific wrongs, such as genocide, torture or racial discrimination. Fourthly, the conventions related to the protection of particular categories of people: women, children, refugees and migrant workers.

(i) *Methods of enforcement*

The classical and still general method of enforcement is by means of the duty of performance of treaty undertakings imposed on the States Parties. It is the domestic legal systems of the States Parties to the given convention which are the vehicles of implementation. Thus the International Covenant on Civil and Political Rights contains express provisions setting forth the duty to ensure that domestic law provides sufficient means of maintenance of the treaty standards. It is a characteristic of such treaties that the means of implementation of conventional duties are a matter of domestic jurisdiction. In this context it is helpful to recall the remonstrance of Sir Robert Jennings that it is "a mistake to think of domestic jurisdiction in 'either/or' terms" [140].

It is also normal to impose monitoring mechanisms in the form of a duty to submit reports and to create an optional competence to consider communications from individuals who claim to be victims of a violation by a State Party of any of the rights set forth in the relevant standard-setting convention. This is the system adopted in respect of the International Covenant on Civil and Political Rights and its Optional Protocol [141].

140. "General Course on Principles of International Law", *Recueil des cours*, Vol. 121 (1967-II), p. 502.

141. I. Brownlie, *op. cit.*, *supra* footnote 134, pp. 125-144.

(G) CUSTOMARY OR GENERAL INTERNATIONAL LAW

The vast majority of States and authoritative writers would now recognize that the fundamental principles of human rights form part of customary or general international law, although they would not necessarily agree on the identity of the fundamental principles. In 1970 the International Court, delivering judgment in the *Barcelona Traction* case, referred to obligations *erga omnes* in contemporary international law and these were stated to include "the principles and rules concerning the basic rights of the human person, including protection from slavery and racial discrimination" [142]. The Final Act of the Helsinki Conference of 1975 [143] included a "Declaration of Principles Guiding Relations between Participating States". This Declaration includes a section on human rights and the following paragraph appears in that section:

> "In the field of human rights and fundamental freedoms, the participating States will act in conformity with the purposes and principles of the Charter of the United Nations and with the Universal Declaration of Human Rights. They will also fulfil their obligations as set forth in the international declarations and agreements in this field, including *inter alia* the International Covenants on Human Rights, by which they may be bound."

It is evident that the participating States recognize that human rights standards form part of general international law: thus the *Digest of United States Practice in International Law*[144] (United States Department of State, 1975, p. 7) sets forth the Declaration referred to in the previous paragraph under the heading: "Rights and Duties of States".

The significance of the role of the "customary international law of human rights" is recognized in the most recent edition of the *Restatement of the Law: The Third*. Under the rubric just quoted the following proposition appears:

---

142. *ICJ Reports 1970*, p. 3 at p. 32.

143. I. Brownlie, *op. cit.*, *supra* footnote 134, p. 391.

144. United States Department of State, *Digest of United States Practice in International Law*, 1975, p. 7.

> "A State violates international law if, as a matter of State policy, it practices, encourages, or condones
> (1) genocide,
> (2) slavery or slave trade,
> (3) the murder or causing the disappearance of individuals,
> (4) torture or other cruel, inhuman or degrading treatment or punishment,
> (5) prolonged arbitrary detention,
> (6) systematic racial discrimination, or
> (7) a consistent pattern of gross violations of internationally recognised human rights." [145]

The literature of human rights tends to neglect the role, or potential role, of customary law. There are, however, illustrious exceptions among whom are Professors Schachter [146] and Meron [147]. In this general context an unresolved issue is the evident need for a synthesis of the concept of human rights and the department of the law of State responsibility concerning the treatment of aliens [148].

(H) The General Principles of Humanitarian Law

In the *Nicaragua* case the International Court at the Merits phase applied "general principles of humanitarian law", based upon Article 3 common to the four Geneva Conventions, to the armed conflict inside Nicaragua in so far as the acts of the United States were concerned. In the words of the Judgment:

> "The Court however sees no need to take a position on that matter, since in its view the conduct of the United States may be

---

145. American Law Institute, *Restatement of the Law, the Third, the Foreign Relations Law of the United States*, 1987, Vol. 2, p. 161, para. 702.

146. O. Schachter, "International Law in Theory and Practice (General Course in Public International Law)", *Recueil des cours*, Vol. 178 (1982-V), pp. 333-338.

147. Theodor Meron, *Human Rights and Humanitarian Norms as Customary International Law*, Oxford, Clarendon Press, 1989.

148. I. Brownlie, *Principles of Public International Law*, 4th ed., Oxford, Clarendon Press, 1990, pp. 526-528.

judged according to the fundamental general principles of humanitarian law; in its view, the Geneva Conventions are in some respects a development, and in other respects no more than the expression, of such principles. It is significant in this respect that, according to the terms of the Conventions, the denunciation of one of them

> 'shall in no way impair the obligations which the Parties to the conflict shall remain bound to fulfil by virtue of the principles of the law of nations, as they result from the usages established among civilized peoples, from the laws of humanity and the dictates of the public conscience' (Convention I, Art. 63; Convention II, Art. 62; Convention III, Art. 142; Convention IV, Art. 158).

Article 3 which is common to all four Geneva Conventions of 12 August 1949 defines certain rules to be applied in the armed conflicts of a non-international character. There is no doubt that, in the event of international armed conflicts, these rules also constitute a minimum yardstick, in addition to the more elaborate rules which are also to apply to international conflicts; and they are rules which, in the Court's opinion, reflect what the Court in 1949 called 'elementary considerations of humanity' (*Corfu Channel, Merits, I.C.J. Reports 1949*, p. 22; paragraph 215 above). The Court may therefore find them applicable to the present dispute, and is thus not required to decide what role the United States multilateral treaty reservation might otherwise play in regard to the treaties in question."[149]

In the result the phrase "general principles of humanitarian law" appears in six passages of the Judgment[150]. It is of some interest that this locution was produced by the Court of its own accord, Nicaragua having, for its own reasons, avoided the introduction of the issue as to whether or not an armed conflict existed.

(I) THE APPEARANCE OF NEW CONCEPTS OF *LOCUS STANDI*

The articulation of principles relating to human rights and fun-

149. *ICJ Reports 1986*, pp. 113-114, para. 218.

150. *Ibid.*, pp. 113-114, para. 218; p. 114, para. 220; p. 129, para. 255; p. 130, para. 256 (twice); p. 148, *dispositif*, para. 9.

damental freedoms is one thing, the discovery of the procedural implications of these developments is quite another. The key question is to what extent, if at all, new concepts of *locus standi* have evolved.

In the *Barcelona Traction* case the Court affirmed the existence of the category of obligations *erga omnes*. In the words of the Court:

> "33. When a State admits into its territory foreign investments of foreign nations, whether natural or juristic persons, it is bound to extend to them the protection of the law and assumes obligations concerning the treatment to be afforded them. These obligations, however, are neither absolute nor unqualified. In particular, an essential distinction should be drawn between the obligations of a State towards the international community as a whole, and those arising vis-à-vis another State in the field of diplomatic protection. By their very nature the former are the concern of all States. In view of the importance of the rights involved, all States can be held to have a legal interest in their protection; they are obligations *erga omnes*.
>
> 34. Such obligations derive, for example, in contemporary international law, from the outlawing of acts of aggression, and of genocide, as also from the principles and rules concerning the basic rights of the human person, including protection from slavery and racial discrimination. Some of the corresponding rights of protection have entered into the body of general international law (*Reservations to the Convention on the Prevention and Punishment of the Crime of Genocide, Advisory Opinion, I.C.J. Reports 1951*, p. 232); others are conferred by international instruments of a universal or quasi-universal character." [151]

It is well known that the Court was indicating a more liberal approach to the concept of legal interest in the wake of the much criticized decision in the *South West Africa* cases (Second Phase) [152].

In the realm of multilateral standard-setting treaties, there can be no question that the condition of being a party, without more,

151. *ICJ Reports 1970*, p. 3 at p. 32.
152. *ICJ Reports 1966*, p. 6.

provides sufficient *locus standi*, even in the absence of material loss. Moreover, the European Commission and European Court of Human Rights have insisted that "the public order of Europe" has consequences in the procedural sphere. Thus, in the *Case of Loizidou* v. *Turkey*[153] the European Court rejected an argument on behalf of Turkey that the régime of reservations to acceptances of jurisdiction should be the same as that of the International Court. The relevant passages of the Judgment include the following:

> "84. In the first place, the context within which the International Court of Justice operates is quite distinct from that of the Convention institutions. The International Court is called on *inter alia* to examine any legal dispute between States that might occur in any part of the globe with reference to principles of international law. The subject-matter of a dispute may relate to any area of international law. In the second place, unlike the Convention institutions, the role of the International Court is not exclusively limited to direct supervisory functions in respect of a law-making treaty such as the Convention.
>
> 85. Such a fundamental difference in the role and purpose of the respective tribunals, coupled with the existence of a practice of unconditional acceptance under Articles 25 and 46, provides a compelling basis for distinguishing Convention practice from that of the International Court.
>
> . . . .
>
> 89. Taking into consideration the character of the convention, the ordinary meaning of Articles 25 and 46 in their context and in the light of their object and purpose and the practice of Contracting Parties, the Court concludes that the restrictions *ratione loci* attached to Turkey's Article 25 and Article 46 declarations are invalid."

In dealing with a related issue, the validity of the Turkish Declaration, the Court observed:

> "93. In addressing this issue the Court must bear in mind the special character of the Convention as an instrument of European public order *(ordre public)* for the protection of individual human

153. European Court of Human Rights, Series A, *Judgments and Decisions*, Vol. 310, p. 29.

> beings and its mission, as set out in Article 19, 'to ensure the observance of the engagements undertaken by the High Contracting Parties'."

At the same time, in the case concerning *East Timor* the International Court was unwilling to permit the *erga omnes* nature of a right to qualify the principle that consent is the basis of the Court's jurisdiction. The reasoning of the Court was as follows:

> "However, Portugal puts forward an additional argument aiming to show that the principle formulated by the Court in the case concerning *Monetary Gold Removed from Rome in 1943* is not applicable in the present case. It maintains, in effect, that the rights which Australia allegedly breached were rights *erga omnes* and that accordingly Portugal could require it, individually, to respect them regardless of whether or not another State had conducted itself in a similarly unlawful manner.
>
> In the Court's view, Portugal's assertion that the right of peoples to self-determination, as it evolved from the Charter and from United Nations practice, has an *erga omnes* character, is irreproachable. The principle of self-determination of peoples has been recognized by the United Nations Charter and in the jurisprudence of the Court . . .; it is one of the essential principles of contemporary international law. However, the Court considers that the *erga omnes* character of a norm and the rule of consent to jurisdiction are two different things. Whatever the nature of the obligations invoked, the Court could not rule on the lawfulness of the conduct of a State when its judgment would imply an evaluation of the lawfulness of the conduct of another State which is not a party to the case. Where this is so, the Court cannot act, even if the right in question is a right *erga omnes*."[154]

There can be little doubt that there is an incremental progression toward an *actio popularis*. There is no inherent limitation of the concept of legal interest to "material" interests and there may be circumstances in which individual States may have *locus standi* in respect of legal interests of other entities such as a non-self-

154. *ICJ Reports 1995*, p. 90 at p. 102, para. 29.

governing territory. This was the position of Judge Skubiszewski in his dissenting opinion in the case concerning *East Timor*[155].

There are occasional developments which are more or less *sub rosa*. Thus in the case concerning *Certain Phosphate Lands in Nauru*[156] at the Preliminary Objections phase the Court was not troubled by the fact that the substance of Nauru's claims related to the period prior to independence. It is true that the Australian pleadings had helped in this direction in that the evidence offered in support of the unsuccessful assertion that Nauru had waived all claims related to the period before independence[157].

In conclusion, it must be stated that, at this stage in international relations, the concept of the *actio popularis* is bound to have certain limits[158].

155. *ICJ Reports 1995*, p. 255, para. 100, citing I. Brownlie, *Principles of Public International Law*, 4th ed., Oxford, pp. 466-467.

156. *ICJ Reports 1992*, p. 240. Cf. p. 253, para. 31.

157. *Ibid.*, pp. 247-250, paras. 12-21.

158. See Bedjaoui, in Mohammed Bedjaoui (ed.), *International Law: Achievements and Prospects*, Dordrecht, Martinus Nijhoff, 1991, p. 1195, para. 61. See also Kéba Mbaye, "L'intérêt pour agir devant la Cour internationale de Justice", *Recueil des cours*, Vol. 209 (1988-II), p. 227 at pp. 316-318.

CHAPTER VI

THE CONCEPT OF STATE RESPONSIBILITY

(A) THE CONCEPT

The third topic in the series of subjects constituting "the mechanisms of public order" is the concept of State responsibility. In its Judgment in the *Factory at Chorzów (Jurisdiction)* case (1927) the Permanent Court stated that:

> "It is a principle of international law that the breach of an engagement involves an obligation to make reparation in an adequate form. Reparation therefore is the indispensable complement of a failure to apply a convention and there is no necessity for this to be stated in the convention itself." [159]

State responsibility is a major concept of customary international law and also constitutes a general principle of law for the purposes of Article 38 (1) *(c)* of the Statute of the International Court. It applies *both* to obligations arising from breaches of principles of general international law *and* to obligations arising from treaties and conventions. State responsibility is, in its operation, closely linked to the procedure for making claims, the mechanisms for peaceful settlement of disputes, and the question of remedies for breaches of obligations.

(B) RULE OF LAW IMPLICATIONS

It goes without saying that the Rule of Law encompasses the concept of responsibility for wrongdoing. It is the particular task

159. (1927), *PCIJ, Series A, No. 9*, p. 21.

of lawyers to ensure that the modalities exist for the effective implementation of a system of State responsibility.

State responsibility is implemented in several ways. A common method consists simply of the making of diplomatic claims with a view to a negotiated settlement or an admission of responsibility and a negotiation about compensation. On 31 January 1972 the British Embassy in Dublin was attacked by a crowd in protest at the shooting of civilians in Derry on the previous day. On 2 February the Embassy was destroyed in a fire after demonstrations by crowds of 20,000 or more. The Embassy had been evacuated previously and the Irish police were unable to protect the building from the expected attack. The Irish Government expressed regret, accepted full responsibility and agreed to restore the property to its original condition. Damage to the contents and the vehicles was the subject of a separate claim for financial compensation [160].

Another common mechanism, employed when there are mutual claims of various kinds relating to a long period, is the "lump sum settlement" in which there is an overall composition of claims with a balance of payable compensation and a waiver of certain classes of claim. Secondly, issues of responsibility may be resolved by an agreed procedure of settlement by mediation, conciliation, arbitration or adjudication.

Thirdly, issues of responsibility or reparation may be resolved by the determinations of the political organs of the United Nations. Thus it has been not uncommon for the General Assembly and the Security Council to make determinations of liability. An example of such a determination is the Security Council resolution of 31 December 1968 [161] related to the armed attack on Beirut Airport by Israeli forces. The Council observed "that the military action by the armed forces of Israel against the civil International Airport of Beirut was premeditated and of a large scale and carefully planned nature", and therefore the Council: "*Considers* that Lebanon is entitled to appropriate redress for the destruc-

---

160. I. Brownlie, *System of the Law of Nations, State Responsibility (Part 1)*, Oxford, Clarendon Press, 1983, p. 105.

161. Resolution S/162 (1968); *Yearbook of the United Nations*, 1968, p. 236. See generally, I. Brownlie, *op. cit., supra* footnote 160, pp. 123-131.

tion it has suffered, responsibility for which has been acknowledged by Israel."

Such determinations may be appropriate in cases in which the facts are indisputable or responsibility is admitted. However, determinations by political organs are in certain circumstances problematical and difficult to reconcile with Rule of Law principles. Resolution 687 (1991)[162] reaffirms the liability of Iraq under international law

> "for any direct loss, damage, including environmental damage and the depletion of natural resources, or injury to foreign governments, nationals and corporations, as a result of Iraq's unlawful invasion and occupation of Kuwait".

Whilst the reaffirmation of the general principle may be uncontroversial, there is the further question of the modalities of deciding specific claims for loss. The United Nations Compensation Commission dealing with claims against Iraq has a procedure which in substance ignores the principle of natural justice referred to as *audi alteram partem*. This principle is formulated as "the right to a fair hearing". The procedure adopted by the Compensation Commission excludes Iraq from the procedure altogether[163].

(c) The Historical Background

It is assumed, for good reasons, that public international law grows out of the practice of States. Nonetheless, there are certain areas in which the framework of concepts and general principles must be derived from a more sophisticated matrix than the casual exchanges of diplomacy. State responsibility provides the most important example of this type of case.

Whilst it may be said that the concepts of just war and reprisals, to be found in the early European doctrine, presupposed a system

162. Adopted on 3 April 1991, para. 16. See also resolution 674 (1990) adopted on 29 October 1990, para. 9, and resolution 686 (1991), para. 2 *(b)*.

163. See Graefrath, *ZaöRuV*, Vol. 55 (1995), pp. 1-68.

of responsibility, the modern concepts and principles did not emerge until the last three decades of the nineteenth century. When the law of State responsibility did develop it owed a great deal to the practice of mixed claims commissions and courts of arbitration. The doctrine developed slowly and in 1884 Hall wrote that "the subject of the responsibility of the State is not usually discussed adequately in works upon international law" [164].

(d) The Nature of State Responsibility

Many principles of international law are concerned with the allocation of powers and relationships which do not generate State responsibility. Thus, for example, a claim to title to a particular parcel of territory, or area of continental shelf or exclusive economic zone, may be contested but such a claim, even if it is proved to be well founded, does not entail State responsibility.

A different situation arises when a claim to territorial sovereignty or other jurisdictional rights results in the use of coercive measures. Thus in the *Anglo-Norwegian Fisheries* case [165], the International Court was asked to give a declaration concerning the legal validity of a system of baselines of a fisheries zone. The United Kingdom, as the Applicant State, also asked for compensation in respect of arrests of British fishing vessels in the waters regarded as high seas by the United Kingdom. In the course of the oral hearings the issue was dropped.

However, it is of interest to recall that, in the context of the proceedings in the *Anglo-Norwegian Fisheries* case, Norway reserved the right to make a claim for damages against the United Kingdom for the harm caused by a refusal to recognize Norwegian sovereignty and the resulting activity by British trawlers in the Norwegian fishing zone [166].

---

164. W. E. Hall, *International Law*, 2nd ed., Oxford, Henry Frowde and Stevens, 1884, p. 198, note 1.

165. *ICJ Reports 1951*, p. 116.

166. Lord McNair, *International Law Opinions*, Cambridge University Press, 1956, II, p. 289. Subsequently, Norway decided not to advance the claim.

(E) The Concept of Imputability to a State

It is frequently stated that responsibility only arises when the act or omission complained of is "imputable" to a State. The concept of imputability is a source of needless difficulty and should be avoided. Imputability is a superfluous concept which implies the inappropriate idea of vicarious responsibility.

The major issue in any given situation is whether there has been a breach of duty. Therefore the content of imputability will vary according to the precise manner in which the relevant legal obligation is defined.

If, in a situation in which this was foreseeable, a crowd attacks foreigners who are present on the territory of Ruritania, and the police fail to intervene effectively or at all, responsibility arises in accordance with customary international law and perhaps also by virtue of available treaty obligations. In this situation the State has failed in its duty to provide adequate protection to foreigners. The failure to do so involves the acts and omissions of its agents, but it is wholly artificial to say that the acts and omissions of the police, or of the crowd, are "imputable" to Ruritania.

(F) The Applicable Law

The normal context for the implementation of State responsibility involves the application of the principles of customary or general international law. In the process some reference may also be made to general principles of law in a confirming, or supplementary, role. However, the position may be varied by the agreement of States. It is not uncommon for special agreements to contain agreed formulations of the principles to be applied in the determination of responsibilities. This was the case when the United States and Britain agreed in the Treaty of Washington (1871) to settle the *Alabama Claims* by arbitration [167].

---

167. See Herbert Briggs, *The Law of Nations*, 2nd ed., London, Stevens & Sons, Ltd., 1953, pp. 1026-1027.

An increasing variant of this is the special agreement which refers to some extent to municipal law as the applicable law. The Iran-United States Claims Tribunal agreement provides as follows:

> "The Tribunal shall decide all cases on the basis of respect for law applying such choice of law rules and principles of commercial and international law as the Tribunal determines to be applicable, taking into account relevant usages of the trade, contract provisions and changed circumstances." [168]

Another interesting choice of law clause occurred in the *compromis* between *Greenpeace Stichting International* v. *The French State* (1987). This arbitration was based on a *compromis* or Special Agreement in which France accepted responsibility for the destruction of the *Rainbow Warrior* in Auckland harbour. The issue in this arbitration was exclusively about the quantum of damage, the compensation for the destruction of the vessel. The choice of law clause stipulated that the applicable law was *either* the law of England, *or* the law of New Zealand, *or* the law of France. No further criteria were indicated. The Decision of the Tribunal is not in the public domain.

It is now possible to move on to examine the conceptual basis of State responsibility.

(G) OBJECTIVE RESPONSIBILITY AND THE ROLE OF FAULT

The question which is debated in the literature from time to time is whether the basis of State responsibility is fault *(faute, culpa)* or a concept of relatively strict liability normally referred to as "objective responsibility".

Of course, no one doubts that either fault or intention *(dol, dolus)*, when proved are *sufficient* to generate responsibility. The question is whether responsibility can exist in the absence of proof of fault or intention to cause harm. The technically correct

168. Claims Settlement Agreement, Art. V; Declaration initialled on 19 January 1981, *International Legal Materials*, Vol. 20 (1981), p. 230.

response is to point out that each individual rule or principle of international law contains a specific content. However, few rules include explicit guidance on the role of fault and, consequently, the relevance of the general principles remains.

As a matter of positive law the position is clear. Both the practice of States and the preponderance of the decisions of international tribunals adopt the concept of objective responsibility. The small number of jurists who favour fault tend to do so because they have misunderstood the reasoning of the Court in the *Corfu Channel* case (Merits)[169]. This misunderstanding arises from the emphasis in the Judgment upon the need to prove knowledge on the part of Albania of the existence of the mines in her territorial sea. In fact, in the light of the subject-matter knowledge was the prerequisite of the legal duty of the territorial sovereign to give warning of the existence of the mines. The Court was simply giving expression to the nature of the particular duty. It was not deciding on the basis of an acceptance of some general theory of fault or otherwise.

In any case, and apart from the question of the legal status of objective responsibility, considerations of sound legal policy militate against adoption of the fault approach. Governments act through agents. Like corporations, they are legal entities and therefore *can only* act through agents. The effectiveness of international duties would be much reduced if the complainant State had to prove some level of knowledge or intention at a high level of government in respect of the acts or omissions of subordinate officials.

(H) PROBLEMS OF APPLICATION OF THE PRINCIPLES

After setting forth some of the general principles it is necessary to turn to the problems of *applying* such principles to the factual and legal complexities presented by the situations arising in practice. By way of illustration four cases will be examined.

---

169. *ICJ Reports 1949*, p. 4.

The first of these is the *Corfu Channel* case (Merits)[170], already referred to. This decision provides a very helpful demonstration of the necessary transition from the generalities of the literature to the particular problems of the marshalling of the evidence, the standard of proof and the application of the relevant legal principles in par-ticular situations. The facts of the *Corfu Channel* case make it an ideal test case for present purposes.

The key facts, as found by the Court, were as follows. As to the facts of the mining, the Court recorded the critical events as follows:

> "On October 22nd, 1946, a squadron of British warships, the cruisers *Mauritius* and *Leander* and the destroyers *Saumarez* and *Volage*, left the port of Corfu and proceeded northward through a channel previously swept for mines in the North Corfu Strait. The cruiser *Mauritius* was leading, followed by the destroyer *Saumarez*; at a certain distance thereafter came the cruiser *Leander* followed by the destroyer *Volage*. Outside the Bay of Saranda, *Saurmarez* struck a mine and was heavily damaged. *Volage* was ordered to give her assistance and to take her in tow. Whilst towing the damaged ship, *Volage* struck a mine and was much damaged. Nevertheless, she succeeded in towing the other ship back to Corfu.
>
> Three weeks later, on November 13th, the North Corfu Channel was swept by British minesweepers and twenty-two moored mines were cut. Two mines were taken to Malta for expert examination. During the minesweeping operation it was thought that the mines were of the German GR type, but it was subsequently established that they were of the German GY type . . .
>
> The Court consequently finds that the following facts are established. The two ships were mined in Albanian territorial waters in a previously swept and check-swept channel just at the place where a newly laid minefield consisting of moored contact German GY mines was discovered three weeks later. The damage sustained by the ships was inconsistent with damage which could have been caused by floating mines, magnetic ground mines, magnetic moored mines, or German GR mines, but its nature and extent were such as would be caused by mines of the type found in the minefield. In such circumstances the Court arrives at the conclu-

170. *ICJ Reports 1949*, p. 4.

> sion that the explosions were due to mines belonging to that minefield." [171]

The consequential findings were that there was no evidence that Albania had laid the mines and Albania had no means of minelaying of her own. There was no reliable evidence that the mines had been laid by a third State. Furthermore, there was no evidence to establish that Albania had direct knowledge of the existence of the mines in the North Corfu Channel in a navigable channel previously swept for mines [172].

The final argument of the United Kingdom had been that the minelaying could not have been done without the knowledge of the Albanian Government. The Court first of all sought to establish the appropriate standard of proof. In the first instance, the Court determined that the existence of control exercised by a State over its territory and territorial waters neither involved prima facie responsibility nor shifted the burden of proof [173].

The Court then continued:

> "On the other hand, the fact of this exclusive territorial control exercised by a State within its frontiers has a bearing upon the methods of proof available to establish the knowledge of that State as to such events. By reason of this exclusive control, the other State, the victim of a breach of international law, is often unable to furnish direct proof of facts giving rise to responsibility. Such a State should be allowed a more liberal recourse to inferences of fact and circumstantial evidence. This indirect evidence is admitted in all systems of law, and its use is recognized by international decisions. It must be regarded as of special weight when it is based on a series of facts linked together and leading logically to a single conclusion.
>
> The Court must examine therefore whether it has been established by means of indirect evidence that Albania has knowledge of minelaying in her territorial waters independently of any connivance on her part in this operation. The proof may be drawn from inferences of fact, provided that they leave *no room* for

171. *ICJ Reports 1949*, pp. 12-13, 15.
172. *Ibid.*, pp. 15-17.
173. *Ibid.*, p. 18.

> reasonable doubt. The elements of fact on which these inferences can be based may differ from those which are relevant to the question of connivance."[174]

The Court then carefully analysed the indirect evidence of Albania's knowledge of minelaying in her territorial waters. Such evidence included the fact that Albania had kept a close watch over the waters of the North Corfu Channel after the earlier incident of May 1946, and evidence and observation on site of Experts of the Court to the effect that any minelaying would have been detectable by the Albanian coastguards.

In the result the Court held that Albania was responsible for the explosions which occurred on 22 October 1946 in Albanian waters. This decision was consequential upon the Court's conclusions on the law and the facts, which were as follows:

> "From all the facts and observations mentioned above, the Court draws the conclusion that the laying of the minefield which caused the explosions on October 22nd, 1946, could not have been accomplished without the knowledge of the Albanian Government.
>
> The obligations resulting for Albania from this knowledge are not disputed between the Parties. Counsel for the Albanian Government expressly recognized that *[translation]* "if Albania had been informed of the operation before the incidents of October 22nd, and in time to warn the British vessels and shipping in general of the existence of mines in the Corfu Channel, her responsibility would be involved . . ."
>
> The obligations incumbent upon the Albanian authorities consisted of notifying, for the benefit of shipping in general, the existence of a minefield in Albanian territorial waters and in warning the approaching British warships of the imminent danger to which the minefield exposed them. Such obligations are based, not on the Hague Convention of 1907, No. VIII, which is applicable in time of war, but on certain general and well-recognized principles, namely: elementary considerations of humanity, even more exacting in peace than in war; the principle of the freedom of maritime communication; and every State's obligation not to allow know-

---

174. *ICJ Reports 1949*, p. 18.

> ingly its territory to be used for acts contrary to the rights of other States.
>
> If fact, Albania neither notified the existence of the minefield, nor warned the British warships of the danger they were approaching." [175]

The Judgment of the Court remains a valuable reminder of the need to avoid generalizing principles and simplistic polarities in the sphere of State responsibility.

The significance of focusing upon the precise character of the legal principles and causes of action involved in the individual case appears again in the case concerning *Military and Paramilitary Activities in and against Nicaragua (Nicaragua* v. *United States of America), Merits*[176].

In this case the basis of imputability was related to the nature of the particular cause of action, and to the type of evidence available. With respect to the direct attacks on ports and installations, and the laying of mines in Nicaraguan internal or territorial waters, these were carried out by United States nationals or by other agents of the United States. The planning, direction, support and execution of the operations involved United States nationals or foreign agents of the United States. On this basis the imputability of these acts to the United States was held to be established[177]. In respect of violations of Nicaraguan sovereignty by overflights, the evidence consisted for the most part of admissions in documents submitted to the Security Council[178], and consequently the attribution of responsibility to the United States created no difficulties.

Responsibility for the paramilitary activities of the *contras* directed against Nicaragua from bases in Honduras and Costa Rica involved the Court in significant distinctions. In particular, the degree of control exercised by the United States was critical. The Court recognized the partial dependency of the *contras* upon

175. *ICJ Reports 1949*, p. 22.

176. *ICJ Reports 1986*, p. 14.

177. *Ibid.*, pp. 45-51, paras. 75-86.

178. *Ibid.*, pp. 51-53, paras. 87-91.

the United States but concluded that the degree of control exercised by the latter did not have the implication that the acts committed by the *contras* in and against Nicaragua were attributable to the United States [179].

The result was that assistance to the *contras* by the United States, in the form of training, arming and financing the *contras*, constituted a breach by the United States of its obligation under customary international law not to intervene in the affairs of another State [180]. In the same way, assistance to the *contras* constituted a breach of the principle of the prohibition of the use of force [181], and infringements of the territorial sovereignty of Nicaragua [182].

In contrast to these determinations, the Court held that the relation of the United States to the *contras* was not so close as to render the United States responsible for breaches of humanitarian law committed by members of the *contras*[183].

(I) MULTILATERAL DISPUTES

It is not uncommon for a dispute brought by State A against State B to relate also to the legal interests and conduct of State C. In a situation in which State C has not consented to the jurisdiction of the Court this gives rise to difficult problems.

The first question which arises is whether there is an "indispensable parties rule" which would make such proceedings inadmissible *simply* on the basis that the remedies asked for by the Applicant implicate the rights and interests of third States absent from the proceedings. The Court has firmly denied the existence of such a rule in the case of *Nicaragua* v. *United States* (Jurisdiction and Admissibility) [184]. There the Court pointed out that other States which consider that they may be affected are free to insti-

179. *ICJ Reports 1986*, pp. 61-65, paras. 109-116.

180. *Ibid.*, pp. 123-125, paras. 239-242.

181. *Ibid.*, pp. 118-119, paras. 227-228; p. 128, para. 251.

182. *Ibid.*, pp. 127-128, paras. 250-252.

183. *Ibid.*, pp. 62-65, paras. 109-116; pp. 129-130, paras. 254-256.

184. *ICJ Reports 1984*, pp. 430-431, paras. 86-88.

tute separate proceedings or to employ the procedure of intervention.

The second question is whether the breaches of international law invoked by the Applicant State involve only joint responsibility as opposed to joint and several responsibility *(solidaire)*. In the case of *Nauru* v. *Australia* an Australian argument to this effect was rejected by the Court, at least as an admissibility argument [185]. In any event the persuasive view of Judge Shahabuddeen, in his separate opinion, was that, even if the responsibility was joint *exclusively*, this would not prevent Australia from being sued alone. In his view, even if Australia could be sued alone, the question whether Australia could be sued *for the whole damage* was a matter for the merits [186].

The third question concerns the principle propounded and applied by the International Court in the case concerning *Monetary Gold Removed from Rome in 1943 (Preliminary Question)* [187]. In the *Monetary Gold* case the Court held inadmissible a claim to a share of the Albanian monetary gold by Italy against three other States in proceedings from which Albania was absent. In the words of the Court:

> "To adjudicate upon the international responsibility of Albania without her consent would run counter to a well-established principle of international law embodied in the Court's Statute, namely, that the Court can only exercise jurisdiction over a State with its consent.
>
> . . . .
>
> In the present case, Albania's legal interests would not only be affected by a decision, but would form the very subject-matter of the decision. In such a case, the Statute cannot be regarded, by implication, as authorizing proceedings to be continued in the absence of Albania." [188]

185. *ICJ Reports 1992*, pp. 258-259, para. 48.
186. *Ibid.*, p. 286.
187. *ICJ Reports 1954*, p. 19.
188. *Ibid.*, p. 32.

In the *East Timor* case[189] the same principle was applied to exclude the claim of Portugal.

However, in other cases, the *Monetary Gold* case has been distinguished. This was the result in the *Nauru* case. There the Court reasoned as follows:

> "In the present case, the interests of New Zealand and the United Kingdom do not constitute the very subject-matter of the judgment to be rendered on the merits of Nauru's Application and the situation is in that respect different from that with which the Court had to deal in the *Monetary Gold* case. In the latter case the determination of Albania's responsibility was a prerequisite for a decision to be taken on Italy's claims. In the present case, the determination of the responsibility of New Zealand or the United Kingdom is not a prerequisite for the determination of the responsibility of Australia, the only object of Nauru's claim. Australia, moreover, recognizes that in this case there would not be a determination of the possible responsibility of New Zealand and the United Kingdom *previous* to the determination of Australia's responsibility. It nonetheless asserts that there would be a *simultaneous* determination of the responsibility of all three States and argues that, so far as concerns New Zealand and the United Kingdom, such a determination would be equally precluded by the fundamental reasons underlying the *Monetary Gold* decision. The Court cannot accept this contention. In the *Monetary Gold* case the link between, on the one hand, the necessary findings regarding Albania's alleged responsibility and, on the other, the decision requested of the Court regarding the allocation of the gold, was not purely temporal but also logical: as the Court explained,
>
> > 'In order . . . to determine whether Italy is entitled to receive the gold, it is necessary to determine whether Albania has committed any international wrong against Italy, and whether she is under an obligation to pay compensation to her.' (*I.C.J. Reports 1954*, p. 32.)
>
> In the present case, a finding by the Court regarding the existence or the content of the responsibility attributed to Australia by Nauru might well have implications for the legal situation of the two other States concerned, but no finding in respect of that legal

189. *ICJ Reports 1995*, p. 90.

situation will be needed as a basis for the Court's decision on Nauru's claims against Australia. Accordingly, the Court cannot decline to exercise its jurisdiction."[190]

---

190. *ICJ Reports 1992*, pp. 261-262, para 55.

CHAPTER VII

THE CONDITIONS FOR THE MAKING OF INTERNATIONAL CLAIMS

(A) The Rule of Law and the Identification of Legal Interest

The Rule of Law requires the effective implementation of the system of State responsibility and such effective implementation calls for the identification of the types of legal interest to be given protection. The law of international claims is concerned with the definition of legal interest and the other conditions of the admissibility of claims.

(B) The Requirement of a Legal Interest

The primary requirement for the making of an international claim is the existence of an interest *recognized by the law*. For reasons of policy there is no equation of damage suffered and the existence of a legal interest. As the International Court stated in its Judgment in the *Barcelona Traction* case: "Not a mere interest affected but solely a right infringed involves responsibility." [191] Thus in that case the Court refused to accept the claim of Belgium to act on behalf of shareholders in a Canadian corporation, whose interests, as it was alleged, had been damaged by acts and omissions on the part of the Spanish authorities.

In the *Northern Cameroons* case Judge Wellington Koo, with some other members of the International Court, classified the issues in terms of admissibility and legal interest [192]. The majority

191. *ICJ Reports 1970*, p. 36.

192. See Wellington Koo, separate opinion, *ICJ Reports 1963*, pp. 44-46; and G. G. Fitzmaurice, separate opinion, *ibid.*, pp. 105, 108-111.

of the Court adopted the position that the issue raised was "remote from reality". The results of the plebiscite in the Northern Cameroons had been approved by the General Assembly of the United Nations which had declared that British administration should terminate on 1 June 1961 [193].

The decision of the Court in the *Nuclear Tests* cases is also relevant. In these cases brought by Australia and New Zealand against France the radioactive fallout resulting from nuclear testing was alleged to violate the sovereignty of the Applicant States. The difficulty here was to present a cause of action which adequately reflected the harm suffered. The Court held that the issue had become moot, that is to say, that there was no issue to try, because French Ministers had made public statements indicating the intention to discontinue the tests [194].

In the case of *Nauru* v. *Australia*[195], key elements in the dispute related to the period before Nauru achieved independence in 1968. This aspect of the case did not appear to create difficulties for the Court. In all probability a contributing factor was that the pleadings of Australia had relied heavily on pre-independence negotiations and transactions as the basis for the preliminary objections, particularly in relation to the question of waiver.

A final example may be taken. In his separate opinion in the *East Timor* case [196] Judge Oda gave his own reasons for voting with the Court in favour of the decision that there was no basis of jurisdiction. In his opinion Portugal simply "lacked *locus standi* to bring against Australia this particular case concerning the continental shelf in the Timor Sea". On Judge Oda's construction of the claim, the case related "*solely* to the title to the continental shelf which Portugal claims to possess as a coastal State". In his view Portugal did not have the status of a coastal State. On this basis the only dispute concerning Portugal was whether it was Portugal

---

193. *ICJ Reports 1963*, pp. 33-34.

194. *Nuclear Tests (Australia* v. *France)* case, *ICJ Reports 1974*, p. 253 at pp. 268-272, paras. 47-59.

195. *ICJ Reports 1992*, p. 240.

196. *ICJ Reports 1995*, p. 90 at pp. 107-118.

or Indonesia which had the status of a coastal State located on the Territory of East Timor. In his words:

> "This is the dispute in relation to which Portugal could have instituted proceedings against Indonesia on the merits. However, any issue concerning the seabed area of the 'Timor Gap' could *not* have been the subject-matter of a dispute between Portugal and Australia until such time as Portugal had been established as having the status of the coastal State entitled to the corresponding continental shelf . . ."[197]

(C) THE EXISTENCE OF A LEGAL INTEREST IS NECESSARY BUT NOT SUFFICIENT

At this point it is useful to recall that *even when* the existence of a legal interest is established, this may not be sufficient. At least three types of factor may supervene to prevent the Court exercising jurisdiction. First, in the *Northern Cameroons* case[198], the majority of the Court invoked the ground of judicial propriety, refusing to decide a hypothetical issue unrelated to any concrete remedial outcome[199]. Secondly, in the *Nuclear Tests* cases the Court held that the issue had become moot in view of the public statements of intention by French officials. Thirdly, in the *Monetary Gold*[200] and *East Timor*[201] cases the very close relationship of the subject-matter of the claims and the legal interest of a third State precluded the exercise of jurisdiction.

(D) THE FURTHER REQUIREMENT OF A CAUSE OF ACTION

The claimant must have a legal interest, that is, an interest recognized as such by the law. In addition the claimant must be able

197. *ICJ Reports 1995*, p. 112, para. 6.
198. *ICJ Reports 1963*, pp. 33-34.
199. Footnote 194, *supra*.
200. *ICJ Reports 1954*, p. 19.
201. *ICJ Reports 1995*, p. 90.

to invoke a cause of action appropriate to protect his legal interest. In many situations the invocation of the appropriate cause of action involves no complications. However, in certain cases the precise formulation of the claim is of considerable significance. A sample of such cases will be presented.

The *Interhandel* case[202] involved an Application by Switzerland against the United States concerning the interpretation of the Washington Accord of 1946 relating to the unblocking of Swiss assets in the United States at the end of the war. Switzerland had presented two claims: a "principal claim" for restitution of Interhandel assets in the United States, and an "alternative claim" designed to raise issues concerning the interpretation and application of two international agreements. It was clearly intended that the alternative claim would avoid the operation of the local remedies rule, on the basis that direct injury to the State was involved. The Court held that the two Swiss claims were substantially the same and upheld the United States preliminary objection based on the failure by Interhandel to exhaust local remedies in the courts of the United States.

In the *Nuclear Tests* cases[203] Australia and New Zealand, as Applicant States, faced the difficult task of selecting appropriate and effective causes of action in relation to a complex factual situation. The problems involved will be examined below in Chapter XIII.

In the proceedings in *Nicaragua* v. *United States*[204] a major element in the drafting of the Nicaraguan Application, and in the subsequent pleadings, was to avoid the ambit of the multilateral treaty reservation in the United States Declaration of acceptance of the jurisdiction of the Court under the Optional Clause. The issue was postponed to the Merits phase and at that stage the reservation was applied with the result that the Court did not have jurisdiction in respect of claims based upon the United Nations

202. *ICJ Reports 1959*, p. 6.

203. *ICJ Reports 1974*, p. 253 ; *ibid.*, p. 457.

204. *ICJ Reports 1984*, p. 392 (Jurisdiction and Admissibility) ; *ICJ Reports 1986*, p. 14 (Merits).

Charter, Article 2, paragraph 4, or upon provisions of the Charter of the Organization of American States [205].

This determination did not prejudice the repertory of causes of action based upon customary international law on which, together with the Treaty of Friendship, Commerce and Navigation, the Court relied in its decision on the Merits. However, in a dissenting opinion Sir Robert Jennings expressed strong reservations concerning the Court's willingness to apply customary law "as it were in lieu of recourse to the relevant multilateral treaties". In particular, Sir Robert found it difficult to discern a principle of customary law existing independently of the provisions of Article 2, paragraph 4, and of Article 51 of the Charter [206].

(E) THE DIRECT INTEREST OF A STATE

As we shall see, a high proportion of claims by States relate to losses caused to their nationals or to national corporations. However, claims are presented in certain cases on the basis of the direct interest of the claimant State. The *Corfu Channel* case (Merits) [207] is a good example of such claims. Apart from the claim for damage to the warships, in respect of claims arising out of the death and injuries of crew members, the compensation claimed included the cost of pensions, and other grants made by the British Government to the victims or to their dependants, together with the costs of administration and medical treatment. Similarly in the case concerning *United States Diplomatic and Consular Staff in Tehran* [208] the Application of the United States requested the Court, *inter alia*, to adjudge and declare:

> ". . . . .
>
> *(b)* That pursuant to the foregoing international obligations, the Government of Iran is under a particular obligation

---

205. *ICJ Reports 1986*, pp. 31-38, paras. 42-56.
206. *Ibid.*, pp. 529-536.
207. *ICJ Reports 1949*, p. 4.
208. *ICJ Reports 1980*, p. 3.

immediately to secure the release of all United States nationals currently being detained within the premises of the United States Embassy in Tehran and to assure that all such persons and all other United States nationals in Tehran are allowed to leave Iran safely ;

(c) That the Government of Iran shall pay to the United States, in its own right and in the exercise of its right of diplomatic protection of its nationals, reparation for the foregoing violations of Iran's international legal obligations to the United States, in a sum to be determined by the Court ; and

(d) That the Government of Iran submit to its competent authorities for the purpose of prosecution those persons responsible for the crimes committed against the premises and staff of the United States Embassy and against the premises of its Consulates."

In the *Nicaragua* case[209] the claims advanced against the United States consisted substantially of claims for harm to the direct interest of Nicaragua as a State. In addition, the Court was asked to declare that the United States was under

> "an obligation to pay Nicaragua, in its own right and as *parens patriae* for the citizens of Nicaragua, reparation for damages to persons, property and the Nicaraguan economy caused by the foregoing violations of international law, in a sum to be determined by the Court".

In this context it may be noticed that a State may have an interest on the plane of international law in movables. In the *Temple* case (Merits)[210] the Cambodian Final Submissions asked for restitution of the sculptures and other items removed from the Temple by the Thai authorities since 1954. The International Court treated the request for restitution as "implicit in, and consequential on, the claim of sovereignty itself"[211].

209. *ICJ Reports 1986*, p. 14 at p. 19.

210. *ICJ Reports 1962*, p. 6.

211. *Ibid.*, p. 36.

(F) THE RULE OF NATIONALITY OF CLAIMS

Most claims by States are made on behalf of nationals and corporations and concern denial of justice, expropriation, arbitrary arrest, maltreatment, and breaches of the standards of treatment set forth in treaties of friendship, commerce and navigation, or treaties of establishment.

In the case of claims on behalf of individuals, the legal interest of the claimant State depends upon the link of nationality. Nationality is thus the criterion of legal interest. The nationality of claims is operated in accordance with the principle of the continuous nationality of claims. The individual concerned must have the nationality of the claimant State at the time of the alleged harm and then continuously until the presentation of the claim by diplomatic means or, if a tribunal is involved, until the date of the award or judgment.

In practice considerable problems are generated when the individual on whose behalf a claim is presented also has the nationality of the respondent State. The question of dual nationality frequently arises in practice in situations in which the individual concerned has changed his or her nationality subsequent to the wrong complained of, but without necessarily discarding the previous nationality.

The practice of States and the jurisprudence of international tribunals speak with an uncertain voice in this area. Two very different approaches co-exist in the sources of the law. British practice is based on the principle that a "State may not afford diplomatic protection to one of its nationals against a State whose nationality such person also possesses". This principle was adopted in the Hague Convention Concerning Certain Questions Relating to the Conflict of Nationality Laws of 1930, Article 4. The other approach is to allow the claim provided that the effective or dominant nationality of the individual is that of the claimant State. This is the principle applied by the United States Department of State. The effective nationality approach is commonly applied by international tribunals.

There are permutations of this problem, for example, when one of the "two States" of a dual national claims against a third State and the latter contends that the "other nationality" of the individual in question is the effective or dominant nationality.

The permutation which creates particular difficulty is presented by cases in which prima facie the individual has one nationality or none. This was the situation in the *Nottebohm* case *(Liechtenstein* v. *Guatemala)* (Second Phase)[212]. Nottebohm had lost his German nationality in 1939. In spite of residence in Guatemala of 34 years, he had not acquired nationality there when he was deported in 1943. The Court adopted the technique applied in the previous jurisprudence in cases of dual nationality, that is, the criterion of "social fact of attachment, a genuine connection of existence, interests and sentiments", to the State of the putative nationality[213]. In the event the Court refused to recognize the validity of Nottebohm's naturalization in Liechtenstein in 1939 for the purposes of diplomatic protection. In other words, the naturalization did not provide a basis for the legal interest of Liechtenstein and the claim was therefore inadmissible.

The decision was based partly on the absence of social bonds of attachment with Liechtenstein and partly on the existence of a collateral purpose for the naturalization, namely, the motive of Mr. Nottebohm to substitute for his status as a national of a belligerent State that of a national of a neutral State in the context of the war which had begun in Europe.

The principle of the dominant and effective nationality has been criticized on the ground that it tends to subvert the status of nationality and increase the possibility of statelessness. The fact remains that international tribunals rely upon the concept fairly often. Thus the Iran-United States Claims Tribunal has adopted the principle in its well-known decision in *Case No. A/18*[214]. However, the Tribunal added a qualification:

---

212. *ICJ Reports 1955*, p. 4.

213. *Ibid.*, p. 23.

214. *International Law Reports*, E. Lauterpacht (ed.), Vol. 75, p. 176.

> "To this conclusion the Tribunal adds an important caveat. In cases where the Tribunal finds jurisdiction based upon a dominant and effective nationality of the claimant, the other nationality may remain relevant to the merits of the claim." [215]

This proviso clearly refers to situations in which reliance upon the other nationality would involve elements of fraud, or estoppel, or fundamental considerations of equity, such as the principle of clean hands.

(G) THE NATIONALITY OF CORPORATIONS

The nationality of corporations and other legal persons of private law is a constant source of difficulty, not least because in such cases "nationality" is a legal construct or link imposed *ex post facto*. More often than not bilateral treaties provide the necessary criteria.

Treaty provisions use a variety of criteria including *siège sociale*, the source of actual control, ownership, and place of creation. An important example is Article VII of the Agreement constituting the Iran-United States Claims Tribunal [216], which provides as follows:

> "For the purpose of this Agreement:
>
> 1. A 'national' of Iran or of the United States, as the case may be, means *(a)* a natural person who is a citizen of Iran or the United States; and *(b)* a corporation or other legal entity which is organized under the laws of Iran or the United States or any of its states or territories, the District of Columbia or the Commonwealth of Puerto Rico, if, collectively, natural persons who are citizens of such country hold, directly or indirectly, an interest in such corporation or entity equivalent to fifty per cent or more of its capital stock.
>
> 2. 'Claims of nationals' of Iran or the United States, as the case may be, means claims owned continuously, from the date on which the claim arose to the date on which this Agreement enters into

---

215. *International Law Reports*, E. Lauterpacht (ed.), Vol. 75, p. 194.

216. *Iran-United States Claims Tribunal Reports*, Cambridge, Grotius Publications, Vol. 1, 1983, p. 9.

> force, by nationals of that state, including claims that are owned indirectly by such nationals through ownership of capital stock or other proprietary interests in juridical persons, provided that the ownership of interests of such nationals, collectively, were sufficient at the time the claim arose to control the corporation or other entity, and provided, further, that the corporation or other entity is not itself entitled to bring a claim under the terms of this Agreement. Claims referred to the arbitration Tribunal shall, as of the date of filing of such claims with the Tribunal, be considered excluded from the jurisdiction of the courts of Iran, or of the United States, or of any other court."

It is of interest to note that the Permanent Court applied the concept of nationality to non-commercial legal entities in the course of applying treaty provisions. Thus in its Judgment concerning *Certain German Interests in Polish Upper Silesia*[217] the Permanent Court held that the City of Ratibor fell within the category of "German nationals" within the meaning of Article 12 of the German-Polish Convention concerning Upper Silesia of 1922. Similarly, the Permanent Court held that the Royal Hungarian Peter Pazmany University of Budapest was a "Hungarian national", for the purposes of the relevant provisions of the Treaty of Trianon, in its Judgment on the *Appeal from a Judgment of the Hungaro/Czechoslovak Mixed Arbitral Tribunal*, 1933[218].

(H) Other Issues Affecting the Admissibility of Claims

(i) *The local remedies rule*

A long-established standard rule of customary law is the principle that a claim will not be admissible on the international plane unless the individual alien or corporation concerned has exhausted the legal remedies available in the State alleged to be the cause of the injury involved. The principle can be, and often is, waived by agreement, and it applies only to cases in which the harm is not in

217. *PCIJ, Series A, No.* 7, pp. 73, 74-75.

218. *PCIJ, Series A/B, No. 61*, pp. 208, 227-232.

the form of direct injury to the State of nationality of the complainant.

The application of the local remedies rule leads to numerous difficulties in practice. The rationale of the principle is itself subject to debate. At one level the rule can be explained on the basis of the more convenient forum. Thus the individual or corporation may find it difficult to persuade the State of nationality to present a claim, and such action is a matter of State discretion. Resorting to local remedies is a procedure within the power of the individual or corporation.

There are, however, substantial countervailing considerations. Most individuals would find litigation in foreign courts practically impossible. If it had been established that the enterprise operating the Chernobyl reactor had been a non-State entity, the claimant hill farmers of the United Kingdom would have had to resort to the courts in the former Soviet Ukraine. It is true that the local remedies rule only applies when effective remedies are available in the relevant national system, but the process of testing this proposition in concrete cases will be complex and expensive. As a matter of good policy, it is arguable that the rule should only be applicable if a prior voluntary link exists between the individual alien and the Respondent State[219]. At the same time this condition of exhaustion of local remedies is clearly established in the law.

In the world of international litigation the rule appears as a legitimate procedural device in the hands of Respondent States. In this context the classification of the subject-matter of the claim is of the first importance. Thus in the *Elettronica Sicula S.p.A. (ELSI) (United States* v. *Italy)* case[220] the first issue was whether the local remedies rule applied to the provisions of the Treaty of Friendship, Commerce and Navigation between the United States and Italy. The United States contended that the breaches alleged involved direct injury to the United States and, consequently, that

219. See International Court of Justice, *ICJ Pleadings*, *Aerial Incident (Israel* v. *Bulgaria)*, 1959, pp. 531-532 (Argument of Mr. Rosenne).

220. *ICJ Reports 1989*, p. 15.

the rule did not apply. The International Court rejected the argument on the ground that the subject-matter of the claim was essentially the alleged damage to the two corporations, Raytheon and Machlett, alleged to be affected by breaches of the Treaty. The second issue to be resolved was whether the local remedies rule applied to a request for a declaratory judgment. The Court found that the claim for treaty violations was not distinct or severable from the claim for damage to the corporations[221]. The issue of principle was thus avoided.

(ii) *Delay in the presentation of claims*

The rubric is, as is commonly the case with general headings, misleading. Thus the literature often refers to the "defence of superior orders", in spite of the fact that there is no defence of superior orders *as such*, though there may be defences of coercion or mistake of law, depending on the facts. So it is with delay. The context is that of the admissibility of claims, and delay in presentation *as such* is not a condition of admissibility. Delay may *in particular circumstances* constitute an implied waiver of a claim.

The other aspect of delay concerns the extent to which the circumstances indicate how the procedural equities fall. Thus, lapse of time will probably not operate if the Respondent State has not suffered any procedural disadvantage. In this connection the conduct of the Respondent State will be relevant. Once the claim has been notified to the Respondent State, there is a presumption against undue delay. Each case will depend upon the particular facts and a judicial determination that a claim is admissible will not preclude further examination of the question of undue delay[222].

(I) Concluding Remarks

The admissibility of claims is often regarded as "black letter law" and therefore not central to the concerns of those, especially

---

221. *ICJ Reports 1989*, pp. 42-43, paras. 51-52.

222. See the Judgment in the case concerning *Certain Phosphate Lands in Nauru (Nauru* v. *Australia)*, *ICJ Reports 1992*, pp. 253-255, paras. 31-36; and see further the *Written Statement of the Republic of Nauru*, July 1991, pp. 47-60.

in universities, whose criteria of significance tend to be related to current intellectual fashions. In reality, the department of "admissibility" comprises concepts and principles which are of fundamental importance: the identification of legal interests, the limits to the judicial function, the causes of action, and principles of procedural equity.

These topics involve the implementation of the Rule of Law in the sphere both of diplomatic protection and also of the work of international tribunals. Careful study of this significant family of subjects reveals that "black letter law" in these areas is by no means cut and dried but involves some sophisticated and difficult issues.

CHAPTER VIII

THE PEACEFUL SETTLEMENT OF DISPUTES

(A) Conspectus: Certain Basic Concepts

It must be self-evident that the legal régime of the peaceful settlement of disputes is a part of the mechanisms of international public order. By way of introduction it is necessary to look at the principles and concepts which form the background.

The first principle is that all Member States of the United Nations "shall settle their international disputes by peaceful means". This is a "Principle" set forth in the United Nations Charter (Art. 2, para. 3) and is generally recognized as a principle of general international law. However, neither the Charter, nor general international law, include a positive duty *to settle* disputes[223].

The term "peaceful settlement" may seem clear in meaning but there are some complexities. Peaceful settlement may result in one of three outcomes: *(a)* an agreed compromise; *(b)* settlement according to law; *(c)* multilateral settlements which may be imposed: see, for example, the Peace Treaties of 1947 and the Geneva Agreement on Indochina of 1954.

The concept of a dispute is approached by the Court in a spirit of realism. The key passages in the *East Timor* Judgment read as follows:

> "The Court recalls that, in the sense accepted in its jurisprudence and that of its predecessor, a dispute is a disagreement on a point of law or fact, a conflict of legal views or interests between parties (see *Mavrommatis Palestine Concessions, P.C.I.J., Series A, No. 2*, p. 11; *Northern Cameroons, I.C.J. Reports 1963*, p. 27; and *Applicability of the Obligation to Arbitrate under Section 21 of the United*

223. See G. G. Fitzmaurice, *Modern Law Review*, Vol. 19 (1956), pp. 4-6.

> *Nations Headquarters Agreement of 26 June 1947, I.C.J. Reports 1988*, p. 27, para. 35). In order to establish the existence of a dispute, 'It must be shown that the claim of one party is positively opposed by the other' (*South West Africa, Preliminary Objections, I.C.J. Reports 1962*, p. 328); and further, 'whether there exists an international dispute is a matter for objective determination' (*Interpretation of Peace Treaties with Bulgaria, Hungary and Romania, I.C.J. Reports 1950*, p. 74).
>
> For the purpose of verifying the existence of a legal dispute in the present case, it is not relevant whether the 'real dispute' is between Portugal and Indonesia rather than Portugal and Australia. Portugal has, rightly or wrongly, formulated complaints of fact and law against Australia which the latter has denied. By virtue of this denial, there is a legal dispute.
>
> On the record before the Court, it is clear that the Parties are in disagreement, both on the law and on the facts, on the question whether the conduct of Australia in negotiating, concluding and initiating performance of the 1989 Treaty was in breach of an obligation due by Australia to Portugal under international law.
>
> Indeed, Portugal's Application limits the proceedings to these questions. There nonetheless exists a legal dispute between Portugal and Australia. This objection of Australia must therefore be dismissed."[224]

The topic of peaceful settlement is dominated by the principle that the consent of the parties is a precondition of settlement. The existence of consent is determined in accordance with sophisticated principles and, in the result, a legal consent may exist which does not coincide with a contemporary political acceptance of the machinery of peaceful settlement.

The principle remains unchallenged in spite of certain apparent exceptions and limitations. Thus it is not uncommon for the political organs of the United Nations to make determinations of legal responsibility and indicate the existence of a consequent duty of reparation (see Chap. VI). Such determinations may or may not provide the basis for the settlement of the relevant dispute. A clearer limitation upon the principle of consent derives from the recent practice of the Security Council in imposing sanctions upon Iraq

---

224. *ICJ Reports 1995*, pp. 99-100, para. 22.

after the illegal invasion of Kuwait. Linked to the sanctions was the imposition of machinery for the assessment and payment of compensation in respect of the consequences of the illegal conduct of the Iraqi Government.

(B) METHODS OF SETTLEMENT

The literature of international law tends to place too much emphasis on adjudication. The experience of international relations offers up an extensive selection of methods of settlement and new variations appear from time to time. It is ironical that methods such as mediation, long familiar to international lawyers, are now fashionably referred to in anglophone circles as forms of "alternative dispute settlement".

(i) *Negotiation*

The normal method of settlement is negotiation leading usually either to a definitive settlement or to agreement on another means of settlement or to a *modus vivendi*. Negotiation has the virtues of flexibility and may involve the infusion of technical considerations unsuited to judicial activity. The occurrence of prior negotiations is not a condition of admissibility but such negotiations may play a useful role in isolating the essential elements of a dispute which is subsequently adjudicated.

(ii) *Mediation and conciliation*

Negotiation is, so to speak, a private transaction. In the alternative there are methods involving third parties, either States or appropriate individuals. Apart from the formal methods of arbitration and adjudication, there are the institutions known as mediation and conciliation. Mediation involves the *direct* conduct of negotiations by the parties on the basis of proposals made by the mediator. The proposals are not binding. In theory mediation is less formal than conciliation.

In reality there is no standard form and each mediation will have its own specific profile, constructed for the needs of the specific case. A recent mediation dealing with sensitive issues between Chile and Argentina was conducted by His Holiness the Pope in the period 1979-1984 [225]. This particular mediation was *ad hoc* but it is normal for multilateral treaties for pacific settlement to provide for a procedure by way of mediation: as, for example, in the American Treaty on Pacific Settlement of 1948 [226].

A standard definition of conciliation is as follows:

> "Conciliation is the process of settling a dispute by referring it to a commission of persons whose task it is to elucidate the facts and (usually after hearing the parties and endeavouring to bring them to an agreement) to make a report containing proposals for a settlement, but which is not binding." [227]

In principle conciliation is more structured and quasi-judicial in function than mediation. However, the precise modalities vary from commission to commission [228]. Some conciliations are similar to arbitrations. The legal basis of a conciliation may be an *ad hoc* agreement, as in the *Iceland/Norway* conciliation of 1981 [229], or in modern multilateral agreements on peaceful settlement, such as the European Convention on Peaceful Settlement of International Disputes of 1957 [230].

(iii) *Arbitration and adjudication*

In its modern form arbitration does not differ essentially from adjudication, although the term arbitration is reserved for the creation of *ad hoc* tribunals with a limited calendar of business and normally devoted to a single dispute. Arbitration involves the application of international law in order to produce a decision binding upon the parties.

225. See E. Lauterpacht, *Mélanges Michel Virally*, Paris, Pedone, 1991, p. 359.

226. Arts. 11-14.

227. See L. Oppenheim, *International Law*, Vol. II, 7th ed. by H. Lauterpacht, Longmans, London, 1952, p. 12.

228. See J. G. Merrills, *International Dispute Settlement*, 2nd ed., Cambridge, Grotius Publications, 1991, pp. 59-72.

229. *International Law Reports*, E. Lauterpacht (ed.), Vol. 62, p. 108.

230. United Nations, *Treaty Series*, Vol. 320, p. 243.

The concept and practice of arbitration are ancient indeed, but it was in the late eighteenth century and nineteenth century that arbitration was revived as a practical mode of dispute settlement. However, some careful distinctions must be drawn. Until the end of the nineteenth century arbitration was not a consistently legal procedure. The mixed commissions and individual arbitrators would often act partly as conciliators, "law and equity" would be applied, and awards were not necessarily reasoned. The *Alabama Claims* case of 1871[231] provided an exception, involving a reasoned award. Since 1899 the difference between arbitration and adjudication, in relation to the essential legal quality of the procedure, has disappeared. After the appearance of a system of permanent international tribunals (in 1920) the practice of *ad hoc* arbitration continued. Standards are now more consistent and since 1907 reasoned awards have been the rule[232].

(C) THE INTERNATIONAL COURT OF JUSTICE AND COMPULSORY JURISDICTION

At the Hague Peace Conferences of 1899 and 1907 efforts were made to codify and to enhance the procedures of peaceful settlement, and a panel of available arbitrators, the Permanent Court of Arbitration, was instituted. More significantly, at the Conference of 1907 plans were adumbrated of a standing Court of Arbitral Justice[233]. In 1920, during the Paris Peace Conference, the difficult problem of the election of members of the Court was solved, and the Statute of the Permanent Court of International Justice was drafted. In 1946 this institution was replaced by the International Court of Justice, which was, in all its essentials, a continuation of the earlier Court.

---

231. See J. B. Moore, *Arbitrations*, Washington, GPO, 1898, Vol. 1, p. 635; *British and Foreign State Papers*, Vol. 62, p. 233.

232. See the Hague Convention for the Pacific Settlement of International Disputes, 1907, Art. 79.

233. Manley O. Hudson, *The Permanent Court of International Justice 1920-1942*, New York, Macmillan, 1943, pp. 80-84.

The new Permanent Court held its inaugural session in 1922. The bases of jurisdiction were three-fold: clauses in treaties, special agreements to submit cases to the Court, and the system of compulsory jurisdiction.

The system of compulsory jurisdiction needs to be explained. It is based upon the so-called Optional Clause, Article 36 (2) of the Statute:

> "The States parties to the present Statute may at any time declare that they recognize as compulsory *ipso facto* and without special agreement, in relation to any other State accepting the same obligation, the jurisdiction of the Court in all legal disputes concerning: [various questions of international law]."

The unilateral declarations of acceptance of this system of jurisdiction would operate conjointly with other declarations, at the common level of overlapping subject-matter, when the declarant State was the object of an Application filed by another declarant. The jurisdiction was "compulsory" only in the ordinary sense that the States Parties to the system had agreed in advance to submit to the jurisdiction in these conditions.

In political terms both in 1922 and in 1946 the conception of compulsory jurisdiction inherent in a standing tribunal of international justice was very radical. The conception continues to be radical. For those States for whom disparities in military and economic power are convertible into advantages in relations with other States *generally*, then appearance in a forum in which the governing principles are impartiality and equality is not attractive.

The role of the International Court (and its predecessor) is conventionally assessed in terms of the system of compulsory jurisdiction and, initially, this approach will be adopted here.

(i) *The deterioration of the system*

The conventional assessment entails the chronicling of the evidence of the increasing debility of the system of compulsory jurisdiction.

(ii) *The incidence of acceptance of compulsory jurisdiction*

By 1934 42 States had accepted the Optional Clause out of a total of 57 States Members of the League of Nations. This was an encouraging level of acceptance. However, it is worth noting that in the first nine-year period of the Court's operation only one out of ten cases begun by application was based upon the compulsory jurisdiction.

When the International Court of Justice opened for business in 1946 the level of acceptance of compulsory jurisdiction was low. In 1946-1947 there were 25 acceptances out of a total of 51 Member States of the United Nations. By 1954-1955, 33 States out of 64 Member States had made declarations. For a long period (1965 to 1990) the proportion of acceptances remained at one-third of the number of Member States of the United Nations. Since 1990 the number of acceptances has slowly increased and currently stands at 58. In the period since 1946 only one permanent member of the Security Council, the United Kingdom, has consented to remain party to the compulsory jurisdiction and the general opinion of learned commentators has been pessimistic[234]. China and the former Soviet Union did not participate at any stage. France and the United States terminated their acceptances in 1974 and 1985 respectively.

(iii) *Qualitative deterioration of the system*

The so-called Optional Clause (Article 36, paragraph 2, of the Statute of the Court) represented a compromise between a system of automatic compulsory jurisdiction for all parties to the Statute and a system reliant exclusively upon specific treaty provisions conferring jurisdiction in relation to certain subject-matter and vis-à-vis the particular parties to those treaties. The compromise involved permitting declarant States to opt into the compulsory jurisdiction whilst at the same time defining the classes of disputes with respect to which the declaration was to apply. This compro-

234. See C. H. M. Waldock, *British Year Book*, Vol. 32 (1955-1956), p. 244; J. G. Merrills, *ibid.*, Vol. 50 (1979), p. 87.

mise was adopted in 1920 and again by the Committee of Jurists sitting in 1945.

This form of compromise meant that the making of reservations to acceptances of jurisdiction was inherent in the system. However, it is probable that the variety and nature of the reservations which were to appear in due course was not fully appreciated. It is true to say that the possibility of making reservations was regarded by the League as an inducement to adhere to the Optional Clause and that the concepts on the basis of which the provision is drafted contain certain sources of inevitable confusion, especially in relation to "reciprocity"[235]. In practice States have imposed time-limits on the duration of declarations and have also reserved the right to withdraw acceptance at any moment by notice to the Secretary-General of the United Nations.

Further evidence of deterioration in the system emerged when certain Respondent States, prima facie subject to the system of compulsory jurisdiction, refused to take part in the process of presenting pleadings and oral arguments[236]. This practice was initiated by Iceland in the *Fisheries Jurisdiction* cases *(United Kingdom* and *Federal Republic of Germany* v. *Iceland)* in 1972-1974[237].

To this picture of dilapidation it used to be normal to add the evidence of a modest performance by the Court in terms of the number of contentious cases actually dealt with. Between 1946 and 1978 the Court dealt with 39 contentious cases and 16 requests for advisory opinions. In the period from 1960 to 1978 the Court's calendar was particularly sparse.

(iv) *The picture of deterioration stands in need of correction*

In general this conventional picture of dilapidation is considerably out of focus. The evidence for this is to be seen in the fact that in the period since 1978 the Court has been busy in spite of

---

235. See H. W. A. Thirlway, *Netherlands Yearbook of International Law*, Vol. XV (1984), pp. 103-107.

236. See G. G. Fitzmaurice, *British Year Book*, Vol. 51 (1980), p. 89.

237. *ICJ Reports 1972*, pp. 12 and 181; *ICJ Reports 1973*, p. 49; and *ICJ Reports 1974*, p. 3.

the fact that none of the assumed causes of debility have disappeared, with the exception of non-appearance.

The picture of dilapidation results to a considerable extent from the link, assumed by writers, between the compulsory jurisdiction and the general welfare of the Court. No doubt the well-being of the compulsory jurisdiction has symbolic significance, but it is illogical to make it the principal measure of the successful operation of the Court. Much of the Court's contentious work relates to compromissory clauses in treaties and to cases brought on the basis of special agreements. Most delimitation cases have come before the Court by means of special agreements[238].

Turning to the practice of making reservations to declarations accepting the compulsory jurisdiction, the significance of the practice is surely exaggerated. As it has been pointed out already, reservations and conditions were always part of the scheme of things, and the flexible régime was seen as an encouragement to adhere to the system. In any event the so-called automatic reservation has not prospered and in the *Nicaragua* proceedings[239] the United States saw no profit in invoking its original automatic reservation.

Finally, there is the significance of the calendar of cases, and especially contentious cases, in front of the Court. The fact is that since 1978 the Court has dealt with 26 contentious cases. More important is the consideration that it is difficult to discern why, at any one period, States take disputes to the Court. Clearly the performance of the Court, and its evident impartiality, provide a basis of confidence. It must also be pointed out that the *number* of cases going to the Court is by no means the only criterion of success. The flow of business is broad-based, both in the sense that it is not confined to one type of jurisdiction or to States of a particular region or ideology.

In this context it is justifiable to emphasize that the disputes taken before the Court have a special character and cannot be

238. See, for example, the *Gulf of Maine (Canada/United States of America)* case, *ICJ Reports 1984*, p. 246; and the case concerning the *Territorial Dispute (Libyan Arab Jamahiriya/Chad)*, *ICJ Reports 1994*, p. 6.

239. *ICJ Reports 1984*, p. 392.

compared to the cases in front of municipal courts. Many delimitation cases involve the permanent status of territory and resources. The appropriate analogy is with issues of public law, and the issue of compensation tends to be secondary.

On occasion the Court has responded to the criticism of writers and others by making changes in its procedure. In particular in 1972 the Rules were revised to encourage resort to Chambers of the Court[240]. The functioning of the Chambers has received mixed reviews, and resort to the Chamber procedure is less fashionable than it was. At the end of the day whether States resort to the Court or not depends not upon procedural embellishments but upon the political habits of mind of Governments, as Sir Gerald Fitzmaurice has pointed out[241].

(D) ARBITRATION AND ADJUDICATION COMPARED

Earlier in this chapter it was stressed that modern arbitration and adjudication between States are essentially the same. This conjunction was the result of the disappearance of the procedural eccentricities of arbitration as it was practised in the nineteenth century. For practical purposes it is the International Court of Justice which provides the paradigm of adjudication and it is useful to notice the factors which still serve to differentiate recourse to arbitration and recourse to the International Court.

It is often said that arbitration is less expensive and more expeditious than recourse to the Court. Experience suggests that the virtues of arbitration in relation to typical inter-State disputes are mythical. The parties to an arbitration must create the tribunal, negotiate the terms of arbitration, and appoint and remunerate the members of the tribunal and its apparatus, including the registrar. In contrast the International Court is free to all, subject to the parties paying their own costs, and provides an experienced

240. See E. Jiménez de Aréchaga, *American Journal of International Law*, Vol. 67 (1973), p. 1.

241. G. G. Fitzmaurice, Institut de droit international, *Livre du centenaire 1873-1973, Évolution et perspectives du droit international*, Basle, Karger, 1973, pp. 278-280.

Registry, the officials of which are accessible and helpful. The International Court also forms part of a political structure, the United Nations, which in principle offers a better guarantee of enforcement of judgments.

Arbitration possesses certain characteristics which, depending on the circumstances, may appear as virtues or vices. First of all, the parties exercise much more control over the conduct of the proceedings in arbitration. Secondly, in arbitration the parties have procedural privacy and there is no procedure allowing the intervention of third States as provided for in the Statute of the International Court, Articles 62 and 63.

(E) The Current Patterns of International Arbitration and Adjudication

By way of conclusion a general survey of the current patterns of arbitration and adjudication will be made in order to demonstrate the variety and extent of the peaceful settlement of disputes in accordance with Rule of Law principles. Whilst this may not appear to be a very original procedure, it is justified because the literature tends to present a segmented picture and it is impressive to review the various patterns as part of a single field. With a certain licence, and allowing for the slow evolution of diplomacy, the term "current" will be used to cover the last 30 years.

(i) *Arbitrations under standing treaty clauses*

A certain type of compulsory jurisdiction arises from standing clauses in treaties providing for arbitration with respect to disputes relating to the subject-matter of the particular treaty. Such clauses can be invoked by one party and without further agreement. In practice, agreement is necessary to compose the modalities of arbitration. By this method several important disputes concerning air services agreements have been settled, as in the *Italy-United States Arbitration* of 1965 [242] and the *United*

242. *International Law Reports*, E. Lauterpacht (ed.), Vol. 45, p. 393.

States/United Kingdom Arbitration Concerning Heathrow Airport User Charges of 1992[243].

On occasion territorial issues of major significance are the subject of compulsory arbitration. An example is the *Arbitration of a Controversy between the Argentine Republic and the Republic of Chile* of 1973-1977[244]. The arbitration was based upon the General Treaty of Arbitration signed on 28 May 1902[245], which had been invoked by Chile. In the event the arbitration was held in accordance with a trilateral Agreement for Arbitration to which the United Kingdom Government was a party.

(ii) *Arbitration* ad hoc *by virtue of a special agreement*

In the last 30 years some major arbitrations have been based upon contemporaneous special agreements *(compromis)* for the resolution of a particular dispute by arbitration. Such arbitrations have often related to issues of delimitation, and especially maritime delimitation.

The *Arbitration between the United Kingdom and France on the Delimitation of the Continental Shelf*[246] of 1977-1978 was based upon an Agreement of 10 July 1975 which composed a Court of Arbitration consisting of five arbitrators of whom one was nominated by the United Kingdom Government and one by the French Government. Apart from the scale of the delimitation exercise itself, the Decision of 1977 made a significant contribution to the development of the principles of general international law.

Other *ad hoc* arbitrations of the recent past include the *Sharjah-Dubai Border Arbitration*[247], the *Guinea-Guinea (Bissau) Maritime Delimitation Case* (1985)[248], the *Guinea (Bissau)-Senegal Maritime*

243. *Award on the First Question*, November 1992 (not published).

244. *Report and Decision*, 18 February 1977; *International Law Reports*, E. Lauterpacht (ed.), Vol. 52, p. 93.

245. *British and Foreign State Papers*, Vol. 95, p. 759.

246. Decisions of 30 June 1977 and 14 March 1978; *International Law Reports*, E. Lauterpacht (ed.), Vol. 54, p. 6; *ibid.*, p. 139.

247. *International Law Reports*, Vol. 91, p. 543.

248. Award of 14 February 1985; *ibid.*, Vol. 77, p. 635.

Boundary Case (1989)[249], and the *St. Pierre et Miquelon Case* (Canada-France) (1992)[250].

(iii) *Arbitration by virtue of provisions in a peace treaty*

In recent times two arbitrations involving substantial and, or, highly sensitive issues have been the result of provisions in peace treaties. The *Rann of Kutch* case[251] involved a dispute about title to a large tract of inhabited territory between India and Pakistan in the Gujarat-West Pakistan region. After the independence of India and Pakistan tension resulting from the dispute as to title caused on outbreak of hostilities in 1965. The Cease-Fire Agreement of 30 June 1965 provided for recourse to arbitration and the Award was rendered on 19 February 1968, and duly implemented.

Another such case was the *Taba Award*[252] which concerned the location of a sector of the boundary between Egypt and Israel. The arbitration was based upon Article VIII of the Treaty of Peace of 1979 between Egypt and Israel but the precise terms and conditions of the proceedings were laid down in a complex Arbitration *compromis*[253].

(iv) *The work of semi-permanent tribunals*

There is a large constituency of semi-permanent tribunals dealing especially with property claims arising from the Second World War. They are based upon peace treaties and commonly involve claims by private interests against a Respondent State. Thus a series of conciliation commissions functioned by virtue of Article 83 of the Italian Peace Treaty. A United States-Japanese Property Commission was constituted in accordance with Article 15 of the Treaty of Peace with Japan. The Austrian-German Treaty of 1957

---

249. Award of 31 July 1989; *International Law Reports*, Vol. 83, p. 1.

250. Award of 10 June 1992; *ibid.*, Vol. 95, p. 645.

251. *International Law Reports*, E. Lauterpacht (ed.), Vol. 50, p. 2. See also J. Gillis Wetter, *American Journal of International Law*, Vol. 65 (1971), p. 346.

252. *International Law Reports*, Vol. 80, p. 226.

253. *Ibid.*, p. 354.

Concerning the Settlement of Property Relations created an Arbitral Tribunal.

Of particular interest is the work of the Iran-United States Claims Tribunal, which was constituted by virtue of the Claims Settlement Declaration dated 19 January 1981[254]. The jurisdiction of the Tribunal is defined as follows in Article II of the Declaration:

> "1. An International Arbitral Tribunal (the Iran-United States Claims Tribunal) is hereby established for the purpose of deciding claims of nationals of the United States against Iran and claims of nationals of Iran against the United States and any counterclaim which arises out of the same contract, transaction or occurrence that constitutes the subject matter of that national's claim, if such claims and counterclaims are outstanding on the date of this agreement, whether or not filed with any court, and arise out of debts, contracts (including transactions which are the subject of letters of credit or bank guarantees), expropriations or other measures affecting property rights, excluding claims described in Paragraph 11 of the Declaration of the Government of Algeria of January 19, 1981, and claims arising out of the actions of the United States in response to the conduct described in such paragraph, and excluding claims arising under a binding contract between the parties specifically providing that any disputes thereunder shall be within the sole jurisdiction of the competent Iranian courts in response to the Majlis position.
>
> 2. The Tribunal shall also have jurisdiction over official claims of the United States and Iran against each other arising out of contractual arrangements between them for the purchase and sale of goods and services.
>
> 3. The Tribunal shall have jurisdiction, as specified in Paragraphs 16-17 of the Declaration of the Government of Algeria of January 19, 1981, over any dispute as to the interpretation or performance of any provision of that declaration."

The applicable law clause (Art. V) is complex and does not

254. *International Legal Materials*, Vol. 30 (1981), p. 230. See also Wayne Mapp, *The Iran-United States Claims Tribunal*, Manchester, Manchester UP, 1993.

refer exclusively to principles of international law. As with all such tribunals, the local remedies rule is excluded.

(v) *The International Court of Justice*

The International Court receives contentious cases from three sources. First, there is the use of unilateral applications to invoke the compulsory jurisdiction. The *Land and Maritime Boundary (Cameroon* v. *Nigeria)* case originated in such an application (in 1994). Secondly, there are cases brought under compromissory clauses in standard-setting conventions. Thus the *Lockerbie* cases[255] were brought by Libya under Article 14, paragraph 1, of the Convention for the Suppression of Unlawful Acts Against the Safety of Civil Aviation of 1971. Finally, a substantial amount of work derives from special agreements on the basis of which particular disputes are taken either to the full Court or to a Chamber of the Court. The important case concerning the *Territorial Dispute*[256] between Libya and Chad was dealt with on the basis of such a special agreement.

This account of the current patterns of arbitration and adjudication has necessarily focused upon the more prominent institutions concerned with the settlement of disputes *between States* on the basis of international law. The pattern could easily be extended by the inclusion of related activities. Thus there are institutions, like the European Court of Human Rights, which have jurisdiction over inter-State disputes, but the applicable law is then the provision of the constituent convention, applied in conjunction with general international law.

---

255. *Questions of Interpretation and Application of the 1971 Montreal Convention arising from the Aerial Incident at Lockerbie (Libyan Arab Jamahiriya* v. *United Kingdom) (Libyan Arab Jamahiriya* v. *United States of America), Orders on Interim Measures, ICJ Reports 1992*, pp. 3, 114.

256. *ICJ Reports 1994*, p. 6.

CHAPTER IX

REMEDIES FOR BREACHES OF OBLIGATIONS

(A) The Concept of Self-help Compared with Remedies

The final topic in the chapters on the mechanisms of public order will be the remedies for breaches of the obligations of international law. By way of preliminary it is useful to point out the distinction between measures of self-help aimed at effecting the *cessation* of the harm as such, and measures the purpose of which is to obtain other legal remedies for the wrong complained of. In the case of declaratory judgments involving injunctive relief clearly the objectives, if not the means, will overlap.

(B) Remedies in the International Court

The purpose is to provide an account of the remedies available in the International Court. Although this approach sounds specialized, the remedies are in fact common to most international tribunals. It is simply that the jurisprudence of the International Court provides the most authoritative and accessible source of material on the subject.

(i) *The remedial competence of the court; in general*

The competence of the Court to indicate remedies is based on Article 36 of the Statute which indicates "the jurisdiction of the Court in all legal disputes concerning: . . . *(d)* the nature and extent of the reparation to be made for the breach of an international obligation", in cases of compulsory jurisdiction by virtue of paragraph 2. No doubt the Court was expected to follow the practice of courts of arbitration in presuming a power to award damages and, apart from special agreement cases, the power of the Court to award damages has gone unquestioned.

In other respects the Court has had to make its own way because the formulation in Article 36 provides no express guidance in respect of declaratory judgments, specific performance and injunctive relief. It is precisely in the remedial sphere that the Court has applied general principles of procedural law. The creative process has been pragmatic, unself-conscious, and somewhat unreflective. The results have been practically useful but rather cryptic in terms of formulation. Parties before the Court have avoided raising issues of competence in relation to forms of judicial relief, except in certain proceedings based upon compromissory clauses. When issues of competence have been the subject of argument, both the Permanent Court and its successor have tended to take a robust line. Thus the Permanent Court rejected an argument that a jurisdictional clause referring to "differences of opinion resulting from the interpretation and the application of" certain treaty provisions did not include claims for reparation[257].

The question of remedies extends beyond the topic of the forms of judicial relief available to include matters which are, practically speaking, cognate. Such matters include the question of *res judicata*[258], the limits of the judicial function in face of a request to the Court to indicate how a Judgment should be carried out[259], and the process by which the Court should determine the object of the claim[260].

The "incidental proceedings" provided for in the Rules of Court also have a remedial role. This is particularly true of

257. *Factory at Chorzów, Jurisdiction, PCIJ, Series A, No. 9*, p. 21. See further C. D. Gray, *Judicial Remedies in International Law*, Clarendon Press, Oxford, 1987, pp. 59-64.

258. See G. G. Fitzmaurice, *The Law and Procedure of the International Court of Justice*, II, Cambridge, 1986, pp. 584-586.

259. *Ibid.*, pp. 555-558.

260. *Nuclear Tests (Australia* v. *France), ICJ Reports 1974*, p. 253.

intervention, where advantages may be obtained both as a consequence of the grant of permission to intervene[261], and also as a consequence of the contents of the pleadings pertaining to a request for permission to intervene which is refused, when the Court is nonetheless informed of the nature and geographical extent of the requesting State's legal interest and acts upon such data during the Merits phase[262]. It is also true of interim measures. In formal terms, a request for the indication of interim measures of protection may appear to have a peripheral and highly contingent role but in practical terms the requesting State may achieve significant gains. If the requesting State can present cogent documentary evidence, and especially if the oral proceedings receive substantial media attention, very useful affirmations of wrongs endured and impending may be made and a wrongdoer effectively exposed. By the same token requests should not be raised without careful consideration and an unsuccessful request may produce adverse effects.

(ii) *Declaratory judgments*

This category is in general use and, though convenient, is also unreliable. A useful starting point is the relevant part of the Court's Judgment in the *Northern Cameroons* case:

> "Throughout these proceedings the contention of the Republic of Cameroon has been that all it seeks is a declaratory judgment of the Court that prior to the termination of the Trusteeship Agreement with respect to the Northern Cameroons, the United Kingdom had breached the provisions of the Agreement, and that, if its Application were admissible and the Court had jurisdiction to proceed to the merits, such a declaratory judgment is not only one the Court could make but one that it should make.
>
> That the Court may, in an appropriate case, make a declaratory judgment is indisputable. The Court has, however, already indi-

261. Case concerning the *Land, Island and Maritime Frontier Dispute (El Salvador/Honduras: Nicaragua intervening), ICJ Reports 1992*, p. 351.

262. Case concerning the *Continental Shelf (Request for Permission to Intervene), ICJ Reports 1984*, p. 25, para. 41; *ICJ Reports 1985*, pp. 24-28, paras. 20-23.

cated that even if, when seised of an Application, the Court finds that it has jurisdiction, it is not obliged to exercise it in all cases. If the Court is satisfied, whatever the nature of the relief claimed, that to adjudicate on the merits of an Application would be inconsistent with its judicial function, it should refuse to do so.

Moreover the Court observes that if in a declaratory judgment it expounds a rule of customary law or interprets a treaty which remains in force, its judgment has a continuing applicability. But in this case there is a dispute about the interpretation and application of a treaty — the Trusteeship Agreement — which has now been terminated, is no longer in force, and there can be no opportunity for a future act of interpretation or application of that treaty in accordance with any judgment the Court might render.

In its *Interpretation of Judgments Nos. 7 and 8 (the Chorzów Factory)* (P.C.I.J., Series A, No. 13, p. 20), the Court said:

> 'The Court's Judgment No. 7 is in the nature of a declaratory judgment, the intention of which is to ensure recognition of a situation at law, once and for all and with binding force as between the Parties; so that the legal position thus established cannot again be called in question in so far as the legal effects ensuing therefrom are concerned.' "[263]

The Court here affirms its competence to make a declaratory judgment and the main point of the decision otherwise is to indicate certain limits to the judicial function, which limits are described by Fitzmaurice as "the question of judicial propriety"[264]. The distinguishing characteristic which the Court appears to rely upon is that a declaration should have a "forward reach". The difficulty is that writers prefer to segregate the "declaratory judgment" from other remedial forms and are tempted to focus upon the difference between a request for a declaration and a claim for damages, or a claim for specific performance. It may be doubted whether this segregation and the distinction it implies can be justified.

There are no problems of form and, as will be shown in due course, the category of declaratory judgments is very diverse in

263. *ICJ Reports 1963*, pp. 36-37.

264. *Ibid.*, pp. 100-108 (separate opinion).

content. Even when an award of damages, or an order for restitution, is made, this is premised upon a finding of legal entitlement. The provisions of Article 36 involve a broad mandate for the Court to resolve "legal disputes" and all judgments are declaratory of the existence of international obligations or of other forms of legal entitlements or of the absence of legal justification.

It follows that there is no useful purpose in seeking to separate out a category of "declaratory judgments". The essential question is to determine the limits to the judicial function. This view is reinforced when consideration is given to the variety of remedial forms sheltering under the umbrella of the declaratory judgment.

(1) The declaratory judgment as a first stage in proceedings

In the case concerning *Certain Phosphate Lands in Nauru*[265], Nauru requested the Court "to adjudge and declare that the Respondent State bears responsibility for breaches of the following obligations . . ." and, finally,

> "to adjudge and declare that the Respondent State is under a legal duty to make appropriate reparation in respect of the loss caused to the Republic of Nauru as a result of the breaches of its legal obligations detailed above . . .".

The Application did not request the Court to proceed to an assessment of damages. Thus the finding on liability, assuming it were favourable, would provide a juncture at which negotiations would provide an appropriate option. A similar two-stage proceeding resulted form the Judgment on the Merits in the *Corfu Channel* case, in which the Court, having made a declaration as to Albania's responsibility, reserved the question of the amount of compensation[266]. The Albanian contention that the Court lacked jurisdiction with respect to the assessment of compensation was rejected in subsequent proceedings[267]. The *Corfu Channel* case was, it may be recalled, founded upon a Special Agreement.

265. *Nauru* v. *Australia*, Preliminary Objections, *ICJ Reports 1992*, p. 240.

266. *ICJ Reports 1949*, p. 36.

267. *Ibid.*, p. 248. The Court relied upon Article 60.

(2) A declaration of some form of legal entitlement

An important mode of declaration relates to the legal entitlement of the parties in their mutual relations. In the *Anglo-Norwegian Fisheries* case the Court found "that the method employed for the delimitation of the fisheries zone by the Norwegian Decree of July 12th, 1935, is not contrary to international law"[268]. In the *Temple* case (Merits) the Court found "that the Temple of Preah Vihear is situated in territory under the sovereignty of Cambodia"[269]. In such cases the primary objective is the issue of entitlement and determinations as to the legality of the conduct of the parties are either not requested or are otherwise marginalized. In the *Fisheries*[270] case the Application included a claim for damages for illegal interferences with fishing vessels, but this was laid aside during the oral proceedings.

(3) A declaration that certain conduct is contrary to international law

The Court has on several important occasions been asked to give a declaration of the illegality of specific conduct of the Respondent State, not simply as a basis for an *ex post* finding of State responsibility, but as a categorical issue, that is, the legality or not of a particular type of activity. At least in the view of the joint dissenting opinion in the *Nuclear Tests* cases, the Australian Application and submissions involved a request for a declaration of the illegality of France's atmospheric nuclear weapons tests[271]. In the case of *Nicaragua* v. *United States* (Merits), the Court made a series of decisions to the effect that certain actions of the United States constituted breaches of various obligations under customary international law, or in some cases breaches of the Treaty of Friendship, Commerce and Navigation[272].

The Court also decided that the United States was under an

268. *ICJ Reports 1951*, p. 143.

269. *ICJ Reports 1962*, p. 36. See also the case concerning the *Land, Island and Maritime Frontier Dispute*, *ICJ Reports 1992*, p. 351 at pp. 610-617.

270. *ICJ Reports 1951*, p. 116.

271. *ICJ Reports 1974*, p. 63 at p. 319 *(Australia* v. *France)*; *ibid.*, p. 494 at p. 501 *(New Zealand* v. *France)*.

272. *ICJ Reports 1986*, pp. 146-148.

obligation to make reparation for all injury caused to Nicaragua by the breaches of the obligations previously elaborated. An additional finding of particular interest was the following paragraph in the *dispositif*:

> "The Court
>
> . . . .
>
> *Rejects* the justification of collective self-defence maintained by the United States of America in connection with the military and paramilitary activities in and against Nicaragua the subject of this case; . . ."

There is no reason to see any qualitative distinction between this type of declaratory judgment and the previous group relating to legal entitlements. Both types satisfy the criterion indicated by the Permanent Court[273] according to which a declaratory judgment was designed

> "to ensure recognition of a situation at law, once and for all, and with binding force as between the Parties; so that the legal position thus established cannot again be called in question in so far as the legal effects ensuing therefrom are concerned".

(4) A declaration that specific acts of implementation of a decision are required

In three cases the Court has responded to requests in Applications by requiring the Respondent State to perform specific acts or to refrain from specific conduct as a consequence of the findings as to the legal entitlements of the Applicant. Thus in the *Temple* case (Merits)[274] the *dispositif* is as follows:

> "The Court,
>
> by nine votes to three,

273. *Factory at Chorzów, Merits, PCIJ, Series A, No. 13*, p. 20; quoted in the joint dissenting opinion, *Nuclear Tests* cases, *ICJ Reports 1974*, p. 319 *(Australia* v. *France)*; *ibid.*, p. 501 *(New Zealand* v. *France)*.

274. *ICJ Reports 1962*, pp. 36-37.

finds that the Temple of Preah Vihear is situated in territory under the sovereignty of Cambodia;

finds in consequence,

by nine votes to three,

that Thailand is under an obligation to withdraw any military or police forces, or other guards or keepers, stationed by her at the Temple, or in its vicinity on Cambodian territory;

by seven votes to five,

that Thailand is under an obligation to restore to Cambodia any objects of the kind specified in Cambodia's fifth Submission which may, since the date of the occupation of the Temple by Thailand in 1954, have been removed from the Temple or the Temple area by the Thai authorities."

Similar orders were made by the Court in the *Tehran Hostages*[275] and *Nicaragua*[276] cases. In the latter, the Court decided "that the United States of America is under a duty immediately to cease and to refrain from all such acts as may constitute breaches of the foregoing legal obligations . . ." (by twelve votes to three).

This "preventive" role is sometimes seen as the specific function of declaratory judgments[277]. Gray is of the opinion that declarations of this type are radical, at least in the context of the competence of the Court[278]. However, it is difficult to discern any significant difference between this mode of declaration and the other types examined above. The form depends on the precise nature of the requests of the parties in the Application. The substance of the matter is that a Judgment is binding and the performance required is the *consequence* of the decision on entitlement.

(5) The declaration as a form of satisfaction

In the *Corfu Channel* case (Merits) the Court found that the action of the British Navy on 12/13 November 1946, the mine

---

275. *ICJ Reports 1980*, pp. 44-45.

276. *ICJ Reports 1986*, p. 149.

277. Charles De Visscher, *Aspects récents du droit procédural de la Cour internationale de Justice*, Paris, 1966, p. 187.

278. *Op. cit., supra* footnote 257, pp. 64-68.

collecting operation, "constituted a violation of Albanian sovereignty". As a consequence the Court stated: "This declaration is in accordance with the request made by Albania through her Counsel, and is in itself appropriate satisfaction." [279]

This finding has been criticized on not very substantial grounds by Charles De Visscher [280]. However, it appears to qualify as a declaratory judgment and the Court, as is its custom, was responding to the request of the party concerned in the matter of remedies.

(6) The declaration of the applicable principles and rules of international law

In the *North Sea Continental Shelf* cases the Special Agreements requested the Court to decide the question:

> "What principles and rules of international law are applicable to the delimitation as between the Parties of the areas of the continental shelf in the North Sea which appertain to each of them beyond the partial boundary determined by the above-mentioned Convention of 1 December 1964?" [281]

The Court had no difficulty in dealing with this case. Although fears have at times been expressed that a readiness to give relatively abstract declaratory judgments might lead to the contentious jurisdiction being used by States to obtain advisory opinions [282], the judicial function in the *North Sea* cases was related in several practical ways to the resolution of specific disputes. This is evident from the terms of Article 1 (2) of the two Special Agreements:

> "The Governments [the respective Parties] shall delimit the continental shelf in the North Sea as between their countries by agreement in pursuance of the decision requested from the International Court of Justice."

279. *ICJ Reports 1949*, p. 35. The issue is not referred to in the *dispositif.*

280. *Op. cit., supra* footnote 277, pp. 190-191.

281. *ICJ Reports 1969*, p. 6.

282. H. Lauterpacht, *The Development of International Law by the International Court*, London, 1958, pp. 250-251.

Declaratory judgments in such cases are closely related to the ascertainment of the legal entitlements of the parties and involve a legitimate and constructive exercise of the judicial function.

(iii) *Claims for damages*

The question which presents itself at this stage is: to what extent, if at all, is the declaratory judgment distinct from judgments involving the award of damages[283]? In all essentials, the answer must be in the negative. The element of compensation, whether this itself be in the form of a declaration that there is an obligation to make reparation, or in the form of a separate phase of the proceedings for the assessment of compensation, is contingent upon a declaration of a legal entitlement of some kind.

It may be recalled that in *Nicaragua* v. *United States*[284] the Applicant State had included in its submissions a request that the Court make an interim award of damages. The Court did not accede to this request, but did not deny the existence of a competence to give such awards.

(iv) Restitutio in integrum

It is doubtful whether this is a separate category any more than claims for damages. In the appropriate cases the Applicant State will request restitution in kind, and if the Court has jurisdiction over the subject-matter, and the relevant legal principles point to restitution or specific performance, then such orders will be consequential upon the finding of a legal entitlement. Such orders were made in the *Temple*[285], *Tehran Hostages*[286] and *Nicaragua*[287] cases. Whether such orders are made depends closely upon the nature of the requests of the parties. If *restitutio in integrum* is not a separate remedy but the natural result of certain forms of

283. Cf. C. D. Gray, *op. cit.*, *supra* footnote 257, pp. 96-97.
284. *ICJ Reports 1986*, p. 143, para. 285.
285. *ICJ Reports 1962*, pp. 36-37.
286. *ICJ Reports 1980*, pp. 44-45.
287. *ICJ Reports 1986*, p. 149.

request for a declaratory judgment, the question of the competence of the Court to give specific performance does not arise, apart from cases based upon compromissory clauses [288].

(C) THE LIMITS OF JUDICIAL REMEDIES

Preliminary objections may be based upon specific issues of the competence of the Court in accordance with the relevant instruments conferring, or alleged to confer, jurisdiction. Apart from issues of jurisdiction, a question of admissibility may be based upon discrete considerations of law and policy. An example of this type of preliminary objection is provided by the principle that the International Court cannot exercise jurisdiction in respect of a subject-matter involving the rights and obligation of a third State without the consent of that State. This is the principle stated by the Court in its Judgment in the *Monetary Gold* case [289].

Other preliminary objections are based upon specific considerations which, it is contended, establish that it would be *inappropriate* to exercise the judicial function even if jurisdiction exists as a matter of principle. This highly controversial area is usually categorized as "justiciability" [290]. From time to time it is contended that the Court should not exercise jurisdiction in respect of "political" disputes [291]. However, this line of argument tends to fail provided the tribunal can discern discrete issues of fact and law, in spite of the political background and ramifications of a particular dispute. This was the approach of the majority of the Court in the *Nicaragua* case [292].

Whilst the question of justiciability involves considerable difficulty, certain specific issues have emerged from the experience of international tribunals and counsel. The subject-matter is volatile

---

288. Cf. C. D. Gray, *op. cit., supra* footnote 257, pp. 64-66, 95-96, where the issue of competence is considered to be problematical.

289. *ICJ Reports 1954*, p. 19.

290. See generally I. Brownlie, *British Year Book*, Vol. 42 (1967), pp. 123-143.

291. See the dissenting opinion of Judge Oda in the *Nicaragua* case: *ICJ Reports 1986*, pp. 219-246, paras. 15-72.

292. *ICJ Reports 1984*, p. 392.

and, in theory at least, extensive. Consequently, it is intended only to provide a sample of the more respectable cases of non-justiciability.

(1) The International Court cannot indicate how a judgment should be carried out[293].

(2) There must be a dispute in existence. In the *Nuclear Tests* cases the Court took the view that, in view of French undertakings to discontinue the series of tests, the object of the claims of Australia and New Zealand had been "achieved by other means"[294].

(3) There must be a *legal* dispute in existence. In the *Nicaragua* case[295] the Court accepted the principle but rejected the United States position that the dispute lay outside the category of legal disputes because it concerned the issue of the unlawful use of force.

(4) It is sometimes argued that certain types of dispute are non-justiciable because the relevant rules or treaty provisions are to be classified on pragmatic legal grounds as not susceptible to judicial examination. This is the position of the United Kingdom and the United States with respect to Chapter VII of the United Nations Charter, in the context of the *Lockerbie* cases[296]. The validity of this position is a moot question.

(5) The precise ground of decision of the International Court in the case concerning the Northern Cameroons (Cameroon v. United Kingdom)[297] was the unwillingness of the Court to respond to a request for a declaration as to the existence or not of certain alleged violations of the Trusteeship Agreement in the conduct by the United Kingdom of the plebiscite in the Northern Cameroons[298]. This request was not related to any

293. *Haya de la Torre* case, *ICJ Reports 1951*, pp. 79-83.

294. *ICJ Reports 1974*, pp. 270-272, paras. 55-59.

295. *ICJ Reports 1986*, pp. 26-28, paras. 32-35.

296. *Request for the Indication of Provisional Measures*, *ICJ Reports 1992*, p. 3 *(Libyan Arab Jamahiriya* v. *United Kingdom)*; *Request for the Indication of Interim Measures*, *ibid.*, p. 114 *(Libyan Arab Jamahiriya* v. *United States)*.

297. *ICJ Reports 1963*, p. 15.

298. *Ibid.*, pp. 33-34.

practical outcome, such as a challenge to the validity of the dispositions which resulted from the plebiscite.

(6) The existence of alternative dispute settlement machinery, which has priority either as a matter of treaty obligations or as a necessary implication from the regular resort by the parties to bilateral machinery, may provide a ground of non-justiciability[299].

(D) JUDICIAL ACTIVITY IN CONJUNCTION WITH POLITICAL MEANS OF SETTLEMENT

The International Court of Justice has from time to time had a role in the promotion of dispute settlement by means of negotiation or providing specific assistance to negotiations. In its Judgment in the Merits phase of the *Nicaragua* case[300], the Court recommended that the parties co-operate with the Contadora process, a regional system of diplomatic negotiation. The *North Sea Continental Shelf* cases[301] were based upon two special agreements, and the purpose of the parties was to facilitate the solution of the problems of delimitation by first of all obtaining the guidance of the Court as to the application of the principles and rules of international law.

(E) NON-FORCIBLE COUNTERMEASURES

It is necessary to turn briefly to the subject of non-forcible countermeasures. The relative inability of the international system to insist on the *settlement* of disputes between States, as opposed to insisting that disputes can only be settled by peaceful means, has inevitably given prominence to the taking of non-forcible countermeasures. Such measures commonly take the

---

299. A similar argument of the United States in the *Nicaragua* case was rejected by the Court: *ICJ Reports 1984*, pp. 438-441, paras. 102-108.

300. *ICJ Reports 1986*, p. 145, paras. 290-291.

301. *ICJ Reports 1969*, p. 4.

forcible countermeasure. Such measures commonly take the form of trade embargoes, the freezing of assets and the suspension of the performance of treaty obligations.

The existence of non-forcible countermeasures as a part of customary or general international law has been acknowledged by international tribunals: see the Award in the *Case Concerning the Air Services Agreement of 27 March 1946* (United States-France)[302], and the Judgments of the International Court in the case concerning *United States Diplomatic and Consular Staff in Tehran*[303], and in *Nicaragua* v. *United States* (Merits)[304]. The subject of countermeasures is still in a state of development and the attendant problems are under study by the International Law Commission. A particular source of difficulty lies in the fact that the purposes of countermeasures include both self-help, that is, cessation of the harm, and redress. It is generally accepted that general international law permits non-forcible countermeasures under certain conditions. The nature of these conditions is still to some extent unsettled.

On this provisional basis, the following conditions appear to be required for lawful countermeasures:

(1) the measures must be intended to obtain redress for the wrong committed;
(2) prior notification of the countermeasures and their purposes must be given;
(3) the measures must be proportionate to the violations complained of;
(4) countermeasures which affect individuals are subject to certain limits deriving from human rights standards which form part of general international law.

---

302. Award of 9 December 1978; *International Law Reports*, E. Lauterpacht (ed.), Vol. 54, p. 304 at pp. 335-341.

303. *ICJ Reports 1980*, p. 3 at pp. 27-28.

304. *ICJ Reports 1986*, p. 14 at p. 127, paras. 248-249.

CHAPTER X

CONTROL OF MAJOR NATURAL RESOURCES

(A) Introduction

The examination of those topics the nature of which justifies the collective description as "mechanisms of public order" has now been completed, and it is necessary to move on to deal with the second major grouping of topics, that is, selected areas of substantive law which have a particular relation to contemporary issues of public order. These areas are as follows: control of major natural resources, title to territory, maritime boundaries and delimitation, and the protection of the territorial integrity and the environment of States.

(B) Expropriation and Control of Major Natural Resources: Classification of the Subject-matter

The episodes of expropriation, regulation of the use of property, and the annulment or modification of concession agreements, which may raise issues of international law when they affect non-nationals, are variously classified in the literature. Essentially the question is one of State responsibility, but this formulation is question-begging, as much depends upon the relevant standards of conduct. However, other classifications employed are just as question-begging. They include "permanent sovereignty over natural resources", "the international law on foreign investment", and "international economic law".

(C) The Treatment of Aliens on State Territory:

The General Principles

The starting point must be the more general issue of the treatment of aliens on State territory, and it is thus necessary to examine, however briefly, the general principles governing this subject.

Apart from the provisions of treaties, there is no duty to allow aliens to enter State territory. There is thus no general freedom of movement in this respect. However, when aliens are allowed to become visitors or residents within the State, certain legal relations arise. The policies and motives lying behind a taking of foreign-owned property are very varied and range from normal programmes of land reform or creation of a public sector in the economy to measures forming part of a pattern of racial discrimination, ethnic cleansing, crimes against humanity, or genocide. It follows that there is no one legal analysis applicable.

When there is a question concerning the treatment of an alien or foreign property, a number of legal contexts could apply either singly or in combination. Such contexts include:

(1) the principles of customary or general international law;
(2) bilateral treaties of friendship, commerce and navigation;
(3) the principles governing regional economic communities;
(4) a regional convention for the protection of human rights; and
(5) the provisions of a relevant trade agreement.

(d) Expropriation: the Policy Issues

A major policy, motivating Governments of various political complexions, has been the establishment of a public sector extending to the more sensitive areas of the economy in order either to implement objectives of economic planning, or to pursue nationalist objectives of excluding or limiting foreign domination of key areas of economic life. A countervailing policy is that of creating an environment attractive to foreign investment by offering various economic inducements and often by the conclusion of an Agreement for the Promotion and Protection of Investments in which it is customary to provide for the conditions in which expropriation may occur in provisions like the following:

> "(1) Investments of nationals or companies of either Contracting Party shall not be nationalized, expropriated or subject to measures having effect equivalent to nationalization or expropriation (hereinafter referred to as 'expropriation') in the territory of the other Contracting Party except for a public purpose related to the internal needs of that Party on a non-discriminatory basis and against prompt, adequate and effective compensation. Such compensation shall amount to the real value of the expropriated investment immediately before the expropriation or before the impending expropriation became public knowledge, whichever is the earlier, shall include interest at a normal commercial rate until the date of payment, and shall be freely transferable. Such compensation shall be made without delay and be effectively realizable. The national or company affected shall have a right under the law of the Contracting Party making the expropriation, to prompt review, by a judicial or other independent authority of that Party, of his or its case and of the valuation of his or its investment in accordance with the principles set out in this paragraph.
>
> (2) Where a Contracting Party expropriates the assets of a company which is incorporated or constituted under the law in force in any part of its territory, and in which nationals or companies of the other Contracting Party own shares, it shall ensure that the provisions of paragraph (1) of this Article are applied to the extent necessary to guarantee prompt, adequate and effective compensation in respect of their investment to such nationals or companies of the other Contracting Party who are owners of those shares."

(E) WHAT CONSTITUTES EXPROPRIATION?

A further necessary preliminary is to ask what is expropriation for present purposes. The essence of the matter is the deprivation by the acts of State organs of a right of property either as such, or by a transfer of the power of management and control. The terminology is irrelevant. A taking without compensation may be described as "confiscation". Many expropriation measures are described as "nationalization". It is the effects of the measure which are legally significant. Even if there is no formal deprivation of title, the use of government intervention to remove assets from the effective control of the owner constitutes an indirect taking. Annulment of contractual rights also constitutes expropriation or its legal equivalent. Particular treaty provisions may establish specialized standards relating to interference with property rights.

In the present context particular significance attaches to the distinction between taxation and expropriation. The significance attaches to the fact that in many legal systems expropriation without compensation is prima facie unlawful whereas taxation is prima facie lawful. The presumption relating to taxation may apply also in international law.

(F) THE CUSTOMARY LAW POSITION AS STATED IN WESTERN SOURCES IN THE PERIOD 1930 TO 1960

As a sort of baseline, an expository device, it is useful to attempt to state the position in customary international law as stated in Western sources in the period 1930-1960. This is not an uncomplicated task. It may surprise some but there was no single, monolithic view among Western jurists. One of the reasons for this is that in the period 1910 to 1930 there had been strong differences of opinion among European States concerning agrarian reform programmes which affected foreign-owned property. These differences of opinion are visible in the records of the Hague Codification Conference of 1930[305].

Broadly speaking, there were two schools of thought in the doctrine and practice of the period 1930 to 1960.

305. See L. Oppenheim, *International Law*, Vol. I, *Peace*, 8th ed., London, 1955, by H. Lauterpacht, pp. 62-63, 350-352.

(i) *The views of Hersch Lauterpacht, 1937*[306]

Some leading jurists, like Hersch Lauterpacht in his Hague Lectures in 1937, have distinguished between large-scale nationalization and small-scale expropriation, and have recognized that, in the case of nationalization of major national resources, compensation would be on the basis of payments phased out over a long period and calculated with reference to the economic position of the State concerned.

(ii) *The Cordell Hull formula, 1938*

The other school of thought, reflected to a considerable extent in the practice of the capital exporting States after the Second World War, insisted that the general principle was that of "adequate, effective and prompt compensation".

In the words of the relevant United States Note of 22 August 1938 to Mexico:

> "The fundamental issues raised by this communication from the Mexican Government are therefore, first, whether or not universally recognized principles of the law of nations require in the exercise of the admitted right of all sovereign nations to expropriate private property, that such expropriation be accompanied by provision on the part of such government for adequate, effective and prompt payment for the properties seized; second, whether any government may nullify principles of international law through contradictory municipal legislation of its own; or, third, whether such Government is relieved of its obligations under universally recognized principles of international law merely because its financial or economic situation makes compliance therewith difficult.
>
> The Government of the United States merely adverts to a self evident fact when it notes that the applicable precedents and recognized authorities on international law support its declaration that, under every rule of law and equity, no government is entitled to expropriate private property, for whatever purpose, without provi-

306. See H. Lauterpacht, "Règles générales du droit de la paix", *Recueil des cours*, Vol. 62 (1937-IV), p. 346. See further S. Friedman, *Expropriation in International Law*, London, Stevens, 1953.

sion for prompt, adequate, and effective payment therefor. In addition, clauses appearing in the constitutions of almost all nations today, and in particular in the constitutions of the American republics, embody the principle of just compensation. These, in themselves, are declaratory of the like principle in the law of nations.

The universal acceptance of this rule of the law of nations, which, in truth, is merely a statement of common justice and fair-dealing, does not in the view of this Government admit of any divergence of opinion." [307]

This prescription on the conditions of compensation is commonly referred to as the Cordell Hull formula after the Secretary of State who was the author of the Note. The United States Note was in response to Mexican nationalization programmes in the 1930s. The Mexican Government did not reject the principle of compensation but maintained that the measure of compensation must depend upon the capacity to pay of the nationalizing State, because otherwise an obligation to pay "immediately the value of the property taken" would deny the State the right to restructure its economy and to introduce economic reforms [308].

As the eminent Latin American jurist, Jiménez de Aréchaga, has explained:

> "The main criticism levelled against this requirement of prompt and adequate compensation is that, although it may be applicable to individual expropriations, it would make it impossible to adopt basic reforms or to take nationalization measures in a wide scale and of a general and impersonal character. The Government of Mexico stated in its reply to the United States that 'the transformation of a country, that is to say, the future of the nation, could not be halted by the impossibility of paying immediately the value of the properties belonging to a small number of foreigners who seek only a lucrative end'." [309]

---

307. Green H. Hackworth, *Digest of International Law*, Vol. III, USGPO, Washington, 1942, pp. 658-659.

308. Mexican Note dated 3 August 1938, quoted by E. Jiménez de Aréchaga in *Yearbook of the International Law Commission*, 1963, Vol. II, p. 238 (para. 2).

309. Mexican Note dated 3 August 1938, quoted by E. Jiménez de Aréchaga in *Yearbook of the International Law Commission*, 1963, Vol. II, p. 238 (para. 2).

It must be appreciated that the Cordell Hull version of the Western position on expropriation does not deny the right of the host State to foreign capital to expropriate as a normal exercise of its territorial competence. Moreover, supporters of the Cordell Hull view of the law recognized that there were exceptions to the compensation rule.

These exceptions are normally stated to be as follows:

(1) the legitimate exercise of police power;
(2) measures of defence against external threats to the State;
(3) confiscation as a penalty for crimes; and
(4) restrictions on the use of property resulting from health and planning legislation, provided such restrictions are proportionate.

In any event, the practice of Western States has been inconsistent in one important respect. If one were to seek to challenge the evidence in favour of the Cordell Hull formula, and the existence of the necessary *opinio juris*, the way to do this would be to commence with an examination of practice in respect of expropriation of the capital exporting States themselves, exemplified by the nationalization practice of the United Kingdom and French Governments in 1946. Thus Professor Jiménez de Aréchaga observed:

> "The practice of States confirms that, in the case of nationalization, the payment of deferred compensation has been offered and accepted, even by countries supporting the traditional doctrine under consideration. France and Great Britain, for instance, have paid compensation for the measures of nationalization of banks, airlines, insurance companies, transportation and steel and coal industries in the form of bonds redeemable, over a number of years, bearing a 3 per cent interest. This formula was accepted by States whose nationals were affected by such nationalization measures, such as Switzerland, United States and Belgium." [310]

310. Mexican Note dated 3 August 1938, quoted by E. Jiménez de Aréchaga in *Yearbook of the International Law Commission*, 1963, Vol. II, p. 238 (para. 4).

(G) THE REQUIREMENT OF LAWFUL PURPOSE

It has been usual for writers and Governments to stipulate that expropriation and its analogues must be for purposes of public utility. However, this requirement is problematical. The more appropriate approach would be to accept that certain forms of expropriation are unlawful, a proposition to be elaborated further below. Unless an act of expropriation does not fall within a specific category of illegality, this being determined by independently relevant principles, then the expropriation is lawful. It is surely a matter for the expropriating State to decide what is required for purposes of public utility[311].

(H) CATEGORIES OF EXPROPRIATION UNLAWFUL *PER SE*

There are certain types of expropriation which are illegal *per se* and not only because of failure to provide for appropriate compensation. These categories include the following:

(1) Seizures forming part of conduct on the part of agents of a State constituting crimes against humanity, war crimes, or acts of genocide.
(2) Expropriation in breach of treaty provisions, as in the famous *Chorzów Factory* case[312].
(3) Measures of unlawful reprisal against another State.
(4) Discriminatory measures intended to cause harm to persons of particular racial or religious groups or nationals of other States. The test of discrimination is the intention of the expropriating Government. The fact that only aliens are affected may be accidental, as the United Kingdom observed in its Memorial in the *Anglo-Iranian Oil Co.* case:

311. See G. Abi-Saab, in Mohammed Bedjaoui (ed.), *International Law: Achievements and Prospects*, Dordrecht, Nijhoff, 1991, pp. 609-610.

312. *German Interests in Polish Upper Silesia* (1926), *PCIJ, Series A, No.* 7, p. 22; *Factory at Chorzów* case (Indemnity) (1928), *PCIJ, Series A, No. 17*, pp. 46-47.

> "The Government of the United Kingdom does not deny . . . that cases may arise in which a measure of expropriation solely affecting foreign nations is dictated by such overwhelming considerations of public utility and general welfare that the measure cannot be said to be directed against or discriminatory against foreigners. In such cases the fact that the expropriation affects foreigners only is, in a sense, accidental. The State cannot be expected to refrain from a measure which is of vital importance for the sole reason that the persons affected are foreigners. However . . . the burden of proof is on the expropriating State to show that these overwhelming considerations exist and the situation is altogether different when the circumstances of the case point cogently to the conclusion that the action taken was embarked upon not in pursuance of a general purpose but with the object of nullifying a transaction which is deemed to be inconvenient or, although more lucrative than was expected at the time when it was entered into, still not as lucrative as the expropriating State would like . . ."[313]

The distinction between expropriation unlawful *per se* and expropriation which is unlawful only if no compensation is provided has significant practical consequences which are intended to reflect the different registers of public policy involved[314]. Thus expropriation unlawful *per se* entails a more rigorous standard of compensation, including a liability for consequential loss *(lucrum cessans)* and, at least when the applicable law is public international law, does not confer a valid title.

(I) THE EMERGENCE OF NEW CRITERIA, 1962-1974

(i) *The prospect of change*

In the last 30 years the version of the law based upon the

---

313. *ICJ Pleadings, Anglo-Iranian Oil Co.* case *(United Kingdom* v. *Iran)*, p. 97.

314. See *Amoco International Finance* v. *Iran, International Law Reports*, Vol. 83, p. 500; I. Brownlie, *Principles of Public International Law*, 4th ed., Oxford, Clarendon Press, 1990, pp. 538-539.

Cordell Hull formula has been seen more and more to have the role of a negotiating stance, and the requirement of "prompt compensation" has not been generally recognized as a standard of general international law. Pressure for a reformed legal régime emerged from the developing States in the United Nations General Assembly and in UNCTAD.

(ii) *General Assembly resolution 1803 on Permanent Sovereignty over Natural Resources of 14 December 1962*[315]

The adoption of this resolution by 87 votes to 2, with 12 abstentions, was recognized on all sides as a significant development. The resolution was in the form of a Declaration on Permanent Sovereignty over Natural Resources. The key paragraphs of the Declaration may be quoted for the sake of convenience:

> "1. The right of peoples and nations to permanent sovereignty over their natural wealth and resources must be exercised in the interest of their national development and of the well-being of the people of the State concerned;
>
> 2. The exploration, development and disposition of such resources, as well as the import of the foreign capital required for these purposes, should be in conformity with the rules and conditions which the peoples and nations freely consider to be necessary or desirable with regard to the authorization, restriction or prohibition of such activities;
>
> 3. In cases where authorization is granted, the capital imported and the earnings on that capital shall be governed by the terms thereof, by the national legislation in force, and by international law. The profits derived must be shared in the proportions freely agreed upon, in each case, between the investors and the recipient State, due care being taken to ensure that there is no impairment, for any reason, of that State's sovereignty over its natural wealth and resources;
>
> 4. Nationalization, expropriation or requisitioning shall be based on grounds or reasons of public utility, security or the national interest which are recognized as overriding purely indi-

315. Text: *International Legal Materials*, Vol. 2 (1963), p. 223.

vidual or private interests, both domestic and foreign. In such cases the owner shall be paid appropriate compensation, in accordance with the rules in force in the State taking such measures in the exercise of its sovereignty and in accordance with international law. In any case where the question of compensation gives rise to a controversy, the national jurisdiction of the State taking such measures shall be exhausted. However, upon agreement by sovereign States and other parties concerned, settlement of the dispute should be made through arbitration or international adjudication;

. . . .

8. Foreign investment agreements freely entered into by, or between, sovereign States shall be observed in good faith; States and international organizations shall strictly and conscientiously respect the sovereignty of peoples and nations over their natural wealth and resources in accordance with the Charter and the principles set forth in the present resolution."

Whilst General Assembly resolutions do not make international law, they are vehicles for the expression of the practice of States. In any event there is strong evidence in support of the conclusion that the adoption of resolution 1803 indicated that the principle of compensation was no longer based upon the "adequate, effective and prompt" formula of Cordell Hull, but upon the principle of "appropriate compensation"[316]. This principle has been adopted as reflecting a consensus of opinion in three arbitral awards: *Texaco* v. *Libyan Government* (1977)[317], *LIAMCO* v. *Libyan Government*[318] and *Government of Kuwait* v. *Aminoil* (1982)[319].

The difficulty is that the phrase "appropriate compensation" calls for interpretation, and the sceptic would say that the development which it represents involves evidence of a state of uncertainty or immaturity rather than a new legal standard. However,

---

316. See O. Schachter, "International Law in Theory and Practice (General Course in Public International Law)", Vol. 178 (1982-V), pp. 296-301, 324; and G. Abi-Saab, in Mohammed Bedjaoui (ed.), *op. cit.*, pp. 611-613.

317. *International Law Reports*, E. Lauterpacht (ed.), Vol. 53, p. 389.

318. *Ibid.*, Vol. 62, p. 141.

319. *Ibid.*, Vol. 66, p. 519.

there is a respectable school of thought supporting the view that the standard, though flexible, retains the character of a legal standard. This was the position adopted, for example, in the *Aminoil* Award, in which the Tribunal observed:

> "The Tribunal considers that the determination of the amount of an award of 'appropriate' compensation is better carried out by means of an enquiry into all the circumstances relevant to the particular concrete case, than through abstract theoretical discussion. Moreover the Charter of the Economic Rights and Duties of States, even in its most disputed clause (Article 2, paragraph 2c) — and the one that occasioned reservations on the part of the industrialized States — recommended taking account of 'all circumstances' in order to determine the amount of compensation — which does not in any way exclude a substantial indemnity."[320]

(iii) *The Charter of Economic Rights and Duties of States of 12 December 1974*[321]

On 12 December 1974 the United Nations General Assembly adopted the Charter of Economic Rights and Duties of States by 120 votes in favour, 6 against, and 10 abstentions. The States voting against were Belgium, Denmark, the German Federal Republic, Luxembourg, the United Kingdom and the United States.

Article 2, paragraph 2 *(c)*, of the Charter provides as follows:

> "Every State has the right:
>
> . . . .
>
> *(c)* To nationalize, expropriate or transfer ownership of foreign property, in which case appropriate compensation should be paid by the State adopting such measures, taking into account its relevant laws and regulations and all circumstances that the State considers pertinent. In any case where the question of compensation gives rise to a controversy, it shall be settled under the domestic law of the nationalizing State and by its tribunals, unless it is freely and mutually agreed by all States concerned that other peaceful means be sought on the basis of the

320. *International Law Reports*, E. Lauterpacht (ed.), Vol. 66, p. 602, para. 144.
321. Text: *International Legal Materials*, Vol. 14 (1975), p. 251.

> sovereign equality of States and in accordance with the principle of free choice of means."

In a general way this provision confirms the standard of "appropriate compensation". Moreover, in spite of its strong emphasis on the national standard of treatment, the provisions of the Charter by implication adopt the standard of appropriate compensation as a requirement of international law. This view of the legal position is adopted by a number of authoritative writers, including Jiménez de Aréchaga [322], Schachter [323] and Abi-Saab [324].

(J) Conclusions on Expropriation

In the discussion thus far it has been assumed that there are existing principles of customary or general international law and a modest analytical apparatus has been deployed on that basis. There is, however, an alternative view which is that the customary law (in its Cordell Hull mode) has fragmented without any effective replacement by an alternative régime. Whether or not this view be accepted, the reality is that recourse to bilateral treaty provisions is now increasingly common. Thus, between 1975 and 1995 the United Kingdom concluded Investment Promotion and Protection Agreements with some 78 States. It is probable that the elements of uncertainty in the customary law help to increase this impetus in treaty-making.

(K) State Responsibility for Breaches of Contract

An area of particularly difficult problems concerns the consequences of action by the State party to a contract which purports unilaterally to annul or modify the terms of a contract, and, in

322. *Recueil des cours*, Vol. 159 (1978-I), pp. 300-302; and *New York University Journal of International Law and Politics*, Vol. II (1978), p. 179 at p. 184.

323. *Recueil des cours*, Vol. 178 (1982-V), pp. 300-301, 321-323.

324. *Op. cit., supra* footnote 311, pp. 610-613.

particular, the provisions of a long-running concession agreement. If the action constitutes a confiscatory annulment, then the principles of general international law governing expropriation of foreign property would apply. If the confiscatory annulment is discriminatory on the basis of race or nationality, the expropriation would be unlawful *per se*.

However, the general view is that a breach as such, as opposed to annulment, does not generate State responsibility on the international plane. There is a minority view visible in the literature according to which the breach of a State contract by the government party of itself generates State responsibility[325]. The essential difficulty with this position is its failure to separate issues relating to the contractual relationship and conduct on the part of the State which goes beyond the relationship and supplants it by the destruction of the subject-matter of the contract as a consequence of an act of government policy.

In most cases the contract itself will contain dispute settlement provisions. Such provisions often have the purpose of excluding the jurisdiction of the municipal courts of both the State party and of the State of national origin of the other party. Moreover, the contract may make a non-localized choice of the applicable law, such as "the principles of natural justice", "general principles of law" or "the principles of international law".

---

325. For the literature : I. Brownlie, *Principles of Public International Law*, 4th ed., Oxford, 1990, p. 548.

CHAPTER XI

TITLE TO TERRITORY (ACQUISITION AND LOSS OF TERRITORY)

(A) Introduction

In this chapter and the two which follow the significance of statehood and the allocation of territory as a public order system will be examined. The allocation of territory and the stability of States in territorial terms depend upon the concepts of title to territory and upon the concept of a boundary.

It is worth pointing out that international peace and stability depend at least as much upon the institutions of statehood and stable boundaries as upon topics, such as the environment, so fashionable in universities. Boundary disputes also have certain relatively eccentric features. First, they are, perhaps surprisingly often, submitted to third party settlement. Issues of sovereignty, as such, are often resistant to negotiated compromise and most States do not regard resortto force as either a realistic or a civilized method of settlement. Secondly, boundary disputes have the peculiarity that the parties are, literally, neighbours and consequently the significance of the method of dispute settlement goes beyond the resolution of the question of title, extending to the need for a definitive solution resulting from a legal procedure to which both parties are genuinely committed, and which will consolidate relations generally.

(B) The Concept of a Boundary

In legal if not geographical terms a boundary is a linear conception. This reflects its primary function, which is to indicate the *allocation of territory* to States. This reference to allocation is not a reflection of legalism but reflects the attitudes of the politicians who make territorial arrangements. There is a significant distinction between delimitation, the determination of the boundary *in principle*, and the separate process of demarcation, the physical indication of the boundary on the ground. As an alignment a boundary is indicated by a *line* described in words in a treaty and, or, shown on a map. When demarcation takes place this involves indication on the ground by cairns of stones, cleared roads in scrub, or concrete pillars.

Natural features do not necessarily provide the effective and precise allocation which is desirable. Thus a river line has to be elaborated in terms of the median line or the *thalweg*, that is, the principal channel or line of deepest soundings. Similarly, a watershed line must be surveyed carefully and then demarcated. Is a boundary which is undemarcated still a boundary? The answer must be affirmative unless final validation by agreement is made conditional upon demarcation.

(i) *Techniques of delimitation*

In practice the processes of delimitation and demarcation tend to be interrelated. The most appropriate technique involves three stages: the agreement on the precise description, the process of demarcation, and then a treaty approving the detailed results of the process of demarcation.

(C) THE RELATION BETWEEN BOUNDARY DISPUTES AND TERRITORIAL DISPUTES

There is an initial question whether there is a distinction between boundary disputes and territorial disputes. The answer is that in principle there must be, but the distinction is only significant in certain circumstances. In practice most territorial disputes, apart from disputes over undivided islands, also involve the establishment of a boundary.

Occasionally, there may be a dispute confined to the determination of the precise location of a *recognized* boundary. The *Taba Award* (1988) [326] related to the 14 boundary pillars forming part of the boundary established originally between Egypt and Palestine in 1907. The Annex to the *compromis* provided that the Tribunal was not authorized to establish the location of a pillar other than at a location advanced by Egypt and by Israel and recorded in Appendix A.

(D) THE CONCEPT OF TITLE; IN GENERAL

The concept of title to territory in international law appears to be multicultural. Moreover, the concept reflects and implements the system of States and the allocation of territory as a basis for the maintenance of stable relations and the avoidance of breaches of the peace. The concept of title includes both original title and rights which are multititular. However, the general approach is essentially multititular and based upon the better right to possess, as opposed to a unititular system, in which title must be traced directly to the original title holder.

(i) *Subsidiary issues*

(1) The doctrine of inter-temporal law

In cases in which evidence of title reaches far back in time, the situation must be appraised in the light of the rules of international law as they existed at the particular period [327].

(2) Critical dates

The critical date is a concept linked to the admissibility and weight of evidence [328]. The critical date is the point at which the dispute has crystallized and is apparent to the parties. Evidence emanating from the parties after this date is presumed to be self-serving and unreliable. However, subsequent actions may evi-

---

326. *International Law Reports*, E. Lauterpacht (ed.), Vol. 80, p. 224.

327. I. Brownlie, *Principles of Public International Law*, 4th ed., Oxford, Clarendon Press, 1990, pp. 129-130.

328. *Ibid.*, pp. 130-131.

dence consistency, and inconsistent conduct and admissions against interest will be taken into account.

(E) MODES OF ACQUISITION AND LOSS OF TITLE

(i) *Methodology: modes of acquisition*

Many textbooks present a standard list of modes of acquisition: effective occupation, accretion, cession, conquest and prescription. Quite apart from the accuracy of the list as such, this methodology does not sufficiently reflect the way in which tribunals work.

(ii) *Roots of title*

(1) Cession and transfer in accordance with a treaty

It is normal for title to be obtained by virtue of a treaty of cession.

(2) The title of successor States in accordance with the principle of uti possidetis

On a succession of States there is a continuity of boundaries in accordance with the principle of *uti possidetis.*

(3) Dispositions in the name of the international community

At various junctures in history territorial dispositions have been made by joint decision of the principal powers of the time. In the years 1919 and 1920 decisions were taken by the Supreme Council of the Allied and Associated States. Within the United Nations system the General Assembly had at least an implied power to administer the termination of a trusteeship status[329].

(4) Renunciation or relinquishment

Renunciation or relinquishment of title is the procedure by which, in the absence of cession, title is renounced in favour of

329. See the *Northern Cameroons* case, *ICJ Reports 1963*, p. 15.

another State or a power of disposition is conferred on another State or group of States.

(5) Adjudication

The decision of the International Court or the award of a court of arbitration will constitute a valid basis of title.

(6) Effective occupation

The concept of "effective occupation" as a mode of acquisition calls for careful explanation. It is a *technical term* denoting the taking of possession as a consequence of the exercise of government authority in an area which does not belong to another State. Whilst the exercise of authority may involve the presence of police or other security forces, this is not necessary. The most important element is the manifestation of State authority by acts normally indicative of sovereignty: the collection of taxes, the building of public roads, the opening of post offices, and the maintenance of public order.

The concept is much more sophisticated and fluid than the classroom definitions make it appear, and the exigencies of the principles of proof and considerations of public order produce constant refinements and permutations in the decided cases. Thus, for example, abandonment — the negative aspect of effective occupation — is not to be presumed, given that title existed at an earlier stage. In some situations the evidence is far from conclusive and it is for the tribunal to appraise the relative strength of the opposing claims. Title here has a necessary relativity in face of the need to achieve finality of decision.

(7) Acquisitive prescription

In principle, effective occupation is related to the assertion of title in respect of *terra nullius*, whilst acquisitive prescription is related to the situation in which, under certain conditions, the definitive title of State A is displaced by a definitive title of State B. In practice the situations which tribunals are concerned with do not conform to these two clearly differentiated models. In reality it is often difficult to know which State arrived first, and there are competing activities over a long period in the same piece of territory.

(8) Acquiescence and recognition

In certain cases evidence of activities in the disputed area may be very thin or ambiguous and in such cases elements of acquiescence or recognition may be decisive of the issue of sovereignty. The *Temple* case (Merits)[330] is a good example of the significance of recognition. In that case the regular use of a map showing the area to be in Cambodia over a long period (1908 to 1958) was regarded by the International Court as recognition or adoption byThailand of the alignment depicted on the map.

(iii) *The practical reality: various forms of evidence taken into account*

By way of conclusion and emphasis, it is clear that tribunals will take all forms of relevant evidence into account. The types of relevant evidence are varied and some of these types will be examined later on.

(F) THE BURDEN OF PROOF

In litigation concerning title to territory each party is in effect claiming title for itself even if one party initiated the litigation and is, formally speaking, the Applicant State. Thus, in the *Temple* case (Merits), the Court stated that, in spite of the fact that Cambodia was the Applicant State, each party would bear the burden of proof on the issues in relation to which it was the proponent[331].

(G) THE EFFECTS OF THE SPECIAL AGREEMENT ON THE ISSUES TO BE DECIDED

It is not uncommon for the provisions of a Special Agreement to specify and restrict the issues to be decided by the Interna-

330. *ICJ Reports 1962*, p. 6.
331. *ICJ Reports 1962*, pp. 15-16.

tional Court or a court of arbitration. Thus in the *Minquiers and Ecrehos* case [332] the Special Agreement indicated that the Court was expected to determine that sovereignty belonged to one of the parties. In other words the Court was requested to provide a definitive outcome *inter partes*.

(H) Particular Categories of Evidence of Title

(i) *Map evidence*

The general approach of international tribunals is to restrict the role of map evidence to that of the corroboration of a conclusion reached on the basis of other evidence. This was the view adopted in the following cases: the *Beagle Channel Arbitration*[333]; the case concerning the *Frontier Dispute (Burkina Faso/Republic of Mali)* [334]; and the case concerning the *Land, Island and Maritime Frontier Dispute* [335]. This appropriately cautious approach does not, however, exclude the possibility of maps being given considerable probative value when certain conditions are fulfilled.

(1) Map evidence and treaty interpretation: maps as parts of the preparatory work

Maps used by the negotiators of the relevant agreement were taken into account by various members of the Arbitral Tribunal concerned with the *Alaska Boundary* case [336], in seeking to identify the channel called the Portland Channel.

(2) Map evidence and the subsequent practice of the parties

A significant role in the interpretation of treaties may be played by the subsequent practice of the parties. In the *Alaska Boundary*

332. *ICJ Reports 1953*, p. 47.

333. *Report of the Tribunal, International Law Reports*, E. Lauterpacht (ed.), Vol. 52, p. 93 at pp. 201-220, paras. 136-163.

334. *ICJ Reports 1986*, p. 554 at pp. 582-586, paras. 53-62.

335. *ICJ Reports 1992*, p. 550, para. 316.

336. *Reports of International Arbitral Awards*, XV, p. 481 at pp. 494-495, 501, 521-522, 530.

case[337] the United States members (Elihu Root, Henry Cabot Lodge and George Turner), in their Opinion on the fifth question before the Arbitral Tribunal, made considerable use of official maps subsequent to the Treaty of 1825 in establishing their interpretation of certain provisions of that instrument.

(3) Contemporaneous practical interpretation by the parties attested by maps of other Governments

"The interpretation placed upon a treaty provision at the time of the conclusion has been found to be important", as Lord McNair has observed[338]. Lord McNair is in this passage referring to the contemporaneous practice *of the contracting parties*. However, it is submitted that the attitude of third States has probative value, the quantum of which will be determined by the particular circumstances. When there is clear evidence of the view of responsible organs of third States, expressed contemporaneously, and in a disinterested context, such view is a form of reliable evidence. Such evidence may take the form of official maps of third States[339].

(4) Maps as evidence of acts of jurisdiction

Maps may be weighed as part of the evidence of a pattern of acts of jurisdiction or administration (or the absence of these). Map evidence played such a role in the *Colombia-Venezuela Arbitration* (1891)[340] and in the Arbitral Award in the *Rann of Kutch* case (1968)[341].

(5) Notoriety and openness of exercise of sovereignty evidenced by maps

It is a commonplace that an important proof of acts of sov-

---

337. *Reports of International Arbitral Awards*, XV, p. 581 at pp. 532-534.

338. *The Law of Treaties*, Oxford, Clarendon Press, 1961, p. 431.

339. *Report of the Tribunal, International Law Reports*, E. Lauterpacht (ed.), Vol. 52, p. 93 at pp. 219-220, para. 161.

340. *British and Foreign State Papers*, Vol. 83, p. 387 at p. 389.

341. *International Law Reports*, E. Lauterpacht (ed.), Vol. 50, p. 2 at pp. 176-177, 514-518.

ereignty and *animus domini* is the openness and notoriety, the public character, of the exercise of sovereignty over territory. In the *Minquiers and Ecrehos* case Judge Levi Carneiro, speaking of the evidence of maps, said: "It may . . . constitute proof that the occupation or exercise of sovereignty was well known." [342]

(6) Admissions and acquiescence in the form of map evidence

In several adjudications maps have been accepted as admissions against interest and evidence of acquiescence when they were made public and given official approval: as in the *Honduras Borders* Award [343] and the *Minquiers and Ecrehos* case [344].

In the *Minquiers* case the Court referred to a chart attached to a French Note of 12 June 1820. In the Note the Minquiers were stated to be "possédés par l'Angleterre". The chart indicated that the Minquiers were British. The Court observed:

> "It is argued by the French Government that this admission cannot be invoked against it, as it was made in the course of negotiations which did not result in agreement. But it was not a proposal or concession made during negotiations, but a statement of facts transmitted to the Foreign Office by the French Ambassador, who did not express any reservation in respect thereof." [345]

(7) The opinion of authoritative official persons as a form of map evidence

Whilst the weight must vary according to the circumstances, most systems of law regard opinion evidence as admissible provided the evidence is that of a person with special skill or knowledge and relates to the sphere of the expertise concerned.

It is the case that tribunals concerned with disputes as to sovereignty over territory have commonly accepted the evidence of maps with an official provenance as evidence of the views of

342. Separate opinion, *ICJ Reports 1953*, p. 105.

343. *Reports of International Arbitral Awards*, Vol. II, p. 1307 at pp. 1330-1331, 1336, 1360-1361.

344. *ICJ Reports 1953*, p. 47 at pp. 66-67, 71.

345. *Ibid.*, p. 71.

Governments and of political figures and officials with special knowledge as to political matters of fact[346].

The weight of evidence will be the greater when the statements reflected in the map evidence are made *ante litem motam*. In the *Labrador Boundary* case[347] the Judicial Committee of the Privy Council stated the following view:

> "The maps here referred to, even when issued or accepted by departments of the Canadian Government, cannot be treated as admissions binding on that Government; for even if such an admission could be effectively made, the departments concerned are not shown to have had any authority to make it. But the fact that throughout a long series of years, and until the present dispute arose, all the maps issued in Canada either supported or were consistent with the claim now put forward by Newfoundland is of some value as showing the construction put upon the Orders in Council and statutes by persons of authority and by the general public in the Dominion."

(8) Maps as evidence of non-official professional opinion; evidence of general opinion or repute

The expert opinions of cartographers and other non-official persons may be admitted as evidence of political facts. Such evidence in the form of maps has been given a certain weight by tribunals concerned with disputes over sovereignty on a number of occasions: as in the Award in the *Island of Palmas* case[348]. On this subject Sir Gerald Fitzmaurice expressed himself as follows:

> "Both sides in the *Minquiers* case adduced evidence tending to show what was the view taken on the question of sovereignty by what might be called non-official but professional opinion — geographers, scientists, publishers of standard atlases, well-known authors, the evidence of maps, etc. Such considerations can never be conclusive. But they may furnish important evidence of general

346. See, for example, the *Sovereignty over Certain Frontier Land* case, *ICJ Reports 1959*, p. 209 at p. 227 (reference to Belgian military staff maps).

347. (1927), 43 *Times Law Reports*, 289.

348. *Reports of International Arbitral Awards*, II, p. 829 at pp. 852-853, 860-862.

opinion or repute as to the existence of a certain state of fact, and *pro tanto*, therefore, may support the conclusion that that state of fact does actually exist."[349]

(ii) *Acts of local administration*

In some decisions of the International Court a significant role is accorded to "routine" or "local" acts of administration, as in the *Minquiers and Ecrehos* case[350]. The acts relied on by the Court in that case included the holding of inquests on corpses found on the islets, the levying of local taxation on property owned by residents of Jersey, the inclusion of the islets in the Jersey census enumeration, and the registration of fishing boats belonging to residents on the islets in Jersey.

However, in other cases a much more cautious view was adopted by the Court as in the *Temple* case (Merits). In its Judgment the Court refused to give any weight to the "very few routine acts of administration in this small, deserted area", on the part of Thailand; such acts were "the acts of local, provincial authorities"[351].

(iii) *Traditional boundaries: evidence of general repute*

A category of evidence recognized by professional international lawyers and also by international tribunals is that of "general repute". This category has three distinct but related components:

First: expert opinion, that is, non-official professional opinion, in the form of the opinion of geographers, cartographers, and historians.

Secondly: general opinion or repute as to a certain state of fact: that is to say, the category known as matters of common knowledge in the law of evidence.

Thirdly: the concept of a traditional boundary. There can be no doubt that there is a concept of the historical or traditional boun-

---

349. *British Year Book of International Law*, Vol. 32 (1955-1956), pp. 75-76.

350. *ICJ Reports 1953*, pp. 65-66, 67-70.

351. *ICJ Reports 1962*, pp. 29-30.

dary in respects of political entities which have a long and well-recorded history.

It is certain that international tribunals accept the category of ancient or original title but, in doing so, will not rely on equivocal evidence. Both parties in the *Minquiers* case invoked an ancient or original title to the islets, but the Court preferred to rely upon relatively modern evidence of acts of possession and the exercise of jurisdiction [352].

In the *Rann of Kutch Arbitration*, the Opinion of the Chairman, Mr. Lagergren, includes the following passage:

> "Reducing the case to its basic elements, three main issues are to be resolved by the Tribunal.
>
> The first is whether the boundary in dispute is a historically recognised and well-established boundary. Both Parties submit that the boundary as claimed by each of them is of such a character." [353]

The text of the Award itself contains a useful affirmation of the significance of boundaries not determined by treaties in international life [354]. The whole question of customary or traditional boundaries has been most helpfully explored by Dr. Kaikobad in the *British Year Book of International Law* [355]. There is a calendar of existing boundary disputes in which, it may be predicted, the concept of a traditional boundary will have a prominent place.

---

352. *ICJ Reports 1953*, pp. 53-57. See also the separate opinion of Judge Basdevant, *ibid.*, pp. 74-79.

353. *International Law Reports*, E. Lauterpacht (ed.), Vol. 50, p. 2 at p. 474.

354. *Ibid.*, pp. 405-409.

355. Vol. 54 (1983), pp. 130-134.

CHAPTER XII

MARITIME DELIMITATION

(A) Introduction

Maritime delimitation is also an area, along with territorial disputes, in which there is extensive recourse to peaceful settlement, usually in the form of negotiation but not infrequently in the form of arbitration or recourse to the International Court. In the Law of the Sea there are essentially three public order systems: jurisdiction over vessels flying the flag of a State (flag State jurisdiction), port State jurisdiction, and the jurisdiction of coastal States in respect of the territorial sea, continental shelf, exclusive economic zone, and fishery zones. It is worth noting that fishery zones, or fishery conservation zones, are lawful under general international law, even though they do not feature in the Law of the Sea Convention of 1982.

(B) The Sources of the Law Relating to Maritime Delimitation

It is necessary to look briefly at the sources of the law relating to maritime delimitation. In the first place the Law of the Sea Convention of 1982 is relatively unhelpful. Articles 74 and 83, relating to the exclusive economic zone and the continental shelf respectively, provide that delimitation "shall be effected by agreement on the basis of international law as referred to in Article 38 of the Statute of the International Court of Justice, in order to achieve an equitable solution". This formulation is inconclusive to a degree.

The law of maritime delimitation consists essentially of the cumulative jurisprudence of the International Court and courts of arbitration, such as the Award of a Court of Arbitration in the *Anglo-French Continental Shelf* case (1977)[356]. The result is a body of principles which constitute general international law as derived from the pronouncements of the International Court. The role of the practice of States is to a certain extent problematical. Parties before the Court are usually assiduous in invoking State practice, but the Court has shown a certain caution in giving weight to practice. The Court appears to take the view that the invocation of other delimitations cannot stand in the way of the complex process of applying equitable principles. But the prima facie relevance of State practice is accepted by the Court[357].

(C) THE APPLICABLE LAW

In the context of arbitration and adjudication it is necessary to determine the relevant applicable law unless this is particularized in a special agreement. If the parties to a dispute are bound by the Continental Shelf Convention of 1958, then Article 6 of the Convention will be applicable[358]. However, Article 6 will not be applicable if there is a special agreement requesting the tribunal to determine a "single maritime boundary"[359].

In cases of first impression, the tribunal may determine the applicable law, in part at least, by reference to the positions of the parties in the course of the pleadings. Thus, in the *Jan Mayen* case, the Court used a practical shortcut in determining the law applicable to the delimitation of the fishery zone:

> "Regarding the law applicable to the delimitation of the fishery zone, there appears to be no decision of an international tribunal

356. *International Law Reports*, E. Lauterpacht (ed.), Vol. 54, p. 6.

357. Case concerning the *Continental Shelf (Libyan Arab Jamahiriya/Malta)*, *ICJ Reports 1985*, p. 38, para. 44.

358. Case concerning *Maritime Delimitation in the Area between Greenland and Jan Mayen*, *ICJ Reports 1993*, pp. 57-58, para. 44.

359. Case concerning *Delimitation of the Maritime Boundary in the Gulf of Maine Area*, *ICJ Reports 1984*, pp. 300-303, paras. 115-125.

that has been concerned only with a fishery zone; but there are cases involving a single dual-purpose boundary asked for by the parties in a special agreement, for example the *Gulf of Maine* case, already referred to, which involved delimitation of 'the continental shelf and fishery zones' of the parties. The question was raised during the hearings of the relationship of such zones to the concept of the exclusive economic zone as proclaimed by many States and defined in Article 55 of the 1982 United Nations Convention on the Law of the Sea. Whatever that relationship may be, the Court takes note that the Parties adopt in this respect the same position, in that they see no objection, for the settlement of the present dispute, to the boundary of the fishery zones being determined by the law governing the boundary of the exclusive economic zone, which is customary law; however the Parties disagree as to the interpretation of the norms of such customary law." [360]

The relevant principles of general international law consist of so-called "equitable principles". The nomenclature tends to confuse the novice. In reality the "equitable principles" are "principles and rules of international law", as the International Court has emphasized [361]. At the same time, it is possible to see the "principles and rules" as providing no more than a framework within which the techniques of equitable delimitation are deployed. This was the view of the Chamber in the *Gulf of Maine* case:

"80. One preliminary remark is necessary before we come to the essence of the matter, since it seems above all essential to stress the distinction to be drawn between what are principles and rules of international law governing the matter and what could be better described as the various equitable criteria and practical methods that may be used to ensure *in concreto* that a particular situation is dealt with in accordance with the principles and rules in question.

81. In a matter of this kind, international law — and in this respect the Chamber has logically to refer primarily to customary international law — can of its nature only provide a few basic legal principles, which lay down guidelines to be followed with a view to

360. *ICJ Reports 1993*, p. 59, para. 47.

361. *North Sea Continental Shelf* cases, *ICJ Reports 1969*, pp. 48-49, paras. 88-90; p. 53, para. 101.

an essential objective. It cannot also be expected to specify the equitable criteria to be applied or the practical, often technical, methods to be used for attaining that objective — which remain simply criteria and methods even where they are also, in a different sense, called 'principles'. Although the practice is still rather sparse, owing to the relative newness of the question, it too is there to demonstrate that each specific case is, in the final analysis, different from all others, that it is monotypic and that, more often than not, the most appropriate criteria, and the method or combination of methods most likely to yield a result consonant with what the law indicates, can only be determined in relation to each particular case and its specific characteristics. This precludes the possibility of those conditions arising which are necessary for the formation of principles and rules of customary law giving specific provisions for subjects like those just mentioned." [362]

(D) The Genesis of the Equitable Principles Governing Shelf Delimitation

In the *North Sea Continental Shelf* cases [363] the International Court had the difficult task of determining the principles of continental shelf delimitation starting with a clean slate, more or less. The Court firmly set aside the equidistance principle, which produced unreasonable results in particular geographical situations, and especially in the situation of a distinctly incised coast such as that of Germany in the North Sea. To discount the equidistance principle was one thing, but to find what to put in its place was quite another.

On behalf of the German Federal Republic it was contended that there should be a *de novo* allocation of sea-bed areas on the basis of a "just and equitable share". Such an approach would have involved a divorce from the geography of coasts and the related concept of a right of the coastal State based upon its sovereignty over the land domain [364]. The Court rejected this approach. The problem which then remained can be summarized as follows.

362. *ICJ Reports 1984*, p. 290.

363. *ICJ Reports 1969*, p. 3.

364. *Ibid.*, p. 22, para. 19; p. 29, para. 39.

Whilst the equidistance principle produced unacceptable results, if applied without modification, it nevertheless represented the general idea that the coastal geography played a major role in delimitation. The difficulty was to devise a set of modalities which might share the virtues both of reference to real geography and of the flexibility called for in view of the protean nature of coastal geography.

The Court devised a two-tiered response. In the first place, the Court placed emphasis on the importance of the land domain, and of coastal configurations, as the basis of the title of the coastal State to shelf areas. In the words of the Judgment:

> "The doctrine of the continental shelf is a recent instance of encroachment on maritime expanses which, during the greater part of history, appertained to no-one. The contiguous zone and the continental shelf are in this respect concepts of the same kind. In both instances the principle is applied that the land dominates the sea; it is consequently necessary to examine closely the geographical configuration of the coastlines of the countries whose continental shelves are to be delimited. This is one of the reasons why the Court does not consider that markedly pronounced configurations can be ignored; for, since the land is the legal source of the power which a State may exercise over territorial extensions to seaward, it must first be clearly established what features do in fact constitute such extensions. Above all is this the case when what is involved is no longer areas of sea, such as the contiguous zone, but stretches of submerged land; for the legal régime of the continental shelf is that of a soil and a subsoil, two words evocative of the land and not of the sea."[365]

Secondly, the Court formulated a set of equitable principles on the basis of which delimitation was to be effected (it will be recalled that the Court was not asked to carry out a delimitation as such). These principles involved an awkward compromise between the realities of geography and the role of equity in modifying the *consequences* of geography. This compromise is encapsulated in the following paragraph of the Judgment:

---

365. *ICJ Reports 1969*, p. 51, para. 96; and see also p. 22, para. 19.

"Equity does not necessarily imply equality. There can never be any question of completely refashioning nature, and equity does not require that a State without access to the sea should be allotted an area of continental shelf, any more than there could be a question of rendering the situation of a State with an extensive coastline similar to that of a State with a restricted coastline. Equality is to be reckoned within the same plane, and it is not such natural inequalities as these that equity could remedy. But in the present case there are three States whose North Sea coastlines are in fact comparable in length and which, therefore, have been given broadly equal treatment by nature except that the configuration of one of the coastlines would, if the equidistance method is used, deny to one of these States treatment equal or comparable to that given the other two. Here indeed is a case where, in a theoretical situation of equality within the same order, an inequity is created. What is unacceptable in this instance is that a State should enjoy continental shelf rights considerably different from those of its neighbours merely because in the one case the coastline is roughly convex in form and in the other it is markedly concave, although those coastlines are comparable in length. It is therefore not a question of totally refashioning geography whatever the facts of the situation but, given a geographical situation of quasi-equality as between a number of States, of abating the effects of an incidental special feature from which an unjustifiable difference of treatment could result."[366]

The telling phrase in this passage is the reference to there not being any question of "completely" refashioning nature. This phrase has a useful candour. This indication of the general philosophy of delimitation must be taken together with the formulation by the Court of the equitable principles to be applied:

"(C) the principles and rules of international law applicable to delimitation as between the Parties of the areas of the continental shelf in the North Sea which appertain to each of them beyond the partial boundary determined by the agreements of 1 December 1964 and 9 June 1965, respectively, are as follows:

(1) delimitation is to be effected by agreement in accordance with equitable principles, and taking account of all the relevant

366. *ICJ Reports 1969*, pp. 49-50, para. 91.

circumstances, in such a way as to leave as much as possible to each Party all those parts of the continental shelf that constitute a natural prolongation of its land territory into and under the sea, without encroachment on the natural prolongation of the land territory of the other;

. . . .

(D) in the course of the negotiations, the factors to be taken into account are to include:

(1) the general configuration of the coasts of the Parties, as well as the presence of any special or unusual features;
(2) so far as known or readily ascertainable, the physical and geological structure, and natural resources, of the continental shelf areas involved;
(3) the element of a reasonable degree of proportionality, which a delimitation carried out in accordance with equi-table principles ought to bring about between the extent of the continental shelf areas appertaining to the coastal State and the length of its coast measured in the general direction of the coastline, account being taken for this purpose of the effects, actual or prospective, of any other continental shelf delimitations between adjacent States in the same region." [367]

These principles and "factors" are open-textured, and in the *Gulf of Maine* case the Judgment of the Chamber provided a more articulate version as follows:

"There has been no systematic definition of the equitable criteria that may be taken into consideration for an international maritime delimitation, and this would in any event be difficult *a priori*, because of their highly variable adaptability to different concrete situations. Codification efforts have left this field untouched. Such criteria have however been mentioned in the arguments advanced by the parties in cases concerning the determination of continental shelf boundaries, and in the judicial or arbitral decisions in those cases. There is, for example, the criterion expressed by the classic formula that the land dominates the sea; the criterion advocating, in cases where no special circumstances require correction thereof, the equal division of the area of overlap of the maritime and submarine zones appertaining to the respective coasts of neighbouring

---

367. *ICJ Reports 1969*, p. 53, para. 101.

States; the criterion that, whenever possible the seaward extension of a State's coast should not encroach upon areas that are too close to the coast of another State; the criterion of preventing, as far as possible, any cut-off of the seaward projection of the coast or of part of the coast of either of the States concerned; and the criterion whereby, in certain circumstances, the appropriate consequences may be drawn from any inequalities in the extent of the coasts of two States into the same area of delimitation." [368]

The development of a substantial case law has to a certain extent elucidated these general criteria.

(E) THE CONCEPT OF NATURAL PROLONGATION

In the *North Sea* cases natural prolongation was used tactically as a *limitation* upon the doctrine of the just and equitable share. But the concept presented a series of problems and it is unhelpful in geological terms and it is question-begging. In any event in most cases adjudicated as a matter of fact there is a geological continuum.

The concept of natural prolongation has been a considerable source of confusion and yet its influence has in practice been limited. In any event it is established that an equitable delimitation and the determination of the limits of "natural prolongation" are not synonymous [369]. Furthermore, when the relevant coasts are less than 400 miles apart, geological features are irrelevant. This proposition appears in the Judgment in the *Libya/Malta* case:

> "The Court however considers that since the development of the law enables a State to claim that the continental shelf appertaining to it extends up to as far as 200 miles from its coast, whatever the geological characteristics of the corresponding sea-bed and subsoil, there is no reason to ascribe any role to geological or geophysical factors within that distance either in verifying the legal title of the States concerned or in proceeding to a delimitation as between their claims. This is especially clear where verification of

368. *ICJ Reports 1984*, pp. 312-313, para. 157.

369. Case concerning the *Continental Shelf (Tunisia/Libyan Arab Jamahiriya), ICJ Reports 1982*, pp. 46-47, para. 44.

> the validity of title is concerned, since, at least in so far as those areas are situated at a distance of under 200 miles from the coasts in question, title depends solely on the distance from the coasts of the claimant States of any areas of sea-bed claimed by way of continental shelf, and the geological or geomorphological characteristics of those areas are completely immaterial. It follows that, since the distance between the coasts of the Parties is less than 400 miles, so that no geophysical feature can lie more than 200 miles from each coast, the feature referred to as the 'rift zone' cannot constitute a fundamental discontinuity terminating the southward extension of the Maltese shelf and the northward extension of the Libyan as if it were some natural boundary." [370]

In many disputes, as in the *North Sea* cases, the sea-bed structure is essentially continuous. In this type of situation the concept of natural prolongation becomes a pleonasm, referring to a legal conclusion as to the limits of the shelf [371]. After all is said and done, where the coasts of the parties are more than 400 miles apart, a fundamental geological discontinuity may still be relevant and even decisive. At the same time tribunals are reluctant to identify distinct natural prolongations [372].

(F) THE ROLE OF RELEVANT CIRCUMSTANCES

The "relevant circumstances" which appear in the *dispositif* of the Judgment in the *North Sea* cases [373] are accorded a low status in the normative hierarchy. Thus they appear after the formulation of "the principles and rules of international law applicable" (para. C) and are referred to simply as "the factors to be taken into account" in the course of negotiations (para. D). In practice, the application of relevant circumstances

---

370. Case concerning the *Continental Shelf (Libyan Arab Jamahiriya/Malta)*, *ICJ Reports 1985*, p. 35, para. 39.

371. See the *Anglo-French Continental Shelf Arbitration*, Decision of 30 June 1977, *Reports of International Arbitral Awards*, Vol. XVIII, p. 3, para. 191.

372. See the *Tunisia/Libya* case, *ICJ Reports 1982*, p. 57, para. 66.

373. *ICJ Reports 1969*, pp. 53-54, para. 101.

tends to be decisive for delimitation. This is especially the case when the tribunal has adopted a provisional median line (as between opposite coasts) and is engaged in the process of correcting or adjusting this median line. In the practice of the Court the following elements have been recognized as relevant circumstances to be taken into account.

(i) *The geographical configuration of the coasts of the parties*

This factor was stressed in the Judgment in the *North Sea* cases[374] as a consequence of the premise that title depends upon the possession of a status as a coastal State.

(ii) *The general geographical context in which the delimitation will have to be effected*

This element, which was introduced by the Court in the *Libya/Malta* case[375], is problematical, and reliance upon it creates the risk of downgrading certain coasts in favour of other coasts.

(iii) *The conduct of the parties*

This factor is well established and was "highly relevant" in the *Tunisia/Libya* case[376] in which the granting of petroleum concessions by the parties had indicated a *de facto* line. Conduct indicates what the parties regard as equitable.

(iv) *The incidence of natural resources when this is known*

This element was approved by the Court in its Judgment in the *North Sea Continental Shelf* cases[377] and also features in the separate opinion of Judge Jessup[378]

374. *ICJ Reports 1969*, p. 51, para. 96. See also the *Tunisia/Libya* case, *ICJ Reports 1982*, pp. 53-54, para. 61; and pp. 63-64, paras. 78-79.

375. *ICJ Reports 1985*, p. 50, para. 69; p. 52, para. 73.

376. *ICJ Reports 1982*, pp. 83-84, paras. 117-118. See also the *Jan Mayen* case, *ICJ Reports 1993*, pp. 75-77, paras. 82-86.

377. *ICJ Reports 1969*, pp. 53-54, para. 101 (D) (2). See also the *Libya/Malta* case, *ICJ Reports 1985*, p. 41, para. 50.

378. *ICJ Reports 1969*, p. 66.

(v) *The need to ensure equitable access to the resources of the area in dispute*

The previous factor was relied upon by the Court in the *Jan Mayen* case to produce the result that the area in which the capelin appeared in fishable quantities was divided equally between the parties. The Court referred in this context to "equitable access" to the capelin fishery resources[379].

(vi) *Security interests*

The International Court has accepted that in principle security considerations may be taken into account, though in a role subordinate to that of the geographical criteria[380].

(vii) *Other factors*

Other factors recognized as relevant circumstances are the unity of any deposits[381], the factor of the perpendicularity of a boundary to the coast, and the concept of the prolongation of the general direction of the land boundary[382].

The International Court has refused to recognize as relevant circumstances arguments based upon relative wealth[383] and upon the relatively greater landmass of a claimant[384]. In its Judgment in the *Libya/Malta* case[385] the Court made it clear that to count as a "relevant circumstance" a factor must relate either to the basis of title or to the objective of States in claiming sea-bed areas. This essay in definition obviously leaves an extensive penumbra of doubt.

---

379. *ICJ Reports 1993*, pp. 70-72, paras. 72-76; pp. 79-80, paras. 91-92.

380. *Libya/Malta* case, *ICJ Reports 1985*, p. 42, para. 51; *Jan Mayen* case, *ICJ Reports 1993*, pp. 74-75, para. 81.

381. *North Sea* cases, *ICJ Reports 1969*, pp. 50-52, paras. 94, 97.

382. *Tunisia/Libya* case, *ICJ Reports 1982*, p. 85, para. 120.

383. *Tunisia/Libya* case, *ICJ Reports 1982*, pp. 77-78, paras. 106-107; *Libya/Malta* case, *ICJ Reports 1985*, p. 41, para. 50.

384. *Libya/Malta* case, *ICJ Reports 1985*, pp. 40-41, para. 49.

385. *Ibid.*, p. 40, para. 48; p. 41, para. 50. See also the *Jan Mayen* case, *ICJ Reports 1993*, p. 63, para. 57.

(G) THE APPLICATION OF EQUITABLE PRINCIPLES TO DELIMITATION OF EXCLUSIVE ECONOMIC ZONES AND FISHERY ZONES

The reasoning of the Chamber of the Court in the *Gulf of Maine* case carried the strong implication that the "equitable criteria" were applicable in principle to maritime delimitation in general[386]. However, that case was concerned with a single maritime boundary within the framework of a special agreement. In any event in the *Jan Mayen* case the Court expressly confirmed that the customary law of delimitation applied to fishery zones and exclusive economic zones[387]. In this context "customary law" is a reference primarily to the equitable principles applied and developed in the decisions of international tribunals since 1969.

(H) THE ROLE OF PROPORTIONALITY

In the *dispositif* of the Judgment in the *North Sea Continental Shelf* cases[388] the third factor "to be taken into account" in the process of delimitation was as follows:

> "the element of a reasonable degree of proportionality, which a delimitation carried out in accordance with equitable principles ought to bring about between the extent of the continental shelf areas appertaining to the coastal State and the length of its coast measured in the general direction of the coastline, account being taken for this purpose of the effects, actual or prospective, of any other continental shelf delimitations between adjacent States in the same region".

A primary difficulty with proportionality is its normative status. In principle this is low and it does not form one of the "principles and rules of law applicable to the delimitation", but is simply "one possibly relevant factor", as the Court emphasized in the *Libya/*

386. See the Judgment, *ICJ Reports 1984*, pp. 290-293, paras. 80-90; pp. 299-300, para. 112; pp. 312-314, paras. 155-160.

387. *Ibid.*, p. 59, paras. 47-48.

388. *ICJ Reports 1969*, pp. 52-53, para. 101 (D) (3); and see also p. 52, para. 98.

Malta Judgment[389]. Moreover, the concept of proportionality cannot provide an independent principle of delimitation based upon the ratio of coastal lengths: if that were the case no other considerations could operate. It must also be pointed out, in case it is not obvious, that proportionality does not produce an alignment. It deals with spatial comparisons and not location.

In the jurisprudence the "factor" or "criterion" of proportionality has normally been applied as an *ex post facto* test of the equitable nature of a delimitation already effected on the basis of other principles and factors, in order to correct any resulting disproportion [390].

The Court's exploration of the precise role of proportionality in the *Libya/Malta* case is incisive and helpful[391]. The eccentric feature of that case is that, having accorded a modest normative status to proportionality overall, the Court went on to give effect to the disparity in the lengths of coasts (as a relevant circumstance) and thus *in effect* reintroduced a more intrusive version of proportionality by the back door.

(I) Disparity in the Lengths of Coasts as a Relevant Circumstance

In the *Libya/Malta* case[392] the Court regarded "the existence of a very marked difference in coastal lengths" as a relevant circumstance, and this position was confirmed in the *Jan Mayen* case[393]. In both Judgments it was emphasized that taking account of the disparity of coastal lengths did not mean a direct and mathematical relationship between the lengths of the relevant coasts[394].

389. *ICJ Reports 1985*, p. 44, para. 57.

390. See the *Anglo-French Continental Shelf Arbitration*, Decision of 30 June 1977, *Reports of International Arbitral Awards*, Vol. XVIII, pp. 57-58, paras. 98-101; *Tunisia/Libya* case, *ICJ Reports 1982*, p. 76, para. 104; p. 91, paras. 130-131.

391. *ICJ Reports 1985*, pp. 43-46, paras. 55-59.

392. *Ibid.*, pp. 48-49, para. 66; p. 52, para. 73.

393. *ICJ Reports 1993*, pp. 68-69, paras. 68-69.

394. *ICJ Reports 1985*, p. 45, para. 58; p. 49, para. 66; *ICJ Reports 1993*, p. 69, para. 69.

In these two cases the disparity of lengths of coasts appears to stand in the place of the original, and less radical, version of proportionality. In the *Jan Mayen* case the distinction of principle between proportionality, and lengths of coasts *qua* relevant circumstance, virtually disappears. In the same case there is an apparent solecism in the use of a principle of equitable access to resources alongside the alleged influence of coastal relationships. At the end of the day the alignment divided the fishery in dispute equally between the two parties[395].

(J) Exclusive Economic Zone and Continental Shelf Delimitation Compared

The provisions of Article 74 of the Law of the Sea Convention of 1982 concerning delimitation of the EEZ between States with opposite or adjacent coasts are identical with those of Article 83 relating to continental shelf delimitation. Moreover, the basis of entitlement of the coastal State to the EEZ is less differentiated from that of shelf areas since the International Court emphasized the distance principle of 200 miles in the *Libya/Malta* case[396]. In general it may be assumed that the principles of delimitation are similar. However, there will be some differences in the balancing up of the equitable factors, more especially when the resources in question are fisheries rather than oil and gas.

(K) Single Maritime Boundaries

In the practice of States in the form of delimitations by agreement the phenomenon of the single maritime boundary appears. Such boundaries divide areas of different status, for example, an EEZ and a fisheries conservation zone of 200 miles. From time to time international tribunals are asked to determine single

---

395. *ICJ Reports 1993*, pp. 79-80, paras. 91-92.
396. *ICJ Reports 1985*, p. 35, para. 39.

maritime boundaries, as in the *Gulf of Maine* case[397]. In that case the Judgment of the Chamber of the International Court applied equitable criteria essentially identical to those applicable to shelf delimitation, whilst emphasizing the need to use criteria suited to a multi-purpose delimitation involving *both* the shelf *and* the superjacent water column[398].

(L) THE GENERAL *MODUS OPERANDI* OF DELIMITATION

A study of the case law of the International Court shows that a fairly consistent *modus operandi* has emerged. This is particularly clear in the *Libya/Malta* and *Jan Mayen* cases.

The *modus operandi* involves five stages:

First: if necessary the area of overlapping claims is divided into separate regions.

Secondly: the distance criterion is applied. In the case of opposite coasts this produces a provisional median line (but this is not an application of the equidistance method). In other cases, a line is drawn which reflects the general configuration of the coasts of the parties.

Thirdly: the application of relevant circumstances may produce a "correction" or "adjustment" of the provisional median line.

Fourthly: the factor of proportionality may be applied *ex post facto* to test the overall equity of the delimitation.

Fifthly: in disputes concerning access to fisheries, the Court may, if it considers it necessary, and as an *ex post facto* test, enquire whether the overall result "should unexpectedly be revealed as radically inequitable, that is to say, as likely to entail catastrophic repercussions for the livelihood and economic well-being of the population of the countries concerned"[399].

---

397. *ICJ Reports 1984*, p. 246.

398. *ICJ Reports 1984*, pp. 326-327, paras. 191-194. See also the *Guinea/Guinea (Bissau)* case, *International Law Reports*, E. Lauterpacht (ed.), Vol. 77, p. 635.

399. See the *Gulf of Maine* case, *ICJ Reports 1984*, p. 342, para. 237. See also the *Jan Mayen* case, *ICJ Reports 1993*, p. 71, para. 75.

(M) THE ROLE OF ISLANDS IN DELIMITATION

There is an issue often pursued in the literature and sometimes in pleadings as to whether islands constitute a special category for purposes of delimitation. The issue is normally presented in the form of a partisan assertion that islands *per se* are incidental features which should not be given a normal entitlement in the context of delimitation. There is no evidence that tribunals treat islands as a discrete category. The determinant is the geographical configurations and relationships overall. Thus a large group of islands may be given less than full effect in one geographical context and no effect whatsoever in another. The latter was the *modus operandi* adopted by the Court of Arbitration in the *Anglo-French Continental Shelf* case [400].

Whilst the general principle is clear, the practice of tribunals has tended to disadvantage islands to a certain degree, in spite of the fact that the coasts of islands prima facie have the same entitlement as other coasts. Islands which fall the "wrong" side of a provisional median line [401] or otherwise do not form part of the geographical framework of the delimitation tend to be disadvantaged (and may be enclaved). Even islands which form part of the framework of delimitation, like Jan Mayen [402], may have their entitlement in effect reduced as a result of reference to the disparity of lengths of coasts as a relevant circumstance.

In the *Libya/Malta* case Malta had argued that the Court should take account of the fact that Malta was an island State and not an island politically linked to a mainland State. The Court's response was as follows:

> "In the view of the Court, it is not a question of an 'island State' having some sort of special status in relation to continental shelf rights; indeed Malta insists that it does not claim such status. It is simply that Malta being independent, the relationship of its coasts with the coasts of its neighbours is different from what it would be if it were a part of the territory of one of them. In other words it

400. Decision of 30 June 1977, *Reports of International Arbitral Awards*, Vol. XVIII, p. 3.

401. *Ibid.*, pp. 87-95, paras. 180-202.

402. *ICJ Reports 1993*, pp. 65-70, paras. 61-69.

might well be that the sea boundaries in this region would be different if the islands of Malta did not constitute an independent State, but formed a part of the territory of one of the surrounding countries. This aspect of the matter is related not solely to the circumstances of Malta being a group of islands, and an independent State, but also to the position of the islands in the wider geographical context, particularly their position in a semi-enclosed sea."[403]

The factor referred to by the Court as "the wider geographical context", which was given effect as a relevant circumstance[404], necessarily reduces the significance of islands. In the same context the deployment of the disparity in coastal lengths as a factor in delimitation may be said to have introduced a relation of the land-mass factor which the Court had rejected as a relevant consideration. The separate opinions of Judges Mosler, Oda and Schwebel contain some incisive criticism of this aspect of the Judgment[405].

(N) AN ASSESSMENT OF THE WORK OF THE INTERNATIONAL COURT

From the outset the Court has insisted that the application of the equitable principles did not involve any question of decision *ex aequo et bono*[406]. Nonetheless, particular exercises in delimitation have provoked individual Judges to complain of equity "freed from the positive law [the Judge] is charged to apply"[407] and that the Court had resorted to "distributive justice"[408]. At a more practical level it may be said that the flexible approach to delimitation and the demolition of the principle of equidistance (even as a presumption in the case of opposite coasts) has probably made negotiation a less tractable method of dispute settlement.

403. *ICJ Reports 1985*, p. 42, para. 53. See also p. 51, para. 72.

404. *ICJ Reports 1985*, p. 50, para. 69; p. 52, para. 73.

405. See H. Mosler, *ibid.*, pp. 120-122; Oda, pp. 135-139, paras. 19-28; Schwebel, pp. 178-187.

406. *North Sea Continental Shelf* cases, *ICJ Reports 1969*, p. 48, para. 88.

407. Judge Gros, dissenting opinion, *Gulf of Maine* case, *ICJ Reports 1984*, p. 388, para. 47.

408. Judge Schwebel, separate opinion, *Jan Mayen* case, *ICJ Reports 1993*, p. 120.

CHAPTER XIII

THE PROTECTION OF THE TERRITORIAL INTEGRITY AND THE ENVIRONMENT OF STATES

(A) Introduction: the Basic Problem

The purpose is to explore to what extent the principles and mechanisms of customary international law are appropriate to deal with the threats to public order and the territorial integrity of States posed by sources of atmospheric pollution. It will be seen that they do not work very well and this for a variety of reasons. The concepts of classical international law, and especially the concepts of physical penetration of harmful agencies across a boundary as a basis of responsibility, do not apply very well to the disseminated and incremental sources of pollution which create problems in contemporary conditions.

(B) The "Applicable Law" Issue

Questions of pollution raise issues of State responsibility and are thus subject to customary or general international law. The legal position may also be affected by relevant multilateral conventions of a standard-setting character. However, it is unhelpful to propose the existence of an autonomous "International Environmental Law" which stands apart from general international law. There is no evidence that such an entity would qualify as an "applicable law" for the purposes of proceedings before international tribunals.

(C) Some Relevant State Practice

There is a considerable quantity of State practice relevant to transboundary pollution, the existence of which is often ignored in the work of academic lawyers. In 1954 the Japanese Government presented claims to the United States in respect of injuries to Japanese fishermen caused by fall-out from thermonuclear weapons testing on Eniwetok[409]. The same issue provoked a Japanese Note to the United States of 20 February 1958. The text of the Note is as follows:

> "In view of this menace posed by nuclear tests to mankind and from a humanitarian standpoint, the Japanese Government and people have consistently had an earnest desire that all nuclear bomb tests be suspended immediately. This desire was stated in a note verbale sent by the Foreign Ministry to the United States Embassy in Japan on September 15, 1957, asking for the suspension of tests on Eniwetok, and also in Prime Minister Kishi's letter to President Eisenhower, dated September 24, 1957.
>
> The Japanese Government regrets that the United States Government, in spite of the desire of the Japanese Government and people, has announced the establishment of a danger zone to conduct nuclear bomb tests. The Japanese Government takes this opportunity to request again that the United States Government consider seriously the suspension of the afore-mentioned tests.
>
> The United States Government states that every possible precaution will be taken to prevent damage and injury to human lives and property in the danger zone and there is no probability of any accidents outside the danger zone. Whatever precaution is taken, however, the Japanese Government is greatly concerned over conducting of nuclear tests and establishment of a danger zone for that purpose in view of the fact that said zone is near to routes of the Japanese merchant marine and to fishing grounds of Japanese fishing boats.
>
> Accordingly, the Japanese Government would like to make clear its view that in the event the United States Government conducts nuclear tests in defiance of the request of the Japanese Government, the United States Government has the responsibility of compensating for economic losses that may be caused by the establishment of a danger zone and for all losses and damages that may be inflicted on Japan and the Japanese people as a result of the

409. Marjorie M. Whiteman, *Digest of International Law*, Vol. 4, April 1965, Washington, pp. 565-566.

nuclear tests. The Japanese Government wishes to reserve the right to demand complete compensation for such losses and damages."[410]

French nuclear weapons tests in the South Pacific in 1966 were the subject of protests from Australia and New Zealand. The New Zealand Note of 27 May 1966 to the French Government reads as follows:

"The Embassy of New Zealand presents its compliments to the Ministry of Foreign Affairs and on the instructions of its Government has the honour to refer to the French Government's announcement of 16 May 1966, in a notice to navigators and an air information publication, of the establishment of a danger zone in the South Pacific in the light of its intention to conduct nuclear weapons tests.

The New Zealand Government has noted this step with grave concern and solemnly reiterates its protest at the holding of nuclear tests in the atmosphere particularly in the South Pacific.

The Government and the people of New Zealand in common with many other governments and peoples are deeply concerned at the prospect of a proliferation of nuclear weapons technology which carries with it the spiralling risks of contamination of the atmosphere and calamitous nuclear hostilities. The Government must regard the checking, not the expansion of nuclear weapons capacity, as one of the most urgent problems of international security. New Zealand has long stressed its opposition to the continuation of all nuclear testing. It welcomed the partial test ban treaty of 1963 as a measure of progress towards more far reaching measures of disarmament and arms control and as a means of halting the contamination of man's environment. The continuation of testing in the atmosphere cannot but hinder the attainment of that objective and contribute also to the difficulties of securing a universally accepted and comprehensive test ban treaty.

Moreover, the New Zealand Government and people cannot but be concerned at a further contamination of man's environment particularly in the South Pacific by nuclear explosions. The Government has welcomed assurances freely given by France

---

410. Marjorie M. Whiteman, *Digest of International Law*, Vol. 4, April 1965, Washington, p. 585.

that it intends to do everything possible to minimize the possibility of a hazard to the health and welfare of the inhabitants of the Pacific Islands. It has appreciated the opportunity offered by the French Government to discuss safety measures with the competent French authorities. It must note, however, that there can be no assurance of the complete elimination of all risks incidental to the proposed tests.

If tests are conducted the New Zealand Government trusts that every effort will be made in accordance with France's announced intentions to minimize the risks involved. In particular it expresses the earnest wish that explosions will take place only in circumstances, especially with regard to meteorological conditions, which afford the greatest possibility of eliminating the risk of fallout on inhabited territories. The New Zealand Government nonetheless must formally reserve the right to hold the French Government responsible for any damage or losses incurred as a result of the tests by New Zealand or the Pacific Islands for which New Zealand has special responsibility or concern.

The Embassy of New Zealand avails itself of the opportunity to renew to the Ministry of Foreign Affairs the assurances of its highest consideration." [411]

Volumes of material produced by the Micronesian Claims Commission are relevant and a number of claims resulted from injuries caused by fall-out. The Commission was a United States Government agency applying legislative standards, pursuant to the Micro-nesian Claims Act of 1971 [412].

Finally, there is the Canadian statement of claim concerning the consequences of the disintegration in the atmosphere of the Soviet Cosmos 954 satellite in 1978. The Canadian claim was based partly on a Convention and partly on general international

411. *ICJ Pleadings, Nuclear Tests* cases, Vol. II *(New Zealand* v. *France)*, p. 22. For other New Zealand Notes see *ibid*., pp. 27-30.

412. Unpublished decisions of the United States Micronesian Claims Commission, 1972-1976 (pursuant to the Micronesian Claims Act of 1971, Pub. L. No. 92-39, 85 Stat. 92, 94 (1971), on file with the United States Department of the Interior and with the United States Foreign Claims Settlement Commission, Washington, DC.

law[413]. The Statement of Claim[414] invokes a standard of absolute liability for space activities in addition to the complaint of violation of sovereignty:

> "21. The intrusion of the Cosmos 954 satellite into Canada's air space and the deposit on Canadian territory of hazardous radioactive debris from the satellite constitutes a violation of Canada's sovereignty. This violation is established by the mere fact of the trespass of the satellite, the harmful consequences of this intrusion, being the damage caused to Canada by the presence of hazardous radioactive debris and the interference with the sovereign right of Canada to determine the acts that will be performed on its territory. International precedents recognize that a violation of sovereignty gives rise to an obligation to pay compensation.
>
> 22. The standard of absolute liability for space activities, in particular activities involving the use of nuclear energy, is considered to have become a general principle of international law. A large number of states, including Canada and the Union of Soviet Socialist Republics, have adhered to this principle as contained in the 1972 *Convention on International Liability for Damage caused by Space Objects*. The principle of absolute liability applies to fields of activities having in common a high degree of risk. It is repeated in numerous international agreements and is one of 'the general principles of law recognized by civilized nations' (Article 38 of the Statute of The International Court of Justice). Accordingly, this principle has been accepted as a general principle of international law."

(D) SOME USEFUL CONCEPTS OF STATE RESPONSIBILITY

At the outset it can be accepted that general international law contains some relevant and useful principles.

(i) *The knowledge and control which a State has over its territory*

The Judgment of the Court in the *Corfu Channel* case (Mer-

413. See the Canadian Note dated 23 January 1979; *International Legal Materials*, Vol. 18 (1979), p. 899; I. Brownlie, *System of the Law of Nations*, Part. i, Oxford, Clarendon Press, 1983, p. 97.

414. *International Legal Materials*, Vol. 18 (1979), p. 902.

its)[415] provides some guidance on proof of knowledge of sources of harm on State territory. The Court observes that the fact of control over State territory does not create a prima facie responsibility nor shift the burden of proof. At the same time the Court held that the exclusive control which a State has over its territory justifies resort to indirect evidence by the claimant State, the victim of a breach of international law[416].

(ii) *State responsibility for private activities*

It may happen that the immediate source of harm consists of activities in the private sector. Indeed, the Chernobyl reactor was, it appears, operated by a private law entity. The law of State responsibility faces such problems without too much difficulty. The State will be responsible in a series of possible scenarios. First, the State concerned may accept responsibility. Secondly, the territorial sovereign may by its conduct approve or adopt the acts of private persons or entities. It was on this basis in part that the Government of Iran was held responsible for the overrunning of the United States Embassy by student militants and the seizure of its inmates as hostages on 4 November 1979[417]. Apart from the two foregoing scenarios, the relevant standard of general international law may stipulate for the exercise of due diligence in control of the activities of private persons or private law entities. In reality, there can be little or no difference between a private sector activity subject to regulatory controls and the operation of State agencies and public corporations.

(E) THE SELECTION OF APPROPRIATE CAUSES OF ACTION: THE *NUCLEAR TESTS* CASES

However, in the sphere of litigation the law does not provide

415. *ICJ Reports 1949*, p. 4.

416. *ICJ Reports 1949*, p. 18.

417. Case concerning *United States Diplomatic and Consular Staff in Tehran*, *ICJ Reports 1980*, pp. 33-37, paras. 69-79.

useful vehicles for pursuing claims as the *Nuclear Tests* cases show. The Australian Application included the following passages:

"The Law

48. In the circumstances which are described in the preceding paragraphs of this Application and which the Government of Australia will set out more fully in its memorial and in subsequent written and oral pleadings, it is clear that a legal dispute exists between Australia and the French Republic.

49. The Australian Government contends that the conduct of the tests as described above has violated and, if the tests are continued, will further violate international law and the Charter of the United Nations, and, *inter alia*, Australia's rights in the following respects:

(i) The right of Australia and its people, in common with other States and their peoples, to be free from atmospheric nuclear weapon tests by any country is and will be violated;

(ii) The deposit of radio-active fall-out on the territory of Australia and its dispersion in Australia's airspace without Australia's consent:

(a) violates Australian sovereignty over its territory;

(b) impairs Australia's independent right to determine what acts shall take place within its territory and in particular whether Australia and its people shall be exposed to radiation from artificial sources;

(iii) The interference with ships and aircraft on the high seas and in the superjacent airspace, and the pollution of the high seas by radio-active fall-out, constitute infringements of the freedom of the high seas.

. . . .

Accordingly, the Government of Australia Asks the Court to Adjudge and Declare that, for the abovementioned reasons or any of them or for any other reasons that the Court deems to be relevant, the carrying out of further atmospheric nuclear weapon tests in the South Pacific Ocean is not consistent with applicable rules of international law.

And to Order

that the French Republic shall not carry out any further such tests."

The essential facts of the *Nuclear Tests* cases[418] were as follows. After originally conducting atmospheric tests in Algeria (1960-1963), France operated a Pacific Tests Centre on Mururoa Atoll, French Polynesia. The programme of tests, including hydrogen bomb tests, lasted from 1966 to 1972. In 1973 reports appeared of a plan for a further series of tests. At this juncture, Australia and New Zealand commenced proceedings in the International Court. The Australian Application of 9 May 1973 requested a declaratory judgment but did not include a claim for damages.

The actual outcome of the proceedings was a procedural fiasco. By 9 votes to 6 the Court decided that the claim was inadmissible. In the first place the Court analysed the pleadings in order to ascertain "the true object and purpose of the claim". The Court determined that Australia was seeking to obtain a termination of the tests and "thus its claim cannot be regarded as being a claim for a declaratory judgment"[419].

The Court then took judicial notice of a series of public declarations by the French authorities, including the President of the Republic, the Minister for Defence and the Minister for Foreign Affairs[420]. The Court evaluated these French Statements and noted that, on the basis of the principle of good faith, unilateral acts could be creative of legal obligations[421]. The key criterion was that of the intention of the declarant. In the words of the Court:

> "43. It is well recognized that declarations made by way of unilateral acts, concerning legal or factual situations, may have the effect of creating legal obligations. Declarations of this kind may be, and often are, very specific. When it is the intention of the State making the declaration that it should become bound according to its terms, that intention confers on the declaration the char-

---

418. *Nuclear Tests (Australia* v. *France), ICJ Reports 1974*, p. 253; *Nuclear Tests (New Zealand* v. *France), ibid.*, p. 457.

419. *Nuclear Tests (Australia* v. *France), ICJ Reports 1974*, p. 263, para. 30. See also *Nuclear Tests (New Zealand* v. *France), ibid.*, p. 467, para. 31.

420. *Ibid.*, pp. 263-267, and pp. 467-472, respectively.

421. *Ibid.*, pp. 267-268, and pp. 472-473, respectively.

> acter of a legal undertaking, the State being thenceforth legally required to follow a course of conduct consistent with the declaration. An undertaking of this kind, if given publicly, and with an intent to be bound, even though not made within the context of international negotiations, is binding. In these circumstances, nothing in the nature of a *quid pro quo* nor any subsequent acceptance of the declaration, nor even any reply or reaction from other States, is required for the declaration to take effect, since such a requirement would be inconsistent with the strictly unilateral nature of the juridical act by which the pronouncement by the State was made.
>
> 44. Of course, not all unilateral acts imply obligation; but a State may choose to take up a certain position in relation to a particular matter with the intention of being bound — the intention is to be ascertained by interpretation of the act. When States make statements by which their freedom of action is to be limited, a restrictive interpretation is called for.
>
> 45. With regard to the question of form, it should be observed that this is not a domain in which international law imposes any special or strict requirements. Whether a statement is made orally or in writing makes no essential difference, for such statements made in particular circumstances may create commitments in international law, which does not require that they should be couched in written form." [422]

The Court concluded that in consequence the object of the claim had disappeared [423]. An alternative view of the case was adopted in the joint dissenting opinion of Judges Onyeama, Dillard, Jiménez de Aréchaga and Waldock [424]. On their construction of the pleadings, Australia had requested a declaratory judgment. The fact that it involved a dual submission (requesting both a declaration and injunctive relief) made no difference. Given that a declaratory judgment had a forward reach, Australia's claims were, on this construction, admissible.

---

422. *Nuclear Tests (Australia* v. *France) (New Zealand* v. *France), ICJ Reports 1974*, p. 267, and pp. 472-473, respectively.

423. *Ibid.*, pp. 270-272, and pp. 475-477, respectively.

424. *Ibid.*, pp. 312-371, and pp. 494-523, respectively.

(i) *The political background of the case*

The political background of the case included a number of problematical elements. The Respondent State, which refused to appear, was a permanent member of the Security Council. A further element, of both legal and political significance, was the radical change in the policy of Australia, the Applicant State, in respect of the testing of nuclear weapons. This element was emphasized by Judge Gros in his separate opinion[425]. In his view there was no rule of law opposable to France concerning the subject-matter[426]. In particular, Judge Gros cited atmospheric nuclear weapons tests by the United Kingdom in Australia (1952-1956) and United States tests in the Pacific in 1962 on Christmas Island with Australian permission. Judge Petrén expressed similar views[427].

(ii) *The sequel in 1995*

In September 1995 there was a dramatic sequel to the decisions of the Court in 1974. In response to the announcement by France of a further series of underground nuclear weapons tests in the South Pacific starting in September 1995, New Zealand requested the Court for an examination of the situation in accordance with paragraph 63 of the Court's Judgment of 1974 in the *Nuclear Tests (New Zealand* v. *France)* case[428]. In paragraph 63 of the Judgment the Court had indicated that "if the basis of the Judgment were to be affected, the Applicant could request an examination of the situation in accordance with the provisions of the Statute . . .".

The Court first of all determined that the "special procedure" envisaged in paragraph 63 was not incompatible with the Statute[429]. The Court then decided that the procedure applied exclusively to nuclear tests in the atmosphere. Accordingly, the

425. *Ibid.*, pp. 276-297, and pp. 480-482, respectively.

426. *Ibid.*, pp. 276-289.

427. *Ibid.*, pp. 298-307, and pp. 483-492, respectively.

428. *Nuclear Tests (New Zealand* v. *France)*, *ICJ Reports 1974*, p. 477

429. *ICJ Reports 1995*, pp. 303-304, paras. 52-54.

"Request" of New Zealand was dismissed[430]. On a simpler analysis, the dispute between France and New Zealand of 1973 was not concerned with *underground* testing and the "Request" of 1995 depended on the limits of the dispute of 1973 and the Judgment relating thereto[431].

(F) State Responsibility and the Environment

A particular difficulty in the sphere of environmental hazards and damage is the selection and deployment of an appropriate cause of action or basis of claim. The process of contamination is often, in physical terms, incremental and may involve complex causal mechanisms. Apart from the finding of a cause of action, the requirement of damage as a necessary condition of claim bears an uneasy relation to the scientific proof of a certain threshold of damage caused by an overall rise in radiation or other forms of pollution and problems of multiple causation then arise.

In the *Nuclear Tests* case brought by Australia against France the Australian Application employed the international law relative of trespass to deal with this problem. Thus the deposit of radioactive fall-out on the territory of Australia was classified as a violation of Australia's territorial sovereignty[432]. In the same context, the concept of "decisional sovereignty" was used, referring to the right of Australia to determine what acts should take place within its territory.

(G) Remedies in Anticipation of Actual Damage

A particular source of difficulty is the controversy on the question whether remedies can be sought in anticipation of actual damage[433]. In general it seems clear that the International Court

---

430. *ICJ Reports 1995*, p. 306, para. 65.

431. See the separate opinion of Judge Shahabuddeen, *ibid.*, pp. 312-316.

432. See *ICJ Pleadings, Nuclear Tests*, Vol. I, pp. 479-490 (Argument of Mr. Byers).

433. See C. D. Gray, *op. cit., supra* footnote 257, pp. 64-66, 95.

can give injunctive relief by way of a declaratory judgment. This was the view of the four Judges of the Court in the joint dissenting opinion in the *Nuclear Tests* cases[434].

It has been suggested that the decisions in the *Nuclear Tests* cases "suggest that an international tribunal cannot grant injunctions or prohibitory orders restraining violations of international law"[435]. This view does not seem to be justified, and declarations are given by the Court which are injunctive in effect.

No doubt requests for interim measures of protection addressed to the International Court have a certain role. Whilst there is a continuing controversy as to their binding character[436], the request, if it is successful, has considerable effects in the political sphere, in part as a result of the media attention and the revelation of facts which the Respondent State finds it difficult to deny. In environmental cases, such effects would have particular value, always provided that credible scientific evidence was available.

(H) STATE PRACTICE IN RELATION TO THE CHERNOBYL DISASTER IN 1986

The Chernobyl disaster provokes sober reflection. The facts were undeniable and the damage, or at least the medium-term damage, was quantifiable. Here there was no incremental source of harm but a vast outpouring of radioactive material which was then borne in the airstream over various parts of Europe.

The aftermath of Chernobyl exhibited a number of striking features. The Soviet Government showed no inclination to accept responsibility, or to offer compensation on an *ex gratia* basis. In any case it was doubtful whether the Soviet Government could

434. *ICJ Reports 1974*, pp. 312-371, and pp. 494-523, respectively.

435. Patricia W. Birnie and Alan E. Boyle, *International Law and the Environment*, Oxford, Clarendon Press, 1992, pp. 150-151.

436. See L. Collins, *Recueil des cours*, Vol. 234 (1992-III), pp. 216-220.

have produced adequate compensation had it been willing. Governments other than the Soviet Government were secretive about the types and levels of radiation. States whose territory had been seriously polluted showed an astonishing reluctance to make claims or even to reserve their rights. A considerable gap between the doctrine of environmental law and the practice of States became apparent.

(i) *The response of Governments to the Chernobyl disaster*

(1) The United Kingdom

The United Kingdom reserved its rights but did not present a claim. In a parliamentary reply given in 1986 the Minister of State, Foreign and Commonwealth Office, observed that:

> "On 10 July we formally reserved our right with the Soviet Union to claim compensation on our own behalf and on behalf of our citizens for any losses suffered as a consequence of the accident at Chernobyl. The presentation of a formal claim, should we decide to make one, would not take place until the nature and full extent of any damage suffered had been assessed." [437]

(2) Sweden

The Swedish Government issued the following statement:

> "In so far as customary international law is concerned, principles exist which might be invoked to support a claim against the USSR. The issues involved, however, are complex from the legal as well as the technical point of view and warrant careful consideration." [438]

The German Federal Republic also reserved its rights [439].

437. *British Year Book*, Vol. 57 (1986), p. 600; 21 July 1986.

438. P. Sands, *Chernobyl: Law and Communication*, Cambridge, Grotius Publications, 1988, p. 27.

439. Patricia W. Birnie and Alan E. Boyle, *op. cit.*, *supra* footnote 435, p. 369.

(3) The Group of Seven

The Group of Seven industrial nations made the following statement on the implications of the Chernobyl accident.

> "2. Nuclear power is and, properly managed, will continue to be an increasingly widely used source of energy. For each country the maintenance of safety and security is an international responsibility, and each country engaged in nuclear power generation bears full responsibility for the safety of the design, manufacture, operation and maintenance of its installations. Each of our countries meets exacting standards. Each country, furthermore, is responsible for prompt provision of detailed and complete information on nuclear emergencies and accidents, in particular those with potential transboundary consequences. Each of our countries accepts that responsibility and we urge the Government of the Soviet Union, which did not do so in the case of Chernobyl, to provide urgently such information, as our and other countries have requested." [440]

This statement does not refer expressly to State responsibility in the legal sense. However, the focus upon the duty to provide information is of legal significance.

(I) Deficiencies in the Approach by Way of Customary Law and State Responsibility

In general, customary law lacks the necessary sophistication both in its formulations of causes of action and in its individualist procedures. The assembling of adequate proof of damage to the individual claimant State is difficult.

Chernobyl and its aftermath casts doubt on the efficacy of the approach to environmental disasters by way of State responsibility. States clearly did not regard the legal approach as being especially relevant. The State responsibility, or liability, approach is about allocation of losses and reparation. It is thus *retrospective*. In the

440. *International Legal Materials*, Vol. 25 (1986), p. 1005.

case of the protection of the environment it is prospective and preventive action which is called for.

International environmental law still consists of treaty provisions and it is far from clear whether any new principles of general international law have emerged concerning the protection of the environment. In its "Request" to the International Court, discussed earlier, the Government of New Zealand invoked the "precautionary principle", summarized in the following passage from the Court's Order:

> "5. Whereas in its 'Request for an Examination of the Situation' New Zealand contends that, both by virtue of specific treaty undertakings (in the Convention for the Protection of the Natural Resources and Environment of the South Pacific Region of 25 November 1986 or 'Noumea Convention') and customary international law derived from widespread international practice, France has an obligation to conduct an environmental impact assessment before carrying out any further nuclear tests at Mururoa and Fangataufa; and it further contends that France's conduct is illegal in that it causes, or is likely to cause, the introduction into the marine environment of radioactive material, France being under an obligation, before carrying out its new underground nuclear tests, to provide evidence that they will not result in the introduction of such material to that environment, in accordance with the 'precautionary principle' very widely accepted in contemporary international law; . . ." [441]

The "precautionary principle" found a sympathetic reception in the dissenting opinions of Judges Weeramantry and Koroma [442]. It is tempting to see the principle as a particular application of the concept of "due diligence" to environmental affairs. The substantial doubt which must remain derives from the supine response of other States in face of Chernobyl. The practice of States immediately thereafter indicates an absence of any precautionary principle in 1986, unless a distinction can be discerned between the operation of reactors and the carrying out of nuclear tests.

441. *ICJ Reports 1995*, p. 290.

442. *Ibid.*, pp. 342-344, and p. 368, respectively.

CHAPTER XIV

THE USE OF FORCE BY STATES

(A) The System of Public Order and the Place of Self-help in the Law

In the period 1928 to 1945 it was established that resort to war was no longer permissible as a form of self-help. The General Treaty for the Renunciation of War, signed on 27 August 1928, provided as follows:

> "*Article I.* The High Contracting Parties solemnly declare in the names of their respective peoples that they condemn recourse to war for the solution of international controversies, and renounce it as an instrument of national policy in their relations with one another.
>
> *Article II.* The High Contracting Parties agree that the settlement or solution of all disputes or conflicts of whatever nature or of whatever origin they may be, which may arise among them, shall never be sought except by pacific means."

This text must be read together with the reservations made by signatory Governments. The reservations, together with the subsequent practice of the parties to the General Treaty, reveal a pattern of general principles and exceptions which in all essentials prefigures the legal régime of the United Nations Charter[443]. Individual States retained the right of self-defence and defensive alliances were legitimate. The General Treaty, often referred to as the Kellogg-Briand Pact, was ratified or adhered to by 63 States, and is still in force.

---

443. I. Brownlie, *International Law and the Use of Force by States*, Oxford, Clarendon Press, 1963, pp. 74-111.

After controversy in the era of the League of Nations the Charter of the United Nations affirmed the prohibition of the so-called "hostile measures short of war": reprisals, pacific blockade, and forcible intervention. The language of Article 2, paragraph 4, of the Charter is clear and comprehensive:

> "All Members shall refrain in their international relations from the threat or use of force against the territorial integrity or political independence of any State, or in any other manner inconsistent with the Purposes of the United Nations."

The system of the Charter represents the normal elements of a public order system, that is to say, a centralized authority with prima facie a monopoly of the use of force and a restrictive régime of self-help by individual States. The policy elements in this régime have been described by the International Law Commission as follows:

> "(2) The absolutely indispensable premise for the admission of a self-contained concept of self-defence, with its intrinsic meaning, into a particular system of law is that the system must have contemplated as a general rule the general prohibition of the use of force by private subjects and hence admits the use of force only in cases where it would have purely and strictly defensive objectives, in other words, in cases where the use of force would take the form of resistance to a violent attack by another. Another element — which, in logic, is not so indispensable as the foregoing, but has been confirmed in the course of history as its necessary complement — is that the use of force, even for strictly defensive purposes, is likewise admitted not as a general rule, but only as an exception to a rule under which a central authority has a monopoly or virtual monopoly on the use of force so as to guarantee respect by all for the integrity of others. Only in specific situations where, by its very nature, the use of force by the agencies of the central authority cannot be resorted to promptly and efficiently enough to protect a subject against an attack by another does the use of means of defence involving force by the subject in question remain legitimate. In view of these remarks, it is obvious that only in relatively recent times did the international legal order adopt a concept of self-defence that, in certain essential aspects, is entirely comparable to that normally employed in national legal systems.

It is in any case obvious that the gradual development of the definition of the concept could only go hand in hand with that of the principle outlawing wars of aggression and conquest, regardless of the times or the circles in which the principle asserted itself in the international law in force."[444]

(B) TITLE TO TERRITORY CANNOT BE DERIVED FROM THE THREAT OR USE OF FORCE

It is a generally recognized principle of customary or general international law that title to territory cannot be derived from the threat or use of force. This principle is a corollary of the Kellogg-Briand Pact of 1928 and of Article 2, paragraph 4, of the United Nations Charter. It was enunciated in a Note of the United States Government dated 7 January 1932 to the Japanese and Chinese Governments, which stated that the United States Government "does not intend to recognise any situation, treaty, or agreement which may be brought about by means contrary to the covenants and obligations of the Pact of Paris . . ."[445]. The principle thus formulated became known as the Stimson Doctrine[446].

The principle is also to be found in various regional instruments such as the Anti-War Treaty of Non-Aggression and Conciliation, signed at Rio de Janeiro on 10 October 1933, and the Bogota Charter of 1948 (Art. 17)[447].

In 1970 the principle was incorporated in the Declaration of Principles of International Law Concerning Friendly Relations and Co-operation among States in Accordance with the Charter of the United Nations. The relevant formulation provides:

"The territory of a State shall not be the object of acquisition by another State resulting from the threat or use of force. No territo-

444. *Reports of the International Law Commission to the General Assembly on the Work of the Thirty-second Session*, International Law Commission, *Yearbook*, 1980, II (Pt. ii), p. 52.

445. I. Brownlie, *op. cit., supra* footnote 443, p. 412.

446. I. Brownlie, *op. cit., supra* footnote 443, pp. 410-423; Marjorie M. Whiteman, *Digest of International Law*, Vol. 2, Washington, USGPO, 1963, pp. 1111-1161.

447. I. Brownlie, *op. cit., supra* footnote 443, pp. 95-99, 116-117.

rial acquisition resulting from the threat or use of force shall be recognized as legal."[448]

The principle of non-recognition of conquest has been applied in the practice of the political organs of the United Nations in respect of Israeli occupation of the West Bank and the Golan Heights and, with dramatic consequences, to the Iraqi attempt to annex Kuwait. In relation to the latter in Security Council resolution 662 (1990) it was decided that the annexation "has no validity". Essentially the same principle is applied when the State resorting to force installs a satellite administration in the guise of an "independent" State, as in the case of the "Turkish Republic of Northern Cyprus".

(i) *Apparent exceptions to the principle*

There are apparent exceptions to the principle which have to be approached cautiously. On occasion the international community recognizes territorial changes which originated in the threat or use of force. Examples include the title of the former Soviet Union to areas formerly part of eastern Poland, and the legality of the possession of Vilnius by Lithuania.

As with most apparent exceptions, analysis reveals that in such cases title derives not from the illegal use of force but from one or more collateral and independent factors. Multilateral recognition may confer title but it is not possible to regard prescription as an acceptable mode of legitimating possession resulting from the unlawful use or threat of force[449].

(C) The Status of the Use of Armed Force as a Justiciable Question

In the *Nicaragua* case the second and third grounds of the inadmissibility of the Nicaraguan claims advanced by the United

448. I. Brownlie (ed.), *Basic Documents in International Law*, 4th ed., Oxford, Clarendon Press, 1995, p. 36.

449. I. Brownlie, *International Law and the Use of Force by States*, Oxford, Clarendon Press, 1963, p. 422 ; and R. Y. Jennings, *The Acquisition of Territory in International Law*, Manchester, 1963, pp. 53-58.

States involved the argument that the subject was exclusively within the jurisdiction of the Security Council. This argument was pressed particularly in relation to the application of Article 51 of the Charter in relation to an ongoing armed conflict[450].

The Court rejected these preliminary objections[451], relying in part on the decision in the *Corfu Channel* case (Merits)[452]. Both the *Corfu Channel* case and the *Nicaragua* case confirm the status of the use of armed force as a justiciable question.

(D) THE GENERAL SCHEME OF THE UNITED NATIONS RELATING TO THE USE OF FORCE BY STATES

The general scheme of the United Nations Charter appears in the following provisions. First of all, the Organization has the purpose "to take effective collective measures for the prevention and removal of threats to the peace, and for the suppression of acts of aggression or other breaches of the peace . . ." (Art. 1, para. 1). The *modus operandi* of such collective measures is elaborated in Chapter VII of the Charter.

Secondly, the threat or use of force by individual States is prohibited as a principle of the Charter in Article 2, paragraph 4. The phrasing "against the territorial integrity or political independence of any States" was inserted to strengthen the guarantee against intervention.

Thirdly, the only exceptions to this régime are as follows:

(i) Article 51 provides (in material part):

> "Nothing in the present Charter shall impair the inherent right of individual or collective self-defence if an armed attack occurs against a Member of the United Nations, until the Security Council has taken measures necessary to maintain international peace and security."

---

450. *ICJ Reports 1984*, p. 392.

451. *Ibid.*, pp. 431-436.

452. *ICJ Reports 1949*, p. 4.

Certain problems attending the concept of self-defence will be examined in due course. For the moment it may be noted that the principle of collective self-defence has been invoked in the context of a number of significant episodes involving the use of force. It is probable that the coalition which went to the assistance of South Korea in 1950 acted, at least initially, by virtue of Article 51[453].

In the context of the conflict in Vietnam the United States Department of State issued a legal memorandum which expressly invoked "the right of individual and collective self-defence against armed attack" and cited Article 51[454]. Again, in the course of the proceedings in the *Nicaragua* case, the United States claimed that the acts in question were justified by the exercise of the right of collective self-defence against an armed attack. The argument was rejected by the Court partly on the facts and partly on the ground that the alleged victims (El Salvador, Honduras and Costa Rica) had made no requests for assistance[455]. Finally, the coalition war mounted in response to the Iraqi invasion of Kuwait was justified on the basis of Article 51 in the *consideranda* of Security Council resolution 661 of 8 August 1990. This and other resolutions invoked Chapter VII of the Charter as the legal basis for various sanctions against Iraq[456].

(ii) Chapter VIII of the United Nations Charter protects the legal status of regional arrangements, which are given a significant degree of autonomy, subject to a general power of supervision on the part of the Security Council.

Article 52, paragraph 1, provides:

> "Nothing in the present Charter precludes the existence of regional arrangements or agencies for dealing with such matters

---

453. See the language of the Security Council resolutions 82 (1950), 83 (1950), and 84 (1950).

454. "The Legality of U.S. Participation in the Defense of Viet-Nam", 8 March 1966; *Dept. of State Bull.*, 28 March 1966.

455. *ICJ Reports 1986*, pp. 118-123, paras. 227-238.

456. See Karel C. Wellens (ed.), *Resolutions and Statements of the United Nations Security Council (1946-1992)*, 2nd ed., Dordrecht, Martinus Nijhoff, 1993, pp. 507 *et seq.*

relating to the maintenance of international peace and security as are appropriate for regional action, provided that such arrangements or agencies and their activities are consistent with the Purposes and Principles of the United Nations."

The provisions of the Inter-American Treaty of Reciprocal Assistance[457] signed at Rio de Janeiro, 2 September 1947, constitute a good example of the powers which may be assumed by a regional arrangement. Thus Article 3 formulates a right of collective self-defence in case of an armed attack and, in doing so, reflects the provisions of the United Nations Charter relating to collective self-defence.

Article 6 relates to a different set of contingencies. It provides as follows:

> "If the inviolability or the integrity of the territory or the sovereignty or political independence of any American State should be affected by an aggression which is not an armed attack or by an extra-continental or intra-continental conflict, or by any other fact or situation that might endanger the peace of America, the Organ of Consultation shall meet immediately in order to agree on the measures which must be taken in case of aggression to assist the victim of the aggression or, in any case, the measures which should be taken for the common defense and for the maintenance of the peace and security of the Continent."

Article 8 lists the measures which may be authorized by the Organ of Consultation that is, the meetings of Foreign Ministers of the parties to the Rio Treaty, including economic sanctions and the use of armed force.

The provisions of the Rio Treaty came into question during the Cuban Missile Crisis of October 1962[458]. The background was as follows. In 1958 the United States had installed intermediate-range ballistic missiles in Italy and Turkey. In 1962 the Soviet Government, which had protested in face of this initiative, began the installation of similar missiles in Cuba. This was regarded as

457. *American Journal of International Law*, Vol. 42 (1948), Suppl., p. 53.

458. See A. Chayes, *The Cuban Missile Crisis*, London, Oxford University Press, 1974.

intolerable by the United States and it was decided to put in place a blockade (described as a "quarantine") to prevent the shipment of so-called "offensive" weapons to Cuba.

The United States intended to seek the approval of the Organ of Consultation of the Rio Treaty and was successful in this diplomatic enterprise. The legal difficulty was to justify such a response in relation to action which, on any possible view, did not constitute an armed attack. When President Kennedy announced the measures to be taken in his speech on 22 October 1962, he stated that the Organization of American States would be asked to invoke Articles 6 and 8 of the Rio Treaty. Thus reliance was placed upon the flexible concept of a threat to regional peace and no reference was made to Article 3, which was conditioned by the requirement of an armed attack.

The régime of the use of force established by the Charter is relatively strict but there are distinct elements of liberalism as a result of the role accorded to the regional arrangements. In any event the action of the OAS in the Cuban missile crisis was not uncontroversial. Thus there was a question whether regional measures could affect the Soviet Union legally. There was also the question of the application of Article 53 (1) of the Charter which requires authorization of the Security Council for "enforcement action".

(E) Multilateralism as a Guarantee of Legality in Decision-making

One of the themes of international security since 1919 has been the assumption that multilateral action is effective and is the only type of action which is likely to be effective. If multilateral action were to be seriously challenged by the opposition of a major power, then the requirement of unanimity (as in the Covenant) or the veto (as in the Charter) was available. More specialized types of multilateral action are available in the forms of regional action and collective self-defence.

The question worthy of debate is whether multilateral decision-making is a guarantee of legality in decision-making. All that can be said is that it militates in favour of legality, but it is by no means a guarantee thereof. A major regional power can use its political and economic clout to ensure an artificial consensus, as in the cases of the United States intervention in the Dominican Republic in 1965 [459] and the invasion of Czechoslovakia by Warsaw Pact forces in 1968 [460]. The former purported to be action of the Organization of American States and the latter was supposedly based upon the provisions of the Warsaw Pact.

(F) Specific Issues: the Concept of Self-defence

The classical source is the diplomatic correspondence relating to the *Caroline* incident of 1837, in which the authorities in Canada had taken action against a vessel used for mounting raids into Canada [461]. The British Government justified the destruction of the vessel on the basis of "the necessity of self-defence and self-preservation".

In a letter of 24 April 1841 from the Secretary of State, Webster, to Fox, later incorporated in a Note to Lord Ashburton of 27 July 1842, Webster required the British Government to show the existence of:

> "necessity of self-defence, instant, overwhelming, leaving no choice of means, and no moment for deliberation. It will be for it to show, also, that the local authorities of Canada, even supposing the necessity of the moment authorised them to enter the territories of the United States at all, did nothing unreasonable or excessive; since the act justified by the necessity of self-defence, must be limited by that necessity, and kept clearly within it."

---

459. Documents in *International Legal Materials*, Vol. 4 (1965), pp. 557-577, 594-596, 1150-1170.

460. Documents in *International Legal Materials*, Vol. 7 (1968), pp. 1283-1339.

461. See R. Y. Jennings, *American Journal of International Law*, Vol. 32 (1938), p. 82 ; Lord McNair, *International Law Opinions*, Vol. 2., Cambridge, University Press, 1956, p. 221.

Lord Ashburton in his letter of 28 July 1842 did not dispute Webster's statement of principle. The formula used by Webster has often been cited but the correspondence made no difference to the legal doctrine, such as it was, of the time. Self-defence was regarded either as synonymous with self-preservation or as a particular instance of it. Webster's Note was an attempt to describe its limits in relation to the particular facts of the incident. The statesmen of the period used self-preservation, self-defence, necessity, and necessity of self-defence as more or less interchangeable terms and the diplomatic correspondence was not intended to restrict the right of self-preservation, which was in fact reaffirmed.

There is a tendency to invoke the Webster formula in isolation, in spite of the fact that it relates to a period before the modern legal régime of the use of force by States had evolved. In reality the formula is vague and question-begging and should be used with considerable caution.

(G) SPECIFIC ISSUES: THE CONCEPT OF ARMED ATTACK

Article 51 is very explicit in its formulation of a condition that individual or collective self-defence is lawful "if an armed attack occurs against a Member of the United Nations". In the first place there is a general issue concerning the relationship of Article 51 and customary international law[462]. The significance of the question derives from the difficulty of reconciling the phrase "if an armed attack occurs" with the thesis, supported from time to time by certain Governments, that anticipatory action is lawful. The partisans of the broader doctrine of self-help contend that Article 51 formally reserves the right of self-defence but does not define its content. Such an interpretation is perverse and would render the exception to the principle stated in Article 2, paragraph 4, substantially subversive of the principle.

---

462. See I. Brownlie, *International Law and the Use of Force by States*, Oxford, Clarendon Press, 1963, pp. 272-275; Y. Dinstein, *War, Aggression and Self-defence*, Cambridge, Grotius Publications, 1988, pp. 169-172; B. Simma (ed.), *The Charter of the United Nations*, Oxford, 1994, pp. 666-678.

At least it can be accepted that the right of self-defence exists in customary international law and this was recognized by the International Court in the Judgment on the Merits in the *Nicaragua* case[463]. The Court, not very surprisingly, adopted the view that the customary law right depended on the existence of an armed attack[464]. Article 51 accordingly falls to be considered as a part of the general evidence of the content of the right of self-defence in customary law.

The crucial question is the identification of instances of an "armed attack" in the presence of often complex facts. Certain indicators can be found in the available sources. Thus minor frontier incidents do not count. The use of a naval blockade certainly involves the threat of force and when the blockade is enforced, an armed attack is necessarily involved.

A legal approach dictates reference to the context, that is to say, the necessity of self-defence and the purposive context which this presents. It is of considerable importance to distinguish action which is intended as a reprisal. The bombing of Libya in 1986 by the United States Air Force was stated to be in response to an attack on United States servicemen in Berlin, for which, it was alleged, Libya was responsible[465]. The bombing of the discotheque in Berlin took place on 5 April 1986, and the bombing of Tripoli and Benghazi took place on 14 and 15 April 1986. The delay in response renders the action eccentric in terms of self-defence. Moreover, there is good reason to believe that one purpose of the United States action was to murder the Libyan Head of State (and a member of his family was in fact killed). Such operations fall outside any legitimate concept of self-defence, more especially when there is no independent assessment of the evidence alleged to justify the action.

Particular difficulties arise when the original incident, as in the Libyan case, took place in one State and the putative action by

463. *ICJ Reports 1986*, pp. 102-103, paras. 193-194.

464. *Ibid.*, p. 103, para. 195 (but see also para. 194).

465. See C. Greenwood, *West Virginia Law Review*, Vol. 89 (1987), p. 933. In the terrorist incident in Berlin one United States serviceman was killed and 50 injured.

way of self-defence occurs in another State. Another permutation of fact concerns the situation in which a State tolerates the presence of armed bands which launch armed attacks against a neighbouring State. There can be little doubt that action by way of self-defence is justified in such cases[466] but the response must be proportionate.

(h) Specific Issues: So-called "Defensive Armed Reprisals"

Professor Dinstein states a principle of "defensive armed reprisals"[467]. In his words:

> "Armed reprisals are measures of counter-force, short of war, undertaken by one State against another in response to an earlier violation of international law. Like all other instances of unilateral use of force by States, armed reprisals are prohibited unless they qualify as an exercise of self-defence under Article 51. Only defensive armed reprisals are allowed. They must come in response to an armed attack, as opposed to other violations of international law, in circumstances satisfying all the requirements of legitimate self-defence.
>
> A juxtaposition of defensive armed reprisals and on-the-spot reaction discloses points of resemblance as well as divergence. In both instances, the use of counter-force is limited to measures short of war. But when activating defensive armed reprisals, the responding State strikes at a time and a place different from those of the original armed attack. In the two hypothetical examples adduced above, the script must be altered as follows: (i) a few days after the Utopian patrol is fired upon by Arcadian troops, an Arcadian patrol is shelled by Utopian artillery, or Utopian commandos raid a military base in Arcadia from which the original attack was sprung; (ii) subsequent to the depth-charging of the Ruritanian submarine by a Numidian destroyer on the high seas, a Ruritanian aircraft strafes a Numidian missile boat a thousand miles away."[468]

466. See Y. Dinstein, *op. cit.*, *supra* footnote 462, pp. 221-229.
467. See Y. Dinstein, *op. cit.*, *supra* footnote 462, pp. 202-212.
468. *Ibid.*, pp. 202-203.

Dinstein states that such action must conform to the *jus in bello*, and also meet the conditions of necessity, proportionality and immediacy. Yet it is difficult to understand how in practice the type of action this writer has in mind can comply with the conditions of proportionality and immediacy.

Whilst Dinstein asserts that this type of armed reprisal can be permissible under Article 51 of the Charter[469] he concedes that "most writers deny that self-defence pursuant to Article 51 may ever embrace armed reprisals". His approach is also in conflict with the opinion of the International Law Commission.

(I) Specific Issues: Forcible Humanitarian Intervention

There is also a minority opinion proposing the legality of humanitarian intervention and the protection of nationals, within the territory of other States.

Professor Franck has expressed such a doctrine in this way:

> "Again, pragmatic escape from the conundrum posed in a 'hard case' requires application of a rule of reasonableness. The strict application of Article 51 *is* reasonable, in almost all cases. An exception may be made, however, where effective government has ceased to exist in the place where the danger to lives has arisen. In that event, however, other normative practice also becomes relevant. A modern customary law of humanitarian intervention is beginning to take form which may condone action to protect lives, providing it is short and results in fewer casualties than would have resulted from non-intervention. This practice does not distinguish between rescuing persons who are citizens of the intervening State, other aliens, or citizens of the State in which the intervention occurs. A State which purports to intervene to prevent danger to its own citizens but ignores the needs of others would be in violation of the new customary norm which it seeks to invoke. Moreover, as with 'anticipatory self-defence', the State which acts in violation of the general prohibition on intervention has the onus of demonstrating the existence of a genuine, immediate and dire emergency which could not be redressed by means less violative of

469. See Y. Dinstein, *op. cit.*, p. 207.

the law. The emerging normative practice also requires an exhaustion of the multilateral remedies established by the Charter system." [470]

In face of such views in the literature, the fact remains that there is no support for this proposition in customary international law. As Professor Oscar Schachter observes:

> "No United Nations resolution has supported the right of a State to intervene on humanitarian grounds with armed troops in a State that has not consented to such intervention. Nor is there evidence of State practice and related *opinio juris* on a scale sufficient to support a humanitarian exception to the general prohibition against non-defensive use of force." [471]

The occasions on which States have invoked humanitarian considerations to justify the use of force within and against another State do not inspire confidence in the new doctrine. Such interventions are commonly based upon a collateral political agenda and involve considerable loss of life, the existence of which is obscured by manipulation of the news media.

The United States intervention in Panama provides a depressing example of this type of operation. In his address announcing the invasion of Panama on 20 December 1989 President Bush justified the action primarily by reference to the "imminent danger to the 35,000 American citizens in Panama" [472]. The Department of State identified the relevant legal principles as follows:

> "The United States objectives were: (1) to protect American lives; (2) to assist the lawful and democratically elected government in Panama in fulfilling its international obligations; (3) to seize and arrest General Noriega, an indicted drug trafficker; and (4) to

---

470. T. M. Franck, "Fairness in the International Legal and Institutional System (General Course on Public International Law)", *Recueil des cours*, Vol. 240 (1993-III), pp. 256-257.

471. O. Schachter, *op. cit., supra* footnote 316, p. 124.

472. See *American Journal of International Law*, Vol. 84 (1990), pp. 545-549; *Report of the Committee on International Arms Control and Security Affairs and the Committee on International Law of the Association of the Bar of the City of New York, The Use of Armed Force in International Affairs: The Case of Panama*, 1992.

> defend the integrity of United States rights under the Panama Canal treaties.
>
> We determined that U.S. military action was necessary to protect and defend the canal, to maintain the ability of the United States to execute its treaty rights and obligations and to protect the lives of American citizens.
>
> We consulted with the duly elected Panamanian government [the government of President Guillermo Endara] which Noriega had illegally kept out of office, and they indicated that they welcomed our assistance."[473]

In addition reference was made to Article 51 of the United Nations Charter.

The United States complained of the death of an off-duty officer who was a passenger in a car which drove through a roadblock at the PDF Headquarters, the beating of another officer and the making of threats of sexual abuse to the same officer's wife. In the resulting invasion 300 Panamanian civilians were killed and 3,000 wounded. A working-class suburb was levelled by the use of excessive fire power. Although it was claimed that the purpose was to restore legitimacy, President Endara subsequently denied that he had been consulted.

The international community was not very receptive to the legal justifications offered by the United States and the United Nations General Assembly condemned the invasion of Panama by 75 votes to 20, with 40 abstentions: General Assembly resolution 44/240 of 29 December 1989. The resolution referred to a "flagrant violation of international law and of the independence, sovereignty and territorial integrity of States". A significant factor in this episode is the failure of the United States to seek the approval of the Organization of American States.

The facts of the Panama intervention must establish the episode as a clear demonstration of the good sense of the present system[474]. Precisely because such interventions are related to a

---

473. *American Journal of International Law*, *supra* footnote 472, pp. 547-548.

474. See I. Brownlie, in Richard B. Lillich (ed.), *Humanitarian Intervention and the United Nations*, Charlottesville, University Press of Virginia, 1973, pp. 139-148.

collateral agenda the achievement of which requires a major political and military penetration of the target State, a great deal of force is necessary, many people are killed (on allegedly humanitarian grounds) and the legitimacy of the government installed is seriously damaged. It is significant that, in relation to the situation in Panama, the United States did not seek a peaceful resolution of the alleged causes of complaint and did not seek to involve the Organization of American States, no doubt because very little support would have been forthcoming.

(J) Specific Issues: Intervention with Consent or on Request

The United Nations Charter does not give recognition to intervention with the consent or on the request of the territorial sovereign, but no useful inference can be drawn from this. General international law recognizes the power of States to consent to activities of other States on their territory, whether these involve the conferment of a right of passage (or overflight), the carrying out of military exercises, the restoration of order in a particular locality, or support to the Government against rebels or terrorists. The principle of consent then operates as an independent principle and it is not as such incompatible with the United Nations Charter.

Certain intractable problems arise from this title to use force. It is not uncommon for the consent to be be granted by a Government the constitutional status of which at the material time is problematical, as in the case of the United States intervention in Lebanon in 1958, or for the "requesting government" to be itself a function and result of the intervention, as in the case of the second Soviet intervention in Hungary in 1956.

(K) Conclusions

The purpose at this stage is to point to the vulnerable areas in the legal régime. The legal régime was clearly intended to restrict resort to self-help and also resort to different forms of armed intervention and reprisal. This was the "intention of the legislator" in 1945 in response to the experience in the period of the League of Nations. There can be no question that important advances have been made. Such advances include the strengthening of the principle that title to territory cannot be acquired by means of the use or threat of force, and the obsolescence of the concepts of "war" or "state of war" as connecting factors.

No doubt the legal régime will always entail problems of application, and rules alone, however carefully formulated, will not induce States to behave in a civilized way. Some of the difficulties of application have been reviewed above. By way of conclusion it is appropriate to point to certain threats to the legal régime relating to the use of force by States which come from outside the régime itself.

Such threats may be tabulated in simple terms as follows:

First, the appearance of new practices in the sphere of recognition which, in conjunction with various forms of political warfare, tend to destabilize otherwise effective Governments, and to provide excuses for intervention allegedly on humanitarian grounds.

Secondly, the use of the Security Council to provide forms of relative legitimacy for collective resort to force by coalitions of States, which resort to force has purposes not limited to those of collective self-defence and not clearly justified by the provisions of Chapter VII of the Charter. The outstanding example of this is the collective measures taken against Iraq after the invasion of Kuwait.

Thirdly, the highly selective application of sanctions by the Security Council in the face of a resort to force by individual States, with the result that the penalty-free delinquent is tempted to argue that the inaction of the Council is evidence of the legality of its actions. This type of reasoning is encouraged in the realms of doctrine by the relativism in the application of legal rules which characterizes some adherents of the Yale Law School.

CHAPTER XV

THE ROLE OF THE SECURITY COUNCIL AND THE RULE OF LAW

(A) The Purpose

The political realignments of the last five years have produced a situation in which the Security Council has acquired a degree of cohesion which has exacerbated the long-familiar problem of the application of double standards by the political organs of the United Nations. In the result the question which has always been on the agenda, the relation of the work of the political organs of the United Nations and the Rule of Law, has become more pressing.

Whilst recent exercises by the Security Council have caused particular concern on the part of international lawyers, it is, of course, necessary to bear in mind the performance of the political organs generally. But it is the Security Council which has the political competence to adopt resolutions which are prima facie binding by virtue of the provisions of Chapter VII of the Charter.

(B) The Role of the Political Organs in Making Legal Determinations

By way of preliminary it is to be emphasized that the political organs frequently adopt a course of conduct based upon legal considerations and intended to have legal consequences. Early in the history of the United Nations the General Assembly adopted the resolution concerning reparation for injuries incurred in the service of the United Nations[475], which was rooted in legal con-

475. I. Brownlie, *System of the Law of Nations: State Responsiblity*, Part i, Oxford, Clarendon Press, 1983, p. 124.

siderations and was related to the Advisory Opinion of the International Court on *Reparation for Injuries Suffered in the Service of the United Nations*[476].

It is fairly common for the Security Council to make determinations relating to State responsibility. Examples include the resolutions concerning the Israeli attack on Beirut airport in 1968[477], and resolution 687 (1991) concerning the attack on Kuwait by Iraq[478]. Another field in which both the Security Council and the General Assembly have made numerous determinations is that of the legality of changes in the status of territory, including the consequences of the use or threat of force in effecting territorial change. The many examples include the presence of a South African administration in Namibia, the unilateral declaration of independence by Ian Smith's régime in Southern Rhodesia, the retention of territory occupied by Israel in 1967, the status of the Bantustans in South Africa, and the status of the area of northern Cyprus occupied by Turkey in 1974.

Such determinations are in nearly all cases normal and necessary and the fact that the political organs make determinations which have legal implications, or which are motivated by legal considerations, cannot as such be the object of complaint or criticism. However, in certain instances the conduct of the political organs gives rise to concern against a background of double standards applied to certain States[479]. It is this element of eccentricity and opportunism which gives rise to concern in relation to the Rule of Law.

(C) JUDGING THE INTERNATIONAL SYSTEM BY MUNICIPAL LAW CRITERIA

Before the criteria which form the practical manifestation of the Rule of Law are set forth by way of reference, it is necessary

---

476. *ICJ Reports 1949*, p. 174.

477. I. Brownlie, *op. cit.*, *supra* footnote 475, p. 128.

478. 3 April 1991, *International Legal Materials*, Vol. 30 (1991), p. 847.

479. See E. Lauterpacht, *Aspects of the Administration of International Justice*, Cambridge, Grotius Publications, 1991, pp. 37-48.

to take care of the objection that it is unsuitable and irrelevant to subject the system of international law and diplomacy to evaluation on the basis of the criteria derived from municipal law. In this context, it is necessary to distinguish two propositions. It is, of course, true to say that the relations of States should not be equated to the relations of legal persons within domestic law, and that, as a consequence, legal concepts should not be translated too readily from the realm of domestic law to the plane of international relations. At the same time there is no reason to refrain from subjecting international law and the sphere of international organization to *analysis* in terms of the values of national legal and political systems.

It would be absurd if it were not possible to evaluate the workings of the international system in terms of the Rule of Law. Indeed, the development of standards of human rights, as well as the procedural standards prevalent in international tribunals as an aspect of general principles of law, demonstrate that domestic law standards, adopted as paradigms or ideals, have penetrated the sphere of international law to a considerable degree.

(D) An Epitome of the Rule of Law

The Rule of Law is not a purely "legal" artefact, since it involves elements derived from political science, constitutional theory, and historical experience. Moreover, it cannot be reduced to a few simple formulations, and it involves a series of conjointly applicable principles or desiderata. For present purposes the following elements are proposed as an epitome of the Rule of Law as a practical concept.

The key elements constituting the Rule of Law are as follows:

(1) Powers exercised by officials must be based upon authority conferred by law.

(2) The law itself must conform to certain standards of justice, both substantial and procedural.

(3) There must be a substantial separation of powers between the executive, the legislature and the judicial function. Whilst this

separation is difficult to maintain in practice, it is at least accepted that a body determining facts and applying legal principles with dispositive effect, even if it is not constituted as a tribunal, should observe certain standards of procedural fairness.

(4) The judiciary should not be subject to the control of the executive.

(5) All legal persons are subject to rules of law which are applied on the basis of equality.

To the elements offered above, it should be added that the Rule of Law implies the absence of wide discretionary powers in the Government which may encroach on personal liberty, rights of property or freedom of contract.

(E) EQUAL SUBJECTION TO LAW

It is not proposed to attempt a general examination of international law and its institutions in the light of this assemblage of criteria, but to focus upon two standards which are particularly relevant to any consideration of the powers of the political organs of the United Nations. The first of these criteria is the requirement of the equal application of the law. An insistence on equal subjection to the law is a shared characteristic of the opinions of a variety of constitutional law theorists.

The workings of the political organs of the United Nations have, particularly in the recent past, produced results which exhibit double standards in the application of the law on a scale which places the principle of equal subjection to law in jeopardy. No doubt the normal criticism of the international system is that it lacks enforcement procedures. There is, however, another dimension to the problem of enforcement. In the past it was only a political contingency which prevented the Security Council from exercising its powers extensively. In reality the powers accorded to it under the Charter are very considerable. When those powers are exercised extensively, the question then arises: What are the legal limits to those powers?

(F) THE POWERS CONCERNED MUST BE EXERCISED IN ACCORDANCE WITH LAW

The second criterion of the Rule of Law which is of particular relevance is the principle that the law itself should be exercised in accordance with certain standards of justice, both substantial and procedural. In the sphere of international organizations, this may be regarded as self-evident. Judge El-Erian has stated the position:

> "Whatever the legal nature of the powers attributed to an international institution, they are specific in the sense that they may be exercised only with respect to certain subject-matters prescribed by the constituent instrument." [480]

There is thus no question that in principle international organizations may act *ultra vires* and thus create the necessity to decide on the legal effect of the illegal acts of organizations [481]. The fact that the international system does not allow for any automatic review of the decisions of organizations has not obscured the real possibility that in certain circumstances the question of *ultra vires* will be dealt with judicially. The validity of the acts of organs of the United Nations thus came into question in the advisory opinion procedure, in the Opinion on *Certain Expenses of the United Nations* (1962) [482] and in the *Namibia* Opinion (1971) [483].

It is a striking fact that the predecessor of the International Court was firmly of the view that the effective application of the Covenant of the League of Nations required the observance of certain procedural standards. In its twelfth Advisory Opinion concerning the *Interpretation of Article 3, Paragraph 2, of the Treaty of Lausanne (Iraq Boundary)* the Permanent Court decided that in respect of an actual dispute laid before the Council of the League the vote of the interested parties did not count for the purpose of

480. M. Sørensen (ed.), *Manual of Public International Law*, London, Macmillan, 1968, p. 75.

481. E. Lauterpacht, *Cambridge Essays in International Law*, London, Stevens, 1965, pp. 88-121.

482. *ICJ Reports 1962*, p. 151.

483. *ICJ Reports 1971*, p. 16.

ascertaining unanimity in the context of Article 5 of the Covenant.

In the words of the Permanent Court:

> "Unanimity, therefore, is required for the decision to be taken by the Council of the League of Nations, in virtue of Article 3, paragraph 2, of the Treaty of Lausanne, with a view to the determination of the frontier between Turkey and Iraq. The question has now to be considered whether the representatives of the interested Parties may take part in the vote.
>
> In this connection, it should be observed that the very general rule laid down in Article 5 of the Covenant does not specially contemplate the case of an actual dispute which has been laid before the Council. On the other hand, this contingency is dealt with in Article 15, paragraphs 6 and 7, which, whilst making the limited binding effect of recommendations dependent on unanimity, explicitly state that the Council's unanimous report need only be agreed to by the members thereof other than the representatives of the Parties. The same principle is applied in the cases contemplated in paragraph 4 of Article 16 of the Covenant and in the first of the three paragraphs which, in accordance with a Resolution of the Second Assembly, are to be inserted between the first and second paragraphs of that Article.
>
> It follows from the foregoing that, according to the Covenant itself, in certain cases and more particularly in the case of the settlement of a dispute, the rule of unanimity is applicable, subject to the limitation that the votes cast by representatives of the interested Parties do not affect the required unanimity.
>
> The Court is of opinion that it is this conception of the rule of unanimity which must be applied in the dispute before the Council.
>
> It is hardly open to doubt that in no circumstances is it possible to be satisfied with less than this conception of unanimity, for, if such unanimity is necessary in order to endow a recommendation with the limited effect contemplated in paragraph 6 of Article 15 of the Covenant, it must *a fortiori* be so when a binding decision has to be taken.
>
> The question which arises, therefore, is solely whether such unanimity is sufficient or whether the representatives of the Parties must also accept the decision. The principle laid down by the Covenant in paragraphs 6 and 7 of Article 15, seems to meet the

> requirements of a case such as that now before the Council, just as well as the circumstances contemplated in that article. The well-known rule that no one can be judge in his own suit holds good."[484]

This reasoning involves the interpretation of the Covenant but, as Sir Hersch Lauterpacht observed: "the Court's vindication of the unanimity rule stopped short of disregarding altogether the general principle of law that no one may be judge in his own cause"[485]. The Advisory Opinion is given prominence in Lauterpacht's examination of the topic of "judicial legislation through application of general principles of law"[486]. The significance of the Opinion lies in the clear acceptance of the view that certain standards of procedural fairness should be applicable when a political organ is dealing with an actual dispute.

Particular difficulties arise when the powers of the Security Council by virtue of Chapter VII of the Charter are involved. It is sometimes assumed, without argument, that if the Council makes a determination of the existence of a threat to the peace or breach of the peace, or act of aggression, it assumes an unlimited consequential discretionary power. And it is true that the Rule of Law experts tend to have difficulties with discretionary powers. Provided the powers have been lawfully conferred it is, so it is said, impossible to regard discretion as incompatible with the Rule of Law. At least a part of the answer to this conundrum is that there is no dichotomy involving discretionary power and the Rule of Law. A discretion can only exist within the law and the real question relates to the ambit of and conditions attaching to the discretionary power.

The few writers who have adverted to the problem are clearly of the opinion that the Council cannot act arbitrarily. Thus Professor Bowett[487] describes the position as follows:

484. *PCIJ, Series B, No. 12* (1925), pp. 31-32.

485. *The Development of International Law by the International Court of Justice*, London, Stevens, 1958, p. 160.

486. *Ibid.*, pp. 158-172.

487. D. W. Bowett, *The Law of International Institutions*, 4th ed., London, Stevens, 1982, p. 33.

"3. *Functions and Powers*

These are stated in Articles 24-26 of the Charter. In conferring on the Council 'primary responsibility for the maintenance of international peace and security', the members of the Organisation agree that it 'acts on their behalf'. The Council thus acts as the agent of all the members and not independently of their wishes; it is, moreover, bound by the Purposes and Principles of the Organisation, so that it cannot, in principle, act arbitrarily and unfettered by any restraints. At the same time, when it does act *intra vires*, the members of the Organisations are bound by its actions and, under Article 25, they 'agree to accept and carry out the decisions of the Security Council in accordance with the present Charter'. This agreement would not extend to a mere 'recommendation' as opposed to a 'decision'."

In this context it is to be recalled that Article 2 of the Charter provides that the "Principles" shall bind "the Organization and its Members". Furthermore, the provisions of Article 24 do not indicate an unfettered conferment of powers, and Article 24 (2) stipulates expressly that:

"In discharging these duties the Security Council shall act in accordance with the Purposes and Principles of the United Nations. The specific powers granted to the Security Council for the discharge of these duties are laid down in Chapters VI, VII, VIII and XII."

Professor Bowett has recently observed:

"There is some judicial support for the view that the acts of the Council enjoy only a *prima facie* validity, a presumption of legality that can be challenged in the final analysis. In the *Expenses* case the Court said:

'. . . when the Organisation takes action which warrants the assertion that it was appropriate for the fulfilment of one of the stated purposes of the United Nations, the presumption is that such action is not *ultra vires* the Organisation'.

Similar language was used in the *Namibia* case, and in the *Lockerbie* case the Court said:

'. . . the Court . . . considers that *prima facie* this obligation [i.e. Article 25] extends to the decision contained in resolution 748 (1992) . . .'

Thus, despite the Court's apparent acceptance of the binding force of Security Council resolution 748 (1992) there is some evidence that, at the merits stage, the Court might reserve the right to question its validity.

It is important that this position should be maintained, and that the Court — or for that matter any other competent judicial body — should not regard itself as precluded from questioning the validity of a Council resolution in so far as it affects the legal rights of States. If this is right, two questions arise: on what grounds would review be proper and by whom should the review be made?"[488]

The conclusion must be that the Security Council is subject to the test of legality in terms of its designated institutional competence. Certain basic criteria therefore apply. A determination of a threat to the peace as a basis for action necessary to remove the threat to the peace cannot be used as a basis for action which (if the evidence so indicates) is for collateral and independent purposes, such as the overthrow of a Government or the partition of a State. Such questions of *vires* are clear enough as a matter of principle, provided the evidence of collateral purposes can be marshalled.

More difficult is the situation in which the Security Council (or the General Assembly) makes a determination which is contrary to principles of general or customary international law. This hypothesis calls for careful identification. The presupposition is that the political organ has made a determination of a threat to the peace, breach of the peace, or act of aggression, which is in principle *intra vires* but then, in the course of implementing this decision, adopts a method of proceeding which is on its face incompatible with general international law and, or, the normal application or multilateral standard-setting treaties.

Initially, it may be asserted that it is question-begging to suppose that any issue of *vires* could arise, because, once the purposes

488. *European Journal of International Law*, Vol. 5 (1994), p. 89 at p. 93.

of Chapter VII are involved, the Council has a wide discretion and this particularly in respect of ways and means. However, this assertion has its own problem of circularity and it is precisely in the sphere of means of implementation that the concepts of purpose and necessity (the colleagues of *intra vires* action) tend to become more open-textured, given that it cannot be *ex hypothesi* necessary to select a method of implementation which is incompatible with general international law.

The position can be clarified by reference to two recent episodes. In resolution 687 (1991) adopted on 3 April 1991[489] the Security Council made the following dispositions:

> "2. *Demands* that Iraq and Kuwait respect the inviolability of the international boundary and the allocation of islands set out in the 'Agreed Minutes between the State of Kuwait and the Republic of Iraq Regarding the Restoration of Friendly Relations, Recognition and Related Matters', signed by them in the exercise of their sovereignty at Baghdad on 4 October 1963 and registered with the United Nations and published by the United Nations in document 7063, United Nations, *Treaty Series*, 1964;
>
> 3. *Calls upon* the Secretary-General to lend his assistance to make arrangements with Iraq and Kuwait to demarcate the boundary between Iraq and Kuwait, drawing on appropriate material, including the map transmitted by Security Council document S/22412 and to report back to the Security Council within one month;
>
> 4. *Decides* to guarantee the inviolability of the above-mentioned international boundary and to take as appropriate all necessary measures to that end in accordance with the Charter of the United Nations; . . ."

It is probable that the alignment as such was disputed and that, therefore, the adoption of a particular alignment by the Security Council involved rather more than a "demarcation". If this be a correct view, then the Security Council has adopted a role which is inappropriate and incompatible with general international law.

489. *International Legal Materials*, Vol. 30 (1991), p. 847. Cf. also E. Lauterpacht, C. Greenwood, M. Weller and D. Bethlehem, *The Kuwait Crisis: Basic Documents*, Cambridge, 1991, pp. 45-50, 73-77.

It is one thing to effect a restoration of Kuwaiti sovereignty on the basis of the status quo prior to Iraq's invasion. It is quite another to impose a boundary in the absence either of bilateral negotiation and agreement or an arbitration or reference to the International Court. Moreover, the position is rendered anomalous precisely because, as resolution 687 makes clear, the intention was to establish "the international boundary", and it is to be presumed that this was to be the alignment justified on the basis of principles of international law.

It is ironical that in the original debate in the Security Council representatives insisted that the Council had no power to determine boundaries [490]. In the words of the United States representative:

> "the United States does not seek, nor will it support, a new role for the Security Council as the body that determines international boundaries. Border disputes are issues to be negotiated directly between States or resolved through other pacific means of settlement available, as set out in Chapter VI of the Charter." [491]

The result of the procedure adopted is incompatible with normal principles of procedural fairness and cannot be regarded as a necessary method of restoring international peace and security in accordance with Article 39 of the Charter. As Sir Hersch Lauterpacht observed:

> "No rule is more firmly embedded in the practice of modern international law than the principle that States are not bound, in the absence of an agreement to the contrary, to submit their disputes with other States to final adjudication by a third party." [492]

Recent dealings between the Security Council and the Government of Libya provide a further example. The key document is

490. E. Suy, *Liber Amicorum Eduardo Jiménez de Aréchaga*, Montevideo, 1995, pp. 441-456.

491. *Ibid.*, p. 445.

492. *The Development of International Law by the International Court of Justice*, London, Stevens, 1958, p. 158.

resolution 731 (1992) adopted on 21 January 1992[493], of which thematerial parts are as follows:

> "*The Security Council,*
>
> . . . .
>
> *Deeply concerned* over the results of investigations, which implicate officials of the Libyan Government and which are contained in Security Council documents that include the requests addressed to the Libyan authorities by France, the United Kingdom of Great Britain and Northern Ireland, and the United States of America in connection with the legal procedures related to the attacks carried out against Pan American flight 103 and Union de transports aériens flight 772;
>
> *Determined* to eliminate international terrorism;
>
> 1. *Condemns* the destruction of Pan American flight 103 and Union de transports aériens flight 772 and the resultant loss of hundreds of lives;
> 2. *Strongly deplores* the fact that the Libyan Government has not yet responded effectively to the above requests to co-operate fully in establishing responsibility for the terrorist acts referred to above against Pan American flight 103 and Union de transports aériens flight 772;
> 3. *Urges* the Libyan Government immediately to provide a full and effective response to those requests so as to contribute to the elimination of international terrorism;
> 4. *Requests* the Secretary-General to seek the co-operation of the Libyan Government to provide a full and effective response to those requests;
> 5. *Urges* all States individually and collectively to encourage the Libyan Government to respond fully and effectively to those requests;
> 6. *Decides* to remain seized of the matter."

This resolution appears to incorporate various other documents by reference, these being described as "requests addressed to the Libyan authorities". The following item is an example of one of the documents referred to in the resolution. It is a British Statement of 27 November 1991 and it reads as follows:

---

493. *International Legal Materials*, Vol. 31 (1992), p. 732.

> "Following the issue of warrants against two Libyan officials for their involvement in the Lockerbie atrocity, the Government demanded of Libya the surrender of the two accused for trial. We have so far received no satisfactory response from the Libyan authorities.
>
> The British and American Governments to-day declare that the Government of Libya must:
>
> > Surrender for trial all those charged with the crime; and accept complete responsibility for the actions of Libyan officials.
> >
> > Disclose all it knows of this crime, including the names of all those responsible, and allow full access to all witnesses, documents and other material evidence, including all the remaining timers.
> >
> > Pay appropriate compensation.
>
> We are conveying our demands to Libya through the Italians, as our protecting power. We expect Libya to comply promptly and in full."[494]

Here again the Security Council has chosen to make dispositions in an area governed by precise principles of public international law. One such principle is that extradition can only take place on the basis of an extradition treaty. In the case of Libya the two States demanding surrender of two Libyan nationals do not have extradition treaties with Libya and have adopted the position that the Convention for the Suppression of Unlawful Acts against the Safety of Civil Aviation done at Montreal on 23 September 1971 is not applicable. Libya has instituted proceedings in the International Court against the United Kingdom and the United States in respect of a dispute over the interpretation and application of the Montreal Convention, proceedings in which the present writer was counsel for Libya.

The proceedings were begun by two Applications dated 3 March 1992, which were accompanied by requests for interim measures of protection. Oral observations relating to the requests were presented on behalf of the Parties on 26 and 28 March 1992. Whilst the Court was deliberating, the Security Council adopted

494. Doc. S/23307, Ann. III.

resolution 748 (1992) on 31 March 1992[495]. The relevant parts of resolution 748 are as follows:

> "*Determining*, in this context, that the failure by the Libyan Government to demonstrate by concrete actions its renunciation of terrorism and in particular its continued failure to respond fully and effectively to the requests in resolution 731 (1992) constitute a threat to international peace and security,
>
> *Determined* to eliminate international terrorism,
>
> *Recalling* the right of States, under Article 50 of the Charter, to consult the Security Council where they find themselves confronted with special economic problems arising from the carrying out of preventive or enforcement measures,
>
> *Acting* under Chapter VII of the Charter,
>
> 1. *Decides* that the Libyan Government must now comply without any further delay with paragraph 3 of resolution 731 (1992) regarding the requests contained in documents S/23306, S/23308 and S/23309;
> 2. *Decides also* that the Libyan Government must commit itself definitively to cease all forms of terrorist action and all assistance to terrorist groups and that it must promptly, by concrete actions, demonstrate its renunciation of terrorism;
> 3. *Decides* that, on 15 April 1992 all States shall adopt the measures set out below, which shall apply until the Security Council decides that the Libyan Government has complied with paragraphs 1 and 2 above."

It was in the light of this second resolution that the International Court decided by 11 votes to 5 not to accede to the Libyan requests for provisional measures of protection[496].

The adoption of resolutions 731 and 748 involved substantial anomalies from the point of view of the Rule of Law. Such anomalies appear at two levels. The Council took the view that a refusal to respond to demands for the surrender of the two suspects by

---

495. *International Legal Materials*, Vol. 31 (1991), p. 750.

496. Case concerning *Questions of Interpretation and Application of the 1971 Montreal Convention arising from the Aerial Incident at Lockerbie (Libyan Arab Jamahiriya* v. *United Kingdom)*, *ICJ Reports 1992*, p. 3 ; *Questions of Interpretation and Application of the 1971 Montreal Convention arising from the Aerial Incident at Lockerbie (Libyan Arab Jamahiriya* v. *United States)*, *ibid.*, p. 114.

Libya constituted a threat to the peace for the purposes of Chapter VII. This determination is itself problematical, but even more problematical is the fact that resolution 731 simply adopts the "demands" of the United Kingdom and the United States, which demands contain no reference to considerations of international law.

Nor do the anomalies end there. The United Kingdom and the United States had made it abundantly clear that they would not accept any recourse to peaceful methods of settlement. Consequently, the demands involved an insistence that Libya accept the version of the facts asserted by the United Kingdom and the United States and, as the documents indicate, the presumption of innocence was not adhered to (see the British Statement set forth above).

Of particular concern is the fact that the subject-matter of the two resolutions involves the rights of two individuals and has ramifications in the sphere of procedural fairness and standards of human rights. Moreover, in the light of the public statements made by senior officials both in the United Kingdom and in the United States there is now a substantial doubt as to whether the two suspects could receive a fair trial either in the United States or in Scotland.

(G) HUMAN RIGHTS STANDARDS

The development of human rights standards both in the context of multilateral standard-setting treaties and in the context of general international law has considerable relevance to the role of the political organs. Human rights standards have produced two different effects, which to some degree involve contradiction and paradox. In the first place, the development of human rights and the erosion of the reserved domain of domestic jurisdiction have caused an extension of the powers, and the willingness, of political organs to seek to intervene in situations involving patterns of breaches of human rights standards and breaches of the principle of self-determination. But as a consequence of this extension of the jurisdiction of organs of the United Nations, the possibility of double standards has increased. The most blatant recent example is the uncensured policy of Turkey to bomb Kurdish rebels both in Turkey and in northern Iraq, whilst the Government of Iraq is forbidden to use force against Kurdish rebels within its own territory[497].

(H) THE CONTROL OF THE CONDUCT OF POLITICAL ORGANS

An important part of the overall picture is the absence of any system of judicial review of the decisions of political organs of the United Nations. There is no compulsory system of review of the acts of organs either by bodies external to them or by individual States. The advisory opinion procedure provides a certain form of review, but it is only occasionally that the majority of States in a political organ will decide to make a request.

(I) PROCEDURAL FAIRNESS AND THE POLITICAL ORGANS OF THE UNITED NATIONS

A further problem derives from the inadequate forms of fact-finding employed in the political organs of the United Nations, combined with a lack of impartiality. This deficiency was pointed out by Mr. Elihu Lauterpacht in 1981[498]. The results of rudimentary forms of fact-finding will not always be unfortunate, because on certain occasions the facts are undenied, undeniable, and a matter of public record. However, several episodes in the recent past have involved actions which were justified by the actors concerned by reference to facts which were by no means easy to verify, which were denied by the State accused, and which at no point were submitted to independent scrutiny.

---

497. Security Council resolution 688 (1991), adopted on 5 April 1991; *International Legal Materials*, Vol. 30 (1991), p. 858.

498. *Proceedings of the American Society of International Law*, 1981, p. 60; and see also E. Lauterpacht, *Aspects of the Administration of International Justice*, Cambridge, Grotius Publications, 1991, pp. 37-48.

A good example of this phenomenon is provided by the United States bombing of Libya in April 1986[499]. In this case, 23 bombers used the most modern ordnance to bomb targets in Tripoli and Benghazi. There was considerable loss of life and injuries among the population, and heavy damage to property, including several embassies. The cause of the bombing raid, according to the United States, was the bombing atrocity in a West Berlin discotheque which killed one United States soldier and injured 230 people. The United States relied upon the principle of self-defence on the basis of Article 51 of the United Nations Charter.

For present purposes, the element to be considered is the absence of any procedural fairness. No fair, or indeed effective, fact-finding was undertaken, and in the Security Council no action was taken in face of a Libyan complaint. The reason for this was the exercise of the veto by the United States, the United Kingdom and France.

The second example of this kind of action concerns the unilateral action taken by the United States against Iraq in response to an alleged plot to assassinate former President Bush in Kuwait in April 1993. On 26 June 1993 the United States attacked the Iraqi intelligence headquarters in Baghdad. The United States reported the action to the Security Council "in accordance with Article 51 of the UN Charter", and stated that the alleged assassination attempt justified the action as self-defence in terms of Article 51. The action, which was described as "proportionate" by United States representatives, consisted of the launching of 23 cruise missiles, several of which caused civilian deaths. The use of force in this promiscuous fashion, involving a spurious appeal to the category of self-defence, has caused increasing concern among international lawyers[500].

Again, for present purposes the lack of any element, however rudimentary, of procedural fairness in relation to the evidence of

---

499. See C. Greenwood, *West Virginia Law Review*, Vol. 89 (1987), p. 933.

500. See G. Gaja, *Revue générale de droit international public*, 1993, pp. 297-320; L. Condorelli, *European Journal of International Law*, Vol. 5 (1994), pp. 134-144.

responsibility for the attempt on the life of Mr. Bush, and of the necessity for action two months later, is disquieting.

(J) Conclusion

This chapter has had the purpose of exposing the existence of certain anomalies in the practice of the political organs in the light of the criteria of the Rule of Law and standards of procedural justice. As is often the case, the identification of the problem is easier than the prescription of a cure. It is probable that there is no simple cure in the form of an institutional reform or procedural device. As in the case of States, so also in the case of organizations and their organs, the legal régime is primarily one of self-limitation.

In the case of the Security Council there is no reason to assume a tension between effectiveness and legality. Common sense would suggest that the authority of a political organ must depend on respect for the Rule of Law and that there is an essential link between operational efficacy and legality.

INDEX

INDEX